DREAMING OF A STRANGER

SHEILA O'FLANAGAN

POOLBEG

All characters in this publication are fictitious and any resemblance to real persons, living or dead, is purely coincidental.

Published 1997 by
Poolbeg Press Ltd,
123 Baldoyle Industrial Estate,
Dublin 13, Ireland

A catalogue record for this book is available from the British Library.

ISBN 1 85371 684 7

Cover photography by The Slide File
Cover design by Poolbeg Group Services Ltd
Set by Poolbeg Group Services Ltd in Garamond 10/12.5
Printed and bound in Great Britain by
Cox & Wyman Ltd, Reading, Berks.

Acknowledgements

(UK No. 19 – Somebody Help Me Out – *Beggar & Co. – March 1981)*

To the team at Poolbeg – Nicole, Paula, Kieran and Philip for their support. Especially to Kate Cruise O'Brien for her belief, her infectious enthusiasm and her thoughtful editing.

To my mother for a lifetime of nagging me to write.

And to Colm for everything else.

A Note on the Author

Sheila O'Flanagan lives in Dublin and has a successful career in the financial services industry. This is her first novel.

1

April 1981

(*US No. 7 – Woman – John Lennon*)

My lover and I sat side by side on the white Caribbean sand. The setting sun shattered into a thousand glittering diamonds as it hit the turquoise blue of the sea, and the only sound was the rhythmic thud of the waves as they broke upon the shore.

My lover and I sat in silence. There was no need for words between us. We were together in body and mind and it was perfection. The electricity between us charged the otherwise tranquil setting. But we would do nothing about that charge until the sun had finally slipped behind the gentle ridge of the island, its dying rays spilling blood into the sea. Then he would lean over to me and breathe quietly into my ear as he always did.

"Jane." The words, coming from just behind me, broke into my dream and shattered it completely.

I looked up from the file that lay open on the desk in front of me. Jessica Fitzgerald laughed. "If you didn't spend half your life in a daze you'd be a brilliant worker," she said. She handed me a sheaf of papers. "All these are fine. Can you get the telexes out before lunch-time?"

I nodded at her. I was still halfway around the world, still in the arms of my secret lover on the white sands of the Caribbean. It was difficult to come back to the fifth floor of the bank's head office in Dublin, where the April rain drizzled miserably outside the opaque windows and there was no lover, secret or otherwise, in my life.

"Are you certain?" Jessica wasn't convinced, I could see it in her eyes. I nodded vigorously, both to reassure her and to rid myself of the image of Sebastian lying bronzed and desirable on the beach beside me.

"I'll have them sent by twelve." I glanced at my watch.

"Hope so," said Jessica. "And when you've done that I need you to do some photocopying for me."

"Do you need that before lunch too?" I asked anxiously. "Only I'm meeting Lucy at half twelve."

"After lunch is fine," said Jessica. "Once you get those telexes off."

"Don't worry." I took the papers to the telex machine while Jessica walked back down the long, open-plan area to her desk.

Jessica Fitzgerald was my boss. She was twenty-six years old, an assistant manager in the International Trade department of the bank where I worked, and she was frighteningly efficient. But she was good to work for. She didn't make you feel stupid if you had to ask a question, she was always helpful and explained things thoroughly so that you were confident you knew what you were doing.

Some people said that Jessica was too helpful. That because she was so popular with her staff she had done herself no good in the further promotion stakes. The word in the bank was that you should always make sure that people knew less than you, that you kept an ace up your sleeve at all times, that you were helpful, but not too helpful. And that you exaggerated your own abilities as much as you possibly could.

At first I'd been scornful of people who said that, but in my two years in the bank I'd realised that they were probably right. I wanted to get promoted soon and I wanted Jessica to realise that I was promotion material.

I sat in front of the big yellow telex machine and typed like a lunatic. A snake of white ticker tape curled its way on to the floor beside me as I punched at the keys. I'd told Jessica that I'd have the telexes done by noon but it meant working flat out to reach an almost impossible deadline.

They were gone by five past. I sighed with relief, stood up and stretched my arms over my head. I tore the top copies from the machine and left them on Jessica's desk. Then I went to lunch.

The wind swirled around Baggot Street. It blew the rain directly into my face and whisked stray papers through the air. I pulled my grey, quilted raincoat around me and hurried down the street.

Lucy was already waiting for me outside

Burgerland. She stood in the shelter of the building, calm and unruffled. Lucy would look calm and unruffled in a hurricane.

Lucy McAllister was my closest friend. We'd been friends since the day we met at St Attracta's Secondary School for girls. I'd arrived at school the first morning feeling very alone. I hadn't gone to St Attracta's Primary School like most of the other girls, and I didn't recognise anyone in the crowd that swarmed around Class 1A. Everyone else seemed to know someone. A group of very pretty girls laughed in the corner together and glanced in my direction. I flushed with embarrassment, wondering if they were sneering at me for some reason. I looked around anxiously.

A small, fair girl sat at a desk near the back of the classroom and ignored everyone around her. She didn't look as though she was keeping a space beside her. She didn't really look at anyone very much. I took a deep breath.

"Are you keeping this space for anyone?" I asked. The fair-haired girl shook her head.

"D'you mind if I sit here then?"

"Feel free," she said. "Don't let me stop you."

"I'm Jane O'Sullivan."

"Lucy McAllister." She looked around. "Don't you know any of these people?"

"No," I said.

"Me neither. It's weird not knowing anybody."

I nodded. "You didn't go to St Attracta's before?"

She shook her head. "The Holy Faith," she said. "But St Attracta's is much more convenient for me. So my folks decided I should change. I didn't want to, really. I liked the Holy Faith."

"I'm sure you'll make loads of friends," I said.

She looked around at the classroom full of girls and sighed. "Maybe."

I couldn't think of anything else to say. I wanted to say something so that she'd realise that I was bright and witty and that I was a good person to know. I pulled at a fingernail.

A tall, severe nun walked into the classroom, introduced herself as Sr Elizabeth, the head, and began to talk to us about our responsibilities as adults.

Lucy yawned and Sr Elizabeth stared at her.

"In this school we expect our students to behave in a mannerly fashion," said the nun. "It is the height of bad manners to yawn when somebody is talking to you. You're Lucy McAllister, aren't you?"

Lucy nodded while thirty girls stared at her.

"Well, Lucy, it's nice to have you in St Attracta's," said Sr Elizabeth. "Hopefully you'll spend your time here profitably and you won't find it all too boring."

Lucy flushed. "Cow," she muttered under her breath.

I gave her a sympathetic smile and she grinned at me.

It's funny how you sometimes click with another person. Lucy McAllister and I clicked. Despite the fact that we were completely unalike in looks – she was like a china doll with her fair hair, blue eyes and pale complexion and I was a sturdy, well-built redhead – we were the same sort of people.

We were both ordinary. Averagely clever, with average looks and an average background. We weren't as popular as the stunningly beautiful Stephanie McMenamin or her select group of friends, but neither were we avoided like some of the other girls. We never did so brilliantly in class that we were envied; but we were never sent to Sr Elizabeth's office with a note from the teacher to say that we were a complete waste of space. We were middle-of-the-road girls. We came from the same sort of families who lived the same sort of lives and we understood each other.

"What d'you want?" asked Lucy as we stood in the queue for our burgers.

"Quarter-pounder, chips and Coke," I said. "No – wait – no chips. I'm trying to cut out chips."

Lucy laughed. Not a very caring laugh, I thought. "Come on, Jane! You can never resist chips."

"I'll have to," I told her. "I hardly fit into my jeans now and I can't afford another pair. I badly need to lose a few inches."

"A small french fries will hardly make any difference," said Lucy. "There's nothing in it worth talking about, anyway."

"All the same," I said as we inched forward. "I'll just have the burger. It's all right for you – you never bloody well put on an ounce."

Lucy grinned. "Metabolism," she said.

We brought our food to a white-topped table in the window. I shivered involuntarily as I watched the rain lash against it.

"So." Lucy unwrapped her burger and daintily

removed the dill pickle. "Have you decided what you're going to do on Friday night?"

I made a face. "Not really."

"Oh, Jane, for God's sake! It's your twenty-first birthday. You must have some ideas."

I took Lucy's pickle and put it on my burger. "No."

"But you can't let your twenty-first go by as though it meant nothing."

It was all right for Lucy. Her parents had thrown her a massive party. Although we were still close friends, her job at the temping agency meant that she met lots of different people. Easily enough to fill the room that Mrs McAllister had hired. And Michael, her older brother, had brought all his friends. I smiled at the memory. It had been a good night.

"It's my folks," I told her. "You know they've organised for us to go to the Walnut Rooms for dinner and a cabaret on Saturday night. They think it's very touching that my birthday and their anniversary should be on the same day."

"I think it's bloody unfortunate," said Lucy.

"Yes, well." I robbed one of her chips. "There's not a lot I can do about it. They've booked a table for twenty. Twenty! All of the aunts and uncles." I took another chip. "They think I'll like it."

Lucy smothered a giggle. "Sounds like a barrel of laughs."

"Fuck off, McAllister," I said.

She smiled and me and removed her chips from my reach. "You're on a diet, remember?"

"I thought maybe we could just go out for a drink," I said.

"Oh, Jane. We do that every week." She crumpled her burger wrapping. "Why don't we at least come into town and then maybe go to a nightclub or something afterwards? You, me and the twins?"

The twins, Brenda and Grace Quinlan, were our other old schoolfriends. They were like one person really, because they were almost identical and you rarely saw one without the other. But we got on well as a foursome and we'd stayed friends even when we'd finally shaken the dust of St Attracta's off our shoes.

"OK," I said. "Will you be talking to the twins or d'you want me to give them a call?"

"You'd better ring them," said Lucy. "I can hardly breathe in that office without them looking sideways at me. Thank God it's only for another couple of weeks."

I didn't know how Lucy could stand going from office to office like she did. I liked knowing that I'd be meeting the same people every day; that I knew where everything was. Lucy was more adventurous than me.

"I'd better get back," she said as she looked at her watch. "They give me such horrible looks if I'm late that I'm quite sure they're plotting something evil."

I laughed at her. "They're probably really nice people."

"Huh," said Lucy. "They're solicitors. How can they be really nice people?"

I worked late that evening. International Trade was a busy department and there was always plenty of work to keep you past five o'clock if you wanted. I worked late whenever I could. I wanted the overtime and there wasn't anything else to drag me out of the office.

God, my life was dreary. Here I was, nearly twenty-one, and I hadn't achieved anything. I lived at home with my parents. I had a safe, but boring, job in the bank. I didn't have any vices. I was still a virgin.

Lucy wasn't. Lucy had lost her virginity in France. When we left school she'd gone au-pairing for a year. Mam wouldn't let me go au-pairing although I desperately wanted to. We had a screaming match about it, but in the end I rang the bank and said that I'd be delighted to accept the position that they'd offered, and Lucy went to France on her own. It didn't bother her in the slightest. She wrote to me once a week to let me know how she was getting on, loving every minute of her time even if she thought that the two children she looked after were over-indulged little brats. Then, one day, a different letter, falling over itself with underlined words and exclamation marks.

"He was <u>tremendous</u>," she wrote. *"I knew that it probably didn't mean anything to him, because it's definitely different with the French, but I just had to, Jane, I just <u>had</u> to. And he was so good-looking and so charming. He brought a bottle of wine and we went out into the country and we did it in the open air! I felt great about it. Mind you, I was terrified that Mme Lemartine would find out about it and send me home! I wasn't worried about getting pregnant, because I had sorted myself out about that the minute I met him! I just knew, you see! You just <u>know</u>, Jane, you'll*

understand yourself. Unless you and your latest have already done the deed! Write and tell me. In the meantime, I am having a great time with Étienne and I know that I'll be heartbroken when it's over."

I crumpled up the paper. I was embarrassed that Lucy could write to me about it and envious that she had managed to lose her virginity in such a romantic way. And that she didn't seem to care that it was in a relationship that was purely for sex. Being in France had changed her outlook on life completely.

How many girls were virgins at twenty-one in this day and age? Hardly any, was my guess. It was just that I was. Still. Despite my best efforts.

I snorted as I thought of my best efforts. In my entire life I'd had three boyfriends and none of them had been remotely close to dragging me to bed. Jesse, an American and my first love at seventeen (which shows that I was a late developer), lasted all of three weeks, the duration of his holiday in Ireland. Then came Frank. My relationship with Frank had been longer-lived but out of a Victorian novel. He was the sort of guy you'd never be afraid to bring home to your parents. He was too good to be true – scrubbed face, straw-coloured hair and a permanent expression of happiness. Frank couldn't cope with my moodier side and we split up after six months. Anyway, Frank wasn't the one. The man who would banish my imaginary lovers forever. I hadn't met that man yet, although I yearned to find him. The one who would make me complete. The other half of myself. When I joined the bank, I almost fainted with the excitement of seeing so many men around my own age walking around the place. This was my opportunity, I thought. This time I would find the man of my dreams.

Actually, I found Dermot. It wasn't his fault that he couldn't live up to my imaginary lovers – to Sebastian or Nicholas or Rupert or Andreas. He did his best, but it wasn't enough. We split up after three months.

So here I was, without a man in my life for the last year. It was stupid to think that I needed a man to feel good. I told myself over and over again that I was happy just as I was, but I wanted someone. I needed someone to put his arms around me and to hold me and to make me feel loved. I ached with the need of finding him.

Mam and Dad were watching TV when I arrived home. I walked into the kitchen and draped my wet coat over the radiator. Pieces of the car that Dad was currently working on were laid out neatly on the kitchen table. Dad was the part-owner of a garage. I was probably the only girl that I knew who could change an oil filter more quickly than shave her legs.

"You're very late," said Mam. "Your dinner will have dried out."

"I didn't think you'd keep any for me," I said. "I told you I might be late when I left this morning."

"I thought you'd ring and let me know." She opened the oven door and took out the plate. "You might want to make some gravy."

The lamb chop was shrivelled and the potatoes dry. Mam was not a cook, she often said so, but she'd be hurt if I didn't eat it.

I brought my food into the living-room with me and settled down in front of the TV. That way, Mam wouldn't bother asking me about my day. She drove me nuts these days. She still treated me as though I was a child when I felt like an adult. Both my parents drove me nuts. They couldn't accept that I was a person in my own right now.

My birthday, for example. I probably wouldn't have had a big party anyway – I wasn't a party sort of person – but I certainly didn't want some family night out to mark my supposed coming of age. I'd been horrified when Mam told me of her plans but I hadn't the nerve, or maybe the heart, to say that I didn't want to be part of a joint birthday and anniversary celebration.

I sighed. I was very hard to please these days.

"Do you know who I saw in the shop today?" Mam worked part-time in the local supermarket.

I shook my head.

"That nice boy you used to know. Frank Delahunty."

"Really?" I was indifferent.

"Yes. He didn't stop at my checkout but I recognised him straight away." She looked pleased. "Why don't you give him a ring?"

"Because I'm not interested in Frank Delahunty any more," I told her firmly. "We split up. He went to London. He probably doesn't even remember me."

"Of course he remembers you." Mam looked affronted that anyone could forget her only daughter. "He was very keen on you."

"I suppose he was," I said. "But it wasn't to be."

"Maybe now that you're older – " She sounded hopeful.

"No."

"But – "

"No," I said. Very decisively.

"Leave the girl alone, Maureen," said Dad, coming to my rescue. "If she isn't interested in the chap, she isn't interested."

I must have been a terrible disappointment to my mother. She'd been beautiful when she was younger. Sometimes when she took out old photograph albums I'd stare at the snaps of her and wonder how on earth she'd produced a daughter like me. And, unlike me, she'd been popular with men. Not difficult, I suppose, when people said that you were a cracker. She was, too. Stunningly beautiful. Small and slender, with golden hair tumbling around her face. How could a woman like that look at her tall, well-built daughter and not wonder what on earth had happened? That was probably why she was always trying to find out about my boyfriends. She was afraid that nobody would ever find me attractive enough to marry, and she wanted me to get married.

I wanted to get married too, one day. But I wanted it to be to the right person, not someone Mam liked, the man that would love me through thick and thin. The man that would protect me.

I was an awful fool when I was twenty-one.

I met Lucy and the twins in O'Brien's on Friday night. Lucy and I arrived at the same time and went upstairs while we waited for the twins. They didn't get out of the department store where both of them worked until after six.

"What'll you have to drink?" I took my purse out of my bag.

"I'll get you one," said Lucy. "It's your birthday after all. And here – " She handed me a gaily wrapped package. "Happy birthday."

"Oh, Lucy, thanks! Will I open it now?"

"Of course," said Lucy. "You're not thinking of sitting here all night without opening it are you?"

I slid my finger under the Sellotape and unwrapped her present carefully.

"It's gorgeous," I said as I held the delicate gold chain out in front of me. "Really lovely."

"Glad you like it," said Lucy.

"Thanks, Lucy." I kissed her lightly on the cheek and fastened the chain around my neck while she ordered the drinks.

"So how are your solicitors?" I asked as we settled into seats in the corner of the lounge.

"I'm sure there are loads of wonderful solicitors," said Lucy. "But I hate this job. Still, I was talking to Anna at the agency yesterday and she said that there were a couple of new jobs coming up soon. I told her I wanted something nice this time and she said she'd see what she could do."

"Any preferences?"

"Human beings," she said.

I laughed. "They can't be that bad."

"I don't want to talk about them," she said. "We're supposed to be having fun tonight."

I drained my glass. "My turn," I said. "Same again?"

The twins arrived as I came back from the bar with the glasses of beer. I got another couple for them and they handed over their present – a beautiful pale cream angora jumper and a multicoloured chiffon scarf.

"Happy birthday, Jane." Brenda lifted her glass.

"Thanks."

"So we've all finally made it to twenty-one," grinned Lucy. "We're all fully-fledged adults."

"Tell that to my mother," I groaned. "She told me not to be home late tonight."

The others laughed. Mam's concern for me was legendary. I suppose it was because I was an only child, but it was stifling all the same. Lucy's mother was far more relaxed than mine. Mrs McAllister never asked Lucy what time she'd be home. And the Quinlan's parents seemed to think that because the twins were together all the time it meant that they'd look after each other. I was the only one with parents who fussed.

"Brenda and I were thinking about getting a flat," said Grace suddenly. "What would you think of that?"

I stared at her. "Would your parents mind?"

"I'm sure they'd prefer if we stayed at home, but you can't live at home forever. Besides, we want to live somewhere that's our own."

"It's a great idea," said Lucy. "Maybe you and I should think of doing it, Jane."

"We were kind of wondering would you like to share with us," said Grace. "It'd be a lot cheaper."

I looked at them in amazement. I'd never thought of leaving home before. Not to live in a flat, anyway. I assumed that I'd move out when I got married, but Dublin girls didn't just up and leave and move into flats.

"What a brilliant idea," breathed Lucy. "It would be fantastic. I'd love to be out of our house. Michael's moved back home while he's saving up for the new bike and Joan and Emily are driving me crazy. My parents aren't too bad, I suppose, but the idea of living somewhere myself – what do you think, Jane?"

"I'd love it," I said. "Have you thought of anywhere?"

"Not yet," said Grace. "But we've been looking at the papers. If we get somewhere purpose-built, it would be best."

"An apartment, you mean," said Lucy. "Not a flat."

"Absolutely. We want to live somewhere nice. Not some crummy tenement in Rathmines."

"Wouldn't that be terribly expensive?" I asked. I hadn't a clue about the cost of renting anywhere. It just seemed to me that a pretty, purpose-built apartment would cost a lot more than any of us could afford. It wasn't as though we were earning huge salaries.

"It would be OK if the four of us did it," said Grace.

I shivered with anticipation. It would be fantastic to be four girls living together in an apartment. It would be freedom at last! We'd be able to do exactly what we wanted, whenever we wanted. I wouldn't have to account for every minute of my time. No more panicking on a Friday night because I'd had a couple of drinks and my clothes reeked of smoke from a pub. Mam went berserk whenever I came home smelling of drink or smoke. She immediately assumed that I'd been on a massive binge. It was terribly unfair of her. I'd only been utterly drunk once before, and that was such a disaster that I vowed never to get into that state again. I shuddered as I remembered leaning over the toilet bowl while my parents stood outside the bathroom door ready to give me an earful when I could stand up again. God, that was awful. I hated being sick. I hated the loss of control. That was why I'd never drunk eight vodkas, two pints and a bottle of wine in a night again.

"So what d'you think, Jane?" asked Lucy.

"I know my parents will go mad," I said. "But I'm all for it."

"Great." The twins looked pleased. "Does anyone have a definite idea of where the apartment should be?"

"Not me," said Lucy. "Although something near town. I need to be near a bus stop so that I can get in early if I've got a job in some out-of-the-way place."

"I don't mind at all," I told them. "Anywhere will do me."

We spent until closing time talking about our flat. Our apartment. It was great. I finally felt grown up whenever I thought about living in an apartment. You couldn't really feel an adult when you lived at home. No matter what, you were always the child. I suppose it's difficult for a mother to think of a child as anything other than someone who needs their love and attention all the time, but I was ready to move on. I knew Mam wouldn't be happy about it. I knew there'd be a scene and I hated scenes, but it would have to be done.

When we were finally thrown out of the pub, Lucy insisted that we go to a nightclub.

"You can't possibly go home yet," she told me. "It's your twenty-first, Jane. It's appalling that you're not having a party."

I sighed. "I told you before I'm not a party person."

"I know, I know." She looked at me in exasperation. "But you've got to make the effort. Come on, let's go to Annabel's."

The twins were all on for Annabel's and I gave in. I couldn't be a party-pooper all my life. We joined the queue outside. The doorman looked long and hard at me before he let me in. I looked too young, I knew. I was the youngest of the four by about three months but I looked at least a year younger than the others. The twins were both elegant girls. Tall and dark, they had a great sense of style. That was why they'd got jobs in the department store – they simply loved clothes. Lucy, who had looked young for her age in school, had found her look in France. Tiny and demure as a teenager, she'd blossomed in the last year. But I was still the same. I hadn't quite managed to tame my wild, curly hair or find a look that fitted me yet. I was growing up inside, but my looks hadn't caught up yet with how I felt.

Annabel's was crowded. We pushed our way into the throng of people on the dance floor.

At least this was better than the cricket club dances of my teenage years. When we were at St Attracta's, everyone went to the cricket club disco on a Friday night and tried to meet the man of their dreams there.

It never worked, of course. Blokes you never saw before would ask you to dance, hold you tightly in their arms and then leave you standing there like an idiot when the music speeded up again. I hated the cricket but I always went. You knew that the night you didn't show up would be the night that he would be there.

We were so naive, I thought, as I danced around my handbag. What chance did anyone have of meeting the man in their life at a bloody disco?

"Would you like to dance?"

The lights had dimmed and the music was slow. He stood in front of me and smiled. The girls grinned at me and gave the thumbs up.

He put his arms around me and I leaned against his chest. He wore a denim shirt. I liked denim shirts. His aftershave was Brut.

"I am a woman in love
And I'd do anything
To get you into my world
And hold you within.
It's a right I defend
Over and over again."

But there had to be more important things in my life than love. I'd tried it, and I wasn't very good at it. Each time I'd gone out with someone, I'd truly believed that this was it. That it was forever. Even with Jesse. I hadn't quite got the hang of simply going out and having a good time with someone. Was everyone as silly as me? I wondered, as I moved around the floor with him and tried to ignore the fact that the button on his shirt pocket was digging into the corner of my eye. Not Lucy – she'd had a few boyfriends since she'd come back from France, and none of them had lasted longer than a couple of months. Not the twins – they didn't seem to need men in their lives. They were different from other people. Not anyone else I knew. I was the sole idiot in town.

"Thanks," he said as the music speeded up again. "Would you like a drink?"

I shook my head. Suddenly I didn't want to be here any more. The girls were standing beside the bar.

"I've had enough," I said. "I think I'll go home."

"Are you sure?" asked Lucy. "It's only one o'clock."

"I'm sure," I said. "Stay if you want to."

She shook her head. "I'm tired, too."

We left together and piled into a taxi outside.

"Riverbrook Estate," said Lucy. "Terenure."

The driver nodded. I sat in the back with the twins while Lucy chatted away to him. I didn't listen to the conversation but leaned my head against the window.

Twenty-one. It had seemed very old when I was at school. Now I realised that it was nothing at all.

2

April 1981

(UK No. 2 – Making Your Mind Up *– Bucks Fizz)*

I stood in front of the mirror in my bedroom and gazed in appalled fascination at my reflection. I looked like a Neapolitan ice cream.

Mam and Dad had bought me a watch for my birthday. It was a neat gold watch with a gold chain. They should have left it at the watch but Mam had also bought me the yellow dress. Some girls with flame-red hair could wear yellow dresses and not look ridiculous, but I knew that I wasn't one of them.

I couldn't understand my mother. She always looked so pretty herself, it was extraordinary that she didn't know what looked well on me. Whenever she bought something for me, I think that she saw herself in it. The yellow dress would have been perfect for her.

I thought about not wearing it, but that would have hurt her feelings. I sat at my dressing-table and wondered if there was anything I could do to salvage my appearance. What I really wanted to do was to wear a pair of jeans and a T-shirt, but that would have caused a riot.

My face stared back at me from the mirror. Grey-green eyes set wide apart, no cheekbones worth mentioning, generous mouth. At least I didn't have freckles. I hated freckles.

I rubbed foundation on to my cheeks and went heavy with the blusher. I didn't bother with make-up during the day but maybe I should have. It would make me better at using it at night. I brushed the silver eyeshadow on to my lids and loaded my lashes with mascara. Then I outlined my mouth with lip-pencil and filled in my lips with the red lip-gloss that had come free with *Woman's Own* that week. I slid my cameo earrings on to my ears, hung Lucy's gold chain around my neck and put on my new watch.

I still looked like a Neapolitan ice cream.

Mam didn't say anything when I appeared downstairs. She must have thought I looked ridiculous. Compared to her, I was a complete mess. She wore a light green skirt with matching jacket and a white blouse. She looked great. Unlike any of the other mothers I knew, Mam was thin. Both Mrs McAllister and Mrs Quinlan were rounded sort of women. They looked like mothers. Mine still looked like a person. I wished she looked more like a mother. It would make it a lot easier for me.

We were late by the time we arrived at the Walnut Rooms and the rest of the family was already sitting at our table. We were escorted to it by a man wearing a dress suit and white gloves which I thought looked silly. I had never been to the Walnut Rooms before, since "Patrons" were supposed to be over twenty-one. The rest of the family frequented it quite a lot for birthdays or anniversaries or, in the case of Mam, a girls' night out with her sisters, Olivia, Judith and Joan, three times a year.

The "Rooms" were really just one room, but it was huge. At one end was a stage and in front of that was a large dance floor, surrounded by tables. The backdrop to the stage consisted of hundreds of strips of foil paper in gold and silver, which fluttered in the draught of the room. Emblazoned across this in huge red lettering was "Stevie Cleere and His Band" and the stage was ready for Stevie and company, silver coloured chairs awaiting their arrival.

Our table was near the stage. It was a big, round table, covered by two tablecloths, one pink and one mauve with a matching pink and mauve flower arrangement in the centre. It was all a little startling to the eye and clashed horribly with my yellow dress.

When we arrived all my relatives stood up and clapped which made me feel hugely embarrassed because people at the other tables turned around to look at us. I could feel my cheeks burn as I slipped into an empty seat. Aunt Olivia kissed me and congratulated the "birthday girl", which again made me flush with embarrassment, and I squirmed uneasily. I looked around the table, trying to avoid the eyes of my relatives and smiling uneasily as I failed.

There were still two seats empty, which surprised me because, as far as I could see, everybody was there. Except Declan, I suddenly realised. Aunt Olivia was sitting beside me. "Where's Declan?" I asked, curiously.

"He'll be here later," she said. "He's picking up Ruth."

Ruth? I didn't know any Ruth. She was not a McDermott, Mam's side of the family, or an O'Sullivan. I'd never heard of her before.

"Ruth who?" I asked.

"Good God, Jane, don't you ever listen to anyone? Ruth is Declan's girlfriend." Aunt Olivia looked at me as though I were an imbecile.

"Nobody told me," I said, defensively. "And I haven't seen Declan in ages."

"Neither have I," laughed my aunt. "Since he met Ruth, I'm not sure he even knows we exist."

They arrived five minutes later. I was sipping my Coke and listening to the conversation around me, when I saw Declan walk into the room, accompanied by a girl I presumed was Ruth.

An amazing girl. Declan was tall, just under six feet and Ruth almost matched him in height. Afterwards, I realised that it was probably because of her footwear, but the first impression was of a tall, thin, pale beanpole. Her hair was waist length and jet black, and fell in a straight sheet around her face. She wore a black T-shirt and long black skirt and a black shawl around her shoulders. She also wore spindly black shoes with an incredible heel which added at least an inch to her natural height. The only colour she wore was provided by a huge silver cross hanging from her neck and her nails and lips, which were post box red. She was incredible. I'd never seen anything like her before. I felt even more foolish in my buttercup yellow dress.

"Hi everyone, this is Ruth." Declan proudly introduced her as they sat down opposite me. He told her the names while she inclined her head graciously in the direction of each person, but didn't speak. "And, of course, my cousin Jane, the birthday girl," he said cheerfully. I tried to smile. She looked at me as though I wasn't really there. "Jane and I used to be great friends when we were children," continued Declan blithely, "but we don't see as much of each other now – do we, Jane?"

"No."

Ruth opened her black handbag and took out a packet of cigarettes and a lighter. I watched her with interest. My parents hated smoking. She lit a cigarette, still without speaking, and took a long, deep drag. Then she exhaled the smoke very, very slowly. She turned and whispered in Declan's ear.

He smiled benevolently at her and kissed her on the forehead. I wondered if he'd noticed that she looked like Morticia in the *Addam's Family*. Declan was such an ordinary-looking person, I couldn't believe that it hadn't struck him that his girlfriend was extremely odd.

"So what do you do, Ruth?" Mam smiled at her.

"I'm a hairdresser," she replied. Her voice was husky and low.

"Really." Mam made it sound as though she had always wanted to meet a hairdresser. "Where do you work?"

"Peter Marks," she replied. "I'm a colouring specialist."

I choked back a laugh. Colour specialist! Specialising in black, no doubt. All the same, I had to admit that she was attractive once you got used to the black. Her skin was flawless, her eyes (after you discounted the make-up) were sultry brown and her neck was long and graceful. Her hands, too, were long and narrow with perfectly shaped nails. As I looked at them, I curled my fingers into my palms to hide my own nails. I didn't bite them much these days but whenever I was nervous I picked at them and they were uneven in length.

The waiter came over and asked her if she wanted something to drink.

"A martini," she said.

"And I'll have a pint," said Declan.

Our family stopped looking at Ruth and began its own conversations. I decided to head for the Ladies.

I stood in front of the long mirror and felt more uncomfortable than ever. In comparison to Ruth, I looked childish. Even if she hadn't been there I would have felt silly but now my sense of discomfort was multiplied a thousand times. My face, which I had thought looked nice when I left the house, now seemed bland and uninspired. My thin-soled sandals were ludicrous. I felt a freak.

They were bringing around the starters when I arrived back at the table. My seat was between Aunt Olivia and Granny McDermott.

"You look very nice, lovey," shouted Granny. She was a little deaf and shouted at everyone now.

"Thanks," I said.

"I like the colour," she said. "Very bright."

I wasn't sure whether this was really meant as a compliment or not. I gave her the benefit of the doubt.

"Thanks, Granny."

"Reminds me of a dress I once had," she continued. I sighed. Granny was a reminiscences person. Once she started, she just went on and on. I think that memories of things in the distant past were more clear to her than memories of things that had happened yesterday. She seemed to be able to conjure up people and places of her youth at will and retreat into their company. Or, as now, inflict their company on you. I listened with half an ear to the exploits of young Rosie McDermott and Ian and Glenda, without really hearing any of it.

Mam was talking to Joan about the supermarket. "People continually try to just walk out," she said. "It's amazing. For the sake of a tin of beans or something. They need better security. And the kids try to rob the sweets all the time."

Dad talked about cars. "It was the carburettor," he told Dick, Aunt Judith's husband. It was always the carburettor, I thought.

"Anyway," said Uncle Kevin, "I thought the best way to do it was to rotovate the garden. Start from scratch. A big job. Worth it, though."

"So I tried on the size fourteen," said Dad's sister, Kathleen. "And it wouldn't go near me! I was so embarrassed. Then she said 'would madam like to try a larger size?' She said it loud enough for the whole damn shop to hear. So I told her no, that I didn't really think it would do for the larger lady."

Judith nodded. "Little upstarts," she said. "I won't go near any of those boutique places."

"It looked lovely, though," moaned Kathleen.

I applied myself to the egg mayonnaise. The conversation was inane. Who cared about dresses and carburettors and rotovated gardens? I hoped I'd never become the sort of person who spent their time talking about their house. I wanted to be – different.

I watched Ruth, who pushed her food around her plate without eating it. I'd have loved to be able to ignore food like that, but once it was in front of me I had to eat it. That was probably why I wasn't a willowy beanpole.

"So how's the bank?" asked Declan, suddenly, looking at me.

"Oh, OK, I suppose," I said.

"Fed up already," he teased. "You're probably too intelligent for the bank."

"Don't be stupid."

"I'm not. You were always clever, Jane."

"You're clever," I said, blushing.

"Not like you." There was real envy in his voice. "I thought it was unfair the way you passed exams without studying for them."

I laughed. "Technique. At least we don't have to worry about them any more."

"Thank God," he said, feelingly. "I hated school."

"I was glad to leave school," said Ruth, suddenly joining in the conversation. "It bored me rigid."

"Where did you go?" I asked.

"Sisters of Mercy," she said, laconically. "Bitches, all of them." I looked around anxiously in case my mother had heard. She wouldn't approve of calling the nuns "bitches".

"Why?" I asked.

"Frustrated virgins," said Ruth. "It's not normal for women to lock themselves away like that."

"But they're not exactly locked away, are they?" I asked reasonably. "Not if they're teaching in the school."

"Not all of them did," she said. "In fact, very few, I think. And they were probably considered racy."

I laughed and she smiled. It changed her face completely. Quite suddenly, I liked her.

"So you work in a bank and you're bored. I work in a hairdresser's, but really I want to sing." I looked at her in alarm, afraid that she might suddenly burst into song there and then.

"Professionally," she added.

"Really?"

"Oh, yes."

"Ruth is a brilliant singer," said Declan. "She's like a female Rod Stewart."

I imagined he was right. That husky voice would sound great on a record.

They cleared away the plates and brought the soup. Aunt Olivia turned to me.

"How's the job?" she asked.

I wished people would stop asking me that. I answered non-committally. She extolled the virtues of hard work. I listened and said nothing.

The main course arrived but Ruth didn't eat her chicken. "I'm a vegetarian," she explained.

"That's silly," said Donal O'Sullivan, who was on the other side of her. "People need meat."

"No, they don't," Ruth said. "You can get all the nutrients you need in vegetables."

"Give me meat and potatoes any day," said Kevin, to a rousing cheer from the assembled men. "It might be all right for you lassies," he added, "but we men need our meat."

Declan looked uncomfortable. I wondered if he was practising being a vegetarian because of Ruth. But he ate the chicken anyway.

The cabaret started. Stevie Cleere and his band played fifties music. Stevie was wearing a gold lamé coat and had his hair slicked back Teddy-boy style. My relatives loved him. I hated it. Declan and Ruth seemed oblivious. He was watched her and she chain-smoked.

Then Stevie Cleere started playing requests. He called out a special one for "The O'Sullivan family at table number three. A wedding anniversary and a twenty-first birthday! Best wishes from everyone!!" A spotlight spun in our direction and highlighted us. I was embarrassed but my parents were delighted. The band played a brief snatch of the *Anniversary Waltz,* then *Happy Birthday,* while the waiter brought a big cake over to the table.

Dad stood up and made a brief speech to the assembled O'Sullivans and McDermotts. He said that Mam had made him the happiest man in the world twenty-three years ago, and again twenty-one years ago, and that his family meant more to him than anything else. I cringed.

Once the cake had been handed around various members of the family got up to dance. I stayed where I was with Granny O'Sullivan, Gramps McDermott, Declan and Ruth.

"Why don't you get up and dance?" demanded Granny, at the top of her voice. "A young girl like you shouldn't be sitting down."

"I hate dancing." I had to remember not to shout back at her, but speak clearly. She hated being shouted at.

"No young one hates dancing. Your mother loved it. Always sneaking out to dances, she was."

I looked at Granny in amazement.

"Wearing too much make-up and shiny skirts. I didn't like it, I can tell you, young Jane. I gave her a good talking-to."

I loved the idea of somebody giving Mam a good talking-to.

"And what did she say?" I asked.

"You know the sort of thing. Girls have to enjoy themselves. I told her that doesn't mean staying out all night and kissing people on the street."

"Who did she kiss on the street?" I asked.

"Martin Farmer," she said. "I never liked him. I was glad when she gave him up."

I'd never heard of Martin Farmer.

"What else did she do, Gran?" This was a great opportunity to get information.

"All the things young girls do. Silly things." Her voice trailed off. She had retreated into the past, her eyes were distant.

"You won't find out anything from Granny," said Declan, suddenly turning around to me. "She's too discreet."

"Oh, I don't know," I said. "She's already told me about another of my mother's boyfriends. Martin Farmer. And I happen to know that she had someone called Fritz for a while. God knows how many else."

"She still only married one person," said Declan.

I made a face at him.

"Come on, Jane." Dad came over to the table. "Time for a dance with my daughter."

"I'm useless at dancing," I moaned but allowed him to take me on to the dance floor.

"You need lessons," he said.

"Nobody dances like this any more," I said. "Lessons would be a waste of money."

"No, they wouldn't. People will always like this sort of dancing. It might go in and out of fashion, but it will last longer than that shaking around you go on with."

"I don't much like shaking around either," I admitted.

"Your Mam likes dancing," he said. "Always did."

"She's good at it."

"So would you be if you practised."

"No I wouldn't, I'm too – too lumpy."

He held me away from him. "Don't be silly," he said. "You're perfect."

I suppose all fathers think their daughters are wonderful, but it was nice to hear my father say so. What's more, he almost believed it. I gave him a hug.

Stevie Cleere introduced "Josefina – with a voice like spun gold". She sounded like Edith Piaf. I hated Edith Piaf.

"You sing better than that," Declan told Ruth, who looked pleased.

Around the table again people had switched places. Joan and Kathleen were beside each other and I eavesdropped on their conversation. Not deliberately, but my back was partially turned and I couldn't help hearing them.

"So if you like him, why didn't you bring him along?" Kathleen asked.

"Not to something like this," said Joan. "This is not my thing, really."

"Oh, I enjoy our get-togethers," said Kathleen. "We hardly get to see each other."

"This family sees each other far too often," observed Joan. "The McDermotts know too much about each other. But if I said I didn't want to come, they'd go mad."

"So what is he doing tonight?"

"I don't know. Sitting in front of the TV, I hope. Missing me, I hope."

They both laughed. I was in shock. It sounded like Joan had a boyfriend. The thought was horrifying. She was old. Joan, I thought, should either be married or single. People her age didn't have boyfriends. It was too ludicrous for words. She was nearly forty, for God's sake! She should have more sense.

I got up and went to the Ladies again. I sat in a cubicle, picking at my nails. What if I never found another boyfriend? What if I was still looking for someone when I was forty? It was a horrible idea. I should be out having fun tonight. With people my own age. Not hanging around with desperate forty-year-olds.

I recognised Judith and Olivia's voices outside.

"He's besotted with her, of course," said Olivia, tensely. "And she's just stringing him along."

"But there's no harm in it," said Judith.

"Of course not. Not yet, anyway. But I would so like him to go out with a normal girl."

"She's probably very nice under all that black," said Judith.

Olivia laughed. "It's hard to tell, isn't it. It's simply that I imagined Declan to pick someone more – oh, I don't know."

"More ordinary?"

"I suppose so."

"He hasn't picked her yet," said Judith comfortingly. "It'll probably peter out. How old is he now?"

"Twenty-two," said Olivia.

"He'll grow out of her. Or she'll change," said Judith. "How old is she?"

"I'm not sure. Something around the same, I suppose."

"I'll bet you any money that by next year she'll have cut her hair and changed her colour scheme," said Judith.

"Hopefully not to yellow," said Olivia, and I could hear the laughter in her voice. "Isn't poor Jane's outfit appalling?"

I froze.

"She's not a raving beauty, is she?" asked Judith.

"It's strange when you consider Maureen at that age," said Olivia.

"Maureen was beautiful," said Judith. "I always envied her. She was so much prettier than the rest of us. Poor old Jane must feel like the proverbial ugly duckling whenever she sees her mother."

"Oh Jane will grow into herself," said Aunt Olivia easily. "Maureen never needed to. She just had an aura about her."

"Do you remember Nick Maguire?" laughed Judith, "and how he kept pushing poems to Maureen through the letterbox?"

"And she hated him." Olivia laughed, too.

"Wonder what became of him?"

Olivia didn't answer, but I presume she shrugged, consigning Nick to the heap of Mam's spurned lovers.

"We'd better get a move on," said Judith. They used the toilets, washed their hands and left. I waited for a few minutes before I moved. Then I wiped the tears from my cheeks.

I was outside my body for the rest of the night, an observer, not a participant. I could see myself sit around the table and laugh at people's jokes, dance with Dad and Noel, even once with Declan. But it was not me who was dancing with them, but somebody being watched by me. I talked to Olivia and Judith and hated them while smiling at them. Hating their pity for me, knowing they were laughing at me all the time. I watched Ruth and filed away her poise and indifference to use myself at a later date. I watched them all as they mellowed through the evening until it was time for us to go home. I could see some of myself in some of them, in a movement or expression, but I didn't want to be like them, talking of their childhood and their houses and trivial things. I was beyond this and I now pitied them for the shallowness of their lives.

The drive home was quiet. We dropped Gramps back to his house where, contrary to his expectations throughout the evening, nobody had broken in and robbed him and where all was peaceful. Mam helped him get ready for bed while Dad and I sat in the tiny parlour. Dad nodded off while I read the paper, the silence of the room only broken by the solemn tick of the clock on the mantelpiece and an occasional snore from Dad.

He was cranky when Mam came downstairs to wake him up. She insisted on driving the rest of the way back home, which terrified me because she was an awful driver. It terrified Dad too, so he kept his eyes shut for the entire journey.

I climbed into bed and pulled the covers around me. It had been a dreadful night. No worse than I'd expected. But I knew now that I had to change my life. They were all sorry for me. I could see that. I needed to become someone else. Someone like Ruth. With panache. I couldn't play it safe any more. At the very least, I would go to Ruth's hairdresser's and get my hair cut.

It would be different when I moved out, of course. When I moved in with Lucy and the twins, I'd be able to spread my wings a bit more. I was going to take my life in my hands and do things. I was going to leave my childhood behind. I was going to grow up at last.

3

May 1981

(UK No. 12 – Can You Feel It – *Jacksons)*

⁂

I didn't get to see Lucy at all the following week. I was up to my neck in work and Jessica was a complete slave-driver. I checked letters of credit and sent off telexes as though my life depended on it. On Friday night, the gang from work decided to go for a few drinks. Jessica said that she was buying – we deserved it. We arrived at the pub at half five and it was already crowded with bank employees. We found a table in the corner and nabbed a few seats. There were five people in our section – Jessica, Peter Mulhall, Lisa O'Toole, Alan Grant and myself. We got on well together although we were very different people. Jessica, Peter and I were the hardworking ones. Lisa really wanted to work in Personnel and Alan was lazy. But great fun.

"Did you hear about Ellen Hamilton?" asked Jessica as she put her glass on the table. "She resigned. She's going to work in RTE."

"Doing what?" asked Lisa.

"Presenting a kids' programme," Jessica told her.

We looked at her in amazement. "Really?" I asked.

Jessica nodded.

"Fair play to her," said Alan. "I couldn't sit around making soppy jokes about kids."

"You'd never last," said Jessica tartly. "TV works to a tight schedule. You're not exactly known for your timekeeping."

We waited for Alan's reaction. "I do my best."

"You're best isn't exactly great," said Jessica. "What makes you late all the time?"

"Exhaustion," said Alan. "I live life to the limits."

Jessica regarded him thoughtfully. "If you live it to the limits you've been doing lately, you'll be in trouble," she warned him. "I've got you off the hook twice already this month."

Alan looked slightly abashed. "I know. You're a pet, Jessica. I promise to be good in work if I can be bad outside it. Anyone for another drink?"

We nodded and Alan went off to order.

"He's mad," said Lisa.

"Takes all sorts," said Peter. "And he's a bit of a laugh."

I liked Alan. In my new, get-it-together life I half-wondered if he was the sort of guy I could go out with. I knew that he wasn't the sort of person I could spend the rest of my life with, but that was a separate issue. But there was no spark with Alan and you needed a spark.

He was frighteningly handsome. His hair was jet black and his eyes were navy blue. His body was tanned and muscular. I felt my heart race.

I didn't know him. I'd never met him before in my life. I met him in St Stephen's Green. I was feeding the ducks. He spoke to me and I knew then. The spark was there. I wanted him. No pretending.

"Are we going clubbing afterwards?" asked Alan as he returned with more drinks. "There's a gang at the other end of the bar going out to Parks."

"I don't mind," I said. "Whatever anyone wants to do."

"I won't," said Jessica, "but don't mind me, I just don't like nightclubs."

I was going to go to a nightclub. No more pretending that I wasn't interested. I was going to go and I was going to have a good time. I got up and went to the loo. Despite the fact that the pub itself had been done up last year, they hadn't bothered much with the toilets and the small area was crowded with girls trying to do running repairs on their make-up while others queued for the two cubicles.

"Fucking ridiculous," said one girl. "All these people and two fucking toilets. What do they think we are?"

I stood in the queue, grateful to be under the air-conditioner. I always felt faint when pubs were crowded and when the air became thick with perfume, sweat and smoke.

I locked the cubicle door. Ever since the night in the Walnut Rooms, I expected to hear people talking about me in the Ladies. It was pathetic, really. I came out and redid my face. I pulled my brush through my hair and wondered how long it would take for it to grow again.

It had been a mistake to get it cut, I thought, as I looked at myself in the mirror. I'd got it done at lunch-time on Monday, but it hadn't been a good idea. My carrotty curls were gone and the hairdresser had created a much sleeker look which relied on masses of mousse and gel. It looked very stylish, but it wasn't me. I wasn't a short-haired person. I would be glad when it grew again.

I pushed my way back into the bar.

"Watch where you're going!" The voice was angry.

"Sorry," I said.

"So you should be, you've nearly drowned me." He looked at me, fury in his eyes.

"Oh, relax," I told him. "It's only a drink."

"It was a drink that took nearly fifteen minutes to get," he said.

I laughed. "You mustn't come here very often," I said. "Look, if it makes you feel any better, I'll order you another one."

"No, thanks," he said. "I couldn't allow that."

"Why not?" I asked.

"Bit unfair," he said. "I only allow girls that I take out to buy me drink. I'm old-fashioned like that."

"Well, you had your chance and you blew it," I told him.

"Maybe you'll go out with me sometime and then I'll allow you to buy me as much drink as you like."

"Maybe I will," I said with a wink as I made my way back to our table.

"Is he from the bank?" I asked, indicating him as I sat down.

"That's Rory McLoughlin," Jessica told me. "He works in the dealing room."

"The dealing room?" I said curiously. "Where they quote us the exchange rates?"

"The very one," said Jessica. "Shower of assholes."

Jessica so rarely criticised anyone that we looked at her in amazement.

"They are," she said. "Think they know everything. Paid too much money, and think they're worth it."

"What exactly do they do?" asked Lisa.

"They buy and sell foreign currency," said Jessica. "You know how there can be a foreign currency amount on our letters of credit? Well, the dealers set the rate that we convert into pounds."

"Oh." Lisa nodded. "Might be interesting."

"It's very fast," admitted Jessica. "I was in the room a while ago. They spend the entire time shouting at each other."

"Why?" asked Lisa.

"Because exchange rates change all the time," Jessica told her. "And if they don't buy or sell at exactly the right time they can lose money."

"Sounds my kind of job," said Alan. "Especially if they pay better."

"You have to be there all the time," Jessica said. "They start at eight in the morning."

"Oh, my God!" Alan rolled his eyes in his head. "The perfect job has just turned into a nightmare."

We laughed. "Actually, they can't do it for very long," said Jessica. "Because it's so high-powered and pressurised, they burn out."

"I feel burnt out and I don't even do that work," laughed Peter.

"You must have to be very good at maths," I mused.

"Absolutely," said Jessica.

"Rules me out, then," I said. "I only barely passed it in my Leaving."

"How the hell did you get a job in a bank then?" asked Lisa.

"My incredible personality," I told her. "And they obviously thought that an A in history would be very useful!"

We ordered some more drink. I was pleasantly mellow by now. I wondered if Lucy would drop in. She'd said that she might, but she was going to an interview at five o'clock and she might just go straight home afterwards. I looked at my watch. Almost eleven. The night had flown.

"Last orders!" shouted the barmen.

"One for the road?" I asked.

My colleagues nodded. I pushed my way towards the bar again.

"Stand clear, stand clear!" He looked at me in mock horror and moved away. "It's the drink spiller," he said.

"You spilled your own," I told him. "Don't blame me."

I shouted my order across the bar. "Are you sure I can't buy you one?" I asked.

He shook his head. "Thanks, but no thanks." He was drunk, but not very drunk. It took a moment for the blue eyes to focus on me again.

"What's your name?" he asked.

"Why?" I returned.

"I'd like to know."

"Why?"

"I don't know. I'd like to know." He looked confused.

"Jane," I told him.

"Jane." He rolled the name around on his tongue. "Jane." He looked thoughtful for a moment. "What rhymes with Jane?" he asked.

I shrugged. "Plain springs to mind," I said. It always did.

"That's too common, besides, it's not true," he said. "No – wait, I have it. Jane – hair aflame, shall we kiss, in a lane."

"What!"

"It's a poem," he said. "I've entitled it 'To Jane'."

"Thanks very much," I said. "You're very thoughtful."

"Don't you like it?" he asked.

"It's the nicest poem anyone has ever composed for me," I said, as I paid the barman.

"Let me help you with the drinks," said Rory.

"If you like."

He came back to the table with me. The gang looked at him.

"I'm Rory," he said. "This is Jane."

Peter grinned and winked at me. "Peter," he said. "And Lisa and Alan. You know Jessica already."

Rory furrowed his brow and looked at her. "Of course I do," he said gallantly, as he took her hand and kissed it. "Jessica. I could never forget Jessica."

"How nice," she said.

He looked around at us. "Do you all work for the bank?"

Alan nodded.

"And a great organisation it is, too," said Rory. He looked around. "Don't go away. I'm getting my drink."

He wandered off and I looked at the others helplessly. "He just tagged on," I said. "Sorry."

"Oh, he's all right," said Jessica. "He probably won't be back anyway. The dealers are a very cliquish crowd."

But he did come back, carrying two pints of Guinness.

"We haven't seen you here before, Rory." Jessica sipped her drink and looking questiongly at him.

"Oh, we usually drink in Larry's," Rory told her. "But this isn't a bad pub. Good company."

Jessica dug me in the ribs and I tried to ignore her.

"So, where do all you guys work?" asked Rory.

"International," said Peter. "Not as exciting a job as yours."

Rory looked pleased with himself. "It's pretty intense," he said, preening.

"D'you ever get to go abroad?" I asked.

"Sometimes," said Rory. "We go to London a bit. I was on a course there the week before last. And there's a forex conference every year. I haven't gone to that yet, but it's held in various countries. It's hard work."

"Sounds it." Peter couldn't keep the irony out of his voice.

Rory ignored it. He turned to me. "How long have you been with the bank?" he asked.

Suddenly, I was interested in him. I don't know whether it was the blue of his eyes, or the lock of red-brown hair that fell into his right eye or even whether it was the scent of an unfamiliar aftershave which wafted from him, but the attraction was there. I felt myself straighten in the seat and look at him more closely.

"Couple of years," I said, opening my eyes wide at him.

"I've never seen you before," he said.

"Nor I you."

We were silent for a moment. The others no longer existed as we looked at each other.

"Are you going anywhere later?" he asked.

"Perhaps." I looked at the others. They looked back, unconcerned.

"Do you want to go for something to eat?"

I did, but I didn't want to abandon my friends. I looked at them quizzically.

"Not me," said Jessica, decisively. "I have to get home. I'm getting up early tomorrow."

"Nor me," said Peter.

"I wouldn't mind a bite," said Alan.

We looked at him, then he winced as Lisa pinched him.

"Come on, then," said Rory, looking at me. "There's a nice little restaurant around the corner."

"D'you mind?" I asked the others.

"Absolutely not." Jessica smiled. "See you Monday."

I followed Rory out of the pub. The air was cold, the warmth of the previous week gone. I shivered slightly and pulled my jacket around me.

"Cold?" asked Rory.

I shook my head. "Not really."

We didn't hold hands or anything as we walked side by side up the street, although we both stopped to look over Baggot Street Bridge. Rory rummaged in his pocket and took out a penny which he threw into the water. I watched him in amazement.

"I always do it," he told me. "Every time I cross the bridge. It's for luck."

"What sort of luck?" I asked.

He smiled at me. "Any sort, really," he said. "Luck in work, usually. But other things too."

We stared at each other for a moment and I moved towards him, but he suddenly shuffled and thrust his hands into his trouser pockets.

"Come on," he said. "I'm starving."

I walked along beside him, struggling to keep up with his long, ranging stride. He was an odd person, I thought, unlike anyone I had ever known before. Supremely self-confident, but strangely disconcerting.

"Slow down, can't you," I pleaded, breathlessly.

He stopped mid-stride. "Sorry," he said, "I always walk quickly."

The restaurant was Italian, small and dimly-lit. There were posters of Italian cities on the walls and lighted candles in Chianti bottles on the tables. It was pleasantly warm with an aroma of garlic and oregano. A waiter who wore a black suit with a deep red cummerbund and green bow tie approached us.

"Mr McLoughlin," he said. "So nice to see you."

"Hi, Mario," said Rory. "Can we have a table for two?"

"For you, of course," said the waiter. "A nice, intimate table, perhaps?"

"That would be excellent," said Rory.

We followed the waiter to a table at the back of the restaurant. He gave us a couple of menus. "Would you like anything to drink?" he asked.

"A bottle of red," said Rory. He looked at me. "That OK?"

I nodded, still half reading the menu.

"Have you decided?" Rory asked me after a minute or two.

"The tortellini would be nice," I said. I hadn't eaten tortellini before, but the menu said beef-filled pasta, so I reckoned I couldn't go too far wrong.

"And for you, as usual, the spaghetti?" Mario looked enquiringly at Rory.

"You know me too well," said Rory. "Perhaps I should have something different one day."

"Perhaps this should be that day," said Mario.

Rory looked at Mario and then at me. "Perhaps." He sounded doubtful. "Oh, what the hell," he said. "Mario, I like the spaghetti. Give me the spaghetti."

The waiter laughed. "Whatever you want."

I didn't know what to say to Rory. I looked at him carefully. He had a strong face, high cheekbones, high forehead, determined chin.

"So what do you do?" he asked me.

"Nothing as exciting as you," I told him. "International trade. I check letters of credit, that sort of thing."

He nodded, but he wasn't listening to me. He closed his eyes.

He had incredibly long eyelashes, the sort any girl would die for. They looked unaccountably soft against cheeks with a five-o'clock shadow. He was unlike any man I had ever met before. He snored gently.

I looked around. Nobody was watching us. I kicked him softly under the table. He grunted, opened his eyes and looked around him.

"Wake up," I said.

"What?" He looked startled. "Oh, shit, Jane – I'm sorry."

"It's OK," I said. "You're tired."

He pealed with laughter and this time people looked at us.

"I'm not tired," he said. "Well, a bit, I suppose. No, my lovely Jane, I've had about eight pints of Guinness tonight and if anything's wrong with me, it's that I've drunk far too much and I've been unbelievably unfair to you. I've dragged you to my favourite restaurant, I haven't been exactly wonderful company and I've had the absolutely disgraceful cheek to fall asleep. I'm very, very sorry."

He looked down at his plate, but not before I saw a glint of amusement in his eyes.

"You're a terrible spoofer," I said easily. "You're not a bit sorry."

He smiled and took my hand. His grasp was firm and confident, his palms dry.

"I am sorry I fell asleep," he said. "That was rude. But I'm not sorry I went to the pub – despite my best intentions – and I'm not sorry I stayed to drink more than I should have, because otherwise I wouldn't have met you and that would have made me even sorrier."

He was amazing.

"I'm not sorry either," I said, finally.

"Good." He unfolded a napkin with a flourish. "Now here comes Mario with our food, why don't we just eat up."

The tortellini were wonderful, cooked in a gloriously light tomato sauce and bursting with flavour. I told Mario as much when he came to check on us.

"I'm so glad," he said, beaming at me. "I will tell the chef."

"The chef is his brother," Rory told me. "They opened last year. It's incredibly good."

"Do you eat here much?" I asked. "He seems to know you very well."

"It's the in-spot for dealers," said Rory. "We all eat here."

"Are all dealers really clever?" I asked.

Rory grinned. "I am," he said, with that self-confident air that I was beginning to recognise, "but not everyone is."

"What do you do when you're not working?" I asked him. It was difficult to make him volunteer any information.

"I play golf," he said.

I groaned. "Not another one."

"What do you mean?"

"Nearly everyone in the bank plays golf. It's so utterly boring."

He shook his head. "It's a brilliant game," he told me. "What else would have you out in the fresh air for four hours?"

"Almost anything," I said.

"Ah, but so much business is done on the golf course," said Rory. "You play any other sport and you don't have time to talk. With golf, it's different."

"Why would you want to do business when you're playing a game?" I asked.

He clucked at me. "You've a lot to learn, young Jane," he said. "If you ever want to get on in business you've a lot to learn."

I played around with my food. "I don't know if I want to get on in business," I said.

"Everyone does," said Rory. "Everyone wants to do well and make pots of money and if anyone says different, they're lying." His tone was strong and sure.

"There are other things," I told him. "Like happiness."

"Anyone who says money doesn't buy happiness is poor," Rory commented. "The only reason they say it is so you can feel good about not being able to afford three holidays a year and a house in Foxrock."

"That's a terrible thing to say."

"But true." Rory sucked a strand of spaghetti from the fork and it sped into his mouth like an express train, scattering tomato sauce as it went.

We both laughed. He took my hand again.

"I like you, Jane," he said.

"I like you too." I looked at my plate.

Rory filled my glass with wine. It was smooth and slid down my throat with ease. The combination of wine and beer was making my head heavy. I'd have a hangover in the morning.

"Dessert, coffee?" asked Mario, clearing away our plates.

"Cappuccino," said Rory. "Do you want anything, Jane?"

"Coffee," I said dreamily.

The walls of the restaurant were expanding and contracting. I blinked a few times to clear my head.

"It's very warm," I said, closing my eyes.

"You going to fall asleep on me now?" asked Rory, who had suddenly come to life.

"No, no," I said. "Just resting."

I don't remember drinking my coffee, but I remember Rory took me by the arm and steered me out of the restaurant. Mario bade us farewell and shook Rory by the hand.

"See you soon, signorina," he called after me.

I ran my tongue around my lips. They were dry.

"Come on," said Rory. "I'll get you home. Where do you live?"

"I'm perfectly capable of getting myself home," I told him, shaking my head in the cool night air. "There's no need for you to put yourself to any trouble."

I really wished I hadn't drunk so much. OK, some Fridays we did give it a bit of a lash, but it wasn't something I did regularly. Three drinks and a couple of Cokes was usually my limit. After all, I was a sensible person.

"I have absolutely no doubt that you'd be able to get home yourself," Rory told me. "But it's late and I don't think it would be a good idea to have you wandering around near the canal at this hour. So please let me see you home."

"I'll get a taxi." I clutched his arm and missed my step.

He caught me and drew me closer to him.

"We'll share a taxi," he said, looking down at me.

He was not my usual sort of person. His face was too hard and he wasn't exactly good-looking. Interesting, maybe, but not handsome.

All the same, I looked into those compelling blue eyes. There was a magnetism there that I couldn't ignore.

He smiled at me and kissed me. In the middle of Baggot Street, with people around us, we clung together in our own world. His mouth pressed harder on mine and my body moulded into his. I might still be a virgin, I thought wildly, but I'm a good kisser.

He groaned slightly, and took his lips from mine. I looked at him thoughtfully. He tightened his hold.

"Now I'm definitely not letting you go home on your own," he said. "Where do you live?"

"Near Terenure," I told him.

"That's OK," he said. "No problem."

"Where do you live?" I asked.

"Blackrock," he answered.

"But really, I live out of your way," I protested. "I can get a taxi myself."

He let me go and held me at arms length. "Is there some reason," he asked, in exasperation, "that you don't want to share a taxi with me? Do I have B.O.? Am I so incredibly ugly that you don't want to be seen with me? Are you afraid that I'll lead you to a fate worse than death?"

I laughed at him. "No."

"Then for God's sake, woman, share a taxi with me."

I bit my lip to stop laughing. He looked so funny in his mock anger.

"Of course I'll share a taxi with you," I said. "I'm just playing hard to get."

"Oh, really," he murmured, pulling me towards him again. "How hard to get?"

"Not very," I answered. "Not very hard to get at all."

Our progress along the canal was slow. Taxis passed us by, and we didn't care. I felt safe and secure in his arms, and I was happy to stop every few yards to kiss him. He tasted of wine and garlic and I supposed I did too. His aftershave was strong and masculine. His hold was possessive and fierce. But he never did more than kiss me, he didn't try to undo the buttons of my cotton blouse, he didn't even slide his hands under my jacket as I'd half expected. He kissed me with an intensity that was almost frightening, but which I returned.

The night air was cold, but I didn't feel it. I was tired, but I didn't notice. When we got to Portobello Bridge, Rory suddenly held me away from him.

"Better get you home," he gasped, "before I do something that I won't be responsible for."

I raised an eyebrow.

"Witch," he said and kissed me again. "Witch."

I held him closely.

He flagged down a taxi and we bundled into it.

I gave my address to the driver, while I burrowed into the crook of Rory's arm.

"I want to let you know that I'm not ready for a steady relationship," he whispered into my ear.

I turned my head to look at him. "Why not?"

"Because I'm a busy person. I work hard. I'm twenty-six years old. I'm not sure I'm ready to settle down."

"Rory," I whispered. "We've had a drink and something to eat. It's hardly a lifelong commitment."

"So long as you understand," he warned. "I don't want you to get the wrong idea about me."

"I like you," I said. "I won't get the wrong idea."

But I more than liked him, I thought, as I finally slid between the sheets of my single bed that night. He interested me more than any other man I had ever met. There was an intensity about him, an energy that no one else I knew possessed. Whether he liked it or not, I was going to see more of Rory McLoughlin. I could feel it, and I knew that somehow our lives would slot together. Even if he wasn't ready for a steady relationship yet. Hell, I wasn't ready for a steady relationship. But I was ready for a bit of fun, and I was sure that Rory would be fun.

4

May 1981

(UK No. 19 – I Want To Be Free – *Toyah)*

I didn't see Rory McLoughlin the following week. We were in a different wing of the building to the dealers and I'd never even been on the dealing room floor. I'd seen pictures of it, of course, they always plastered them into the Annual Report, pictures of people holding two phones to their ears and trying to write at the same time. Progressive. Dynamic. Hard-working.

I was put out that he hadn't bothered to call, despite both our assurances to each other that we weren't looking for a long-term relationship. The least he could have done was phone me, I thought miserably. I tried to forget about him. I was still stuck in the groove of thinking that each man I met should be forever. I did my best to shove him into the back of my mind and not to jump like a frightened gazelle every time the phone rang.

Jessica Fitzgerald teased me gently about him, although I swore to her that we had only gone for something to eat and that nothing had happened.

"Nothing?" she asked, her voice unbelieving.

"Not the sort of thing you're thinking about, anyway," I returned. I took my pen and ran through a checklist of numbers.

"Stop pretending to work," said Jessica. "I can't believe you didn't get up to anything with Rory."

"Why ever not?" I demanded. "It's not as though he's really my type."

"Because everyone wants to get off with one of the dealers," she told me. "They earn good money, they have a great life and most of them are good-looking."

"Rory McLoughlin is not good-looking," I informed her. "Not in my book, anyway. He's interesting, though." I was pleased to be able to say all this without blushing.

"I'll be watching you," she said, picking up a file from my desk. "And if you spend your time taking personal phone calls, I'll know I'm right."

I made a face at her retreating back. I was a bit disappointed that Rory hadn't called, although I didn't want to admit to it yet, not even to myself.

I bent over my letters of credit and read through the documents, turning over the sheets of paper with frantic speed.

Lucy's phone call distracted me.

"Busy?" she asked me, with the air of one who is not.

"Pretty much." I glanced up to see if Jessica was watching me.

"Can you talk?"

"You talk, I'll listen."

"Well, look, Jane, I think we should do the flat-hunting tonight and tomorrow. I can do it tonight, so can Brenda and Grace."

"Do you have anywhere in mind?" I idly circled an error in the papers. Could nobody ever get things right? This would have to be done again.

"We've three," said Lucy.

"Three!" I was surprised. I hadn't realised that the girls had gone so far without me.

"Yes. The ones I told you about off Waterloo Road. They look great, Jane. Real apartments. Then there's a flat in Donnybrook Village – that's the downstairs of a house – and there's a purpose-built flat over some shops on Morehampton Road. All very convenient for work, don't you think."

"Convenient for me, certainly," I said. "But you're out in Tallaght."

"Only until the end of next week," Lucy said. "Anyway, let's face it, Jane, I could be anywhere. So where I live doesn't really matter. Besides," she coughed self-consciously, "Dad is buying me a car."

"A car!" I was overwhelmed with jealousy. "A car!"

"Yes. It's my twenty-first present. He couldn't get it before now. It wasn't in."

"Where's he getting it?"

Lucy was silent for a moment. "Your Dad's place," she said.

I wished that my father, the garage owner, had bought me a car for my birthday. The watch Mam and Dad got me was lovely and I'd no reason to complain, but a car would have been superb. Why, I wondered, couldn't my family have as much money as the McAllisters? My Dad worked hard enough. It seemed terribly unjust.

"What sort of car?" I asked casually.

"Only a Mini," said Lucy, but she could hardly keep the pride out of her voice.

"I'm delighted," I said. "That means we'll be able to drink and you can drive."

"It means that I can live wherever we like," Lucy reminded me. "And I like the idea of Donnybrook. It's always seemed nice and classy."

I laughed. Jessica glanced up at me and I immediately started checking papers again.

"Better than Rathmines, anyway," Lucy said firmly. "So can you meet us?"

"What time?"

"Sixish?"

"OK. Where?"

"Do you want to meet in the Burlington?" asked Lucy. "We can look at the apartment there first and then walk up to Donnybrook."

"No car yet?" I asked, disappointed.

"Not till tomorrow," said Lucy. "Your Dad is giving it a service."

"Good old Dad," I said, cheerfully. "At least you'll be sure it'll go. Unless I find some important engine part lying on the table after tea. It has been known to happen."

"Funny ha ha," said Lucy. "Look, I've got to go. I'll see you later, OK."

"OK," I said. "Mind yourself."

"À bientôt," said Lucy.

I grimaced. Her habit of ending conversations in

her newly-acquired fluent French always reminded me that she was the one who had spent the year away, not me. I wished, oh how I wished, that I'd been allowed to go. I hated the way she could chatter in French – not that there was anyone on the Riverbrook Estate who could chatter back, but it was amazing to listen to her all the same.

I looked at my watch. Four o'clock. I rubbed my eyes and sat back in my chair. Three flats to look at sounded great. I only hoped that I could persuade my parents that I wouldn't turn into some wild, permissive person as soon as I moved out.

I hadn't yet broached the subject of the flat with them. They couldn't actually do anything about it now, of course, I was old enough to make my own decisions, but I hated being at odds with Mam and Dad. This was still my greatest problem. That I hadn't been a rebellious teenager, that I hadn't really caused them endless nights of grief. I'd never dyed my hair, or worn outrageous clothes or safety pins through my nose. So when I told them that I wanted to do a perfectly simple thing like stay out overnight (as I had when Lucy had come home – we'd stayed at her brother Michael's place), or go away for a weekend, they always spent ages asking me to explain in minute detail where I was going and who I would be with. That's all very well when you're seventeen, but a bit much when you're twenty-one.

The only way Mam and Dad would ever see me as an adult was if I left home and lived my own life. It wasn't that I didn't care about them, didn't love them in my own way. It was simply that I couldn't possibly live with them any more.

I hated it when Mam complained about the state of my bedroom. It was my room, surely she shouldn't care if I left tights on the floor? I hated it when she criticised my hair. It was my hair, I could wear it however I liked. I hated it when she wanted to know where I was at every moment of the day. I wanted my freedom. The bliss of putting my key in the door whatever time of the day or night I liked and not hearing the whispered "Is that you, Jane?" I couldn't wait to move into the flat.

The girls were already at the Burlington when I arrived. Brenda and Grace looked uncannily alike. They both wore their department store skirts and blouses, blue skirts and blue and white striped blouses. I would bet anything that customers took a double take when they moved from Ladies' Separates (Brenda) to Evening Wear (Grace). They would wonder how on earth the salesgirl could move from one side of the floor to the other so quickly. Despite the fact that the girls usually wore their hair differently, they were identical tonight. I blinked at them. It took a moment to decide who was who.

"Hi, Jane," smiled Brenda (the gold chain with the initial B the giveaway for those that needed it). "Want a drink?"

Lucy looked anxiously at her watch. "I said we'd be there by a quarter past six," she said. "It's nearly that now. Maybe we should just go?"

"I don't mind," I said. I slipped my jacket back on. "Let's head off."

"The ideal thing about here," said Lucy, as we reached Waterloo Mews, the apartment block off Waterloo Road, "would be how near it is to everything. The hotel, the pubs, the shops – "

"And work," I said. It would be ideal for me.

"What about the other flats?" asked Grace. "Aren't we going to look at them?"

"Oh, sure," said Lucy. "But what do you think, girls? If this one is OK, will we just go for it?"

"If they'll let us," said Brenda. "I think this would be the best."

"We haven't even seen it yet," said Grace. "Wait until we look first. It might be an awful tip."

But the apartments were new, and still smelled of fresh paint and new carpets. The block was five storeys high, in warm red brick with black wrought-iron balconies protruding from each apartment. The sun shone weakly, casting a watery glow across the face of the building.

I liked the look of the apartment block. It looked stylish and modern and I liked the idea of moving into a purpose-built block rather than taking over part of a house.

The letting agent was waiting for us in the lobby.

"There's a security camera." He waved his hand in its general direction. "Follow me, will you."

We trooped after him.

"Third floor," he said, "it's quicker to take the stairs."

The stairs were carpeted in pale green. I thought it might get dirty very quickly, and then I mentally slapped myself for such a domesticated, middle-aged thought.

"Number Thirty-Three," intoned the agent. "This way, ladies."

We fell in love with the apartment instantly. It was impossible not to. The door opened into a small hallway, off which were four doors.

The agent flung one open. "Living area," he said. "Very bright and spacious. Gets the evening sun." The rays flickered over the floor.

"It's lovely," I whispered to Brenda, who nodded. The room was decorated in pale blue and grey. China blue wallpaper on which hung some pretty water-colour prints, smoke-grey carpet and natural pine furniture. The agent was right. It was a bright, airy room.

"Kitchen in here."

The kitchen was a small room off the living room, a room to stand up in, not for sitting in. It was white and green, white formica cupboards with green handles, white ceramic tiles with a green leaf pattern.

"There's a waste disposal unit in the sink," said the agent.

"Nice," murmured Lucy.

He led the way back into the hallway. "Bedrooms here." He opened two of the doors. "One slightly bigger than the other. Both with fitted wardrobes."

We wandered around the bedrooms. Both were decorated identically, yellow and mauve. A bit bright for my taste, but pretty nevertheless.

"I like it," said Brenda.

"And this is the bathroom." He opened the last door. "No window in here, but an extractor fan." He switched it on as though it were an astounding feat of engineering.

"I love it," said Grace.

"I'll leave you to look around for a few minutes," he said.

We wandered through the apartment again, thrilled to bits with it. I'd no desire whatsoever to see any crummy half house in Donnybrook or flat over shops. This was the one I wanted. I stepped out of the sliding doors on to the balcony. The evening sun was disappearing from it now, but later in the summer it would get the full benefit of its westerly aspect. Despite the fact that we were near Baggot Street and Leeson Street the sounds of the cars were muted and distant. Birds chirped at each other from the copse of trees in the grounds. It was perfection.

I turned back inside. The girls were still wandering around the apartment, exclaiming with delight over any little item that took their fancy.

"I bought it for you." He looked at me.

"What on earth do you mean?"

"I want you to have somewhere of your own. A bolthole, if you like."

"But, Armand – "

"No, please, Jane. It is important. You are my life, you know that. But I am in France, you are here. It is necessary for you to have somewhere of your own, no?"

"Of course I want somewhere of my own. But I can't possibly – "

"No, please. A gift. From me. From the bottom of my heart."

"Armand – "

"Jane, you cannot refuse this of me. Whether we stay together or not, this is still my gift to you. For all you have done. For the love you have given me."

"It's too much."

"Don't be silly. I already have two houses, a villa in St Tropez, an apartment in New York. Surely one little apartment here, in your town, is not too much? I want to give it to you. I love you."

"I love you too."

We melted into each other's arms. Time stood still. The evening sun slipped below the balcony as his lips found mine . . .

The twins returned to the living-room, smiling. "What do you think?" asked Brenda.

"I love it," I said. "I feel part of it already."

"Me too," said Grace. "Isn't it cute?"

"And there's quite a lot of space," said Lucy, who had come back into the room. "It doesn't feel at all poky or anything, does it?"

"How much?" I asked, "compared to the others?"

"Fifty pounds a month more than the house, thirty more than the flat over the shops." Lucy checked her notebook.

"Can we afford it?" I asked. I knew, divided by four, that I could afford the rent. I was earning the most money and the rent on the apartment wasn't much more than I gave my parents, anyway. Of course, I'd have to pay for food and all the other expenses that I didn't have to worry about at home, but I knew I could manage. I'd got very good at managing finances.

"We can," said the twins. "Once we keep up our commission levels," added Brenda. "And we're good at selling. Did you know that the take in my department is up over 10% on this time last year?"

Brenda was extremely proud of her sales ability.

"And mine by 12%," said Grace. "Although we have two new salesgirls as well as me."

"And you, Lucy?" I asked.

"No probs," said Lucy. "I'm employed by an agency now, not the individual companies. I can manage."

"So will we go ahead?" I asked.

Although Lucy had organised the viewing, everyone waited for me when it came to making the decision.

The girls nodded happily.

The agent was standing in the kitchen looking out of the window. I cleared my throat as I entered the room. He turned to me.

"Have you decided on anything, girls?" he asked.

"We'd like to take it." I tried to keep my voice calm.

He smiled at me. "Good," he said. "There are a few things we have to sort out."

He listed all the things he needed. References, a bank statement, a deposit. I protested. He told me that they needed all these things to make sure that we didn't do a runner and leave the place in a mess.

"Once your references check out, then we'll be ready," he told me. "Then you can sign the lease and we're in business."

"How long will all this take?" I asked.

"Only a week." He smiled suddenly and looked altogether more human.

We had hoped that we'd have everything signed and sealed that evening, and it was a bit disappointing not to be given the keys there and then. But we resigned ourselves to it. Besides, I still had to break the news to my parents.

We had a celebratory drink in the Burlington. Lucy rang the other flat owners and told them that we wouldn't be out to look at their places, then we talked about housekeeping, division of labour and electricity bills.

Brenda and Grace said that they'd take the smaller bedroom, since they were used to sharing. Lucy and I were happy to take the other one, although the smaller bedroom actually had a bigger window, and I liked big windows.

I decided not to say anything to my parents until we heard back from the agent that everything was OK. We couldn't see what could go wrong, but I couldn't allow myself to believe that we'd actually got it until he rang.

I spent the next few days in a rash of feverish excitement, waiting for his call. Jessica put my edginess down to the fact that I hadn't heard from Rory, but for once in my life I wasn't pining for some man. The idea of the apartment was far more appealing than anything to do with Rory McLoughlin.

So when we bumped into each other in the staff canteen later that week I was offhand, and he looked surprised when I brushed by him without stopping to talk. From my vantage point at the table near the window I was able to observe him more or less unseen and I could tell that his eyes had followed me and that he was watching me.

Stuff him, I thought, as I speared a chip (why did they have to be so soggy, they drooped over the fork). If he's interested, he can do the running. If he isn't . . . well, if he isn't, there are plenty of people who are.

I didn't care that currently there weren't any interested men. Anyway, once we had our apartment I could see a vista of weekend parties and any number of men stretching out into my future.

Kevin Spencer, the letting agent, rang me the following Thursday to tell me that everything was in order and that I could sign the lease at lunch-time on Friday. I was the only one who could get the time to call in to his office, and so I was the only one who was going to sign the lease. That meant that I would be the one responsible for it. The responsibility was awesome. This was the single most adult thing I'd ever done in my life.

So I called around, sat in the stylish office and waited for him to appear with his folder and his pens and I signed the lease on Apartment 33, Waterloo Mews, off Waterloo Road, Dublin 4.

I walked out with the keys, throwing them up and down in my hand, trying to look casual, until they slid out of my grasp and into the gutter. I scrabbled after them in a panic and pushed them safely into the side pocket of my handbag.

I phoned the girls, told them that I'd the keys, and asked them when they wanted to move in.

Lucy, Brenda and Grace all said that they could

move in straight away. Brenda told me that her father had offered to move their things, Lucy had taken delivery of the car and said that she was already packed, I was the only one who hadn't even had the nerve yet to mention the subject at home.

Mam and Dad were already sitting at the dinner table when I arrived home. Mam took a plate of pasta out of the oven for me. I wished that she wouldn't bother making food for me. I was never sure what time I'd be home and it was ludicrous for her to cook meals that I might not eat. But she did, time and time again, despite my protestations. I eyed the congealed pasta in despair before realising that this was the last time, I could eat it with good grace because I wouldn't be coming home any more.

It was like plastic in my mouth, although I didn't know whether that was because it had dried out in the oven or because I was too nervous to eat.

I broached the subject when Mam poured out her second cup of tea.

"Lucy and I are thinking about moving into a flat." I kept my voice ultra-casual.

"Don't be ridiculous," said Mam. "You don't need to move into a flat."

"Why?"

"Because you've a perfectly good home here. There's no need for you to throw money down the drain renting a flat. Besides, they're all damp and horrible."

"Not this one," I said. I was still keeping my voice casual.

"You mean you've looked at one?" Mam was horrified. "Without telling us first?"

"There wasn't any need to tell you anything," I protested.

"Well, don't bother thinking about it any more," said Dad. "Your Mam's right. It's an awful waste of money. Better stay here and save up for a house."

They hadn't a clue.

"We're, um, actually thinking of moving in this weekend," I mumbled.

"You're what?" Dad put his cup carefully into his saucer and regarded me thoughtfully. I hated it when he regarded me thoughtfully.

I cleared my throat. "I'm moving into an apartment this weekend," I told them. "With Lucy and the Quinlan twins."

"And you didn't think to discuss this with us?" Mam was angry.

"There was nothing to discuss, surely." I tried to sound reasonable. "I mean, I was going to move and so I went to look at the apartment and – well – ." My voice petered out.

"It would have been nice to mention it at home before you did anything." Dad folded his newspaper and put it on the table beside him. "Why didn't you say anything until now?"

"No reason," I said. "We weren't sure we'd actually get this apartment or anything, so I didn't think there was any need to say it until – " I faltered. "It didn't seem worth mentioning."

"You're leaving home and you didn't think it worth mentioning," said Mam. "That's wonderful."

I sighed deeply. I knew that the conversation would turn out like this. But this way, it was a *fait accompli*. There was nothing they could do. If I'd discussed it earlier, they would have found a thousand reasons why I should stay at home a bit longer. And I, feeling guilty, might have stayed.

"So where is this flat?" asked Dad.

"It's not a flat," I said strenuously. "It's a purpose-built apartment. It's lovely, Dad, really it is. It's off Waterloo Road."

"Convenient for work," he said. I shot him a grateful glance.

"You won't feel like you've even left work," said Mam. She stood up and started to clear away the dirty dishes, crashing them into the sink. I bit my lip.

"When exactly do you intend to move in?" asked Dad.

"Over the weekend," I said. "Mr Quinlan said he'd move Brenda and Grace's things and Lucy can pile her stuff into the car."

"Do you want a hand, then?" asked Dad. "I suppose our car is big enough for almost everything."

I smiled at him. "Thanks," I said.

"Is that all you have to say to her?" Mam, abandoned her dishwashing and looked at Dad. "That you'll help her move."

"I don't see that we can exactly stop her, do you, Maureen?" he asked her. "After all, she is twenty-one. She's an adult."

Mam sat down. "I know," she said.

I didn't know what to say. Part of me understood how she felt but I had to live my own life. Dad could recognise that. Why couldn't she?

The atmosphere was a touch icy for the rest of the

evening. Dad tried to keep it light, but Mam was fretful and annoyed. When I went to bed that night, I could hear the murmur of their voices through the wall. I supposed they were talking about me. I pulled my pillow over my head and tried to go to sleep.

When I came home from work the next day, I found most of my possessions neatly packed in brown cardboard boxes. I looked at Mam in surprise.

"I had nothing to do this afternoon," she said lamely. "I thought I'd help."

I hugged her, and she buried her head in my shoulder. "Be careful," she said fiercely.

"Of course I'll be careful." I looked at her in amazement. "What do you take me for?"

She held me at arm's length. "It's not that I don't trust you," she began.

" . . . but," I added.

"But." She smiled at me. "OK, I trust you."

"Thanks." I kissed her on the cheek. "Do you want to help me pack?"

Mam was a good packer. I don't know why, because it wasn't as if she ever went away anywhere. Maybe it was because she was naturally neat and tidy, but she folded my clothes far more professionally that I ever could myself. We took clothes out of my wardrobe and then she went into the spare room and called out to me that I had almost a hundred jumpers in there and how many of them did I want?

I followed her into the bedroom and looked at the mound of knitwear on the bed.

"Anything else in there?" I asked, peering into the wardrobe. I smiled suddenly, for there it was, where it had been for the past four years, my gossamer-light deb's dress. Still shimmering in the evening sunlight, still elegant.

"Don't suppose I'd fit into it now," I said, regretfully, looking down at my body.

"Oh, you probably would," said Mam loyally.

"Don't think so," I said. "I've grown."

We laughed, sharing the joke.

I selected some jumpers from the pile. "I'll leave some of the others," I told her. "Anyhow, I might come back and stay the night from time to time. I might need some clothes here."

She nodded, happy with my remark. I'd no real intention of returning home, but I owed her something.

The great move took place on Saturday morning. For the first time in about ten years, I was awake on Saturday before eleven o'clock. My eyes snapped open at about nine, and I was out of the bed and under the shower by half past. I stood under the heavy flow of water, allowing it to course through my hair and trail down my body. I closed my eyes and dreamed of freedom.

We had already decided on the sequence of events. At the moment, I was the only one with a key. I would get three more cut on the way over to the apartment and be there by half past eleven. I told them that I would wait, that I wouldn't go into the apartment before they arrived, but the twins said not to be stupid, to go in and put on the kettle.

As it turned out, I was there by eleven o'clock. Mam and Dad both came with me, they wanted to see where I was living. I opened the door and showed them in, bursting with pride.

The sun hadn't yet come around to the living-room and the balcony was still in shade. But the rooms were bright and new, and both my parents approved of the apartment. Mam particularly liked the intercom and video which meant that we could see someone at the door before we let them in. She thought that it was superb security. Dad liked the sink disposal unit. Both of them liked the balcony and promised some flowers in pots for it. Dad lugged my gear upstairs and I hauled the boxes into the bedroom that I was to share with Lucy.

Mam and Dad left before the others arrived and for that I was truly grateful. It meant that I had ten minutes in the apartment by myself, feeling proprietorial. I walked from room to room. It was perfectly silent in a way my home never had been. There was no ticking clock, or humming fridge or gentle hissing of an immersion heater.

I stood in front of the full-length mirror in the tiny hallway. Jane O'Sullivan, apartment dweller. Adult. It was great. I laughed aloud with the excitement of it all.

The shrill blast of the intercom sent me into orbit. When I stopped shaking I picked up the receiver. The video screen flickered into life. Brenda and Grace waved at me. I pressed the button and heard the buzzer of the main door as the twins disappeared from view. The intercom buzzed again and Mr Quinlan's face appeared. "Let me in," he said. "I've got all their clothes!"

The Quinlans piled into the apartment, filling the hallway with luggage.

"What a lovely place," said Mr Quinlan, giving it a cursory glance. "Hope you'll be very happy here, girls."

"Thanks, Dad," said Brenda.

"I'll be off then," he said. He didn't bother to stay and check out everything like my parents had. He seemed totally uninterested.

"See you, Dad," said Grace. "I'll phone you later."

"Do you have a phone here?" he asked.

I shook my head. "Not yet."

"Oh, well, the hotel is near enough if you need to call," he said. "See you, Jane."

He picked his way through the hallway, climbing over the boxes.

"I'll pull them out of the way," promised Grace. "God, Jane, isn't this great!"

I hugged her. I couldn't help it.

"Where's Lucy?" asked Brenda.

I shrugged. "No sign," I said. "Probably still in bed." I walked over to the balcony and flung open the doors. "Although how she could possibly sleep – " I stepped outside and leaned over the balcony rail. Behind me, I could hear the Quinlans pulling boxes around the apartment.

Outside, the sky was blue, the air warm. The traffic was a distant hum and there were no children's voices. We were in our sophisticated, adult world. 33 Waterloo Mews.

Lucy's green Mini hurtled up the road and screeched to a stop outside the block. She climbed out and looked up, pushing her blonde hair out of her eyes.

I waved frantically at her. "I'll open the door for you."

"Come down and give me a hand," she yelled. "I can't carry all this myself."

More boxes were hauled into apartment 33, which was beginning to look like a construction site.

"Before we do anything," Lucy reached into one of the boxes, "let's celebrate!" She pulled out a bottle of Asti. "Not exactly vintage champagne," she said, "but it fizzes and makes a popping noise."

"Brilliant!" cried Brenda.

"I've got glasses," I said. "Dad gave me a collection. He gets loads of them from petrol companies."

I rummaged around and found the box full of glasses. I tore off the cellophane and took them out.

"Better rinse them," I said.

"Don't be daft," said Lucy. "It's alcohol. It'll kill any germs."

She pulled the foil wrapper from around the cork. "Ready?"

She eased the cork out of the bottle and it popped pleasingly. She filled the glasses. We stood in the middle of the living-room and clinked the glasses together.

"To the apartment," I said.

"The apartment," the others echoed.

"To girls on tour!" cried Lucy.

"To us."

We spent the day unpacking. It was very

domesticated really and not at all exciting, but we had a great time. I hated hanging up clothes at home. By the afternoon, everything I possessed was neatly hanging on rails in the wardrobe.

We unpacked crockery and cutlery, our books and our clothes. Brenda played her cassette recorder at a level that probably would have had us instantly evicted, except that nobody had yet moved into the apartments beside us.

Ludicrously, for a Saturday night, we sat in. Lucy and I drove up to the Chinese takeaway and brought back curries and sweet and sour. We sat in front of the Quinlan's portable black and white, eating Chinese, drinking the wine we had bought and revelling in our freedom. Then we sat around in a circle, and talked until four in the morning before we fell, exhausted, into bed. I was happier than I'd been in ages.

5

June 1981

(UK No. 13 – Ain't No Stoppin' – *Enigma)*

The rain fell unremittingly from the cloud-filled sky, splashed through the trees and cascaded across the pavements, forming wide oil-streaked puddles that filled the potholes in the roads. People scurried home, heads down, holding a sea of coloured umbrellas over them.

Raindrops plopped from the flat roof over the doorway of Waterloo Mews and joined the rivulet running frantically past the building; the torrent into which I stepped, soaking my feet completely.

I swore gently. It was not being wet that was the problem – I was wet through already, but it was the cumulative effect of being wet and cold in a month which was supposed to be summer that made me mad. I hated Irish summers. Each year, the promise of warm, sunny days. Each year, the reality of grey skies and stiff easterly winds.

I pushed open the entrance door and hurried up the stairs to our apartment, the plastic shopping bags bouncing off my legs.

The relief was immense when I finally got myself and my bags into the apartment. I shook my wet hair and slipped off my sodden coat and shoes. I opened the bathroom door. A forest of damp tights and drying knickers met me. I hung my coat on the back of the door, dumped my umbrella in the bath and carried my bags into the bedroom.

It had been a good day's shopping. I'd bought a new skirt and blouse in Pamela Scotts and a new pair of shoes in Fitzpatricks. The skirt was lilac, calf-length but with a long slit up the side. It was both demure and seductive and, teamed with the crisp white blouse, it looked devastating. My shoes were lilac too, totally unwearable during the day but they would knock 'em for dead at night. They were high-heeled, spiky and hard to wear, but I knew that they were fabulous. I didn't mind suffering for my appearance.

I made some coffee and drank it in the living-room, as I looked out of the window at the dismal vista outside. The white plastic chair looked forlorn, a puddle of rain in its seat. The terracotta pots were miserable along the balcony, their purple and yellow pansies beaten into the clay by the sheer volume of rain. I leaned my forehead against the window and gazed into my coffee cup.

A month since we'd moved in together and it was working well. A few minor quibbles about leaving half-opened bottles of milk on the table and not in the fridge; a bit of a barney over Lucy's habit of borrowing everybody else's make-up; occasional quarrels about whose turn it was to hoover the carpet, but overall we got on well together.

Sometimes days passed without actually seeing each other. Brenda and Grace left first in the morning. They walked down to Grafton Street and always had a cup of coffee in Bewley's before they started work. So I sometimes missed them. I was the last to leave because my journey to work was the shortest. In fact, I probably spent the most time in the apartment. Lucy had a new (but not serious) boyfriend and she went out with him occasionally; the twins often went out at night together. I liked sitting in, though, even when I was alone.

I was tired today. It was Saturday. The twins were at work and so was Lucy, currently temping in a travel agency. So I could afford to stretch out on the sofa and drape my legs over its padded arms. I had been out late the night before with the crowd from work. We'd done the pub and then Annabel's, which was now very convenient for me because I could stagger home. There was a reason for our revelry – Jessica had been promoted and was now manager of the entire department. One up for the working girls, I'd told her.

She'd grinned and said it was hard work. It was true, she told me, that you had to be twice as good for half the recognition. I was glad that Jessica's niceness hadn't got in the way of her promotion, it gave me some faith in the system.

Surprisingly, I was becoming more interested in work myself. Up until now, I had seen my job as simply a way to pay for my social life and I'd wanted promotion for the higher salary. But I was getting good at it, able to anticipate problems and stave them off and even to solve them when they did arise. I enjoyed the challenge now and I wanted to be busy. I liked having to call our correspondent banks in places like Caracas and Rio. It made me feel as though I really had a global job, instead of one situated in Dublin, Ireland. Jessica's promotion made me realise that I could get on too and believe in my work.

I lay down on the sofa and closed my eyes. It would be nice to be somewhere like Caracas or Rio now, I thought, listening to the incessant thud of the rain against the window. At least it would be warm.

The house was white, dazzling against the bright blue background of the sky. Its front was pillared and impressive, a flight of pink-tinged marble steps led up to a double doorway. Almond trees surrounded it, the nutty kernels wrapped in green fur. The scent of frangipani perfumed the air.

We sat around the pool, fanned by the breeze drifting up from the coast. The waiter brought long drinks in frosted glasses, decorated with an array of fruit.

My husband removed his sunglasses and took a drink.

"To you, my darling," he said.

I raised my glass. "Happy anniversary."

We locked eyes. He stood up. His body was lean and sinewy, the colour of mahogany. He kissed me. It was deep and passionate. I groaned. We broke our embrace. He started to shake me by the shoulder. Why was he shaking me by the shoulder?

"Jane, wake up." It was Lucy shaking me by the shoulder. I blinked at her, squinting.

"Wake up," she repeated.

I sat up. It took a minute to orientate myself. I was angry at Lucy for dragging me out of my dream.

"What do you want?" I asked, crossly. "I was having a lovely dream."

"Oh, well," she said. "If you don't want to hear something miles better than the best dream you can imagine . . . "

I looked at her. I couldn't believe there was anything she could tell me that was better than lying around the sun-kissed villa of Rio de Janeiro.

"When can you get your holidays?" she asked.

I shrugged. "Not sure," I said. "I haven't actually put in for them yet although I'm supposed to. But everybody else had plans and I didn't so I didn't bother to fill in anything."

"Can you get them next week?" asked Lucy.

"When next week?" I asked.

"Next Monday," she said.

"Do you mean take Monday off?" I couldn't believe she was asking me to take Monday off.

She sighed deeply. "Of course," she said. "God, you're thick."

"If you told me what it was about," I said, tartly, "I'd have a better idea of what I can and can't do. Anyway, I can't take Monday off because I haven't asked for it."

Lucy looked at me as though I was mentally subnormal. "If you want to go to Majorca you'll have to take it off," she said.

I stared at her. "Majorca?"

She bubbled with the excitement she had been suppressing. "Yes. If you can get the holidays and if you have a hundred pounds to spare."

"What do you mean?" I asked.

She smiled at me. "There's a special offer in the Travel Agents," she told me. "A cancellation. We didn't get it until nearly closing time and by then it was too late to sell to anyone. For a hundred pounds a head, we can get an apartment in Palma Nova. Flight goes out tomorrow night."

"Tomorrow night!" I felt like a parrot.

"Eleven o'clock." Lucy flopped on to the floor and smiled at me.

We looked at each other like children who had broken into a sweet shop. I had two hundred pounds in my bank deposit account, even after today's shopping expedition. I could afford to go. I could go. If I could get the holidays. If I could get in touch with Jessica, perhaps. And if I could find my passport.

"Where's my passport?" I asked, in a panic. "I need a passport, don't I."

"Yes, you do," said Lucy.

"But how will they get us the tickets?" I asked. "If the flight's going tomorrow?"

"They'll leave them at the airport for us," said Lucy. "They do it all the time. I just go in and hand over the money and they give us the tickets and away we go."

How could I get in touch with Jessica? I wondered frantically. I would have to let her know. If I went without telling anybody, they would probably fire me.

But nobody else was on holidays next week, so it shouldn't be a problem. Unless they wanted to be pigheaded about it. Why should they be, though? After all, it wasn't as though there was any reason to stop me. Somebody else could do my work.

"I have to contact Jessica," I said. "I'll have to let them know."

"Do you have a phone number?" asked Lucy.

"No. I don't think so. Maybe. I'm not sure."

"Jane!" cried Lucy, in exasperation. "Get your act together. Now can you go or not? Can you take the holidays, do you have the money, do you have a passport? Answer carefully, one at a time."

I sat and gazed at the wall in front of me. "I'm not sure, yes, yes but I don't know where it is." I thought a bit more. "I have no clothes," I told her. "Nothing summery, anyway. I bought stuff today but it's Irish weather stuff, not continental stuff."

"It doesn't matter," Lucy told me. "You'll only be wearing a bikini and shorts."

I shivered with excitement. "I don't have a bikini," I said blankly.

"Aaargh!" cried Lucy.

"OK, OK," I said. "I'm sorry. I'll get organised."

I rummaged in my handbag. I knew that somewhere in there was Jessica's address. Maybe her phone number was there too.

"I'd better try and get Jessica first," I said, emptying the contents of the bag on the floor. "God, I hope I can go."

Until now the furthest abroad I had been was a school trip to Brussels. It had been interesting, even fun at the time, but it was hardly in the same league. I couldn't imagine that tomorrow I might get on a plane, out of here and into the sun! It was almost too much to take in.

"Here it is," I cried. "Her address. And – " I paused, triumphantly, "her phone number!"

"Great," said Lucy. "Do you want to phone her now?"

"I'll go straight away," I said. "And I'll phone my folks as well. Oh, Lucy, this is brilliant!"

She smiled at me. "I know," she said. "Will I look for your passport while you're phoning?"

"Yes." I pulled on my wet coat. "I think it's in the bottom of my bedroom locker somewhere."

I raced out into the rain. I didn't mind that the back of my neck was cold and damp. We always used the phones in the Burlington whenever we wanted to make a phone call. The hall porter looked at me dubiously as I walked inside. I knew I looked a wreck but I didn't care.

Jessica was in, she was only too pleased to let me take two weeks holiday starting Monday. "Have a great time," she told me. "Send a postcard and don't overdo the duty-free."

Mam was less enthusiastic. She wanted to know who the tour operator was, where exactly we were staying, why the other couple had cancelled, how we intended getting to the airport, what time the flight left and returned and how did Lucy know that there was a room in the hotel for us.

I tried to answer her questions, but obviously I couldn't tell her everything. I suggested that perhaps she and Dad might like to drive us to the airport and collect us when we got back. That way she'd be sure we left and sure we returned. Would that make her happy, I asked.

"Phone me tomorrow as soon as you have all the details," Mam said. "We'll see what we can do then."

I hurried back to the apartment. Lucy was waving the green passport at me. "Horrible photo," she said.

"Get stuffed," I told her. "Jessica said 'yes'! I can go!"

We hugged each other and danced around the living-room. Suddenly the sound of the rain on the windows was welcome, a reminder of what we were leaving behind.

"How hot will it be?" I asked.

"I'm not sure," Lucy told me. "It was bloody hot in Paris last year, but I don't know what it will be like in the Med."

The Med! It sounded fantastic.

"But it will be hot?" I asked anxiously. "It's always hot in Spain, isn't it?"

"God, yes," said Lucy. "Like summer is meant to be."

Brenda and Grace were green with envy when they came home to find us packing suitcases.

"You lucky cows," said Brenda feelingly as she surveyed the selection of T-shirts and light summer skirts taking up the living-room floor. "I'd love to be going on holiday."

"Bitches," said Grace. "I hope it rains."

She didn't mean it. The twins were two of the kindest people I knew. They offered us a selection of their own clothes. Decent of them, but Brenda and Grace were tall and willowy and, although I was tall, no stretch of the imagination would describe me as willowy. Lucy was smaller, and slight, but she borrowed a couple of long T-shirts which she said would look nice with a belt around the middle. "Make a nice dress," she said.

"Bring lots of suntan lotion," warned Grace. "Everybody runs out of it."

"It's cheaper over there," said Lucy. "So all the girls in the agency tell me, anyhow."

"We can buy some in the duty-free," I said.

Our cases were packed by nine o'clock. I laid out the clothes I wanted to wear tomorrow. I couldn't sleep that night. I tossed around in the bed and listened to the continuing rain. I couldn't wait for the following day.

Mam and Dad had agreed to drop us to the airport. They called around to the apartment at eight o'clock and Dad carried our bags down to the car. They hadn't been in the apartment since I moved in. Mam looked around with interest at the signs of our habitation – mounds of clothes waiting to be ironed, a scattering of books and magazines, Grace's clothes-design drawings. She examined the pots of plants on the kitchen window ledge and opened the cupboard door.

"You should have more vegetables," she said.

"I'll eat them on holiday," I promised.

The airport was crowded. Lucy found the holiday rep and asked about our tickets. My heart was pounding; I was terrified the girl wouldn't have a clue what we were talking about. After what seemed an age, Lucy returned, waving the tickets at me. So we were definitely going!

Long queues of people snaked around the check-in desks. We looked around for the one marked "Palma". It had the longest queue. I joined it immediately, terrified (stupidly) that somehow we might miss the flight if we didn't get in the queue straight away. There were hordes of people in the airport and the noise and bustle was tremendous.

"You don't have to stay," I told my parents.

Mam looked anxious. "I should stay until you take off," she said.

"That's not for nearly two hours," I said. "Don't waste your time. We'll be fine."

"Come on, Maureen," said Dad. "Let's leave them to it."

So they left. Mam hugged me and told me to have a great time. Anyone would think, I mused, that I was going away for good. It was only a holiday.

It took ages to check in, but finally we had our boarding passes and we went through to the duty-free.

"Don't buy booze here," said Lucy. "It's cheaper abroad. Everyone says so."

"What should I buy?"

"We have to get sun protection, don't we," said Lucy.

We stocked up with Ambre Solaire. I bought a bottle of *Charlie* and Lucy, who had a love affair with it since France, bought *Diorissimo.* I bought a huge bar of Cadbury's Fruit & Nut and Lucy bought an enormous Toblerone. Then we went to the bar and ordered Bacardi and Coke as a fitting holiday drink.

I felt a bit overdressed. I was wearing my olive green jump suit which was very stylish, but not great in a crowded airport. Other people wore shorts and T-shirts. Lucy wore a light blouse and a pair of jeans, but she always looked comfortable and smart no matter what she wore.

As the hand of the clock pushed around towards eleven, I felt my stomach flutter with anticipation. We were still sitting in the terminal building at eleven-fifteen. People began to shift around in their seats, coughing, clearing their throats and looking at their watches.

Eventually the flight delay was announced. Our flight would leave at midnight. There were groans from the assembled throng, but Lucy and I didn't care. We ordered another couple of drinks.

"No point in worrying about it," said Lucy. "It happens all the time."

I was glad that Lucy had the experience of her month at the travel agency behind her. She knew what was going on. Last week a couple had stormed into the agency, complaining that their hotel had been infested with cockroaches and that the food had been atrocious. Lucy confirmed that sometimes people ended up in awful accommodation, or the wrong apartment block or even, sometimes, the wrong resort.

"Still," she said. "Unless you shell out a fortune for the holiday, why get into a frazzle about it?"

I knew that if my holiday had gone wrong I would

get into a frazzle about it, but that was the difference between Lucy and me. She was always relaxed, no matter what happened. I let things get to me. Anything that went wrong, anything that didn't go to plan, upset me. I was anxious now as I tapped my fingers on my thigh and looked out of the panoramic window at the huge aircraft coupled to the bridgeway.

I presumed it was ours, but I wondered who on earth AirHols were. I had assumed that we would be travelling Aer Lingus. I had never encountered the charter flight market before.

"Want another?" asked Lucy, as she drained her plastic glass.

I shook my head. "It'll send me asleep," I said. "Maybe later."

Children were getting cranky. A baby cried, setting off another child. People looked around in irritation while parents anxiously tried to quieten their offspring.

We were delayed again. The people in the boarding area beside us filed on board the AirHols plane. I grimaced. That plane had been our plane. Hijacked, now, by the crowd at gate B26.

We watched it taxi slowly away from the building. We could see the movement of people behind the windows. It passed ponderously past our window and out of view. It was almost impossible to believe that this white painted bulk could ever get into the sky, let alone stay there.

Five minutes later it thundered along the runway and up into the night sky. Were we waiting for a plane to come in? wondered Lucy. If it hadn't arrived yet it would take at least half an hour, maybe even an hour, before we could board it.

"Let's have another drink," I said.

While we sipped our drinks another plane, ChartAir, slid into the bay.

"Maybe this is it," I suggested, half hopefully, half nervously. I was hopeful because I didn't want to sit in the airport for much longer, but nervous because ChartAir was painted bright pink and I had very little confident in a pink aeroplane.

It was another half-hour before two air hostesses in pink uniforms and gold badges emblazoned ChartAir, called our flight.

There was a mass rush towards the steps as people struggled to get on to the plane first. Lucy told me to wait, that most people liked to rush but that there was no point. There were seats for us, she said, they were allocated, the flight wouldn't go without us. But I found it very difficult to sit calmly in my seat and watch people board the plane.

Eventually, the crowd thinned out and Lucy stood up. I jumped up beside her. We presented our boarding passes and walked down the bridgeway to the plane.

Our seats were near the front. Bright orange upholstery clashed with pastel pink paintwork inside. I wasn't convinced about the safety of the aircraft. My only other flight had been Aer Lingus, with its pictures of shamrocks, harps and colleens on the inside of the plane and its Irish music piped through the cabin. ChartAir were playing Hits of the Sixties. It didn't seem quite in keeping with my idea of air travel.

They went through the same preflight routine, though, checked that we were belted in, banged the overhead lockers closed and pointed out the emergency exits – in the unlikely event that we would need to use them.

"Better be unlikely," I muttered to Lucy as I read the safety leaflet. "I'm too young to die."

"Honestly, Jane," Lucy was blasé about air travel, "it's safer than travelling by car."

"That's what everyone says," I retorted. "But at least the car is on the ground."

"It's a pity it's dark," mused Lucy. "It's so much nicer when you can see what's happening."

The plane rumbled along the runway. Images of crashes flashed through my head. I wished I hadn't read *Airport!* quite so recently.

"Do they use noise abatement procedures here?" I asked Lucy but she didn't bother to answer me.

The jet engines suddenly roared into life, their whine becoming more and more anguished. I could feel the plane wanting to move forward, gathering power. I gripped the seat. Then we were off and running, gathering speed with every second. It would be OK if we could travel like this and stay on the ground, I thought. I liked the speed, it was the height that bothered me.

Then we were in the air. The lights of the city formed a sparkling web of yellow and white far below us.

"Oh, Lucy, it's gorgeous," I breathed, then jumped with nerves as the undercarriage of the plane bumped into place. I clutched at her sleeve and she laughed at me.

"Relax," she said. "We're on holiday!"

I felt in the holiday mood now. The plane climbed higher into the blackness of the sky. Ethereal patches of grey cloud skimmed past the window. Already the land below was distant and invisible.

I settled back in my seat, feeling a little more relaxed and opened my magazine.

Lucy closed her eyes and let out a sigh.

Air hostesses rushed up and down the plane, offering drinks and more duty-free. Some people near the back started to sing and were asked to stop. I was enjoying myself immensely. They brought our meal around after about an hour and it was thoroughly disgusting. A limp lettuce leaf and some cottage cheese, followed by something that I couldn't identify but which might have been a sausage and then a pot of custard. I would have complained except for the fact that it wasn't really costing us anything.

"Airline food is always dreadful," said Lucy knowingly. She hadn't eaten any of it. "Especially charter flights."

I dozed off after the meal, but it was hard to sleep with all the activity going on around me. The people in the seats behind us were a family and one of the children kept kicking the back of my seat. Every so often I turned around and eventually caught the culprit's eye. I looked stonily at him and he curled up, frightened.

Dawn was breaking as we touched down at Palma airport. I nudged Lucy in the side and pointed at the sea. The Mediterranean. Even the name was full of glamour. The plane circled the airport. I could see the toy-sized cars and vans hurtling along the main road beneath us. I held my breath as we swooped down, watching everything magnify in size as we dropped from the sky. Then finally we landed, and I realised that the plane was still travelling very fast. The engines roared again and I held tight to the arm-rest. Quite suddenly the plane slowed down and taxied sedately to its resting-place.

It was ages before they let us off, but when they did the wall of warm air hit me like a physical blow.

"My God," I said to Lucy who was just behind me. "It's early morning and it's warm already."

"Isn't it lovely?" She squeezed my arm. "Don't you think it's fabulous."

I revelled in the warmth. I couldn't believe that this was real, that Spanish people had this sort of heat in the air all the time.

"We've probably come at a warm time," I said. "It's not like this every day, I suppose."

Mam had told me that the evenings would probably be cold. She'd insisted I pack an Aran jumper. If this warmth was anything to go by, the Aran jumper would be staying in the bottom of the case for the entire holiday. I hugged myself with delight.

We were here, in a foreign country, ready to have fun.

It wasn't exactly fun in the airport, it took nearly an hour before they piled us all into the huge blue and green coaches parked outside the building.

The tour rep clambered inside and fired off a volley of rapid Spanish to the driver who laughed sourly, then spat out of the door. The rep counted us a few times, then called out our names. It was like a school trip.

Eventually, though, we pulled away out of the airport and on to the main road.

I thought that Lucy was right and that we probably would be killed on the roads. The drivers drove with an abandoned enthusiasm that would have had them arrested at home. Nobody else seemed to notice except me. The tour rep was utterly unconcerned. She sat beside the driver and read through a ring folder, ignoring anything on the roads.

It was bright now. The landscape was rugged and dry. Tall, yellow apartments loomed from the centre of sandy fields. It was extraordinary.

Then, into sight, came the sea, sparkling as the early morning sun spilled on to it. Thousands of fragments of light breaking up as the swell of the water moved to and fro. I caught my breath at its beauty.

The light was so different, I thought. The air was clearer, without the grey that clung to Dublin. The houses were brilliantly white, with red and orange tiles and brightly coloured hibiscus in clay-filled gardens.

We passed an olive grove where a caricature of a Spanish peasant leant against a spindly tree. He wore faded denim dungarees and a torn straw hat, and he was drinking a bottle of water.

"This is fantastic," I said. "Absolutely fantastic."

As we approached the resort, the tour rep began to tell us about the area. She warned us to keep topped up with sun protection cream and gave us other boring bits of information that were completely irrelevant.

Lucy and I were the last to get off the coach, the only two people staying in the Aparthotel Sol y Playa, a huge concrete building which stretched so high that it seemed to spear the blue sky above.

We lugged our cases into the foyer. The rep told us to come to her informal client get-together later that day and we ascended in a creaky lift to our room on the twelfth floor.

The view from our balcony was almost wonderful. Our vision of the sea was somewhat marred by the edifice of the Apartments Maria opposite, but we could still see a chink of the aquamarine water. Below us was the apartment's own square of blue, the pool, around which hundreds of sunbeds were arranged in a neat display.

I stood, barefoot, on the balcony and turned my face towards the sun. I felt like a flower beginning to unfurl.

Apartment 33 and the rain streaking down its windows was already a distant memory.

Our holiday had begun.

6

July 1981

(UK No. 16 – Piece of the Action – *Bucks Fizz)*

I stood at the edge of the pool and curled my toes around the tiles. I bent my knees slightly and tried to ignore the searing heat of the sun on my burned shoulders. Actually, they weren't so sore now although they had been agony a couple of days before.

We hadn't realised that the sun would be so strong. Tanya, the tour rep, had warned us at her client meeting about the sun and we took her advice to heart, at least as far as covering ourselves in sun-tan lotion was concerned. But we used oil, not cream, and it was like sitting in an oven carefully basted. We underestimated the burning power of the sun. We imagined it was the same as a very hot day at home, but after we got burned we realised it was very, very different.

So two days into our holiday we had spent almost the entire day sitting inside the hotel bar, sipping drinks and looking at the sunbathers outside without being able to join them.

Since then we'd abandoned the oils, switched to creams and covered our shoulders and thighs. Now we had light tans, our skins were healing and we could spend time outdoors again.

I loved Spain. Palma Nova was a brash loud resort and the average age of the tourists must have been twenty or twenty-one. I would have liked somewhere a little more sophisticated – Happy Hour in the Lady Diana pub every night had a limited appeal – but you couldn't say that there weren't enough places to go.

Lucy and I tried to visit places where Spanish people themselves might go, but there weren't too many of them. I'd assumed, part of my schoolgoing mentality, that if you visited a foreign country you should try and see some of it. But Palma Nova wasn't exactly a centre of culture. Still, once we accepted that we were only there for the suntans and nightlife, we had a ball.

We ate in the hotel each evening at seven o'clock, spending about an hour and a half over our meal. We always ordered wine because it was so cheap and because we felt incredibly sophisticated when the waiter topped up our glasses. Lucy tried to speak Spanish to him, and by now she had picked up a few words. He spoke French which was significantly better than his English so she managed to chatter to him in a mixture of both, much to his amusement.

His name was Salvadore and he was from Barcelona. He told us that we should visit his city which was "muy, muy magnifico" and we assured him that we would. I meant it. I was sure that there were lovely places in Spain.

To satisfy my desire for exploration, we went on an excursion to the centre of the island, and to the capital of Palma where we visited the cathedral and the working port. Having done both of these things, Lucy declared herself finished with the cultural aspects of our visit and said that she was going to devote the rest of her time to sunbathing.

"And maybe I'll pick up one of these gorgeous men," she said, as she rubbed after-sun into her reddened skin.

The men were a revelation. Some were skinny, weedy and unattractive, but there were a number of well-built, muscled bodies, tanned to a deep mahogany who paraded in front of us every day in the tiniest of swimming togs.

I leaned forward and dived into the pool. The water was shockingly cold after the heat of the afternoon. I stayed underwater, as close to the bottom as I could until I reached the other end of the pool where Lucy was dangling her legs. I pulled them gently, not enough to drag her into the pool which she would have hated, but enough to make her scream at me.

"Don't do it," she yelled, "or I'll kill you."

"Pull her under," called Jaime. "She's too lazy."

I waved at him and he wandered over to the pool.

"Come on in," I said. "It's lovely."

"Yes, yes, I know," he replied. "Once you are in the water it is lovely. Only thinking about it is not so lovely."

"A big strong man like you," I joked. "No problem." I splashed a little water at him. "Come on, Jaime."

He thought for a moment, then belly-flopped into the water beside me, surfaced and put his arms around me.

I liked Jaime de Boer. We'd met him and his brother Wim earlier in the week. They had been drinking in the CocoLoco Tropical Bar when we walked in.

The CocoLoco was designed to look like a huge coconut. The tables were made of straw and the seats were shaped like halved coconuts. Palm trees grew inside the bar and brightly-coloured parrots and macaws squawked at the clients.

Lucy and I sat at the bar and ordered Tequila Sunrises. We were sipping the long drinks when the de Boer brothers started chatting us up. It was fun to let them, the brothers had superb manners.

They were both probably only after a bit of holiday fun but, Lucy told me, so were we. Not that much fun, I mouthed at her, but she just laughed.

So we talked to Wim and Jaime and went with them to the Razzmatazz Nite Club where we danced until three in the morning, when they left us back to the hotel, kissing us both in the foyer before they left.

We didn't see them the next day, but the day after that they turned up at the hotel pool and had turned up every day since. We had sunbathed together. It was much more exciting having Jaime rub sun cream into my back, instead of Lucy doing it. He would massage it gently into my shoulders and rub it carefully into the nape of my neck, before running his fingers slowly down my spine until I tingled with the pleasure of it.

Jaime pulled me under the water and wrapped his legs around my body. I pummelled him fiercely until he released me and I surfaced again, gasping for air.

"You didn't give me a chance," I protested, but all he did was kiss me, slowly, on the lips.

I hauled myself out of the pool and sat beside Lucy, slicking my hair back from my forehead.

"Where are we going tonight?" I asked.

It was Friday. We were going home on Sunday and the brothers were going home later that night.

"CocoLoco," said Wim who was busy plaiting Lucy's hair.

"We should go for a meal first," said Jaime. "It would be nice, don't you think."

"Lovely," I said. I was tired of the ApartHotel Sol y Playa's food but Lucy and I had eaten there every night because our food was paid for and we hadn't had time to save up for the holiday.

"Where will we go?" she asked.

"There's a nice restaurant near the beach," suggested Jaime. "It's called El Condor."

"Is it English?" asked Lucy.

"Why do you want everything to be English?" asked Wim.

"I don't," she protested. "I simply wondered."

"It's a mixture," said Wim. "We've eaten there a couple of times. There is a good variety of food."

"Sounds OK to me." I didn't mind where we ate.

"Good," said Jaime. "There is no point in going too early for eating. Maybe eight o'clock."

"Eight," said Lucy, aghast. Lucy loved food. Unfairly, she never put on an ounce of weight.

"It is more civilised," said Wim. "Eating early is silly. We will meet for a drink at seven and eat at eight."

"That's fine," I agreed.

"If we're eating later, then I'm going to have a snack now," said Lucy firmly.

We laughed at her but she didn't care, so we followed her to the bar where she ordered an omelette. A *tortilla*, she said, pronouncing it torteeyah.

"I'll have a ham sandwich," I said.

"Un bocadillo con jamon," ordered Lucy.

I sighed. Lucy could be very irritating. All the waiters answered us in English.

When we'd finished, we sat by the pool again. I loved it by the pool. It was crowded and a bit noisy but I loved being warm and I loved swimming out of doors.

Every morning of our holiday I woke up expecting to find that grey clouds had rolled in over the sky and that the temperature had plummeted to the levels I was used to. But every morning I blinked in the brilliant sunshine and the temperature remained resolutely in the nineties.

Lucy and I would go down to the restaurant, usually too late for breakfast, but we'd order coffee and croissants which we took back up to our room and we'd breakfast sitting at our balcony table. It was blissful.

"Are you coming to the beach now?" Wim drained the beer which he had ordered.

Lucy and I exchanged glances. "It's a bit late," said Lucy. "And we've got good spots at the pool. I'd prefer not to move."

"Me either," I said. "But you go ahead if you want to."

"I want to have a swim in the sea," said Jaime. "We'll see you later."

"Fine," said Lucy. "Do you want a drink in the Coco before dinner?"

"That's an after-dinner place," Wim objected. "How about upstairs at the Eagle's Nest?"

We nodded. There was a lovely view from the upstairs of the pub.

"See you later, then," I waved at them as they left.

Lucy and I sat in silence for a while. It was pleasantly peaceful sitting under the sunshade.

"Nice guys," she said, suddenly.

I nodded. I liked Jaime.

"Do you love him?" asked Lucy.

"What?" I was startled.

"Jaime – do you love him?"

"Do you love Wim?" I asked.

She shrugged.

"I don't love Jaime," I told her. "I like him. I like him a lot, but I don't love him."

She sighed deeply. "Thank goodness for that," she said. "I thought you'd fallen for him."

"What d'you take me for?" I asked. "We're on holidays. They're Dutch. What's the point in falling for him?"

"Well, you know you, Jane," she said. "You fall for everyone."

I stared at her. "Rubbish," I said.

"It's not rubbish," Lucy retorted. "You're always falling for people."

"No, I'm not."

"Don't be silly." Lucy traced her finger around her glass. "You do."

"Who?" I asked, indignantly. "Who, pray tell, have I recently fallen for?"

She had the grace to look slightly abashed. "Not recently," she said. "But, Jane, you lose your heart too easily."

She listed my boyfriends who seemed to me to be very few. Particularly since most of them had been so short-lived, I told her.

"But you were crazy about them at the time," she pointed out. "Each time you meet someone you think that this is it."

I blushed. She was right. Every time I went out with someone, I would almost immediately visualise spending the rest of my life with him. I couldn't help it.

"What about you?" I asked. "You were on and off again with Cian O'Connor for nearly two years."

"But I never loved him," said Lucy. "I went out with him and sometimes I enjoyed it, but I never believed that this was my one true love or anything like that. You think that way all the time."

"There's nothing wrong with thinking about it," I said, defensively.

"Of course not," said Lucy. "But you're only twenty-one, Jane. There's more to life than meeting a guy and getting married."

"I know that," I retorted.

"So you haven't decided that Jaime is the one for you and your life will be a wasteland if he leaves you."

"I know that he is not the one for me and that he will be going back to Holland and I will never see him again." I spoke the words clearly, enunciating each one distinctly so that Lucy would understand me. "I am not stupid, Lucy."

"OK," she said. She looked worried. "I'm concerned, that's all."

I was touched by her concern but still irritated. Just because she had a couple of no-strings-attached flings she felt that she could lecture me on men. And because she had lost her virginity to whoever he was in France, without losing her heart. I could do that too, I thought, fiercely. Sex was a physical thing, it didn't have to mean a lifelong commitment.

"Don't get me wrong," Lucy said. "I don't mean to lecture you, Jane."

"You're always lecturing me," I said. "But that doesn't mean that I'll listen to you."

She grinned at me, and took me by the hand. I squeezed it. We understood each other.

"What are you going to wear tonight?" she asked, turning the conversation back to things that really mattered.

I wore a royal blue cotton dress which highlighted my tan and brought out the copper in my hair. I liked myself with the suntan, it made me look so much healthier and, I admitted to myself, prettier. I took the sun more easily than Lucy, although her dusting of honey was gorgeous and she looked almost Scandinavian with her long, blonde hair and golden skin. She wore an emerald green skirt and a deep pink shirt which would have looked awful at home but which was ideal on holiday.

I painted my lips scarlet and rubbed Vaseline over the lipstick to make them look wet and alluring. I hung my Majorcan pearl earrings from my ears and twirled in front of the mirror to admire myself.

"You're gorgeous," said Lucy sarcastically. I stuck my tongue out at her.

"Let's go," I said.

The Eagle's Nest was at the edge of the beach and a quieter pub than most of them because it didn't have a Happy Hour and it didn't sell cocktails.

Wim and Jaime were waiting for us. They looked superb in their faded jeans and white shirts, with their fair curly hair and bright blue eyes.

"Hello, ladies," Jaime stood up and pulled two chairs out for us. "What would you like to drink?"

We both had Bacardis while the brothers drank beer. We sat in silence, looking over the bay. It got dark quickly in Spain, the sea and sky were already black and the coloured lights of the town reflected off the water like glittering beads. The sea thudded gently against the beach beneath us with a rhythmic soothing sound which would soon be deafened by the music from the bars and the nightclubs. The breeze from the sea was warm and pleasant.

"Have you enjoyed your holiday?" asked Lucy, who could never stay quiet for very long.

"Oh, it was good," Wim replied. "Especially since we met you." He leaned forward and kissed her on the cheek. Lucy offered him her lips and he kissed her again, while I squirmed in my seat.

"And you?" Jaime looked at me. "Did you enjoy your holiday?"

"Oh, yes," I replied, trying to ignore Lucy and Wim.

"Me too," said Jaime. He leaned toward me but I picked up my glass and took a large gulp of Bacardi. So he didn't kiss me but he touched me gently on the back of the neck which almost sent me into orbit anyway.

I wondered whether Jaime expected to make love to me tonight. It was their last night. He hadn't suggested it before, even though I had met him alone for a drink once or twice while Lucy went off somewhere with Wim. But maybe he would feel that tonight would be the right time. He probably felt that he could get away with it more easily on his last night because he wouldn't have to face me the next day.

I took another sip of my drink. Did I want him to make love to me? It's hardly making love, I told myself sternly. It's just having sex. Would he want to have sex with me, then? And if he did, would I let him. The condoms which Lucy had handed me just before we left the apartment were in my bag. I had looked at her, horrified, as she had given them to me.

"Better safe than sorry," she'd said, smiling.

I didn't know where she'd got them and I didn't ask. But she obviously intended going to bed with Wim. Where, I didn't know. I couldn't see us all going back to the Sol y Playa with Lucy and Wim in the bedroom while Jaime and I sat in the living-room. I blushed as I thought about it.

Why was life so difficult? I wondered. Or was it

me that made it difficult? It seemed straightforward enough for Lucy. See a man, go out with him, have a good time, say goodbye. Sex for me was all caught up with love and romance. I wondered if I was the last old-fashioned girl on the planet.

Of course, I didn't believe that you had to be a virgin when you got married. No, I thought you'd need to have a bit of experience, just so's you'd know what was what, but all these surveys that showed that girls had lots of partners before marriage scared me. How would I find loads of men to go to bed with? Anyhow, I couldn't let a man that I wasn't serious about see me naked. There were too many little podgy bits of flesh for that!

Lucy and Wim came up for air and smiled at us. My hands were shaking as I put my glass back on the table.

"Will we go and eat?" Jaime looked at me.

"I don't mind," I said, and the others nodded.

We walked down the steps and on to the street. The pubs were all brightly lit now, drumming out music into the streets, flashing neon lights to entice you inside. Shops were open, their merchandise spilling on to the pavement so that you couldn't help looking at it. Lucy and I had already bought sombreros, sunglasses, T-shirts emblazoned "Majorca", flip-flops and huge donkeys to bring home to the twins.

The El Condor restaurant was at the end of the strip, tucked back a little from the street and with only a few tables outside.

"Out or in?" asked Jaime.

"Oh, outside," I said.

I loved eating out of doors. It was great to eat with the warm evening air around you as you watched the nightlife.

We sat down at a table. The waiter came outside and handed us the menus.

The brothers knew what they wanted straight away. Jaime ordered a mixed salad followed by calamari. Lucy informed him that calamari was octopus and he said that he knew that already but he liked it. She made an agonised face. Wim ordered soup and chicken. Lucy and I dithered over our choice until Wim demanded that we make a decision unless we wanted to starve. Eventually we decided to have salads for starters. Then we'd try the *paella,* because the food at the hotel had been very un-Spanish and we reckoned we should at least attempt a local dish. Jaime ordered two bottles of Rioja and some mineral water.

The waiter returned with our starters and I popped a piece of tomato into my mouth, wondering why they tasted so much better here. Mam would have been amazed by the amount of salads I was eating. I thought, although I wasn't sure, that my skin had improved because of it. I'd already resolved to change my eating habits when we went home.

The *paella* was nice too, although I didn't like seeing whole shellfish arranged around it. I could never eat anything that looked as though it might have once been alive. Lucy laughed at me as she expertly removed the meat and ate it.

We talked about home, about our jobs, about our

families, about our countries. Jaime and Wim were very proud of The Netherlands and they had only good things to say about it.

"Amsterdam sounds lovely," said Lucy, shovelling rice into her mouth. "I'd love to go there some day."

"But you must, of course," said Wim.

She nodded and applied herself to her food again.

The wine was heavy and made me a little woozy. I drank some more mineral water. I wished that alcohol didn't make me so tired, it was very antisocial.

We finished our meal and called in to the CocoLoco for some cocktails. Then we played crazy golf on the little course beside it. Lucy was utterly useless at crazy golf but I was good at it and, despite the alcohol, won, much to everyone's surprise.

"Natural talent," I said, with false modesty as I tapped the ball into the hole at the eighteenth.

"What do you want to do now?" Wim looked at Lucy and me.

"Whatever you like." Lucy put her arms around him and pulled him close to her.

"Maybe we should split up for a while," suggested Jaime. "Jane and I will go for a walk and meet you back at the hotel later."

"Fine by me," said Lucy.

I bit the inside of my lip. Did Jaime have an ulterior motive, I wondered. Did he just want to get me on my own?

So what if he did, I told myself. Wouldn't you like to be on your own with him?

Jaime took me by the hand and led me away from the crazy golf.

"Where would you like to go?" he asked.

"I don't mind," I said.

We walked towards the beach.

"It's not much of a beach," said Jaime, as we stepped on to the sand. "I think it's man-made."

"Maybe." I slipped out of my high-heeled sandals and walked barefoot on the sand.

"Give me those," said Jaime, taking the sandals.

I walked to the water's edge and allowed it to lap gently over my toes.

"It's lovely and warm," I said.

"I'm not going to paddle," said Jaime. "I will get my jeans wet and I have to wear them on the plane."

"Are you sorry to be going home?" I asked.

He smiled. "Yes," he said, simply.

We walked along the beach in silence. I enjoyed the feeling of the water on my feet. Earlier in the week the skin on my feet had peeled disgustingly, but now they were smooth and tanned. Healthy brown feet with smooth pink and white soles.

"Will you be sorry to go home?" asked Jaime.

I nodded. "I like it here," I said. "I suppose I couldn't possibly live somewhere like this, but I love the weather."

"It is a bit hot for me," said Jaime. "Every night it is so hot I cannot sleep."

"I couldn't the first few days," I admitted. "But now I can. Anyway, we don't usually get to bed that early and you can sleep beside the pool."

"Always the practical one," Jaime said.

"I can't help it," I protested.

"You should be not practical sometimes," he told me.

"Impractical," I corrected.

"Thank you," he said.

We reached the crop of rocks that jutted out into the sea. It was dark here, and quiet, the sound of the town muted by the distance. I sat down on one of the rocks and examined my toes.

"What are you doing?" asked Jaime.

"Nothing."

He sat beside me, and put his arms around me. Although I had been expecting it, I jumped.

"Jane," he protested.

"Sorry," I muttered. "Didn't mean it."

He caught me under the chin and turned my face to his. We gazed into each other's eyes. He was very attractive. I felt my heart begin to thump in my chest.

His lips came down on to mine, soft but demanding. I responded to him, wrapping my arms around his neck. He shifted position on the rock and pulled me towards him.

"Ouch," I said, as my sandals hit me on the back of the head.

"Sorry." He fumbled around, trying to put them down somewhere.

"Give them to me." I broke from his embrace and placed my sandals on a smooth-topped rock. I stood beside him and looked at him again.

He gripped me by the hair and I moved towards him. His body was warm and strong. I could feel myself tremble with desire for him. How much desire,

I wondered, as his hands slid gently down my back. How much do I want him?

His hands moved downwards, to my buttocks, pulling me closer. I could feel him, hard, against me. Oh God, I thought.

He kissed me on the neck, on the shoulders, moved his head down to my breasts. I felt my nipples harden through the cotton of my dress as he brushed his lips over them. He clasped a breast in his hand.

"You're so lovely, Jane," he said.

My dress was long, too long. He fumbled for the hem of it, trying to touch my thighs. I was shivering with lust, I wanted him more than I had ever wanted anyone in my life.

"Wait," I said.

Deliberately, I pulled my dress over my head and stood in front of him in my snow-white bra and pants. He caught his breath as he looked at me. I felt in control now, this was my decision, my choice.

I undid the buckle of his belt and slid the zip of his jeans, pulling them down. He watched me in amazement.

"If we are doing this," I said, keeping my voice steady and free of the embarrassment that I still felt, "then you must wear something."

The Dutch are very pragmatic. He had a condom in his jeans pocket.

Then we were moving together again, in a rhythm echoed by the waves on the sand. I felt myself open for him, accept him, feel him. It was an interesting experience, I thought. Pleasurable, yes, but not mind-blowing. Not what Lucy had written home about, but something that was worth doing. We were lying on the sand now, and he was on top of me, moving faster and faster until suddenly he cried out and was still. I quivered.

"You were fantastic," he said. "I have never known anything like it."

"Really?" I said. All I had done was move with him. Was that all it took?

"Absolutely," he said. "It was the best thing ever for me."

"I'm glad you liked it," I said.

"Did you?" asked Jaime, who was now pulling his jeans on again.

I took my dress from its place on the rocks and pulled it over my head again.

"Yes," I said. "But I've got sand in my hair."

"You look lovely with sand in your hair," said Jaime. "You are lovely."

"I don't believe a word of it," I said. "You've probably got an even lovelier girlfriend at home."

He smiled at me. "No girlfriend," he said. "I promise."

"Well," I said, as I gathered my shoes. "I don't mind if you have, Jaime. It was just a holiday thing between us, wasn't it?"

"But a good holiday thing," he said, anxiously. "Don't you think?"

"A great holiday thing," I told him, and kissed him on the nose. "Now let's get back and find the others."

Lucy and Wim were in the hotel bar. She had a self-satisfied smile on her face, and she looked questioningly at me as we sat down beside them.

"We went for a walk on the beach," I said. "What did you do?"

"Oh, stayed here," said Wim, casually. "You were gone a long time."

"Were we?" I asked. "I didn't notice."

"Too busy to notice," said Jaime and I kicked him on the ankle.

Lucy giggled and I kicked her too.

We had a drink in the bar and then it was time for Jaime and Wim to go back to their apartment. We walked down with them, and sat on the steps, waiting.

Jaime kept his arm around me, while Wim held Lucy's hand.

Eventually, their bus arrived and they said goodbye. I was glad they were going tonight. Now that I had lost my virginity to Jaime, I was uncomfortable about meeting him again.

"Write to me," said Lucy as Wim climbed on to the bus.

"Of course," he said.

"Goodbye," I said to Jaime, kissing him lightly on the lips.

"Goodbye," he said. "I'll always remember you."

The bus drove away and Lucy and I stood side by side.

"Well?" she demanded, looking at me.

"Well, what?" I said nonchalantly.

"Well, did you?"

"Did I what?"

"Jane O'Sullivan, you look like the cat that got the cream. You must have!"

"Must have what?"

"You know perfectly well what."

"Lucy," I said. "I took your advice. I didn't get too involved."

She looked disappointed.

"All the same, he was a great lay!"

"Jane!"

"Well, let's face it, I'm not likely to see him again, am I? What else would you call it."

"Did you enjoy it?"

"It was OK," I said.

"Only OK?" Lucy looked disappointed for me. "Wim was great!"

I thought about it afterwards. I had deliberately stayed uninvolved because Lucy was right, I lost my heart too easily and there was no future in losing my heart to Jaime de Boer. But I had freed myself from the shackles of my virginity and I was grateful to him for that. All the same, I still dreamed about the one true love, the man who would cherish me, and love me, and protect and care for me till the day I died. I wondered what he was doing now.

7

August 1981

(UK No. 18 – New Life – *Depeche Mode)*

Two weeks after we came back from holidays, Jessica called me into her office.

"I've some news for you, Jane," she said as she sifted through a green-coloured folder, "you're going to be transferred."

"Transferred!" I looked at her in horror. I didn't want to be transferred. I liked my job in the International department and I was working really hard now. I knew that I was doing well, that my productivity (that awful word they kept throwing at us all the time) had soared, that I was getting more and more done in less and less time. I couldn't understand why they were transferring me. It was completely unfair.

"I don't really want to move," I said, twisting the gold ring I'd bought in Majorca around my middle finger. "I like it here, Jessica, all my friends are here."

She smiled sympathetically. "I realise that, Jane," she said. "And I know that nobody likes to move. But you have to take this as an opportunity. It's good for staff to be moved around. You know that I was in the banking department before I moved here."

"Is my work not good enough?" I asked, nervously. Maybe it was only me who thought that my productivity had soared and I was making loads of mistakes. I didn't think so, but I couldn't think of any other reason to transfer me.

"It's nothing like that at all," said Jessica. "Absolutely not. I'm very pleased with your work, Jane, and I would prefer to keep you in the department if I could. But they need someone in Settlements and your name came up as a conscientious worker."

I was glad my name was linked with concentiousness, but that didn't make it any easier. And Settlements. Settlements sounded extremely boring.

"It won't be boring at all," assured Jessica. "And – " she paused, raising an eyebrow at me, "you'll be next door to the dealing room."

I made a face. For some reason, Jessica seemed to think that I fancied Rory McLoughlin. Ever since we'd headed off together from the pub she'd made barbed comments about him to me, despite everything I said to her. In spite of my own original premonition that we would have some sort of relationship.

"That was months ago," I informed her. "I haven't even seen him since."

That wasn't strictly true because I'd seen him from

time to time in the canteen, but I'd ignored him. If he was really interested in me he could come looking for me. The fact that he hadn't had convinced me that it had been a once-off thing and I didn't care. Besides, I was much more confident since my holidays. I really didn't mind too much about Rory McLoughlin.

"You and he made a great couple," said Jessica, wistfully. "I thought it was the start of something when you went to eat with him."

"You thought wrong, then," I said, coolly. I was pissed off with Jessica. She could have kept me in the department if she'd really wanted to. All this guff about Rory McLoughlin was just to salve her conscience. I didn't know why she wanted me out of the department, but she must have done. I wondered who my replacement would be.

I moaned to the girls when I went home that evening. It had been, for once, a glorious day and they were sitting on the balcony when I got home. Lucy was carefully trying to retain her tan, rubbing Johnson's Baby Oil into her legs, while the twins had smeared themselves with Hawaiian Tropic. The apartment stank of coconut.

I dragged a chair on to the balcony with them, enjoying the warmth of the sun.

"Almost like Spain," said Lucy, in satisfaction, as she stretched out her oiled and gleaming legs.

"Not nearly as hot." I plopped down into the chair.

I poured out the story of my transfer and they were understanding and sympathetic.

"Can't you say that you just don't want to go?" asked Grace, who was drawing on a large block of paper. I looked over her shoulder. It was a design for an evening dress and it looked stunning.

"That's lovely," I told her. "No, the bastards can transfer you wherever they like. If I complain, I could probably end up in a branch in Athy or something."

"Better not complain, then." Lucy closed her eyes.

"It's so unfair, though," I moaned. "I was getting on really well."

"Maybe it'll be better in the new department," said Brenda, "Perhaps you'll like it even more."

"I doubt it," I said. "And it means that I have to start making new friends again and everything."

"I have to do that every time I start a job," murmured Lucy. "It's not so bad, really."

She was now the secretary to the managing director of a distribution company. It was a three-month assignment while his own secretary was on maternity leave. Lucy enjoyed the job. The company had a beautiful suite of offices in a Georgian building around Fitzwilliam Square and they had a key to the park so that she could lie on the grass at lunch-time and bask in the sun. Because so much of the company's business was overseas, it was essential that Lucy could speak French and she was completely fluent by now.

"Maybe you should change jobs altogether," suggested Brenda, idly. She looked at Grace's drawing. "If you make the collar a little higher here . . . " she suggested. Her twin nodded in agreement and her pencil flew over the paper, making the alteration.

"What could I do?" I asked. "I'm not much good at anything."

"I thought you were good at banking," said Lucy.

"Oh, it doesn't mean much, really," I said. I was depressed and nothing they could say would cheer me up.

"Rubbish," said Grace, holding her drawing away from her. "What do you think, girls?"

It was lovely. The evening dress was long and filmy, with a high collar at the back and a plunging neckline at the front. There was no doubt that the twins had real fashion sense.

"Can you make it up?" I asked. "I bet you anything people would pay a lot of money for it."

"It's only for fun," said Grace.

Lucy opened her eyes, took her feet down from the balcony rail and looked at the drawing.

"Why don't you study design properly?" she asked. "You'd do really well."

Grace shrugged. "I'd like to," she said. "But it would be too expensive. Maybe in a couple of years."

"Frank went on to Milan to study," I said. "And I never heard from him again. I wonder how he's getting on."

"Unless he's great, he probably won't make any money out of it," said Brenda. "Only one or two people break into the big time."

"I'll tell you what," I said as an idea came to me. "Why don't you make up the dress and I'll wear it to our Christmas party, and when one of the top brass ask me where I got it I'll say that I have a friend who's in design. Maybe they'll give you a loan and set you up in business."

Grace looked doubtful but Brenda thought that maybe it was a good idea.

"What we'd really like," she confided, "would be to have our own shop and sell clothes. Not all our own designs, of course, but expensive clothes."

I could see how they would make it work. Both girls had developed a wonderful sense of style and looked superb no matter what they wore. Brenda and Grace could buy clothes from Dunnes Stores or Penneys and make them look as if they'd bought them from Pat Crowley or the designer rooms at Brown Thomas.

"Maybe I'll make it up anyway." Grace, head to one side, looked critically at the drawing.

"If you make it, I'll pay for it," I said.

"OK," said Grace. "You're on."

We sat on the balcony until the sun slid down behind the tall houses opposite. Lucy went in to have a shower, she was meeting a few friends from the temping agency later. Brenda and Grace asked me if I'd like to go to the Burlington for a drink, but I decided to stay at home and read.

I was getting edgy again. I hadn't had a boyfriend in ages and it didn't look as if I'd find one soon. I was being transferred in work. Everyone else seemed to have an idea of what they wanted out of life but I didn't. The silence of the apartment when the girls had gone was oppressive. I pulled on a jumper and went outside for a walk.

I walked up Waterloo Road, then turned right on to Leeson Street and back along the canal. This was my regular evening walk. It usually took half an hour because I always sat on one of the seats and stared into the murky canal water, or watched the swans glide effortlessly along.

My stomach hurt and I knew that I was narky because I'd started my period. Its arrival usually made me feel depressed for a day or two, but I was quite relived this time because I'd had the niggling worry that I might be pregnant. I'd kept the lid firmly on that idea as much as I could, but when I realised that I was nearly a week overdue I got into a terrible panic and prayed like a mad thing.

"Please, God, don't let me be pregnant, I'll never do anything like it again." "Please, Our Lady, I'm sure you don't want me to be pregnant, to bring an unwanted baby into the world, I swear I'll never do it again." And finally, "Please, St Jude, patron of hopeless causes, I promise, fervently, never to do it again."

Once it had actually come, I realised that I'd been incredibly silly to have worried. We'd taken precautions, after all, and it was probably only my guilty conscience that had delayed it.

I was a mixture of relief and hormonal imbalance that evening and I went to bed early before the rest of them came home.

"It's a girl," the nurse said, putting my child on my chest. "Congratulations!"

My husband leaned towards me. "You clever girl," he said, kissing my sweat-soaked cheek. "You have given us a daughter. This is the most wonderful day of our lives."

My daughter was beautiful, clear skin, deep blue eyes and a soft, downy covering of golden hair.

"We will call her Gloria," said my husband. "Because she is so glorious."

"Don't be ridiculous," I said. "Her name is Samantha."

"No, it should be Melissa."

"Or Fiona."

"Or Lucy."

"Lucy is my friend. You can't call our baby by my friend's name."

"Why not?" he asked, suddenly nasty. "She'd a wonderful girl and she's absolutely superb in bed."

I snapped my eyes open, my heart thumping. Lucy was snoring gently in the bed opposite me. I was soaked in sweat because the room was sweltering. I crawled out of the bed and opened the window to let in a waft of warm night air.

I started work in the Settlements department the following Monday. I was very nervous as I took the lift up to the fifth floor and stepped out into my new department.

Rosaleen Corcoran, the twenty-nine-year-old Head of Settlements, came over to me as I stood uncertainly by the lift.

"Jane, isn't it," she said, brightly. "Come on in. It's lovely to have you here. We're absolutely up to our necks, it's so busy."

I looked around me. The Settlements area was large and everyone had a computer terminal on their desk. We didn't have a computer at all in

International Trade. There was a constant hum of noise and a clicking of keyboards as information was inputted into the system.

Rosaleen led me to a grey steel desk with its own terminal.

"This is your desk," she said. "What do you know about computers?"

I shook my head. "Nothing, I'm afraid," I said. I felt very stupid.

"Not to worry, we'll train you in. There are a number of different jobs you have to do and you'll be fully trained in everything. It's vitally important for you to be quick and accurate."

She launched into a detailed account of my work and the work of everyone else in the department while I looked around me. My desk was in a good position, near the window so that I could look out over the city. The view was superb, I could see Dublin Bay in the distance beyond the jumble of houses, buildings and railway tracks. My old desk had been on the second floor of a different block and had simply overlooked other offices.

"We rotate people within the department," said Rosaleen. "It's for your own good and for security reasons as well. If we left people too long in one area, then they might become indispensable and we can't afford for that to happen."

I nodded wisely.

"Now," Rosaleen looked around her. "Lorna Mulcahy will train you in, she's a good worker and a good trainer as well." She called her over. Rosaleen told Lorna that I was to be trained on input and then left us.

Lorna was a tall girl, well-built, with heavy glasses and severely-cut hair. She didn't waste any time in small talk, but sat me down in front of the terminal and showed me the trading tickets and what to do with them.

It seemed simple enough to me, and I wondered why I'd been transferred to do such boring work.

Suddenly, Lorna let out a cry and waved a ticket at me.

"Asshole," she said. "Why do these guys insist on doing this!"

She showed me the ticket. The writing was illegible anyway, something I'd discovered already, but Lorna was adept at reading it. I didn't know what was wrong.

"He's put in a rubbish payment instruction," she explained. "This ticket shows somebody buying French francs and selling dollars. The instruction on the ticket is to pay the dollars to London and the francs to New York. Total rubbish. They have to pay the dollars to somewhere in New York and the francs to somewhere in Paris." She held the ticket up to me. "This is one of the commonest mistakes they make. They're so fucking careless."

I was amazed at her. She was so annoyed about it all. It was just a mistake, I thought, why such a fuss about it?

Lorna pushed her seat away from the desk and strode toward the dealing room with me following in her wake.

I'd never been in the room before, and I looked in amazement at the activity. There were about fifty people in the room, sitting at long desks surrounded by flickering screens which were filled with a meaningless jumble of numbers. The noise was tremendous, the dealers shouted at each other and voices were coming from somewhere through loudspeakers. I hadn't a clue what was going on.

Lorna picked her way through the room and stood in front of one of the desks. Rory McLoughlin looked up at her, and at me.

"Well, hello, girls," he said. He leaned back in his chair and hung his telephone over his shoulder. "To what do I owe the pleasure?"

"This is Jane," said Lorna, "she's starting here today. And one of the things I am teaching her is not to accept this kind of fucking garbage from dealers." She waved the ticket in front of him. "What the fuck do you call this?"

I'd never heard so much swearing in one sentence before.

"Keep you knickers on." Rory sat upright. "What's wrong?"

"You're trying to pay fucking French francs to fucking New York," said Lorna, "and fucking dollars to London. Any chance you could give me an instruction that bears some fucking resemblance to the trade you've done?"

Rory laughed. "I'm sorry, my sweet," he said. "I was thinking of something else. You know, it's fucking busy in here today, Lorna, and I'm writing fucking millions of tickets so if I get one wrong now and again, it's not a fucking crime. You don't have to come here and lose your head entirely, you know."

"You're giving Jane a very bad example," said Lorna. "It's not our job to correct your mistakes."

"But you do anyway, don't you?" Rory stood up and kissed Lorna on the head. "I really am sorry."

She was suddenly mollified and blushed. "OK," she said. "Be careful next time."

Rory looked at me. "So you've joined us," he said. "Nice to see you."

"You leave Jane alone." Lorna punched him in the shoulder. "She's a nice girl and she doesn't need any grief from you."

"OK." Rory winked at me. "I'll see that I'm nice to her all the time."

"He's OK, really," said Lorna as we went back to our desks. "In fact, he's one of the better ones. Most of them think writing the ticket is a complete waste of time. They're completely inaccurate and they don't give a damn. One day, all of this will be computerised anyway and they'll probably have to input the tickets themselves but, in the meantime, we do it."

She sat down at the desk again.

"What would have happened if you didn't spot the mistake?" I asked, curiously.

"The computer spits it out at you," said Lorna. "You can override it and tell it to accept the deal, but then someone else should spot it when the contract is printed. Rosaleen probably told you that we rotate around the department, so that one day you might be inputting and another checking contracts. Actually, I could have asked somebody else to bring that ticket to Rory, but I reckoned you'd probably like to see the dealing room."

"It's huge," I said. "And is it always so noisy?"

"Nearly always," said Lorna. "There's so much going on, you see."

"And do people talk like that all the time?" I asked.

"Like what?" asked Lorna.

"You know," I said. "Swearing all the time."

She looked at me in amazement. "Does it bother you?"

"Not exactly," I said carefully. "We didn't have so much occasion for it in International Trade."

Lorna laughed. "You catch it from the dealers," she said. "They're really awful. And the only way to get their attention is to yell and shout and curse at them too. Otherwise, they'll leave you standing there and completely ignore you. You have to be tough to work here."

We spent the rest of the morning inputting deals, then Lorna showed me around the rest of the department. She explained all the different jobs that I might have to do and introduced me to the different people. They seemed like a nice bunch, although I wished I was back in International Trade, doing what I was good at. It was terrible to be inexperienced again, not to know instinctively what was right and what was wrong in a given situation. I'd to keep asking Lorna things and it made me feel very stupid.

I went to lunch with three of them, Lorna, a girl called Martina whose job I hadn't yet seen, and two other inputters, Clive and Séan.

Clive and Séan both wanted to be dealers. They said that there was nothing better than the buzz you got when you walked into the dealing room. And everybody knew that the dealers earned twice and three times as much as everyone else. Every time a vacancy arose, both Séan and Clive applied for it. They hadn't got it yet, but they were confident that one day they would.

"Do vacancies come up that often?" I unwrapped a rectangle of sugar and dropped it into my coffee.

"Fairly often," said Séan. "The dealers leave, you see. They get offered jobs in other banks for better money and they go. It's becoming a much more exciting job than it used to be."

"Wasn't it always like this?" I asked.

Clive shook his head. "Currencies used to have fixed levels against each other," he said. "But now they change all the time. The dealers have to buy and sell them all the time and try and make money doing it. And it will get busier and busier. It's the job to be in."

Not for me, I told the girls that evening. It was madness. I'd gone into the dealing room again that afternoon. It was obviously not as busy as it had been that morning because half a dozen of them were playing some sort of indoor cricket with a rolled-up newspaper and the side off a brown cardboard box.

"They're all completely nuts," I said. "Like children."

Lucy was in good form because she was going to France with the MD for three days. They would stay at the Georges V hotel, which was the most exclusive in Paris, and everything would be paid for. We were all madly envious.

Grace was working on the evening dress. She'd bought a swathe of material in a magnificent jade green which she said would look fabulous with my eyes, and she pinned it on to a dressmaker's dummy which she'd also bought. The colour was fantastic and I couldn't wait to wear the dress. I'd given Grace the money for the material but she refused to take any payment for the dummy or for making up the dress. It would be a showcase of her work, she told me.

Brenda and Grace decided that they would open a shop together. Not immediately, they said, but some time within the next five years. They would work really hard and save as much money as they could.

"Maybe you should move back home," said Lucy.

"Not yet," replied Brenda. "But if we buy the shop, then we might have to."

"It doesn't cost us that much more to live here," said Grace, "but there'd be more space at home."

It was true that the dressmaking was making serious inroads into the space in the apartment. The twins' bedroom was almost taken over by material, and we had to wear shoes indoors all the time in case we stepped on lost pins by mistake. But none of us wanted to give up the apartment. It was still the best thing we had ever done.

I was on one of my evening strolls when I bumped into Rory McLoughlin again. Somehow I'd expected that he'd make an opportunity to talk to me at work, but he never had. I felt a bit hurt when I thought about it, but I tried to dismiss him from my mind. All the same, I was thinking about him when I turned into Baggot Street to buy some milk and literally bumped into him.

"Hello there, Jane." He caught me by the shoulders.

"Hi," I said unenthusiastically. "What are you doing around here?"

"We went for a pint in Searson's after work," he said. "I was going home. What are you doing?"

"Getting some milk," I said.

"Bit of a trek in from Terenure," said Rory.

I looked at him blankly.

"I'm sure there must be shops closer to you than here," he added.

"Oh, I don't live in Terenure any more," I said. "I'm living in an apartment off Waterloo Road."

"Really?" he asked. "That's great."

"Why?"

"You're very prickly, Jane," he said. "I think it's great when people move from home, that's all."

"Have you?" I asked.

He looked abashed. "Unfortunately not," he said.

"I'd better get back," I told him. He made me uncomfortable.

"Ah, don't go, Jane. Come and have a drink with me."

"You've already had a drink," I said.

"I've had two pints and a rock shandy," said Rory, "I can manage one more."

"Look, I don't really see the point," I said. "It's not that I dislike you or anything, but – " I lifted my shoulders helplessly.

"Why does there have to be a point?" asked Rory. "Come on, I'll tell you my life story if you tell me yours."

Men were always asking me to tell them my life story, I thought. As if there was anything worth telling.

I didn't know whether I wanted to go for a drink with Rory or not. I liked him, but I didn't want to be some sort of stopgap for him between real relationships. He obviously wasn't interested in me or he would have asked me out weeks ago. And, if the talk in settlements was to be believed, he already had a girlfriend.

"Come on," he said, persuasively, "one drink."

I sighed. One drink wouldn't do any harm, I supposed, and I hadn't had a drink with a man since Jaime de Boer.

"Where do you want to go?" I asked.

"I'm easy," he said. "Anywhere you prefer?"

"The Burlington," I said.

He made a face. "That's not a real pub."

"I know, but it's where I want to go. Take it or leave it." I was being incredibly rude, I thought.

"I'd better take it, then," said Rory as he linked me by the arm.

The hotel lounge was crowded and I sat down in a corner while Rory got the drinks.

"So, what do you think of Settlements?" He handed me a beer.

"It's OK," I said, "but I preferred it where I was before."

"Change is good for you," Rory told me, "and any of the dealing areas are good fun."

I didn't think deciphering a dealer's scrawl was particularly good fun and said so.

"We're all hopeless writers," he said. "But we make the money, so who cares?"

"Does anyone else in your family work in a bank?" I asked him.

"Don't be daft." He took out a cigarette and lit it. "Dad is an accountant. Mum is a housewife. Both my brothers work in offices but I don't exactly know what they do. I don't care, either. My sister is married." He took a drag of his cigarette. "No – I'm the one and only high-flyer in the family."

"My Dad owns a garage," I said. "Mam works in a shop."

"My mother never worked." He smiled lazily. "Just as well, we'd never manage if she was out. Anyway, Dad had a heart attack last year so she's very concerned that he doesn't overdo things."

I nodded and took another sip of beer.

I'd two glasses of beer while he had one pint and another rock shandy. He said that he tried not to drink too much on weekdays, it was only on Fridays that they went out and got mouldy drunk.

"I was pretty pissed when I took you to that Italian restaurant," he said. "I'm sorry about that, Jane, it wasn't very nice of me."

"Oh, I enjoyed it," I said, offhandedly.

"It wasn't fair," he said. "I've been a bit embarrassed about it ever since. I didn't like to get in touch with you in case I'd done something really terrible."

"You didn't do anything terrible," I laughed.

"Sure?"

"Absolutely."

"What did I do?" he asked.

I looked at him. "Don't you remember?"

He studied the back of his hand. "Not terribly well."

"You kissed me," I said.

"Really?"

I nodded.

"My breath must have been terrible," he said. "I'd drunk millions of pints and smoked hundreds of cigarettes. I'm sorry."

"I'm not," I said.

He smiled suddenly, and I liked him.

"So, what sort of kiss was it?" he asked.

"An ordinary sort of kiss," I said.

"Like this?" he pecked me gently on the cheek.

"Not exactly."

"Like this?" he kissed me lightly on the lips.

"Not really."

He let out a deep sigh. "I can't imagine what sort of kissing I was doing then," he said.

"Like this," I said, and kissed him.

"Jesus," he said, breaking free. "You'll get us barred."

"You did ask," I said.

"Maybe we should go outside and you could show me again," said Rory.

We paid for the drink and walked out of the hotel. It had grown a little chilly since earlier, and I hugged my jumper to me. Rory put an arm tightly around me as we stepped out on to the street. We walked down towards the canal, and he led me to a tree on the canal bank.

"So," he said, "you were showing me something."

I leant up against the tree and kissed him again. Our lips parted and his tongue entered my mouth, exploring it, finding the gap between my teeth. I felt myself go dizzy with pleasure. He pressed closer to me and I held him tightly. He slid his hand under my jumper and touched my breasts lightly.

I could feel myself grow warm with wanting him. I squirmed with pleasure, pressing myself still closer.

"God, Jane," he breathed into my ear. "You're fantastic."

"Thanks," I gasped.

He moved away from me. "I'd better stop," he said. "You drive me insane with desire."

I giggled. "Sounds good."

"But not here and now,' he said.

"OK." I tidied my jumper. I was shaking.

"You're some cool lady," he said. "Can I see you again?"

"You see me every day," I said.

"No." He stepped away from me. "I didn't mean it like that, Jane. I mean, will you go out with me?"

"Of course I will," I said.

He hugged me, fiercely. "You're the most incredible person I've ever met," he said. "I want you all for myself."

"I'm glad," I said. "Because I want you too."

We looked at each other and he started to kiss me again. Even when I'd been with Jaime, I hadn't felt anything like this. If he'd asked me, I would have allowed Rory to make love to me on the spot, never mind where we were. If I wasn't in love with him, I most certainly wanted him.

"I'll walk you home," he said. "I won't be responsible for my actions if I don't."

So we walked back to Waterloo Mews where he left me in the porch, depositing a very chaste kiss on my nose before he went. It was only when I went inside that I realised I'd forgotten the bloody milk.

8

September 1981

(UK No. 1 – Tainted Love *– Soft Cell)*

I banged on the door of the bathroom and told Brenda to hurry up. The twins were going out with some of the girls from the department store where they worked and had hogged the bathroom since six o'clock. I was meeting Rory at eight and I wanted to wash my hair, have a shower and smother myself in perfumed body lotion. Lucy, unusually, had decided that she would stay in. Often, if I was going out with Rory, she would go out with the twins; once or twice she had come out with Rory and myself, but for some reason they didn't really get on and those nights were uncomfortable for all of us. Lucy seemed not to care that she wasn't going out with anyone. The job at the distribution company took up all her time, sometimes she even worked Saturdays. She hadn't been working this Saturday but she claimed that she was too tired to even consider going out.

Rory and I were meeting in Searson's and then going to his favourite Italian restaurant La Bamba, where we had eaten that first night, for something to eat.

I looked at my watch. Nearly half past seven. I would be late. I banged on the door again.

"Keep your hair on." Brenda emerged from the bathroom with a large pink bath towel wrapped around her. "I'm finished."

"About time," I grumbled, "you've probably used up all the hot water."

It was a constant nightmare on Saturday nights. Last person into the shower usually ended up having a tepid flow at best. But since Lucy hadn't bothered tonight I was hopeful that there would be enough hot water left.

I stepped into the shower and the jet of water hit me. Warm, not scalding, but acceptable. I tipped a generous amount of shampoo into my hand and massaged it into my scalp. My hair was beginning to grow again, I noticed, with pleasure. Although I'd enjoyed the experiment of having it short, I never really felt that it was quite me, and it was nice to be able to twist it into a little knot on the back of my head again. I smothered myself in Badedas gel, enjoying its herby smell. I stood under the flow of water and hopped around the shower trying to shave my legs. This was never very successful and I expected that one day I would fall, break a leg and drown under the water, but I did my best. I hoped that I hadn't left any tell-tale tufts at my ankles.

The water began to cool and I turned the taps rapidly. I hated cold showers with a vengeance. I took my own towel from the back of the door and wrapped it around me.

"I have your hairdryer," called Brenda, from her bedroom. "I'm nearly finished."

I sat in front of the mirror in my bedroom and began to pluck stray hairs from my eyebrows.

"Here you are," Brenda rushed into the bedroom. "Sorry. Ours is broken."

"I hope you have a wonderful time," I said sourly.

"Get a grip," said Brenda.

"Oh, sorry," I said, truly contrite. "I didn't mean to snap."

Brenda smiled. She never took offence. "No worries," she said.

I dried my hair and applied my make-up. I'd learned a thing or two about make-up in the last few years and I could now apply it so that it looked very natural. I still tended to wear greys or browns on my eyes, but I didn't apply it as heavily and I could make my eyes look wider and brighter. When I was finished I was pleased with how I looked. I took my white blouse and lilac skirt from the wardrobe and put them on. Because we were only going as far as Searson's, I was able to wear the lilac shoes too.

I sprayed myself liberally with Charlie, behind my ears, on my throat, on my wrists, behind my knees and between my breasts.

Lucy was sprawled on the sofa in front of the TV when I walked back into the living-room. She was wearing a pair of baggy jeans and a sweatshirt.

"You look great," she told me.

"So do you," I teased. "Sure you don't want to

come with Rory and me?" I didn't really want her to come but I had to make the offer.

"No, thanks," she said. "I'm fine here."

I felt bad leaving her sitting in on a Saturday night. After all, when we'd taken the apartment first we'd always gone out together. Now I was going out with Rory and the twins had something else to do, and I didn't think it was fair on Lucy.

"I honestly don't mind," she said.

"But you're stuck here on your own," I said.

"Jane – I don't mind," said Lucy. "Really. If I did, I'd say so."

"I still think you should get a boyfriend," I told her. "It's not natural for you to be on your own."

"I'm perfectly happy," said my friend. "Now will you go, you'll be late."

I walked out into the late September air. The evenings were getting shorter and shorter now, the nights coming sooner and the air growing cooler. I hated the idea that we were moving towards winter. Once October came and the clocks went back, I always wanted to hibernate. It was so unnatural to get up in the dark and come home in the dark, and it made me ill-tempered.

But tonight was balmy. I'd flung a long white cardigan around my shoulders which was slightly at odds with my skirt's long slit. My shoes hurt, but they looked so good I pretended not to care. I was glad, though, when I reached Searsons, only five minutes late.

I hated being late. It wasn't part of my personality at all. If anything, I was the sort of person who would arrive early for dates and lurk in the toilets until the appointed hour.

I looked around for Rory but he hadn't arrived yet. Rory, unlike me, was rarely on time for anything. It drove me nuts.

My relationship with Rory was strange. It was very physical, although we hadn't gone to bed together. It was sparky. He was always testing me with weird questions or telling me dealing room anecdotes. It was fun, because he knew how to enjoy himself and spent lots of money when we went out. But I wasn't comfortable with him yet and I didn't know how long we would last.

I sat down in a corner of the pub where I could watch the door and ordered a vodka and white.

I kept half an eye on the door and watched the other people in the pub. I always loved watching people in pubs, they never seemed to notice that they were being observed. I settled back in the red velvet seat and watched the couple opposite me. They were having a row. The girl kept her head down and stared at the table while he looked away from her, unconcerned. Every so often she took a tissue and wiped at her eyes. Poor thing, I thought, I wonder what he's done.

The doors swung open and I looked up expectantly, but there was no sign of Rory, the people coming in were a mixed gathering of men and women.

I glanced at my watch. A quarter past eight. Where the hell was he? He had, as far as I knew, intended to eat at half eight. Had he booked the table at La

Bamba? I asked myself. I wasn't sure. It wasn't the sort of restaurant where you normally had to make a reservation.

He'd show up before half eight anyway, I thought. Rory liked his food. I would tell him that he was growing a paunch, and poke at it gently and he would grab me by the hands and tell me that it was more of him to love me.

But he still hadn't shown up by half past eight. I toyed with my drink, not wanting to order another until Rory arrived. Where on earth was he? It was unlike him to be quite this late.

I wondered if I should go down to the restaurant and see if he was there. Maybe I'd got it wrong. Maybe he'd said to me that he would meet me in the restaurant and that we'd go to Searson's afterwards. Suddenly, that seemed the most likely explanation. All the same, I thought I'd give him a couple more minutes. Just in case. Give him time to arrive at La Bamba, too.

So I waited until nearly twenty to nine before I got up. The barman looked at me sympathetically as though he thought I'd been stood up. I had been feeling a bit stood up earlier, but now I realised that I'd made a mistake I didn't feel too bad.

I walked down the street to the restaurant and pushed open the door. Mario greeted me effusively, as he always did.

"Signorina, most lovely to see you," he said, clasping me by the hand. "Where is Signor McLoughlin tonight?"

I felt the blood rush from my head. "I – I'm not

sure, Mario," I said. "I was to meet him and I'm not sure where. But we were going to have something to eat here later, so I thought he might be here."

"He has no reservation signorina." Mario looked concerned. "And we are quite full tonight."

"Would we need a reservation if we were to eat now?" I asked.

"I could make room for you, signorina," said Mario.

"But I'm not sure of the time," I said. "I think I'd better leave it for now, Mario. I'll check out the pub for him."

"OK," said Mario. "If he comes here, I will tell him."

"Thanks," I said and fled out of the restaurant.

I'd never been so embarrassed in my life. How dare he do this to me, I thought, holding my hands to my flaming cheeks. How dare he put me in this position. I stood on Baggot Street wondering what to do now. Should I go back to Searson's, where the barman would think I was mad? Should I wander around and hope to bump into Rory? I wasn't all that enthusiastic about wandering anywhere in these shoes. And where would I wander? Where could he be?

Perhaps, I thought, perhaps he'd had an accident. Maybe even now he was lying injured in the road. He must have had an accident, I thought. Otherwise he would be here. Or maybe he was sick. He'd had a bit of a cold yesterday, he'd been coughing down the phone lines which drove him mad. Maybe his cold was worse. We didn't have a phone so he couldn't contact me. Perhaps he was lying in bed now, fuming because he couldn't get in touch with me.

OK, I thought, that was the most likely thing. I'd walk to the Burlington, look up his phone number, and call his house. I didn't know his phone number by heart because I'd never had to call him at home. We arranged all our dates in the office. I knew his address though, so it would be easy to look up.

It took me ages to walk to the Burlington, because I now had a blister on my heel. This always happened with the lilac shoes, I thought viciously. I would have liked to take them off but I didn't think it would look good.

The Burlington was crowded. There was some sort of function going on and hordes of people swarmed around the foyer. The men were in tuxedos and the ladies wore brightly-coloured cocktail dresses and flitted around like butterflies.

I pushed through the crowd to the bank of telephone booths and picked up a phone book, easing my blistered foot out of my shoe as I did so.

The sheer number of McLoughlins made my heart sink. And, of course, although I knew Rory's address, I didn't know his father's name so I had to look through the entire list. Eventually I found it: Peter McLoughlin, the address and the phone number. I slid money into the phone and dialled.

The phone purred at the other end but nobody answered it. I stood there wondering whether anyone would answer, wondering whether Rory's parents were there, but there was nothing. Only the purring sound.

I replaced the receiver. Fuck you. I angrily brushed the hot tears from my eyes. Where are you?

I didn't know what to do. I went into the Ladies and sat in a cubicle. I tore off a strip of toilet paper and stuck it inside my shoe to protect my foot. Then I emerged and reapplied my lipstick. I would ring Searson's, I decided, in case he was there now. I looked at my watch. A quarter past nine. Maybe he'd said nine o'clock, not eight o'clock.

I phoned the pub and asked to speak to Rory McLoughlin. The barman called out his name. I could hear the hum of conversation in the pub, a sudden shrill laugh, then footsteps to the phone.

"He's not here," said the barman.

"Oh," I said. "OK. Thank you."

I replaced the receiver again. Obviously, wherever Rory was, it wasn't in Searson's or La Bamba. The only thing for me to do was to go back to the apartment. I'd get a Chinese takeaway and Lucy and I could sit together, eat and watch TV.

Pleased with my decision, furious with Rory and miserable that he hadn't shown up – for whatever reason, I called into the takeaway and ordered a chicken curry and a sweet and sour.

It was nearly ten o'clock by the time I got back to Waterloo Mews. I opened the apartment door carefully and walked into the living-room. There was no sign of Lucy. Maybe she'd gone out. Maybe she'd decided to go into town and meet the twins after all. I went into the kitchen and put the food on the worktop.

A sound from the bedroom disturbed me. She'd gone to bed already. Probably couldn't stand being at home alone. Poor Lucy. Sorry as I felt for myself, I felt sorrier for her.

I pushed open the bedroom door and stood, shocked. Lucy was in bed, all right, but she wasn't alone. I could see the outline of another person beside her, almost on top of her. I gasped audibly. As they realised that they were no longer alone, Lucy cried out in fright.

"It's only me," I muttered, completely embarrassed. "I didn't realise . . . " My voice trailed off.

I didn't recognise the man in bed with Lucy. He was older than her, a good deal older, in his thirties at least. He started to laugh.

"Shut up." Lucy dug him in the ribs.

I stumbled back into the living-room, tripped over my own feet and sprawled across the floor.

"Are you OK?" Lucy stood behind me, pulling her dressing-gown around her. I sat up and looked at her.

"I'm fine," I said.

She gazed at me. "I'm sorry," she said. "I wasn't expecting you home so soon."

"Who is that?" I hissed. "In the bedroom."

She looked abashed. "It's Nicholas," she said.

"Nicholas?"

"Nicholas Clark. He's the MD of the company I'm working for at the moment."

"Oh, my God." I looked at her, aghast. "Lucy, you told me he was married."

"He is," she said.

"Oh, Lucy!"

"Look, it's no big deal," said Lucy. "We're not madly in love or anything."

"How could you?" I asked.

"How could she what?" Nicholas Clarke walked into

the room. He wore a black polo neck and tight-fitting jeans. Despite his greying hair, he was very attractive. I could see why Lucy had gone to bed with him.

"Nothing," I muttered.

He put his arm around Lucy and kissed her lightly on the forehead.

"I'd better go," he said. "I'll see you Monday."

"OK," she said.

"Goodnight, Nick."

"Goodnight." He took up a black leather jacket from the sofa and put it on. He waved at both of us as he went out the door.

I turned on Lucy and shouted at her. Had she no sense? What if she got pregnant? She was only going to get hurt, wasn't she? What about her future? What about Nick's wife? And family?

When I'd finished my diatribe I burst into tears.

Lucy looked at me calmly, went into the kitchen and filled the kettle. I stayed, sobbing, on the sofa. She returned five minutes later with cups of tea.

"It's not up to you to criticise me." She handed me one of the steaming cups. "It's my life, Jane."

"But Lucy – you'll ruin it!" I cried. "It makes no sense."

We sat in silence for a moment.

"Do you love him?" I asked.

She sipped her tea and gazed into the cup. "I don't know," she said. "I like him a lot, and I fancy him like mad, but I don't know whether I love him."

"But he's married, Lucy!" I cried. "How could you possibly even consider going out with a married man?"

"I didn't really mean to," she answered. "It just happened."

"And was this the first time you – ?"

She shook her head. "No. We went to bed together last week. Remember when I was working late?"

"Where did you do it?" I asked.

"In his car."

"Oh, Lucy." I didn't know what to say.

She begged me not to give her grief. She told me that he was probably quite happily married. She didn't think that he would leave his wife and she didn't think she wanted him to. But there was something about him that attracted her and she couldn't get him out of her system.

"He's so sexy," she said. "Everything he does excites me."

"But you should resist temptation," I told her.

Lucy laughed. "You sound like the nuns," she said.

"They probably weren't entirely wrong," I muttered.

"Look," said Lucy, "when he breaks my heart I'll come to you and say that you were right all along. But at the moment, we're together and that's that. I don't want to talk about it, Jane."

"OK." I was silent. I couldn't, absolutely couldn't, condone her behaviour. There was some girl out there, Nick's wife, who didn't know that her husband was sleeping with someone else. I couldn't take that. Nick would go home to her and kiss her and say that he'd been working late and she would never know that he'd been in Apartment 33, Waterloo Mews.

"She might not care." Lucy interrupted my thoughts at exactly the right moment.

"Has he said that?" I asked.

She shrugged her shoulders. "Only that they're going through a rough patch."

"But Lucy, don't you think he's using you?"

"I don't know," she said, making a face. "I suppose we're using each other."

I put my arm around her shoulder. She was my friend, my best friend and no matter what, I would stick by her. She took my hand and squeezed it. We sat together for a moment, then she looked at me and said suddenly, "What the hell are you doing home now anyway? Did you and Rory have a row?"

The memory of my own evening, which had been completely blotted out by my discovery of Lucy and Nick, came flooding back. I bit my lip. I'd meant to say that we'd got our times mixed up and that I'd missed him, or something, but I blurted it out.

"He stood me up!" Then, again, I burst into tears.

Lucy put her arms around me and rocked me gently. She handed me a tissue while the tears flooded down my face. The shame and the humiliation of what Rory had done was almost too much for me to bear. I couldn't look at her.

"The bastard!" she said, "I'll fucking kill him."

Because she swore so seldom, it always sounded twice as bad coming from Lucy.

I sniffed, self-consciously. "Maybe I made a mistake," I said. "Maybe I got the time wrong, or the place wrong."

"If you'd done that, then surely he'd have come

around here looking for you," said Lucy. "I'd have answered the door."

"Maybe he did and you didn't notice." I was suddenly hopeful.

"I don't honestly think so, Jane," she said. "If there was a chance I'd say so, but Nick and I were in the living-room until only a few minutes before you came in."

"That was my only hope," I said disconsolately. "Unless he's been in an accident or something."

"D'you think that's very likely?" asked Lucy. "Was he driving?"

"No," I said.

We sat in silence. The big clock on the bookshelf ticked loudly in the background. I sniffed.

"Was that Chinese I saw in the kitchen?" asked Lucy.

I nodded.

"What did you get?"

"Curry and sweet and sour."

"Do you think it'll still be hot?"

"Enough, I suppose."

"Come on, then," said Lucy, "I never knew a problem that wasn't solved by eating."

So we ate the Chinese and opened a bottle of wine and sat in together, and I decided that best friends are absolutely essential to get you through life in one piece.

I didn't hear from Rory on Sunday, although I stayed around the apartment all day hoping that he might drop by. I couldn't believe that he wouldn't try to get in touch with me somehow and I still worried that something might have happened to him. I read through the Sunday newspapers carefully, looking particularly closely at the small stories in case there was one about a young man who had walked under a bus.

There was nothing in the newspapers and I had to assume that Rory was all right. I raged and wept all day Sunday, and the girls kept out of my way because I was in truly awful form. Lucy went home to her parents for the day and the twins went to a fashion show in the Mansion House, so I was alone with my thoughts. Horrible, vicious thoughts about what I would do to Rory McLoughlin when I met him.

I didn't sleep on Sunday night and I was out of bed early on Monday. I tried not to rush into work. The dealers were always at their desks by eight o'clock at the latest because the financial markets were already open on the continent and they had to be ready to trade, but none of the settlements staff ever arrived before half past.

I usually strolled in about a quarter to nine, having allowed everyone else in the apartment to use the bathroom first. Today I could easily have been in by eight but I made myself sit down and have coffee even though I'd been first up.

I spent ages getting ready for work. I chose a calf-length black skirt with pencil-thin pleats and a figure-hugging cream top to wear over it. It was my most slimming outfit. The cut of the skirt hid my bulging stomach and its length hid my stocky legs. I dusted my face with translucent powder and blusher and applied a very light covering of eyeshadow. I didn't normally wear make-up to work and I didn't want to look as though I'd made a special effort, but I did want to look sexy and attractive so that Rory McLoughlin would know exactly who it was and what it was he had passed up.

I arrived at the fifth floor, walked over to my desk, switched on my computer terminal and pulled out my chair at the same time.

The rose was sitting at the edge of my desk in a small cut-glass vase. Propped against the vase was a gift card which simply said "Sorry". It was signed Rory.

I felt the tears prick behind my eyes, and my bottom lip trembled. It was a lovely apology, but was it enough?

"Jane! What a lovely flower!" exclaimed Rosaleen as she walked past.

"Wish anyone I knew would send me roses," said Lorna wistfully.

"It's only one rose," I said, "no need to get carried away." But I lifted up the vase and sniffed at it appreciatively.

I sat at my desk and glanced through the paperwork without ever seeing what was written. Whatever it was that had prevented Rory from meeting me, he was upset about it. I wondered was he suffering pangs of guilt now, as he sat in front of his Reuters screen looking at the shifting numbers. Was he thinking about me, wondering whether I'd got the flower? Wondering whether I would forgive him.

It depended on why he had left me in the lurch, I

decided. I touched the red petal. It was soft and delicate.

I waited almost half an hour before I picked up the phone.

"Dealers," he said.

"Hi, dealers," I responded.

"Jane." He sounded worried.

"I got your flower."

"Do you like it."

"It's very pretty."

Silence.

"I'm very sorry about Saturday night," he said.

"So you fucking should be," I told him angrily.

"Really, Jane, I am sorry."

"Where were you?"

"My pal Jimmy rang to see if I would play football with him on Saturday afternoon," said Rory. "So I said I would. It was out in Greystones which was a bit of a pain, but it was a good game and we had a laugh. Then Jimmy went over on his ankle and we thought he might have broken it, so I had to bring him to Casualty and wait. You know yourself what Casualty is like. Hold on a minute, will you?"

The phone went silent and I could visualise him at the other end shouting an order to one of the brokers. It was almost impossible to have a conversation on the phone with Rory.

"Anyway," he returned to the conversation a minute later as though nothing had happened, "we were ages in Casualty and then I brought Jimmy home and we had a couple of drinks, and the next thing I knew it was nine o'clock. It was too late to meet you then, although I rang Searson's to see if you were there. Oh, fuck, Jane, I'll call you back in a minute."

The phone went dead. I fumed at my desk for a few minutes, then started work. There was no point waiting for him to call me.

His touch on my shoulder made me leap like a gazelle.

"Hi, there," he said. I swung around. He had never come out to me on the settlements floor before.

"Hello."

"I meant it when I said I was sorry," said Rory. "You mean too much to me to allow you to hate me."

"I don't hate you," I said. "How could I hate you?"

"Easily," said Rory.

"I never hate people," I lied.

"Stand up," he ordered.

"What do you mean 'stand up'," I asked.

"Exactly that."

I sighed exaggeratedly, but carried out his request. I reached his shoulder, Rory was very tall. And strong. He played rugby and soccer, very unusually.

He put his arms around me. "This is the bravest thing I've ever done," he said, and kissed me in full view of everyone.

9

October 1981

(UK No. 2 – It's My Party – *Dave Stewart/Barbara Gaskin)*

The Hallowe'en party was Grace's idea. She said it was atrociously bad form that four girls living together hadn't yet had a major party. Hallowe'en, she argued, was the perfect time and, what was more, we could make it fancy dress.

I wasn't keen on the idea of a fancy dress party. I always liked getting dressed up for parties, but not fancy dress. I could never think of anything to wear.

Brenda and Grace said that there were loads of things you could wear, and they were ready to make anything we wanted. Brenda decided to go as Robin Hood, Grace said that she would go as Maid Marian. I pointed out that we should all go as ghosts or vampires, but the girls refused anything sepulchral. Lucy got into the spirit of things and said that she would go as Mary Shelley.

I had no ideas whatsoever. The twins told me that I would have to think of something pretty damned quick if I wanted them to make me an outfit.

We sat in the apartment as the rain washed down the patio door. It had rained solidly all week and we were immune to the noise of the sluicing water. Lucy was compiling a list of invitees.

She had decided to ask about a dozen people from the distribution company. A few sales reps (mainly men) a couple of secretaries (girls) and a mixture of other people from the office, including Nicholas Clark.

"How about Mrs Clark?" I asked archly.

"Get stuffed, Jane," said Lucy.

Most of the twins' invitees were female, because most of the staff in the department store were female. They'd asked about ten people and only two of them were men.

"It's up to you to redress the balance," giggled Brenda. "You can ask only men, Jane."

"No problem," I said confidently. "Although I'll have to ask some of the girls as well."

But I was lucky. There were a lot of men in settlements, and I wanted to ask some of my International Trade friends too. By the time we had finished compiling the list, we had about forty names.

"Will they all fit in here?" I asked, looking around the apartment. "There isn't a whole lot of room."

"Better to have it too full," said Lucy. "Probably half the people won't arrive anyway."

I was getting more enthusiastic about the idea. It would be a bit of fun.

Rory thought so too when I told him about it. "I'll come as Antony," he said, "you can be Cleopatra."

"Aren't people always going to fancy dress parties as Antony and Cleopatra?" I asked.

"I don't mind," he said. "Go as whatever you like."

I wasn't sure whether he actually meant it or whether he was annoyed with me. The problem with Rory was that it was difficult to work out what he meant sometimes. He would get offended at something trivial, and ignore something which I thought a horrible insult. Our relationship was prickly, but fun. That was why I liked going out with him. He was unpredictable.

My parents liked him. The week after he had stood me up – an episode which had already becoming a standing joke – I suggested that we might drop in to my parents on the way to the movies.

Mam was delighted to see me with a good-looking man like Rory and she was thrilled when I told her how well he was doing in the bank and what an important job he had. Dad liked him too, although he was less convinced about the job.

"Sounds mad to me," he said, wiping his glasses, "but times are changing, I suppose."

I sighed deeply. My parents spent a lot of time talking about changing times.

"Do you want to see some photos of Jane when she was younger?" Mam beckoned Rory to sit down beside her.

"We haven't time, Mam," I moaned. "Really, we haven't."

"Of course we have," said Rory, wickedly. "I'd love to see photos of you, Jane. Before you got all old and wrinkly."

I made a face at him as Mam went off to get the photo album.

"She was a lovely baby," she said, as she opened the book.

"Oh, not baby photographs," I complained. "Really, Mam."

But Rory exclaimed over them all. Pictures of me in my pram (I thought they'd have long been thrown away), my first day in school, my First Holy Communion (looking almost saintly, I thought), my Confirmation, holiday snaps, family snaps, and a photograph of me in my deb's dress, holding Michael McAllister's hand.

"Who's that?" asked Rory.

"Jealous?" I teased.

He squeezed me and leaned toward me. "Of course."

"It's Lucy's brother," I told him. "He's married now."

Michael McAllister had married an absolutely stunning German girl called Ulrike whom he had met in London. Ulrike was the typical German, blonde hair, blue eyes and rosy cheeks. We poured over the photographs for a while. I was surprised to see how much I had changed over the last few years. I was still a well-built person, but I had lost a lot of the puppy fat I'd had earlier. My face was thinner too, and altogether more adult. Funny, when I was seventeen I thought I'd known so much. I'd been so sure of my opinions. Now I realised that I'd known nothing at all.

My parents insisted on telling Rory stories about

me as a child. How I'd fallen from the garden shed into the rosebushes beneath, emerging with ripped skin and covered in blood so that Mam had almost fainted when she'd seen me; the night I had walked in my sleep and had tried to get out of the house and into the back garden because I thought that the flowers needed to be watered; the time when I had eaten four jam doughnuts at one go and had been sick all over the kitchen floor

"I wish you'd stop giving away all my secrets," I said. "Come on, Rory, we'll be late for the movie."

"What are you going to see?" asked Mam.

"The Empire Strikes Back," I said, glumly. "I'd rather go and see something a little less like a western."

"It's a good movie," said Rory, unrepentantly. "*Star Wars* was good, Jane, you have to admit that."

"I thought it was garbage," I told him. "But I'll sit through the sequel for you."

"That's my girl," he said.

We left my parents and drove into town. Rory had his father's car, a silver Golf. Next year he would be getting a company car.

The movie was OK, I thought, nothing special. Rory never tried to kiss me or hold me in the cinema, his attention was totally focused on the screen. Occasionally he would drape his arm across the back of the seat and twist my hair, but in an absent-minded sort of way. He bought loads of popcorn which he ate throughout the movie, offering it to me from time to time.

But he kissed me after he drove me home. He

parked in the shadow of the huge beech tree which had given the apartment block its name, and reclined the driver's seat.

Rory was a superb kisser. He could drive me to a frenzy with the touch of his lips. His tongue nuzzled me as he breathed gently into my ear. I wondered sometimes where he had learned, because he could do things to me that no one else had ever done. When I was with him, close to him, I never wanted to leave him.

His hand travelled up my thigh, barely caressing me, sliding to the inside of my leg and higher. I caught my breath as he touched me and I felt myself quiver. I reached for him, under his shirt and ran my fingers through the matted hair of his chest. Our breathing was fast, impatient. I wanted to make love to him. I was glad that I had done it already, with Jaime, because now I knew what to expect.

"We'd better not," I gasped, as he undid the buttons of my blouse and cupped my breasts in his hands. "Not yet, Rory."

"Why not?"

"Do you have anything?" I asked.

He was silent. "No." He broke away from me.

We looked at each other. He looked away first.

"I want to sleep with you, Jane," he said. "I love you."

I had waited to hear him say the words. Sometimes I wondered if he ever would say them. He was so self-possessed, so independent, so interested in work and his friends and life in general. I was afraid that he wasn't really interested in me.

"Really?" I asked.

"Of course," said Rory. "Who wouldn't?"

I moved towards him again, and he buried his head in my breasts.

"I'll do something about it for the next time," I said.

"Promise?" he asked.

"Yes."

I did up my blouse, straightened my skirt and reclaimed my shoes from under the car seat.

"Do you want to come in for coffee?" I asked.

He declined. He'd better get home, he told me, his father went mad when he was out with the car.

I went to the family planning clinic after work the next day. They were very nice to me, very understanding and put me on the pill. I walked out of their building feeling self-assured and in control.

When I got back to the apartment I saw Dad's car parked outside and my heart beat faster. My parents never called around to me. What on earth could be wrong?

Lucy and Dad were sitting at the table in the living-room drinking tea. Dad stood up the minute I walked in and I felt that he could see straight through my bag to the packet of pills which were burning a hole in it.

"What's the matter, Dad?" I asked, seeing the immediate worry on his face.

"Your Mam is in hospital," he said, "they're doing tests on her."

I was white-faced. "Why?" I asked.

"She had pains in her chest," he told me, "and the doctor decided that she had to stay in."

"Oh, my God." She had already died of a heart attack in my mind. I couldn't help imagining the worst. I swayed on my feet.

"She'll be fine," said Dad. "I came over to take you in to see her."

I hated going to the hospital. Hospitals reeked of illness and death.

Mam didn't look too bad when I saw her. I tried not to look at the drip hanging from her arm and searched her face for any signs of tiredness instead. She said that she felt fine now and was embarrassed at being in bed. There was nothing wrong with her, she told us, she was probably just tired.

Rory was great that week. He came home to the apartment with me every day and waited with me until Dad called around to take me to the hospital. He didn't try and pressure me into going out anywhere. He could see how worried I was.

And I was worried. Shaking with fear, in fact. I had never, ever thought that either of my parents might become ill. Not at this stage in their lives when they were still quite young. I wanted Mam to be all right. I wanted them to find nothing wrong with her, though I was secretly convinced that it was hopeless.

As it turned out, I need not have worried. Our fears about heart attacks were entirely unjustified. Mam had torn a muscle in her chest. They kept her in to be certain, but everything was OK.

We had Sunday lunch together for the first time since I'd moved out. Dad drove us out to the Downshire House Hotel in Blessington. We'd often gone there when I was smaller and when we'd been for Sunday drives around the lakes.

We sat at a corner table in the dining-room and waited for the menus.

"I'm glad you're OK," I said, looking at Mam. "I was really worried."

She smiled at me. "I knew there was nothing really wrong," she said. "I felt it. And, of course, I prayed to Our Lady."

I tried to hide my impatience. Although I prayed in times of crisis myself, I didn't really believe in God any more. And I could never understand why Mam prayed to Our Lady and to the saints. If you were going to pray at all, you should go directly to God. But I said nothing. When I was younger, I would have argued with her. I was more tolerant now. Living away from home helped a lot.

"What are you having?" asked Dad, looking down the menu.

"The sole," I said. "And the *gratin* potatoes."

"Are you sure you want fish?" asked Mam, who thought that fish was a penance food.

"I like sole," I told her. "We have it at work quite a bit."

"I like your boyfriend," said Dad, casually. "Have you known him long?"

"Since before I went on holiday," I replied. "But I only really started going out with him after we came back."

"Just be careful." Mam folded and unfolded her napkin.

"What on earth do you mean?" I asked.

"Exactly that. Don't let him do anything you don't want to."

"Really, Mam!" I was annoyed with her.

"Well, it's important to keep yourself for the right man," she said.

I blushed hotly.

"Maybe he is the right man," I said.

"Maybe he is, but you'll have to be sure," said Mam. "You don't want him to take advantage of you."

"He won't take advantage of me." I looked down at the table. "Nobody will."

"Make sure of that," said Dad firmly.

What would they say, I wondered, if they knew that their darling daughter had already been taken advantage of, as they put it? Willingly been taken advantage of in a completely reckless holiday romance. Poor Rory was bearing the brunt of their parental angst.

I played with my cutlery and tried not to get flustered, but I was glad when they started gossiping about the family. I didn't really listen, although I heard what they were saying. I was wondering whether Rory would become part of our family. Would he be included in the gossip this time next year?

I was sure now that Rory was the man for me. We had our differences. He was notoriously late for things; if he didn't enjoy something then he would walk out and leave. He didn't suffer fools gladly and he worked (in my view) far too hard, but he was definitely the one for me. We liked the same things – if not the same movies. We liked restaurants and pubs, we liked reading thrillers, we liked cars. We liked travel and we wanted to have lots of money. Since I'd worked in the bank, I'd realised how many people had money and had a better life because of it. And now I was used to money. Not having it myself, but seeing it every day in the numbers which came across my desk. Rory bought it and sold it and I transferred it around the world. It seemed to me that if I was rich, I would be happy.

I was happy now, though. Or I would be, I thought, if I had something to wear for our fancy dress party tonight. I sat on the edge of my bed and chewed the corner of my lip. I'd spent the week in and out of the hospital so I hadn't had time to think about the party. Brenda mentioned it occasionally to me but I'd been too distracted to worry about it. I'd told her that I'd think of something. But here I was, two hours to go and nothing to wear.

The apartment looked great. Brenda and Grace had bought witches, masks and cut out ghostly shapes from white paper and stuck them around the walls. Lucy had hollowed out pumpkins which she'd bought in Kilmartin's in Baggot Street and we had filled baskets with fruit and nuts. We were going to light candles instead of using the lights. It would look great, I thought. We'd bought gallons of Pedrotti and made fruit punch for the guests, who were expected to bring the rest of the drink themselves. We were half hopeful that they would actually arrive in time and not spend the entire night in the pub first. We'd suggested nine o'clock. Nine o'clock. It was seven and I still hadn't decided what to wear.

I'd thought that I would be able to dress up as a clown or something, but when I saw Brenda, Lucy and Grace's costumes I knew that my clown effort would look tacky and juvenile.

Grace was Maid Marian, in a long flowing dress and a blonde wig. Brenda dressed up as Robin Hood in a green pointed hat, green tunic, leggings and boots. They'd made the outfits themselves and they looked fantastic.

Lucy barged in wearing nothing but her bra and pants but she had her dress over her arm and with her hair was a sheet of gold.

"Have you thought of anything yet?" she asked brightly.

I shook my head. "Looks like I'll just be in jeans and a jumper," I said.

"You can't do that!" Lucy was shocked. "It's our party. You have to dress up."

"But as what?" I asked. "I can't think of anything."

She rummaged through my wardrobe, pulling clothes off hangers.

"What about the green dress?" she asked. "The one Grace did for your Christmas party."

"I can't wear that yet," I said. "Don't be daft. Besides, there'll be people from the bank here, I can't wear it now and wear it again at Christmas."

I pulled out the drawers and tipped the contents on to the bed.

"Why don't you wear your pyjamas?" asked Lucy. "That'd be good. The men would like that. Wear as little as possible."

"Rory would enjoy that," I said.

"Here you are, Jane." Brenda burst through the bedroom door carrying a swathe of silver chiffon. "You can be a sort of ghost."

I took the material from her.

"What is it?" I asked.

"We ran it up during the week," she told me. "You were so tied up because of your Mam and everything. We didn't really know what to do, so this is just a ghostly outfit."

"Oh, Brenda," I said, touched that they had bothered. "Thank you."

She smiled. "Don't mention it. I think it'll look lovely on you."

I held it up against me. "It's great. Thanks again." I let out a sigh of relief. Thank God I had something.

I brushed my hair back from my head and secured it with a beaded comb. I did my sultry make-up look, silver eyeshadow and pillar-box red lips. I varnished my nails and wore my mauve shoes. I felt a bit underdressed in comparison with the others. Lucy looked fabulous as Mary Shelley, and the twins were brilliant. But I could hardly complain.

"You look fine," said Grace.

"Rory won't be able to keep his hand off you," promised Brenda. "He'll think you're great."

He did. He arrived before everyone else. I answered the door and he whistled appreciatively. He slid his arms around me. "Good enough to eat."

"Well, you needn't try eating her now," said Lucy tartly. "She's supposed to be keeping an eye on the sausages."

We were cooking cocktail sausages for later. I gave a shriek and went to check them.

People arrived reasonably promptly and soon the apartment was thronged. It looked fantastic with the flickering candles and the eerie pumpkin faces.

Despite my best efforts, we had ended up with more women than men but that didn't seem to bother anybody. The music was loud but nobody complained. We'd invited the occupants of the apartments all around us. Everybody brought drink so that there were piles of bottles and cans in the kitchen.

Nick Clarke arrived with a bottle of champagne which he popped and passed around between as many as he could. He looked extremely handsome and I could see why Lucy fancied him. He was older than anyone else there and he looked at us as if we were a bit crazy, but we were young and we were having fun.

Jessica, Peter, Damien and Alan had all come from International Trade. Rory invited all of the dealers along because I told him we wanted lots of men, so the room was full of them, still using all their jargon so that nobody had a clue what they were talking about.

Still, they were very bright and outgoing and kept the party fizzing along nicely. Shane Goodman, the corporate foreign exchange trader, was chatted away to Nick, telling him that he should be hedging his dollars forward. Nick nodded wisely, as though it meant something to him.

Brenda and Damien sat in a corner of the room,

each with one half of the same apple in their mouth. Grace chatted happily to the guy who lived in the apartment upstairs. We had never even met him before; his name was Greg and his parents owned the apartment. He was doing engineering at college. I told Grace to hang on to him, looked like he was loaded.

The sausages were very successful. When I brought them into the living-room everybody fell on them. The buzz of the conversation grew louder, we kept the music fast and upbeat and we reckoned that the party was going well.

"I haven't spoken to you all evening." Rory interrupted my conversation with Jessica and pulled me into his arms. "Everyone is having a great time but I'm left talking to people I don't know."

"You were nattering away with the other dealers," I told him. "I knew better than to interrupt you. All this garbage about cross rates and swissy prices and arbitrage and long bonds."

He laughed at me. "I'm sorry, what do you want me to talk about?"

"Oh, I don't know," I said, putting my arms around his neck. "My beautiful body, maybe?"

"I could talk about that all right." He pulled me closer to him. "But why talk about it? Why not do something about it?"

"Like what?" I whispered, nibbling at the end of his ear.

"You're driving me crazy," he said, "absolutely crazy."

"Jane, what have you done with the bottle opener?" cried Grace, "you had it last!"

Reluctantly, I slipped away from Rory and found the opener. Lorna was looking through our selection of music. "Anything slow?" she asked me, "I want to dance with Martin."

"Who's Martin?" I asked.

She nodded towards one of the reps Lucy had invited. I couldn't see why she wanted to dance with him, not my type at all, but I gave her a slow and smoochy tape which she slipped into the cassette recorder.

"For your eyes only
Will see me through the night."

I allowed Rory to fold me into his arms. It was as though we were alone together. We clung together, barely moving. I rested my head on Rory's chest. He stroked my back. I was perfectly at peace.

"Can't live, if living is without you."

"That's how I feel." I looked up at him.

His dark blue eyes glittered in the candlelight. He leaned forward and kissed me.

I knew that I would make love to him that night. I was ready, he wanted to, we would have the opportunity. Well, maybe. If we could find a place in the apartment that wasn't already taken by somebody else.

I led him to our bedroom. It was empty, apart from the mound of coats on the beds. I locked the door behind me.

"Are you sure you're ready?" asked Rory.

"Of course," I said.

I wondered if he thought that he was my first

lover. As far as I was concerned he was, Jaime wasn't a lover, he was my experience.

I lowered the straps of the slip over my shoulders.

"Take it off," he commanded.

I let it fall to the floor, trying to keep my stomach sucked in as much as I could. I was happy that my body was in better shape than it had been a couple of years earlier, but my stomach was still a disaster area.

"Take them all off," said Rory.

I wasn't embarrassed. I stood naked in front of him.

"God," he said. He pulled off his own shirt and trousers. Somebody banged on the bedroom door.

"Go away," I shouted.

I heaved all the coats on to Lucy's bed and we got into mine. We burrowed under the covers. Rory kissed every part of my body that he could reach. I reached out and grasped him.

"Be gentle with me," he whispered, and I giggled. I was glad that he had made a joke, it made it easier.

Rory was more aggressive than Jaime, more dominant and quicker. But he held me tightly afterwards, stroking my hair, my back and my thighs. He told me that he loved me.

"But will you respect me in the morning?" I asked mischievously.

"I will still love you in the morning," said Rory.

It was the most romantic thing anyone had ever said to me. If ever I had any doubts about Rory McLoughlin, they had been banished that night. He was the man for me. I wanted to marry him.

10

November 1981

(UK No. 20 – Why Do Fools Fall In Love? – *Diana Ross)*

An icy wind whistled up Burlington Road, swirling dead leaves on the pavement, making my eyes water. I hugged my fleecy jacket around me and tried to insulate myself from the bitter cold. It was cold enough to snow, and they had forecast it last night, but this morning the sky was clear and blue. Frost glittered crisply on the pavements. It had stayed deceptively sunny all day; only when stepping outside did you feel the deadly bite of the Arctic wind.

I scurried across the road and let myself into the apartment, my freezing hands hardly able to hold the key. One day I would buy myself a new pair of gloves. I usually bought them around Christmas every year and lost them by January.

Greg from apartment 43 ran down the stairs as I came in. He nodded at me, asked was it cold and, when I said yes, shivered in anticipation. I liked Greg. We had seen him a couple of times since the party.

He'd called down to the apartment a couple of times since, simply to chat. He still seemed interested in Grace, although he had the same problem as all men did with the twins. It was impossible to know which one he was dating. The twins were beginning to take more of an interest in men, too. Until now, they had seemed to be totally happy with each other's company, very disconcerting unless you knew them. But Grace had been out a couple of times with Greg. Brenda went out very occasionally with one of the buyers in the department store.

Our lives were progressing very satisfactorily, I mused, as I skipped up the stairs to the apartment. Rory and I saw a lot of each other. I loved him more and more every day and I think he felt the same way. Sometimes I was plagued with doubts. He was such an active person, had so many different things to do. He didn't talk about us very much. Sometimes I panicked because he was never on time for anything and had to be reminded if we were going anywhere. But he said that he just had a short attention span, it was because of work, nothing to do with me.

We had been to my parents' house a couple of times. Rory was always extremely courteous to Mam, and to any of my relatives we happened to meet there. They all thought he was the nicest young man they had ever met.

The only person he didn't really get on with was Lucy. I thought that Lucy was plain jealous of the fact that I had a stable loving relationship while she was still having an affair with Nick Clark. She never said anything to me, but I knew that she wanted Nick to leave his wife and move in with her. It worried me. I wanted Lucy to be happy. I was so happy myself, I couldn't bear to think of her being badly treated or miserable. Maybe it'll work out, I thought, as I opened the apartment door. Maybe by next year we'll all be in happy relationships. None as happy as mine, though.

The heating was on in the apartment which meant that someone was home already. I pushed open the living-room door and walked inside.

Lucy sat at the pine table, her head in her hands. I dropped my bag on the floor and rushed over to her.

"Lucy," I said, "are you all right?"

She shook her head, her blonde hair a curtain which hid her face.

"What's the matter?" I asked.

She sniffed loudly, and a tear dropped on to the table in front of us. I hadn't seen Lucy cry in years.

"Come on, Lucy, you can tell me. I'm your best friend." I pulled up a chair and sat beside her. I took her wrists in my hands and tried to pull them away from her face.

She looked up and shook her hair back. Her eyes were red and her cheeks blotchy and swollen from her tears. She looked awful.

"Tell me," I ordered.

"That bastard!" She sniffed again and a tear slid out of her eye and down her cheek. She scrubbed at her face with a crumpled tissue.

"Who?" I asked, already knowing the answer. "Nick?"

"Of course, Nick," she snapped. "Who else?"

"What has he done?"

She buried her head in her hands again. I watched her anxiously.

"Lucy?" I said, softly. "What has he done?"

He's got her pregnant, I thought to myself. It was the one thing I feared for myself and the only thing I could imagine that would send Lucy into this despair. Bad enough for me, though, I could always marry Rory. But what on earth would Lucy do?

"His wife is pregnant," she cried, suddenly. "His fucking wife is pregnant."

I looked at her and sighed deeply. Not as bad as if she were pregnant.

"How could he?" She looked up at me. "How could he? He told me he wasn't sleeping with her any more." She started to cry again, great gulping sobs. "He said that they hadn't had sex in over a year. That's a joke. Her baby is due in April."

"You couldn't expect him not to have sex with her," I said, trying to be reasonable. "They're living in the same house."

"But he said that he didn't sleep with her," sobbed Lucy. "He swore he didn't sleep with her."

I didn't know what to say. All along I had imagined that this was how the affair would end, but I couldn't say I told you so to Lucy. I wanted to, but I couldn't say it. I kept quiet. I wished there was something I could do.

She hiccoughed, and wiped her eyes again.

"Would you like a drink?" I asked. "Brandy, whiskey, vodka – tea, coffee?"

She shook her head. "It's like when you're a kid,"

she said, "and you do something your mother doesn't approve of. And she says that it'll all end in tears. And it does, Jane, it fucking does."

I wanted to cry, too, Lucy was my friend. I cared about her. I wanted to kill Nick Clarke myself.

"He's not worth crying over," I told her. I knew that the words were trite and stupid. "You'll find someone else, Lucy."

"I don't want someone else," she sobbed. "I want him, Jane. I love him."

I put my arms around her and hugged her. I knew how she must feel. If Rory ever two-timed me, I would feel like this. But I was lucky, because Rory loved me and you don't cheat on people you love. So Nick, the bastard, hadn't loved Lucy and hadn't loved his wife either.

"How did you find out?" I asked. "About her being pregnant?"

She gulped. "He told me," she said. "He said he couldn't see me on Thursday because he was going with her to a prenatal class."

I wanted to choke him.

"Don't worry, Lucy," I said helplessly.

"I'm not worried," she said. She stood up and walked over to the window, "I'm just so very fucking stupid." She leaned her head on the glass. "You warned me, Jane. You warned me against him and I didn't want to listen. But you were right."

I shifted uncomfortably in my chair. Knowing I was right was one thing, being told it was different.

"I just didn't think it would work," I said. "I might have been wrong."

She smiled at me, a watery smile. "But you didn't lecture me and I'm very grateful. You were right and you said what you had to say and you left it at that, Jane. I really appreciate it."

I was embarrassed. "Come on, Lucy. You'd do the same for me."

"I won't have to," she said. "You've got Rory. You're lucky."

I didn't say anything. I was lucky and I knew it. Men like Rory didn't come around every day.

"Why don't we go out?" I suggested. "Have a few drinks, get something to eat? Just the two of us? We haven't done that in ages."

She made a face. "I don't really feel like going out," she said. "I've got a bit of a headache and I look awful."

"So take some Panadol for your headache and wash your face," I told her. "Come on, Lucy. Let's do it."

So we went to the Leeson Lounge and had a few vodkas, then wandered along to La Bamba for something to eat. Mario welcomed me as a favoured customer now, as I was, because I went there so often with Rory. It was funny but before I met him I had hardly ever gone to a restaurant for something to eat. Captain America's had been the limit of my sophistication. But I was growing used to walking in to La Bamba and having my coat taken and the menu put in front of me while Mario went off to get mineral water without being asked.

"It's my treat," I told Lucy when I saw her look at the prices in the heavily-bound menu. "Have whatever you like."

We had ravioli and lasagne and tons of smelly garlic bread which cheered us up immensely. I was a little show-offish with Lucy. I asked Mario to recommend a decent wine, not plonk, to prove to her that I was now the sort of person who drank decent wine. I wanted to show her the kind of life I led with Rory. We had a good time. We called into Searson's for one on the way back to the apartment and were in giggling form by the time we got home.

Lucy was in a better mood the next morning. She decided to tell the agency that she wanted to switch jobs, that she couldn't work for Nick's company any more. She dropped me outside the bank before driving into town so that I was early and able to get a lot of work done before the deals of the day filtered through.

It was one of the hectic days. The dollar soared against the deutschemark, interest rates were all over the place and the dealers shouted and screamed at each other, wrote illegible tickets and frantically tried to make money.

Rory and I had intended to go for a drink after work, but I knew that it was highly unlikely on a day like this one. On days like this, the dealers went off together to talk about their trades, and where they thought the markets were going, and how they had managed to turn a loss-making situation into a profit-making one.

Half of the talk was nonsense and I rarely joined Rory if he was going out with the lads. I got irritated listening to them. They thought they knew everything. I secretly felt that they knew nothing.

I hardly got to talk to Rory at all that day, just a brief hello when I went into the dealing room with a query on a ticket. So the next day I was delighted when he left a note on my desk which read *"Sorry, too busy to think, do you want to go to London for the w/e, love, Rory."*

I rang his extension and said "yes" and he told me that he had already organised the tickets. He'd arranged to meet some clients over there, he said, they were going to a football match on Saturday, but we would have Friday night together and most of Sunday.

I was a little put out at this. An evening and half of Sunday wasn't much, but at least he'd asked me, and he'd bought the tickets.

Mam phoned me at work that afternoon. I was busy and I didn't have much time to talk but I had to tell her.

"He's what?" she asked. I could hear amazement in her voice.

"He's bought tickets for us to go to London," I told her, "for the weekend."

"This weekend?"

"Of course." I altered a trade ticket. One of Rory's. He'd got the currencies mixed up.

"So I suppose you're going then?"

"Why not?" I asked.

"Where are you staying? With friends?"

"No," I told her. "The Inn on the Park. It's a very flashy hotel, Mam, and Rory's paying for that too."

"That's very nice of him, I suppose."

"Of course it is." I cradled the phone on my shoulder as I inputted data. "Rory's very good to me."

"I know that," said Mam. "I like him. I'm just not sure that – "

"Mam!" I interrupted her. "We'll be fine. I'll be fine. Don't worry."

"It's not that I'm worried," she said, "but – "

"Listen to me." I interrupted her again. "We're going away for the weekend. Loads of couples do that. It's quite normal. Please don't spoil it for me."

I could almost see her frown. I heard her sigh and I grinned to myself. She wanted to ask me about the sleeping arrangements, but she was silent and I wasn't going to volunteer anything. I was an adult. I could make my own plans. Besides which, I was taking my pill religiously every evening before I went to bed and I was confident that at least I wouldn't get pregnant.

Of course when Rory and I got married, then it would be different. I would wait for a year or so, there was no point in starting a family too soon, but I wanted to have children. I was an only child, so I wanted to have at least two, but I wasn't sure about it. I'd seen films of women in childbirth. It seemed awfully painful and I wasn't into pain.

We caught the six-fifteen to Heathrow. I hadn't been to London since I was a child, when Mam and Dad had taken me over for Easter. We'd gone on the ferry. We'd seen all the sights, done all the tourist things. I still remembered the hugeness of it all compared with Dublin.

I liked London. I liked the variety of the buildings, the incredible number of people, the bustling, hurrying nature of the city. We took a taxi to the hotel. Rory had been given some sterling by the bank for expenses, so it didn't cost us anything.

The hotel was fantastic. A liveried doorman stood outside the entrance and held the door open for us. A porter brought our bags up to the room. I bounced up and down on the double bed while Rory raided the little fridge and opened a snipe of champagne.

This would be the first time that we had spent the night together. We had, of course, made love again since the night of the Hallowe'en party, but only a couple of times, and there had never been the opportunity for us to spend an entire night together.

"What do you want to do?" I wriggled suggestively on the bed.

"What do you think?" Rory grabbed me.

After a very satisfactory interlude Rory suggested that we have a shower.

"Together?" I asked.

"Of course," he said.

We stood under the jet of water together, revelling in the warmth. Rory tipped some shower gel into the palm of his hand and smoothed it all over me, starting at my shoulders and finishing at my ankles. It was exotic and sensuous. I did the same for him, working the soap into a white lather in the black hairs of his chest. We held each other closely, our bodies slipping against each other.

"I love you, Jane," he said. "I really love you."

"I love you too," I said.

We went to the hotel restaurant for dinner. It made La Bamba look cheap. The tables were covered in crisp white linen tablecloths. Waiters glided between the tables, carrying plates covered in silver domes. The menu was written on expensive parchment. I felt that we should be whispering, it was all so lavish.

We sat in a companionable silence observing our fellow diners. They were mostly businessmen in navy and grey suits, but at the table directly opposite us sat a middle-aged woman, beautifully dressed, impeccably made up and elegant. She added colour to the somewhat drab diners.

We went back to the room and sat on the bed watching TV. It was very loving and I felt as though we were married already. Mrs Rory McLoughlin. It had a good sound to it.

I'd expected that we would spend the whole night making love, but Rory fell asleep after the first time and snored gently beside me. I rolled him over on to his side, but he kept rolling back again. Eventually though, he turned towards me, put his arms around me and slotted beside me like a spoon as we both fell asleep.

He was to meet his London clients early the next morning. They were taking the tube to Highbury to watch Arsenal play. I had absolutely no interest in football whatsoever. Dad had never followed a particular team so it never really entered into the equation at home. Any time he did watch football, it was in the pub. None of my boyfriends had any interest either, so terms like "offside" meant nothing to me. Rory couldn't believe I knew so little. He knew the name of everyone on the current Arsenal team, Arsenal teams of the past, other clubs team members had played for and every manager the club had every employed. I thought it was a load of rubbish and said so.

However, I left him happily wearing his Arsenal scarf on Saturday morning. I went shopping. I walked down to Piccadilly Circus and then up Oxford Street, calling into every single shop on the way. I liked shopping in London, the sheer number and size of the shops was breathtaking. I spent all day in the shops. I was utterly exhausted by the time I made it back to the hotel, weighed down with plastic bags full of goodies. I wasn't sure what time Rory would be back. He'd said that he was going for a few pints after the match so I lay back on the bed and waited for him to return.

By seven o'clock, I was fed up and hungry. I knew that Rory lost his sense of time when he'd had a few drinks. But I thought it would be different when we were away together. I watched *Columbo* and ate the large Toblerone from the minibar.

By eight o'clock, I was really pissed off. What could they be doing? Surely he would remember that I was on my own and come back.

By nine, I had looked at the room service menu and ordered a burger and chips. Rory was paying for the room, he could pay for the food as well, I decided, as I speared a chip in anger.

By ten, I was worried about him. London wasn't like home after all, anything could have happened to him. Perhaps he'd forgotten where he was staying,

He arrived back at around eleven, eyes red, cheeks flushed. He reeked of stale beer and cigarette smoke. His scarf was wrapped loosely around his neck and he staggered through the door. He smiled at me before he flopped down on the bed.

"Where on earth were you?" I asked.

He yawned widely and stared at me.

"Where were you?" I repeated.

"On the piss," he grinned, vacantly. "Had a great time."

"I'm very glad," I said, tartly. "I thought you'd be back before now."

He opened his eyes to look at me. "Why?"

"I just did."

"We were at a match," he said, as though that explained everything. "How could I be back before now?" He closed his eyes again.

"Have you had anything to eat?" I asked.

He snored gently in reply. I poked him in the back, but he simply rolled over and ignored me.

I watched him lying there, angry and frustrated. What was the point of coming to London together if we were going to be apart all day – if he was going to sleep the minute we got together again? Did he not find me attractive? Was there something wrong with me? Obviously there must be, because otherwise he would have drunk two pints and come back to the hotel.

I climbed into bed beside him and lay there wide awake, a rigid mass of anger and confusion.

We had to check out by noon the next day, and our flight was at two-thirty. I woke him at eleven. He prised his eyes apart and looked at me blearily.

"Wha' time?" he asked.

"Time to get up," I said, shortly.

He reached out and pulled me to the bed. "Come back in," he said.

"No."

He sat up. "What's the matter?"

I was horrified to realise that I was on the brink of tears. I bit my lip and turned away from him.

"Jane?" He caught hold of my arm. "What's wrong?"

"I thought you'd be back earlier last night," I said, choking back a sob. "I waited for you for ages."

"But you knew I was at the match," he said, his voice surprised. "You knew I was with the lads. We went for an Indian afterwards."

"How was I to know that?" I asked.

"You should have guessed."

I suppose I should. Impossible for a gang of men to get together at a football match and not get pissed and go for something to eat.

"I didn't realise," I said lamely.

"Silly girl," said Rory. "Come on, we've time."

I fell towards him and climbed back into the bed. Our lovemaking was fast and frantic.

We barely had time to check out. I was embarrassed, certain that the receptionist knew that we had just made love. It was a rush to get to the airport. Our flight was on time. Rory was very considerate towards me, asked me if there was anything I needed, insisted that I sat beside the window, pandered to my every whim. When the air hostess asked if there was anything we wanted, he asked for Panadol.

When I was back in the apartment that evening I

couldn't decide whether I'd enjoyed the weekend or not. I had certainly enjoyed the flights over and back, I loved aeroplanes, even though take-off scared me. I'd enjoyed our exquisite dinner on Friday night, but I still felt peeved that Rory had left me all day Saturday on my own, that he couldn't really understand why it had bothered me.

Still, it was part of getting to know each other. And it wasn't as though he was having fun all the time, he was with clients, after all. But if we did decide to get married, I hoped that he'd give up this desire for football and drink and realise that I was far more important to him than either.

11

December 1981

(UK No. 10 – Wedding Bells – *Godley & Cream)*

We were all going home for Christmas Day. Given the chance, we would have stayed in the apartment and had Christmas dinner together, but we knew that our parents would go absolutely mad if we did.

We decorated the apartment, though. We pooled our money to buy a small tree which we stood in a wastepaper bin, propped up with books. It smelled gorgeous; the entire apartment was enveloped in the heady, outdoor smell of the fir tree. Brenda and Grace made wreaths of holly leaves and fir cones, and I bought a big inflatable Santa Claus which we blew up and stood in the corner of the room. The presents were placed in a pile under the tree.

It looked very festive and it would have been wonderful to spend Christmas Day there, but we decided that it wouldn't be worth the hassle to try and insist. Anyway, none of us would have been able to cook the dinner.

The week leading up to Christmas was hectic. The Settlements staff night out was on the Thursday. We got merry in Henry Grattan's, stuffed ourselves with food in a Chinese restaurant and finally fell down Leeson Street. It was a brilliant night. I got back to the apartment at about four o'clock.

Lucy woke me at half past eight, just as she was leaving. I hauled my eyes apart and looked at her through the gelled clump that was my hair.

"It can't be time to get up," I moaned and she laughed unsympathetically.

"You woke me up when you got in," she said, heartlessly. "I'm enjoying waking you up now."

"Bitch!" I called after her retreating back, throwing back the bedcovers and staggering into the bathroom.

Why on earth did we go out on a Thursday night, I wondered as I massaged shampoo vigorously into my hair and tried to stay standing under the spray of water. Whose idea was it?

Not only had we gone out on Thursday night, but tonight was the official bank party. This was for all staff, it was the one to which I would be wearing the dress that Grace made, and it was held in the Shelbourne. I had been looking forward to it, but the way I felt now I wasn't quite so sure. I couldn't see how I could possibly stay awake long enough to go to another party.

I made hundreds of mistakes at work that day. For some reason, I was totally unable to remember the code for sterling and kept trying to input any sterling transactions as Irish pounds. The computer rejected them each time with a beep which was instantly recognisable. Rosaleen kept looking across at me, I know that she was counting the number of errors I made.

I wasn't the only one, of course. Settlements was full of white-faced people who could barely keep their eyes open. The dealers rang the phones simply to wake us up.

"How are you today?" My phone rang. It was Rory.

I grunted at him.

"That bad?"

"I feel terrible," I said. "My eyes hurt, my head hurts and I can't input anything right. Rosaleen keeps looking at me and I'm sure she's going to write something awful on my appraisal."

We had our annual staff appraisal every Christmas. Our annual bonuses were paid depending on how good the appraisals were. I'd hoped that mine would be good, I knew that I'd worked hard and that I was accurate and careful. All the same, I was afraid I could blow it all today.

Rosaleen had been at the party, but she'd drunk 7-Up in the pub and had gone home after the Chinese. Rosaleen didn't believe in having fun.

"Don't worry," Rory told me. "You'll be fine."

I did feel better later on that evening and I had another shower before I got ready for the party.

Lucy did my hair for me. It was long enough to put into a neat French plait at the back of my head, which instantly made me look older and more sophisticated. I did my make-up carefully, applying just a touch of khaki eyeshadow to the corner of my eyes before filling the rest with my usual grey. Brenda had bought a lovely blusher a few days earlier which she said would look great on me, so I tried it out. It did look good. It made my cheekbones look higher and my face thinner.

Grace helped me into the green dress. She was very hopeful that somebody would like it and I was sure that they would. I just wasn't certain that, despite my assurances, I could get someone in the lending department interested enough to consider advancing the twins money for dress design.

The high collar at the back suited me and my hairstyle. I wore earrings which Aunt Olivia had given me for my twenty-first, drop pearls in a silver setting. I put on the silver chain that Rory had bought me the week before – a pre-Christmas present he'd called it. I smothered myself in Dior's *Cristalle* which I had bought on the way to London. I borrowed Grace's silver gate bracelet because I didn't have any silver bracelet of my own and I wanted to keep my jewellery consistent.

"Let's look at you," she said. I stood up and twirled around. The bodice of the dress was tight and the skirt full. It was a good party dress, I said, although I'd have to be careful not to eat too much, otherwise I might burst.

"Have you put on weight?" demanded Grace as she hauled at the zip.

I had to admit that I was a few pounds heavier. Going out with Rory meant eating and drinking more and I wasn't getting any exercise except sex. I was determined that I would diet after Christmas.

Rory called around for me in a taxi to bring me to

the party. Although we thought we would be early, there were plenty of people already at the bar. We pushed our way through the crush to get a drink.

"Hair of the dog." Rory handed me a Bacardi and Coke.

"I need the entire dog," I muttered.

He went off to join the dealers while I stayed with my own crowd. Jessica came in, looking very pretty in a black cocktail dress, accompanied by Neil Dawson from the Baggot Street branch. Lorna had made a real effort and was wearing her hair differently, in a softer, less severe style which made her look much more feminine. Michelle wore a long, slinky ball gown which made me feel that Grace's dress was too fussy. But everyone had admired it so far and, when I told them all that my flatmate had made it, they were really surprised.

I stayed chatting to Jessica while Neil wandered off.

"How are you getting on in Settlements?" she asked, sipping her drink.

"Not bad," I told her. "But I preferred International Trade."

"Really?" she said. "I thought you liked the people in Settlements better."

"Not really, "I said. "They're OK, no different. Nobody like you, Jessica. Nobody who takes an interest."

"I thought that one person was taking an interest." She nodded over at Rory who was deep in conversation with Shane.

"Oh," I said. "I didn't think you meant Rory."

"He's taking quite an interest, though, isn't he?" she said, wickedly. "It's the talk of the bank."

"Is it?" I was surprised. "Loads of people in the bank are going out with each other."

It was difficult for it not to happen. There were so many people of a similar age that inter-office affairs happened all the time.

"But Rory is such a good catch," said Jessica.

"You said that to me before," I told her. "Anyone would think you fancied him yourself."

She blushed furiously and I looked at her in amazement. "You don't fancy him yourself, do you?"

She shook her head vigorously. "I'd better tell you," she said. "I went out with him once."

I looked at her in shock. "When?"

"When he joined first. It was ages ago, Jane, and we only went out twice. He was younger than me and it didn't work out. But I've stayed fond of him."

"He never said anything," I told her.

"He's probably forgotten," said Jessica blandly.

I supposed it was reasonable to assume that Rory had gone out with other people in the bank, but I'd never asked him about it. I'd tried to talk to him once before about his previous relationships, but he was always dismissive about them, said they didn't matter. I hadn't realised that Jessica could be one of them.

"It really meant nothing," she said again, uncomfortably. "I shouldn't have mentioned it."

"It's OK," I said. "Don't worry about it." I wasn't worried. Jessica wasn't Rory's type.

The hotel staff came around at that point and tried to usher us in to the dining-room. I moved with the throng. I sat at a table with the Settlements crowd and the dealers were at the other side of the room, but that didn't matter because I knew that Rory and I would get together later.

Helium-filled silver balloons were tied to the backs of the chairs. A huge Christmas tree, decked with shining balls and sparkling white lights, took up the corner of the room. We all crowded around the tables, exclaiming in delight.

"Love your dress, Jane," said Martina. "It's absolutely fantastic."

"Sure is," said Rita. "Where did you buy it?"

"My flatmate made it for me," I told her. "She wants to be a dress designer."

"I wish she'd design something for me," said Martina. "It's the nicest dress I've seen."

I was pleased, both for me and for Grace. "I'll tell her that," I said. "Thanks."

After the meal we got up and danced. I stayed with my own crowd for an hour and then Rory came to claim me. We danced together, a public affirmation of our status as a couple.

It was the best Christmas party ever. In the raffle I won a £10 voucher for Brown Thomas, although I couldn't imagine what I could possibly buy there for a tenner, and Rory won a bottle of sherry, which he said that I could bring over to Mam and Dad for Christmas.

"My parents don't drink it," he said. "I know your mum likes sherry."

"She'll be thrilled," I told him. "Thanks."

I'd met Rory's parents a couple of weeks earlier.

They seemed nice enough people, but his mother was more distant than mine and I couldn't help thinking that his father rather looked down on me. Rory had two brothers and a younger sister, although I hadn't met any of them yet. That was the one thing that bothered me about our relationship. If it was to be the one, if we were to get married, surely I should meet his family first. It wasn't as though they could stop us, of course, I simply felt that it would be the proper thing to do.

Rory's family wasn't as close as mine, though. Mam, Aunt Liz, Aunt Olivia and Aunt Joan met regularly. The various cousins knew each other very well. When we were smaller, we holidayed together a lot. The McLoughlins weren't like that at all. Rory had aunts and uncles, but he said he didn't see them much and he never thought about them. I couldn't imagine a family like that.

He held me close as we danced together. I could feel the warmth of his hand, smell the musky scent of his aftershave, sense his breathing with the rise and fall of his chest. I rested my head on his shirt and he held me still closer.

"I don't know if it's cloudy or bright
'cause I only have eyes
For you,
Dear"

I echoed the words softly under my breath as we swayed slowly in time to the music.

"I only have eyes
For you."

The church was crowded for Midnight Mass. Outside, frost glittered and sparkled on the black tarmac. Inside, fan heaters blasted warm air on to the congregation. A huge crib took up one side of the altar.

"Adeste Fideles." The choir began the hymn, filling the church with rich sound. The priests marched in a procession around the church, carrying a doll to symbolise the Christ child. Father O'Herlihy, the parish priest, laid it in the manger.

It was a ritual that had been part of my life since I was nine years old and first deemed old enough to be allowed to Midnight Mass. I looked around me. I hadn't been to Mass since I left home. Since I didn't believe in God and since I thought the ritual was very silly, there didn't seem to be any point, but there was something very comforting about Midnight Mass. I listened to the priest and felt guilty about my relationship with Rory. But we would be married one day, I thought. We love each other. It's right for us to sleep together. All the same, I felt terribly uncomfortable. Why did the Church have to make us feel like sinners all the time? I asked God. Surely He didn't want people to go around in a perpetual haze of guilt.

When we got home Dad made us Irish coffees and Mam heated up some mince pies. It was lovely. We wished each other a happy Christmas and went to bed.

The smell of roasting turkey wafted up to my bedroom in the morning. It was one of those aromas which brought me back to my childhood.

I was standing in the kitchen, watching Mam peel potatoes.

"Why do you take the skins off?" I asked.

"Because you have to do that to roast them," she told me.

"Why are you scraping bits out?"

"They are the eyes. You have to get rid of them."

"But they'll be blind!" I cried. "They won't be able to see."

I smiled at the memory as I walked into the kitchen again.

"Can I do anything to help?

"Peel some potatoes," said Mam, and didn't understand why I started to laugh.

I peeled potatoes, prepared the sprouts and scraped the cranberry sauce out of the jar and into a sauce boat.

"Are you going to wander around in your dressing-gown all day, or are you going to get dressed?" asked Mam.

"I'm going to get dressed, of course," I said. "But we have to give presents first. I always do that in my dressing-gown."

She smiled at me. "OK," she said, wiping her hands on her apron. "Let's see if your dad is ready."

Dad was sitting in the living-room watching *Miracle on 34th Street*.

"Do you want to do presents?" I asked.

He nodded, so we sat down in front of the tree and exchanged gifts. I watched my parents anxiously. I had spent a lot of time trying to get something they would like.

Dad was delighted with the stereo headphones I bought him. He liked to listen to music and watch TV at the same time, which drove Mam mad, so I had decided that this way he could do both. Mam was a bit put out to see that she only had a box of chocolates as her gift, until she opened the envelope inside the gift-wrap and saw a voucher for a full-day beauty treatment at one of the Grafton Street salons.

Her face lit up and she kissed me on the cheek. I knew she would like it, she always looked so well when she was made up and dressed up but she never spent time on herself these days.

Mam had bought me a lovely silver-blue jumper, decorated with silver stars. Dad had bought me a book. I opened the present that Rory had given me the day before. I knew that it couldn't be anything like an engagement ring, because the box was too big, but secretly I hoped that it might be. It wasn't. It was a beautiful gold chain from which hung a wishbone.

"How pretty!" exclaimed Mam.

"That chap really likes you," said Dad.

I slipped the chain around my neck and wished Rory was with me now. I felt a great ache of longing for him. I wondered if he had opened my present to him, a huge watch which told the time in almost every capital city in the world.

I went upstairs, had my shower and dressed in the new jumper and a black velvet skirt I'd bought especially for Christmas. I brushed my hair into a new style so that it fell over one eye. Looks cool, I thought.

When we sat down to dinner, Mam suggested that I pin it back out of my eyes.

"It's meant to be like that," I said, peevishly. I wasn't used to being criticised. In the apartment, we gave each other tips about how to look better, but we never told anyone to brush their hair out of their eyes.

In fact it was quite strange being home. My bedroom didn't seem like mine any more. I'd taken the pictures off the wall when I moved out. The wardrobe was empty except for the few bits and pieces I'd left behind and what I had brought with me for the three days I was staying at home. Mam and Dad had assumed I would stay with them until I went back to work, and I didn't have the heart to say that I wanted to go back to the apartment.

But after three days I was mad to go back. It was hard to be treated like a child when I was used to making my own decisions. I went down to Lucy's house on St Stephen's Night, just to get a break, and my parents wanted to know what time I'd be back. She said it was just as bad at her place, and the two of us wondered whether we could return to the apartment straight away. But we couldn't. It would have broken their hearts.

The day after St Stephen's Day, all the aunts and uncles came over for dinner. It was a traditional family get-together, held in a different house every year. I looked around at all of them and was a bit disappointed that I didn't have any brothers and sisters. When I got married, Christmas in my house wouldn't be the same huge social gathering. Sisters stay close, I thought, watching them. Brothers can sort of take it or leave it.

I looked at my watch and wondered whether Rory would call. He was in Scotland for Christmas. his family owned a house there and spent every Christmas "holed up in the highlands", as he called it. There wasn't a phone in the house, so he couldn't call easily. The nearest phone was in the village, three miles away. He said he would try to phone, but that if it was raining he wouldn't bother. I told him that he'd better bother. I'd checked the weather forecast. It was pouring, apparently.

I sat and tried to join in the conversation but I was bored with it. I didn't care that Phoebe Sinclair's eldest daughter had got a first at university. I didn't even know who Phoebe was, it turned out she was an old school friend of Aunt Olivia.

"And Juliet O'Hara's girl has gone to live in the States," said Aunt Liz. "She married a doctor."

"I never liked Juliet," said Mam. "She was a snob."

"Only because her family were rolling in it," reminded Aunt Liz. "Do you remember, they had a girl who came in and cleaned for them every day?"

Mam nodded. "They treated her like a slave," she said. "She was a lovely girl."

"Do you remember Agnes Delaney?" asked Aunt Olivia, suddenly. "I saw her in town the other day. Pasted in make-up and trying to look half her age. Actually looked twice it."

"Stop being bitchy," I said. "You're assassinating every character of your youth."

Aunt Liz laughed at me. "You'll enjoy doing that when you get older, young Jane," she said. "Bet you could say a few choice things about people you went to school with."

I pursed my lips, then smiled. "Stephanie McMenamin – tart," I said brightly.

"Jane!" exclaimed Mam.

"Well, she was," I said. "I never liked her. Always showing off."

"Didn't she get married?" asked Mam.

I nodded. "She has a baby daughter and she's expecting her second," I said.

"My God!" said Aunt Olivia. "She's only your age?"

"Yes," I replied. "She got married the year we left school. To the same guy she was going out with since she was about fifteen. Kurt Kennedy. She lives on Riverview Estate."

I had seen Stephanie a few times since we left school. At first I had been madly envious of her. A gang of us had gone to the church the day she married Kurt and had watched jealously as she had walked down the aisle looking radiant, her blonde hair swept up and her long veil trailing down her back. Kurt had looked debonair and handsome and I remember thinking that I could fancy him myself.

The last time I saw Stephanie she'd been pushing her daughter in a pram, hurrying for a bus. She hadn't looked half as glamorous then.

I knew about marriage. I knew it wouldn't always be perfect. That there would be days when I would probably regret it. Days when it would be a hassle. But I still wanted Rory to ask me.

What about you?" asked Aunt Joan, breaking into my reverie. "Are you thinking of getting married yet, Jane?"

I blushed. "Not yet," I said.

"Are you sure?" teased my aunt. "You don't sound convinced."

"Tell us about your boyfriend," demanded Aunt Olivia. "What's he like."

"Really," I protested, "you sound like you're vetting him or something."

Mam laughed. "They're just raging because you've a handsome young man dancing attendance on you," she said. "They think he sounds great."

"Have you been telling them?" I asked.

"Just a bit," she said. "Well, you *are* my daughter."

"His name is Rory," I said. I didn't need much encouragement to talk about Rory. Saying his name conjured up his face. This was the longest I had gone without seeing him since we started going out together. I told them about him, how hard he worked, how generous he was, how good-looking he was.

"He sounds great," said Aunt Liz, warmly. "But don't get married too young."

"Who said anything about getting married?" I demanded. "We've only been going out together."

Aunt Liz shook her head knowingly.

"She's right," said Mam, suddenly. "Don't rush into anything, Jane. Enjoy your life."

"I *am* enjoying my life," I said forcefully. "I'm having a great time in the apartment with the girls. We go to work during the day and go out at night."

"Every night?" Mam sounded concerned.

"Don't be daft," I said. "You know we don't. But we go out at the weekend, sometimes together, sometimes with boyfriends, and it's great."

Aunt Olivia nodded. "I would have loved to live in a flat on my own when I was younger," she said, wistfully. "You're very lucky, Jane."

"I think so, too," I said, and got up to answer the phone which had begun to ring.

"I thought you'd never call," I said to Rory. "I've missed you."

"Sorry," he said. "I couldn't really get away before now. What are you doing tonight?"

"I'm sitting in with my family. They're reminiscing about the old days and telling me to have fun while I'm young."

"Sounds OK to me," he said, cheerfully.

"I told them I was having fun," I said.

"I thought you were missing me," he said. "How can you be having fun?"

"Well, I usually have fun," I amended. "When will you be home, Rory?"

"I'll be back on New Year's Eve," he said. "Do you want to go out?"

"Of course I do," I said. "What did you have in mind?"

"Oh, anything once it's with you," he said, making my heart somersault.

"You say the nicest things," I told him.

"I know."

We chatted for a while longer and then I went back into the living-room.

"I know you want to have fun," said Aunt Liz,

looking at my happy face. "But it seems to me that he has you in the palm of his hand. I take it that was your Rory."

"That was my Rory." I sat down and tucked my legs under me. "He misses me."

They laughed. "Who misses who?" asked Aunt Olivia but I ignored them.

On New Year's Eve, Greg from apartment 43 invited us up to his apartment for a party. We accepted with alacrity, although I told Lucy that I'd be seeing Rory first.

"No problem," she said. "We're all going to the Burlington for a drink then straight up to Greg's place."

"Straight up?" I asked.

"Straight up," she answered. "I promise we won't barge in on you." She winked lasciviously and I made a face at her. But I was glad that Rory and I would have some time on our own in the apartment.

He called around at half past eight, looking incredibly desirable in his denim jeans, denim shirt and black leather jacket. I felt myself melt the moment he walked through the door.

The girls went off to the pub, telling us that they would see us later.

"Don't forget to come to the party," reminded Lucy as they walked out of the door.

"We won't." I closed the door behind them, delighted to be on my own with Rory at last.

We fell upon each other as though we had been apart for years instead of days. We laughed at ourselves and our desire. I opened a bottle of wine and put on some music and lay in his arms, happier than I had been in days.

It felt so perfect. So right. I closed my eyes and allowed him to stroke my cheek.

"I have a present for you," he said, suddenly.

I sat up. "Another one," I said. "You're spoiling me."

"I've nobody else to spoil," he said. "Besides, I like giving you presents. You're like a child when you get something."

"You're the only one who gives me presents," I said. "And I do so love them."

"Well, I was going to give you this one on Christmas Day," he said, "but then I couldn't give it to you and not be there."

"Hand it over," I commanded. "Give me the goodies."

He laughed and took the box out of his jacket pocket.

I knew at once that this was it. It had to be. I schooled myself not to be disappointed if it was another chain, or a bracelet or a pair of earrings. Rory might not be ready for marriage yet. He might think that we were too young. He might think that I would like a small gift of jewellery. Not a ring. He wouldn't know that I would be devastated.

I opened the box and looked inside. The ring nestled against the navy blue velvet, sparkling gently. The diamond was very beautiful. It was a solitaire in a raised setting and it glittered in the lamplight.

"Oh Rory," I breathed. "It's fabulous."

He searched my face. "Do you like it?"

"Oh, yes."

"It's an engagement ring," he said.

"I can see that," I told him.

"I wanted you to be sure what it was."

"I'm certain what it is," I said.

"So?" asked Rory.

I took the ring out of the box and slipped it on to my engagement finger. I turned my hand from side to side so that shafts of light sparked out from the diamond.

There were tears in my eyes as I looked at Rory. "I love you," I said.

"But will you marry me?" he asked.

It was the question I had been waiting for since I was about thirteen. When I realised that girls got married. And Rory, my beloved Rory, had asked me. We hadn't casually chatted about it and decided to get married one day in a very sensible sort of way. He had bought a ring and given it to me and asked me.

"Of course I'll marry you," I said, looking up at him again. "I've always wanted to marry you."

We went into the bedroom and made love. I wore nothing but my engagement ring in bed.

"I love you," I said.

"I love you," said Rory.

We were still there in each other's arms at midnight. We heard the sounds of people entering Greg's flat above, the steady hum of voices, the thud of music and the shrill laughter of a party. But we had stayed where we were, content to be together. So when they stopped the music and started counting down to the new year we were still together, holding each other tightly.

I was engaged to be married, I thought, proudly. Engaged to Rory. My new life was about to begin.

12

February 1986

(UK No. 1 – When The Going Gets Tough – *Billy Ocean)*

Jessica dumped a file on my desk and grinned sympathetically. "Busy?" she asked.

I looked up from the documents I was checking to see if she was joking. I was very busy. "What does it look like?" I demanded. "I'm up to my neck. I'll never get this lot finished by five o'clock."

"That can wait," said Jessica. "I need you to check these now."

I glanced at my watch and then at the file. It was crammed with paper.

"Turnstone Industries," I said. "That's Jake's." I looked over at the empty desk where Jake Loomis normally sat.

"But Jake is at the conference and I need someone to do this now," said Jessica.

"I know Jake is at the conference," I snapped, feeling rage well up inside me.

I'd wanted to go to the conference. It was called

"International Banking in the Eighties" and, even allowing for the hype of the brochure, it had looked very interesting. I meant to ask Jessica about it as soon as I saw the brochure but she was at a meeting so I left it on my desk for later. I couldn't find it the next day. I looked around for it for a while, then Rory rang me about something or other and I forgot all about it. Until Jake Loomis casually mentioned that he was going. He'd taken the brochure from my desk. "I assumed you weren't interested," he said blandly when I challenged him about it. I thought about making a fuss and demanding to go too, but it wasn't worth it. I was spitting mad all the same.

After I married Rory, the bank transferred me back to International Trade because they needed someone with experience in the department. Most of the people I'd originally worked with had either resigned or been promoted to other areas. Jake Loomis had come from Personnel and he was ambitious. I knew more about the work than he did, I was more conscientious than he was and I was more efficient than him – but he was the one at the conference and I wasn't.

"Jane?" Jessica was staring at me.

"I don't see why I should have to – "

"Jane, I'm not asking you, I'm telling you."

I gritted my teeth. "Fine."

I pulled the file towards me and started work. None of the documents was properly checked and everything was out of sequence. That little shit, I thought bitterly.

I flew through the work. I had to. Rory and I were

going out tonight and we were leaving on the dot of five. Rory would go crazy if I was late. Bill Hamilton, the most senior executive in the corporate treasury division, had invited a number of people to dinner in his house. We were invited because Rory had been promoted at Christmas. So we couldn't be late.

I still had a couple more documents to check when Rory rang me at ten to five from reception.

"I'll be down in a minute," I said. "I'm almost finished."

But it was nearly ten past by the time I hurtled down the stairs and into the marble foyer. Rory's face was black as thunder as we hurried down to the car park.

He was already sitting on the edge of the bed when I emerged from the shower. He looked great in a new charcoal grey Hugo Boss suit, pale cream shirt and Pierre Cardin tie. He tapped his watch and sighed.

"All right, all right," I said. "I'll be ready soon. Keep your shirt on."

"I don't want to be late," said Rory. "This is a very important dinner, Jane."

"I know it is." I switched on the hairdryer. "I won't be long."

We had plenty of time. The invitation said half-seven for eight and it was only a quarter to seven now. He was driving me nuts. Rory, who had never been on time for anything in his life before, was now the one telling me to hurry up!

I did my face and took the purple satin dress from the wardrobe. It was last year's dress but it was one of my favourites. It made me feel very sexy and sophisticated and that was how I wanted to feel in front of Rory's colleagues.

"Do up my zip," I asked Rory, who still sat on the bed.

"Breathe in," he said, as he hauled at it.

"I am."

"Breathe in a bit more."

I sucked in my breath and he tugged the zip.

The fabric rucked unflatteringly around my stomach even though I tried to smooth it out, and it strained across my chest. I looked as though I'd explode through it any minute.

Rory looked at me critically. "You're letting yourself go a bit."

"Give me a break," I said as I tugged at the dress again. "I haven't worn this in ages. It's probably just a bit of weight since Christmas."

"Christmas was eight weeks ago," he informed me. "You should have lost any pounds by now."

"Well, I haven't," I snapped, annoyed with myself for putting on weight and annoyed with him for being so direct about it. "And I can't possibly wear this dress. I'll have to find something else." I was close to tears. I had been so organised and now it was all a shambles. I was going to have to rethink my entire outfit. If I ever got out of this bloody dress. I was embarrassed about putting on weight although I usually added a few pounds in the winter. I lost them again in the summer but that wasn't much use now.

I was irritated at the way Rory was looking at me. As though I was some fat lump trying to squeeze into a dress five sizes to small. This dress was my size. Usually.

"I'd better wear the black," I said, rummaging around in the wardrobe. "It's stretchy."

"I never thought I'd see the day when you would be going for comfort, not style," said Rory.

"Fuck off, will you," I said in temper. "There's nothing wrong with the black dress."

"It's a boring dress," said Rory. "Anyone can wear black."

I couldn't stand Rory criticising how I looked. I never said anything derogatory to him about his appearance. I ignored him and pulled it off the hanger, smoothing in out on the bed.

"Well, I can't wear it," I said, "there's a stain on it." I wanted to kick and scream in frustration.

By the time I'd found a suitable dress (navy blue, a couple of years old and normally slightly loose on me) Rory had decided that we were late. He hustled me into the car and ignored the fact that I'd stepped in a puddle, so my feet were wet. I didn't say anything but switched the heater on full blast to try and dry them.

He gunned the car along the dual carriageway. The driving rain smashed against the windscreen and the wipers raced across it frantically. I shivered. I wasn't looking forward to tonight any more.

The panic of having to race around and find something else to wear had given me a headache. I leaned back in the comfortable seat of the BMW and closed my eyes. I tried to relax my shoulder muscles and breathe slowly, but I was terribly tense and I couldn't seem to empty my mind like you are supposed to.

"Fuck!" exclaimed Rory and swerved suddenly.

I snapped my eyes open. "What's wrong?"

"Fucking cyclists. No lights. In this weather. He deserves to be knocked down!"

I peered out of the back window but I couldn't see anyone. "You didn't hit him, did you?"

"Don't be ridiculous. If I'd hit him, he'd know all about it." Rory slammed the car into fifth.

I said nothing. It wasn't worth talking to him when he was in this sort of mood.

Bill and Karen Hamilton lived in a five-bedroomed, detached, redbrick house off the Stillorgan dual carriageway. It was an exclusive development of only twenty houses, all slightly different and designed to appeal to people with money. They had integrated garages, landscaped gardens and mock-Georgian porticoes over the front doors. The cobble-locked driveways were big enough for two cars and most of the people living in Huntswood Heights owned two cars. All of the houses had high hedges or trees enclosing their gardens, keeping them very private.

"Come on," said Rory, as he switched off the engine. "Let's hurry."

We ran up the driveway together, holding our coats over our heads. It was a horrible night. I pressed the doorbell and heard it chime at the back of the house.

Karen Hamilton opened the door. She was a stunning girl who looked considerably younger than thirty-three, which was how old Rory had told me she was. She was tall and thin with a long, graceful neck and a perfect oval face. Her hair was almost jet black and cascaded down her back in rippling glossy waves. She had dark brown eyes and black straight eyebrows. Her skin was sallow and glowed with a tan from a winter week in the Canaries. She wore a red wool dress which clung tightly to every curve of her body, its plunging neckline accentuating the deep V of her breasts. A ruby pendant rested in the hollow and drew your eyes inexorably towards them.

Rory's eyes almost popped out of his head when he saw her.

"Hello, Karen," I said, when he failed to speak.

"Jane." Karen's voice was low and throaty. "It's wonderful to see you."

A bit of an exaggeration. Karen Hamilton had only met me once before. They way she spoke it was as though her only joy in life was seeing me again. I smiled at her.

"Come in," said Karen, "before you get soaked."

We stepped inside the house. The hallway was wide and the carpet deep and warm. The walls were papered in a creamy abstract design hung with prints from the New York Metropolitan gallery, lit by unobtrusive spotlights.

"We're in the lounge." Karen sashayed down the hallway ahead of us.

The other couples were already there and I felt Rory's intake of breath as he realised that we were the last to arrive. Bill Hamilton stood in front of the gas effect fire, a glass of whiskey in his hand.

"Ah, Rory." He put the glass down on the mantelpiece. "You made it. And the lovely Jane." He extended his hand and I took it. He shook hands with a firm, decisive grip.

"What can I get you?" he asked.

"Could I have a Bailey's with ice?"

"Certainly," said Bill, "and you, Rory?"

"Gin and tonic, please."

I looked around the room while Bill busied himself with the drinks. It was huge, divided by double doors which led to the dining area. The understated decor could only have been achieved with a lot of money.

"Do you know everyone?" Bill asked me, as he handed me the drink.

"She knows me," smiled Graham Kirwin, the Chief Dealer and Rory's boss. "And she knows Suki."

Suki was Graham's wife, a beautiful Eurasian girl he had met when he was working in Frankfurt. I had met her once or twice before, but I didn't know her very well.

"Hi." She smiled.

The others introduced themselves. All of the men worked in the treasury department. All of the wives were drop-dead lovely. I felt clumsy and unattractive in my navy blue dress.

"Well, now that we're all here, I'd like to congratulate Rory McLoughlin on his recent promotion," said Bill as he lifted his glass, "and all of you on putting in such a good year for the bank."

"Hear, hear," said Bernard McAleer.

"And I'd like to thank the wives, especially," said

Bill. "Sometimes wives have to put up with an awful lot. Late hours, hard work, et cetera. So I'd like to thank them too."

"Absolutely," said Lorraine, Bernard's wife.

What a load of crap, I thought. All the same I raised my glass and smiled at Bill. He was about forty, going grey, and with a paunch which was escaping over the top of his expensive trousers.

"Of course, Jane still works for us." He smiled at me. "And you're doing very well, I believe."

"Thank you," I said. He was patronising me. I hated being patronised. I wasn't doing that well. I'd been promoted last year but I reckoned it was well overdue. I was good at my job, but it was very hard to feel that it was important when Rory earned nearly three times as much as me – before bonuses. Bill made some more comments about the bank and its staff and how wonderful we all were. I supposed they taught them all that motivational stuff at their management meetings. I shifted uncomfortably from one foot to the other.

"So, tell me, Lorraine," said Karen as she moved across the room and adeptly divided the men from the women, "where did you get that fabulous outfit?"

"It's a Karl Lagerfeld," she said, "I bought it in London."

"It looks superb on you," said Karen.

"Yours is lovely too," said Linda Sherry. Linda was the most ordinary-looking of the girls; the only one that didn't look as if she'd stepped off a catwalk.

"Thank you, my dear," said Karen. "I bought it in Terenure, would you believe."

"Really!" Lorraine looked surprised. "Very elegant."

"Thanks. It's a nice shop, near the village. Called *Les Jumelles.*"

"Oh, I think I know it," said Linda.

"I do," I said. "The girls who run it are friends of mine."

I was delighted. The shop, which they had opened a couple of years ago, was obviously attracting the right sort of clientele. These girls could afford to spend money.

"Did you buy that dress there?" asked Lorraine, as she arched one of her fine eyebrows.

I blushed furiously. Lorraine was making some sort of dig at me and I didn't like it.

"No," I said shortly.

There was a moment's silence, then Suki asked Karen about her recent holiday.

My attention wandered from the conversation and I looked around the room again. Everything in it was of the highest quality. The carefully polished fittings shone. The carpet, like the one in the hallway, was deep. I was conscious that my heels were making little marks in it.

The girls continued to chat about holidays. Karen had been to the Canaries. Lorraine and Bernard had been skiing in Kitzbuhel.

"It was brilliant," said Lorraine. "The snow was fantastic and the nightlife was even better. Some of those ski instructors!" she laughed knowingly.

"I've never been skiing," I said regretfully, deciding that I should make an effort to join the conversation, "although Rory says we must go some time."

"Go now while you don't have children," said Lorraine. "Once you start a family, you don't get a moment to yourself."

"Don't talk to me!" said Linda cheerfully. "Do you know what Charlie did the other day?"

She launched into a story about her son, a tin of paint and the cat next door. Linda was good at telling stories and she had us in fits of laughter.

"Another drink, girls?" asked Bill. We nodded.

"I meant to give up drink for January and February," moaned Lorraine. "I put on far too much weight over Christmas."

"I think you look great," said Fiona Roche. "A bit of weight suits you."

Actually, Lorraine looked like a stick insect to me. I couldn't imagine how she thought she was even slightly overweight. I could see her shoulder blades clearly through her dress. They started to talk about diets and I listened carefully. Tomorrow, I thought, I would start one of my own. No more crisps or sweets in front of the TV. What I needed was less food and more exercise.

When we'd married first, Rory and I joined a squash club. Neither of us was very good but we had fun bashing the ball around. But now Rory was far too busy to bother with squash and I'd stopped going to the club on my own. I'd start again, though. Maybe when Lucy came home she would join the club too. The last time I'd talked to her she hinted that she was thinking of returning to Ireland. She'd spent the last few years in Paris as a PA to the director of an Irish company there, but she was tired of France and she said she was looking for a job at home. She'd visited home quite a bit, and I'd been over to Paris a couple of times which was fun, but I missed our easy companionship at home. She'd gone to France shortly after I got engaged, to forget about her disastrous affair with Nick Clarke. She'd stayed because she liked it so much. Then, being Lucy, she'd found a boyfriend and moved in with him. I got the impression, the last time we talked, that the relationship was floundering and I wondered if that was why she'd hinted at coming home.

I yawned, and quickly covered my mouth with my hand.

"Don't tell me you're tired!" exclaimed Karen. "Or is our conversation boring you?'

"No, not at all," I said, hastily. "I think it's the heat from the fire."

"It was such a cold night I rather thought you'd like some warmth," remarked Karen. She leaned down and lowered the setting on the gas fire. "Is that better?"

"It's fine," I replied in embarrassment. "There was no need to lower it for me, honestly."

"Oh, I like to give my guests whatever they want," she said, making me feel as though I'd just put her to an immense amount of trouble. "Do you want to go in and eat?"

I said that I would love to eat, although I wasn't very hungry. I still had a headache and my stomach wa queasy, but the others said that they were starving. Karen smiled brilliantly at Bill and asked him if he was ready for food.

"I thought you'd never ask!" he cried.

"Excuse me a moment, then," said Karen, and disappeared into the kitchen. I admired her ability to be a wonderful hostess and to cook a meal for us all while being so relaxed. If it was me, I knew that I would be in a complete tizzy, running in and out of the kitchen, with a red face glowing from the steam.

Karen sauntered back into the room a few minutes later, smiled radiantly at us and led us into the dining-room.

"This looks great." Linda sat down at the shining mahogony table.

"Appearances are everything," laughed Karen.

I knew what Linda meant. The table was beautifully presented. The wood gleamed warmly, the cutlery shone and crystal wine glasses sparkled under the subdued lighting. A lovely floral centrepiece gave off the faint scent of orchids.

"What's for dinner, darling?" asked Bill, as he unrolled his napkin and shook it vigorously.

"Wait and see," said Karen.

The door to the kitchen opened and a girl walked into the room, carrying two bottles of wine. I almost fainted when I saw her because I recognised her instantly. It was Louise Killane, one of the girls I had gone to school with. I squirmed in my chair. What on earth was she doing here?

"Louise is our chef this evening," said Karen.

I looked up in surprise. I had assumed that Karen would be doing all the cooking herself. I didn't realise that people actually got somebody in to do the cooking for them. And Louise Killane! I hadn't seen

Louise since we'd left school and I had no idea what she had planned to do. But obviously she'd studied cookery, even though as far as I remembered she hadn't done Domestic Science at school.

She took the wine to the sideboard, opened the bottles and poured a little into Bill's glass for him to taste.

"Perfect," he said, "go ahead."

She poured the wine delicately into the glasses. When she came to my place I saw the flicker of recognition in her eyes, but she said nothing, just filled my glass.

"She's a wonderful cook," said Karen, when Louise had left the room. "She does a lot of private functions and parties. I was at a charity dinner recently and Louise had done the cooking. Absolutely superb."

I was interested to taste Louise's cooking, although I was still feeling dodgy and the drink hadn't settled my stomach. I despaired of my recent habit of getting headaches and feeling ill whenever I went out. I couldn't understand it.

Louise came back into the room carrying bowls of soup. The bowls were a delicate white porcelain, decorated with a simple gold band. My heart sank as I saw the soup.

Leek and potato, Louise murmured as she put the bowl in front of me. Green soup, I thought, as I looked at it. I hated green soup. The only soup I liked was vegetable or tomato. I had a big psychological problem with green-coloured soup, especially when a blob of white cream sprinkled with chives floated on the top of it.

I took my spoon and swirled the cream through the liquid. Now that food was in front of me I felt queasier than ever.

I took a piece of bread from the basket that Karen had passed around and buttered it. Perhaps if I had a bit of bread I'd feel better.

I ate the bread and toyed with the soup. Louise would feel hurt if I didn't drink it. That was the worst of soup. With a main course you could play with the food and hide the bits you didn't like under something else, but a full soup bowl was a dead give-away. All the same, I drank about half of it and hoped that it would be enough.

Louise didn't say anything when she came back to collect the bowls, but I heard the quiet intake of breath when she saw mine. I felt terrible about it.

"So, Jane," said Graham. "How are things in International Trade?'

I looked up from the table and smiled at him. "Very well," I said. "We're very busy."

"That's good news," said Graham. "And your team is getting the work done?"

"Absolutely," I replied.

"I think you're great to keep working," drawled Fiona. "I couldn't."

"I like working," I said defensively, even if it was only half true.

"I do a lot of voluntary work," said Lorraine, "but I feel that I should leave paid work to people who really need it."

I felt as though I had been slapped.

"But, of course, we all have children," said Linda,

smiling at me. "When Jane has a family, she'll probably find it far too demanding to keep working."

I looked gratefully at her. "That's probably right," I said.

"How old is your eldest now, Bill?" Don stretched back in his chair.

"Would you believe Gary is nearly fourteen?" said Bill. "I can hardly believe that myself."

Karen certainly didn't look old enough to have a fourteen-year-old son. She looked in great condition. She must have worked out every day to keep a figure like hers. I resolved to join a gym myself as soon as possible.

The door opened again and Louise carried the dinner plates to the table. "Poached salmon," she said, placing the plate in front of me.

Oh, Louise, I thought despairingly, why couldn't you have cooked something else?

Normally I liked salmon, although it wasn't my favourite fish. But it sat there in the middle of the plate covered in golden butter and the smell of it made me want to be sick.

Why did I feel so bloody awful? Sweat prickled my back. Please, God, I begged, please don't let me be sick tonight. Rory would never forgive me. Louise spooned some tiny buttered potatoes and some creamed carrots on to the side of my plate.

"Thanks," I whispered. She smiled, very faintly, at me.

I couldn't keep my mind on the conversation. I listened to the words but I couldn't join in. I was concentrating on eating as little as possible but trying to arrange the food so that nobody would notice. I was hot, my head was pounding and I could feel my scalp sweating. I knew that my face was burning. I wiped my damp palms on the side of my dress. The buzz of chatter around the table was loud and it seemed to echo around the room. I sipped the glass of mineral water beside me. Maybe I've got the flu, I thought desperately.

"Of course, Singapore is such a fabulous place," Suki said, her voice coming from a great distance. "Have you ever been to the Far East, Jane?"

I shook my head, unable to trust myself to speak without throwing up. I'd never lost the horror I had about being sick, the terror of feeling my stomach heave and being able to do absolutely nothing about it. I could see it now, being sick on top of that beautiful table. Spraying the flower arrangement with vomit. I closed my eyes.

"Excuse me a moment," I said, and dashed upstairs to the bathroom.

I threw up into the toilet basin, gasping for breath as my undigested dinner came out the way it went in. I tried desperately to be sick as quietly as I could. My head felt as though it would explode, but I felt a bit better. I flushed the toilet and sat on the edge of the bath for a few minutes. After awhile I stood up and splashed some cool water on my face. I squeezed some toothpaste from the tube on the bathroom shelf and rubbed it on to my teeth with my finger. Then, with a shaking hand, I redid my lipstick. I checked my dress to make sure that I hadn't spotted it but it was OK.

I went back downstairs again and rejoined the dinner table.

"Are you all right?" asked Linda as I took my seat beside her.

"Of course." I kept my voice as firm as I could.

Rory looked at me quizzically. "What were you doing up there?" he muttered. "We were going to send up a search party."

"Nothing." I looked down at the plate in front of me.

Louise had replaced the salmon with dessert – a sumptuous, rich, chocolate gateau. My heart fell when I saw it. I'd been hoping that maybe Louise wouldn't have done a dessert, that she'd bring out a cheeseboard which I could have ignored.

Everyone else tucked in with gusto. I picked up my fork and cut a sliver. As a chocolate cake it was superb. As something to put into my sensitive stomach it was a disaster. I only ate half, and made a joking comment about having to diet.

"It's a bit late now," guffawed Rory, "since you can't fit into your clothes."

I looked at him in horror. How could he say something like that in front of other people? How could he make fun of me in this way? He was telling them the story of the purple satin dress. The girls laughed. I tried to pretend that I didn't care. I'd kill him when I got him home.

"But the dress you're wearing is beautiful," said Linda, when they had finished laughing.

"Rory is right, though." I tried to sound unconcerned. "I really must lose a few pounds."

"I know a few good diets," said Karen. "I'll copy them for you, Jane, help you lose that surplus."

"That's very decent of you, Karen," said Rory as he smiled at her. "I'm sure Jane would be delighted."

I wanted to kill him.

"Why do we worry about our weight so much?" asked Lorraine. "Men don't care at all. Look at my husband." She gazed fondly at Bernard, who was an advertisement for good eating. "He's a bit on the plump side but it doesn't seem to worry him in the slightest."

"Men look better with a bit of bulk," said Don Roche.

"I agree." Bill patted his ample stomach, the result of too much corporate entertainment and too little exercise.

I hoped that Rory would never end up like that. I felt sick again.

Louise came around with coffee and put a salver of mints on the table. She took away my half-eaten chocolate gateau without a word.

"Would anyone like a brandy or a port?" asked Bill.

I nodded. A brandy might settle my stomach.

"Are you sure?" asked Rory. "You don't usually like brandy."

"I thought I'd have one this evening," I said shortly. "You don't mind, do you?"

"Not at all." He looked at me curiously.

The golden liquid seared its way down my throat. I sipped it carefully as I felt it warm me.

Karen led us back into the lounge, where we sat

around the coffee table. I'd found it easier to sit up at the dining table. The sofa was very deep and soft and I felt uncomfortable.

They talked about the bank, gossiped about the staff, chatted about holidays, while I concentrated on not keeling over. I looked down at my engagement ring and watched the sparkling of the diamond come in and out of focus. I closed my eyes.

It happened quite suddenly and I couldn't prevent it. With an abrupt heave, I felt myself be sick again. I stood up, knocked Fiona's glass out of her hand and threw up all over the pale pink carpet. I stood there, like a character in a horror movie, spewing dinner in every direction.

The girls leaped out of the way, while the men looked on in shock.

"I hope it wasn't the salmon!" cried Karen.

I couldn't answer her, I was too busy being sick. I wanted to die with the shame of it.

Rory put his arms around my shoulder. "Are you all right?" he asked, his voice tight.

I couldn't answer him, I heaved again, splattering the sofa.

"I'm sorry," I gasped, as I finally stopped. "I'm truly sorry."

"Don't worry about it," said Karen, her voice insincere. "It'll be fine."

I had disgraced myself and my husband. No matter what concern Rory was showing now, he would be absolutely furious with me later and I could understand that. Of course, it wasn't my fault but that was hardly the point.

"Do you want to go upstairs?" asked Bill.

"A bit late for that," said Karen.

"Maybe we'd better just go." Rory was dangerously calm. "I'll take her home. I'm terribly sorry, Bill, Karen."

"Not your fault," said Bill, "can happen to the best of us."

Karen went into the kitchen and returned with kitchen towel and a bucket of water. She started to try and clean her carpet.

"Let me do that," said Rory.

"No – it's fine, I'll do it." Karen looked as though the McLoughlin family had already done enough.

The other men tried to ignore it. The girls clustered around me sympathetically.

"You will be all right," said Suki, in her lilting voice. "Are you feeling better now?"

"Yes," I said, although I still felt absolutely awful.

"Come on, then," said Rory grimly. "We'd better go."

"I'll get your coats." Bill left the room.

We were hustled out into the rain and I was grateful for the cold night air.

"Get in," said Rory as he opened the car door.

"I'm sorry," I said, miserably.

"Why didn't you say you weren't feeling well before we went out?" he demanded. "You could have stayed at home instead of embarrassing me like that."

He switched on the ignition and the car sped down the road. I leaned my head against the cool window.

"I didn't do it deliberately," I said. "I felt OK earlier."

"So why did you have to wait until we got to Bill and Karen's before making an exhibition of yourself?" he demanded. "Really and truly, Jane, you've probably destroyed my career."

"Don't be fucking stupid." I lifted my head to look at him and felt dizzy again. "It was an accident, that's all. Bill said it could happen to anyone."

"Bill was trying to be diplomatic," snapped Rory.

I wished it hadn't happened. I would never be able to meet those girls again without dying of shame. I understood how Rory felt.

He went on and on at me in the car. He moaned at the show I'd made of myself and of him. "And we were late getting there," he said as he opened our front door. "My God, Jane, if you wanted to ruin my life you went the right way about it."

I stood in the hallway and looked at him. "It wasn't my fault," I said again. "Can't you get that into your head? You're going on at me as though I deliberately decided to puke on somebody's carpet. Don't you realise that I am absolutely, completely and utterly mortified? You keep talking as though it's only you that's upset. Well, I'm fucking upset and I don't feel well. So piss off and leave me alone."

I stormed upstairs to our bedroom and fell on to the bed in a paroxysm of weeping.

Rory didn't follow me. I could hear him stalk around downstairs, slam the fridge door shut, turn on the TV. I was really sorry about what had happened but I wasn't going to let him blame me. As though I could have done anything about it. He could have been more sympathetic, I thought miserably. He could have cared more about the fact that I was sick than the impression we were making. Those bloody people were probably laughing at me. My back was coated in sweat again. I lay on the bed and wanted to die.

Eventually, I went downstairs again and took a couple of Hedex.

"They'll probably make you even more sick," said Rory.

"Nothing left to be sick with," I mumbled as I swallowed a capsule.

He put his arms around me. "I'm sorry," he said, "I didn't mean to get at you. It wasn't your fault."

I smiled lopsidedly at him. "Thanks."

He kissed me on the head, although it was a very half-hearted sort of kiss. "Come on," he said, "I'll put you to bed. Let's hope you feel better in the morning."

I slid beneath the duvet and allowed the coolness of the pillow to soothe my burning cheeks. I hoped I'd feel better in the morning, too. Right now, I was afraid I was going to die.

13

March 1986

(UK No. 11 – How Will I Know – *Whitney Houston)*

I stood in front of the mirror in the bedroom and looked at my naked body. I could see the difference. At least, I thought I could see the difference. I hoped that the almost imperceptible swell from my breasts to the bottom of my stomach was because of my pregnancy and not because I was fat anyway.

It had taken three more days before the penny dropped. Even though Rory and I had talked about starting a family and I'd stopped taking the pill about six months earlier, I simply hadn't realised that I was pregnant. Now that I finally was, I wondered whether it was such a good idea. I didn't know if I was ready. I was even less sure about Rory.

Rory was determined to make as much money as he could before he was thirty-five. He got into the dealing room by half past seven every day, checked the news reports and thought of clients to call and of new and more inventive deals he could show them.

He was more wrapped up in work than in his home life but I couldn't blame him. Dealing was very intense. I'd no doubt that he loved me but I often wondered if it came to a choice between me and a foreign exchange deal which he would choose. I tried to participate in his work life as much as I could. I entertained clients with him whenever he asked, which was rare. I wanted to be a supportive wife.

Rory was thrilled when I told him I was pregnant. I was surprised at how happy the news made him. He wanted to go out for a meal to celebrate. I reminded him what had happened the last time we went out together and he laughed at me. In some ways I think he was pleased that he could go to Bill Hamilton and say "Bill, the reason my wife puked all over your beautiful home was because she's pregnant." It was a lot better than thinking I might have done it because of the food.

Karen Hamilton rang me after Rory broke the news.

"I'm thrilled for you," she said. "Having a baby is a wonderful experience."

If it was all that wonderful, I'd thought, feeling sick at the time, why hadn't she had a few more? Afraid that she wouldn't regain her superb figure, probably.

"And when your baby is born, I hope you'll join one or two of my committees Jane. We do a lot of work, fund-raising, that sort of thing."

I gave her a non-committal answer. It wasn't that I disliked Karen but I didn't feel comfortable with her, and I really didn't want to become part of her set. I hoped that she'd told Louise Killane why I'd been ill. I didn't want her to think it was because of her cooking.

I rummaged through my wardrobe. I could still fit into some of my clothes, but most of them were beginning to get a bit tight around my waist and I knew that sooner or later I was going to have to buy maternity clothes.

No clothes shopping today, though, I'd things to do. Exciting things like collecting clothes from the dry cleaners and getting my shoes heeled. Then I would come home and cook Rory's lunch. Rory would be back from golf by about two and he'd be ravenous.

I took down my track suit bottoms and a sweatshirt from the wardrobe and put them on. Rory was always starving when he came home from golf. I hadn't regained my appetite yet. I wasn't sick any more but food held absolutely no interest for me. It seemed to me, too, that Rory was eating more. He kept suggesting that we go out to eat, to save me cooking, but I'd no interest in going out.

I was a bit worried that Rory would get pissed off with me. I knew that I wasn't much fun at the moment. I hoped that the lethargy would pass, but right now I was exhausted all the time. I think it was because we were so busy in work and I used up all my energy there. I wanted to get my revenge on Jake for going to the conference instead of me, although the opportunity hadn't presented itself yet. It was important for me, too, to stay efficient at work. I didn't want them saying that I was taking advantage of being pregnant. Actually, I was pretty useless at being pregnant. It wasn't much fun for Rory either, because he was such an outgoing person and he didn't like the fact that I wanted to be at home all the time, but he tried to be understanding. He succeeded mostly, but I stretched his patience sometimes.

I collected the laundry and my shoes and then made Rory's lunch. He wasn't home by two o'clock, which was irritating, because the spaghetti bolognese was nearly ready and I couldn't stand the smell of it. I sat curled up in the living-room and read *"You and Your Baby"*. The photographs were very off-putting.

Where the hell was he? The clock on the mantelpiece ticked solemnly. Three o'clock. I turned off the ring under the sauce and threw the pasta into the bin. He'd probably stopped for a couple of pints. Maybe he'd decided to have something to eat, as well. He could have bloody rung me to let me know.

The spring sunshine filtered through the curtains and across the polished pine floor, showing up a film of dust. My fault, of course.

I should do a bit of housework. Even if I was feeling a bit down, that was no reason to allow the house to go to rack and ruin.

Our house had been brand new when we'd bought it. It was about a mile outside Rathfarnham village in a small development around a tiny green. I'd enjoyed decorating it. I had great fun picking wallpapers and curtains, carpets and rugs. I felt very grown-up.

The phone rang and I jumped out of the chair. At

last, I thought. He would be ringing to say he was on his way. I grabbed the receiver.

"Jane?" The voice was breathless and crackling.

"Lucy? Is that you?"

"Who do you think it could be?" she asked.

"You haven't called in ages," I complained.

"I have been *très très* busy," she said. "Sorry, Jane."

The last time Lucy had rung me was New Year's Day.

"What's new?" I asked, cheered at the sound of her voice.

"I'm coming home," she told me.

"Really?"

"Really."

"That's great news, Lucy." I was really pleased. "I can't wait to see you. Have you got a job here or anything yet?"

"Yes," she replied happily. "I send off a few CVs back in January and, believe it, or not, one of the companies has made me a brilliant offer. It's a great opportunity to come home."

"What about Eric?" I asked.

Eric was Lucy's French boyfriend. She'd been living with him for the past two years.

"Eric and I have split up," she said abruptly.

"Oh, Lucy," I said. "I'm sorry."

"It's not so bad," she said. "I knew that it wasn't going to work, Jane. That's why I didn't marry him."

All the same, I could hear the disappointment in her voice.

"Any news yourself?" she asked.

I didn't think it was the time to tell her I was

pregnant. "Nothing that can't wait for a good old natter when you come home," I said brightly. "When are you coming?"

"Sunday week," she told me.

"Do you want me to pick you up?" I asked. "Or are your parents doing it?"

"Would you meet me?" She sounded pleased. "That would be great. I'm coming in at a quarter past three."

"I'd love to meet you," I said. "What's your flight number?"

She told me. "It'll be fun being back home," she said. "It's funny, but I only started missing it in the last few weeks and now I can't wait to get back."

"Where are you going to live?"

She groaned. "I'll have to move in with my folks for a couple of weeks," she said. "I don't have anything else. But I want to buy an apartment somewhere. I've got used to apartment living over here."

"It's not quite the same," I laughed. Lucy lived in a beautiful apartment in a town outside Paris. The building was old, the rooms were huge and the apartments reached by a rickety old iron lift which creaked its way up each storey. I'd visited Lucy's apartment twice and had absolutely loved it. I could see why she was entranced by living in France. The town of St Just was exactly like a fairytale town. Narrow cobbled streets, tall cream-coloured buildings and little corner shops. Then, about a kilometre from Lucy's apartment, a very modern train station with efficient trains which could hurtle you to the centre of Paris in about half an hour.

"I'll phone you again before I leave," said Lucy. "You can help me house-hunt when I come back."

"Love to," I said.

I replaced the receiver and hugged myself. I was delighted that Lucy was coming home. Since she'd gone, I didn't have a close girl friend anymore. I met the twins, of course, but it wasn't the same thing. Those girls were like one person. They didn't need a close friend. We had some laughs, but I never felt that I could confide in them the way I could in Lucy.

I head a meow outside the kitchen. A chocolate-coloured tabby sat on the back step and pawed at the glass of the patio.

"What do you want?" I asked as I opened the door.

The tabby stalked into the house, wrapped himself around my legs and left half his coat on my track suit. I leaned down and stroked him on the head.

I didn't know where the cat had come from, but he had turned up about a year ago, soaking wet and mewing pitifully. I'd taken him in and fed it, much to Rory's disgust.

"You'll never get rid of it," he told me sourly.

He was right. The cat adopted us. He turned up every day for a feed and spent hours lying on the windowsill outside the kitchen catching the rays of the sun.

I liked him, though. He was company. I liked the way he would roll around in the grass, the way he chased butterflies, the way he shinned up our side wall and looked, disdainfully, at the dog next door.

I'd christened him Junkie because he ate absolutely everything. Any food that we would have thrown out, Junkie eyed as a gourmet meal. Food that you'd never have considered giving to a cat – cheese, yoghurt, tomatoes and pasta – Junkie ate it all. None of this poached fish or chicken lark for him.

"Want some bolognese?" I spooned some of Rory's dinner into the cat dish.

Junkie purred appreciatively and set to work as he demolished the food and vibrated with happiness at the same time.

"Glad someone appreciates it." I wandered back into the living-room.

I lay down on the sofa and closed my eyes. A few minutes later, the purring furball that was the cat jumped on to the sofa beside me and settled down for a sleep too.

The lights flickered and gleamed over the still waters of the Caribbean. A warm south-westerly breeze fluttered through the palm trees. I sat on the pier and sipped my margarita.

He came up behind me and touched me on the shoulder. I jumped.

"Why are you alone?" he asked.

"I don't know."

"The most beautiful girl in the world and you are sitting in the dark drinking alone. That cannot be right."

"I'm not alone," I told him. "My husband is here."

"Really? And where might he be?"

I gestured vaguely towards the bar. "Getting a drink, probably."

"I see." His hands were dry, and gentle as they massaged my shoulders.

"Please don't do that," I said.

"Somebody should," he told me.

The sound of the car pulling into the driveway jerked me awake and I sat upright, causing the cat to leap from the sofa and meow with fury.

"Sorry, Junkie," I gasped. I rubbed my arm which he'd caught with his claws. I glanced at the clock. Gone six. I'd been asleep for ages and the light was fading. I heard the heavy thud of the car door closing and the sound of Rory's key in the front door.

I blinked a couple of times to clear the sleep from my eyes. I'd be casual when Rory came in, I thought, even though I was furious with him. What sort of time was this to come home, when he had left for his round of golf at eight-thirty this morning? He had left me on my own all day which was completely unfair.

He poked his head around the living-room door. "Hi," he said.

I knew at once from the sound of his voice that he'd been drinking. This made me even more annoyed.

"Where have you been?" I asked him.

"Where do you think?" He came into the room. "Playing golf."

"Until now?" I asked. "Bit of a long round."

"Don't be silly," he said. "We played our round. We had to wait for half an hour for the tee, then we got going. Very slow, though. A lot of people on the course. Then we went for something to eat afterwards."

"You might have told me you were going for something to eat," I said. "I made you spaghetti bolognese."

"Oh." He looked discomfited for a moment. "Doesn't matter, I can eat it now. I'm starving again." He sat on the edge of the sofa. "I'd a great round," he said. "I played a brilliant lay-up shot to the third and then a super little pitch to within, oh, I'd say, three inches of the hole for a birdie. The lads were raging. Then, at the fifth – "

"I don't really care," I interrupted him. "I'm sure you had a wonderful time. Although it seems to me you spent more time on the nineteenth than on the course."

"Oh, give it up, Jane," he snapped. "Of course we had a couple of pints afterwards. It's not a crime."

"Well, you shouldn't have driven home," I said. "It's not right."

"Christ Almighty, listen to her. You've become such a moan, it's not real. All you ever do is nag at me."

"I don't." I was hurt. "I'm merely saying that you shouldn't drink and drive."

"What you're saying is that you don't want me to drink at all," said Rory. "That's what you're saying."

"No, it's not. Not at all. I don't mind you having a drink but there's a time and a place. And it's not fair, you going off on the piss on a Saturday leaving me completely on my own all day."

"You probably slept through the whole day," said Rory. "That's all you ever do. Sleep."

Tears stung the back of my eyes. Of course I slept a lot. I was pregnant and I was tired. It was dreadfully unfair of Rory to claim that my tiredness was the reason he'd been out all day.

"You could have rung me," I protested. "You could have called and said that you wouldn't be back for lunch."

"If I'd done that you would have moaned at me more," said Rory. "Nobody else's wife gets into the rage that you do."

A tear slid down my cheek. "I don't get into a rage," I said forlornly.

"You never stop giving me grief," said Rory. "No matter what I do. You hate the fact that I'm in work so early, you hate the fact that I have to meet clients for lunch, you hate coming to dinner parties with me – "

"I don't hate dinner parties," I protested.

"Tell that to Karen Hamilton," said Rory.

There was an angry silence. "You know perfectly bloody well that I puked at Karen's party because I am pregnant with your child," I said. "You're being horrible, Rory."

This was always his ploy when he came home a bit pissed. Attack is the best form of defence, he'd told me once. Generate an argument about something else and you'll distract attention from whatever it is you're defensive about.

He stalked out of the room and I could hear him running the water for a shower. The state he was in he'd probably slip and drown, I thought bitterly, and I wouldn't care.

I sighed deeply. I knew that I was right. I went around the house closing the curtains and switching on the lights. Junkie curled up in front of the fire. I made myself some tea and toast.

I listened to the sound of the running water upstairs

and fumed silently. His life would have to change with the arrival of the baby. It was all very well to be out and about whenever he felt like it, but he couldn't continue on like that when our child was born. There would have to be more give and take. The trouble was, that wasn't the way he'd been brought up. His mother had been the sort of woman whose life had revolved completely around her home and family. She was a brilliant cook, made all her own clothes and had the house sparkling clean all the time. The two sons, Jim and Paul, were well looked after. They didn't have to do anything around the house and neither did Rory's father. His contribution was the weekly pay cheque. It was all very different from my own upbringing. Rory and I used to have terrible arguments because I'd try to get him to do a bit of ironing or hoovering. As far as he was concerned, it was nothing to do with him. The most I managed to get him to do was the occasional bit of cooking and to put his dirty washing in the laundry basket instead of on the floor.

I pulled the sofa closer to the fire. I could understand why he would be fed up with my tiredness, I was fed up with it myself. Rory returned to the living-room wearing his dressing-gown.

"Is there any food left?" he asked shortly.

"There's still some bolognese in the pot," I said, "but I'll have to make more pasta."

"Don't bother," he said. "I know how to make pasta. You sit there with your feet up."

I couldn't figure out whether he was being sarky or not. It was always hard to tell with Rory. I switched on the TV and watched Noel Edmonds.

Rory came in with a plate of spaghetti bolognese which he perched precariously on the arm of the sofa. "Sure you don't want some?" He waved a forkful of pasta in front of me.

I shook my head.

We sat in tense silence. Rory took the remote control and flicked through the channels, never staying on one for more than a minute. I didn't say anything when a blob of bolognese slid off his fork and landed on our cream-coloured sofa.

It was a horrible evening. We couldn't be nice to each other. I was too annoyed and Rory kept falling asleep because of the drink. His eyes were bloodshot when he was awake.

I made more tea at half past nine, and shook him by the shoulder to see if he wanted any.

"Leave me alone," he muttered.

I wanted to cry. Was this what it was all about? I asked. Was this it? Was this what I'd expected when the priest asked, "Do you, Jane, take Rory?"

My wedding day had been perfect. It was the stuff that dreams are made of. I'd truly believed that everything I wanted had come true.

We were married on the June bank holiday weekend. The sun blazed from a clear sky, not even a cotton puff of cloud marred its brilliant blue. I could feel the heat from the pavement through the thin-soled sandals I was wearing, and I was immensely glad that I'd decided against the huge taffeta ball gown that Mam had liked and had chosen the mid-length lace dress that Grace preferred.

She designed and made my dress, of course. Off-white, calf-length, lace over silk. A little sequinned bolero jacket over it, no veil but an arrangement of silk flowers in my hair.

I was ecstatic that day. Rory actually gasped when he saw me and I knew that, for once, I did look beautiful.

"The bride always looks beautiful," Mam said, with tears in her eyes, "but you are really lovely, Jane."

We hugged and kissed and I felt closer to her than ever before.

The reception was in the Burlington. I'd spent so much time there when we lived in the apartment, it seemed the natural choice. We had a ball, the food was great, the band fantastic and nobody had made a fool of themselves which had to be a first for any wedding I'd ever been at.

Then we went on honeymoon – a two-week idyll on Lanzarote which suited us perfectly. Since then, Rory wanted his holidays to be less sun and more action, but our honeymoon had been perfection. We stayed in a self-contained villa in a very upmarket complex near Playa del Carmen. We lay in the sun together, swam in the pool together, sat on the beach together, spent every moment together and not once been bored or tired or annoyed with each other.

So why was I so bloody miserable now, when it had been so wonderful in the past? Maybe we were just going through a phase. Perhaps my hormones were messed up because of the baby. Perhaps Rory was feeling the strain too. Maybe I was so caught up in myself that I was ignoring my husband. The books and magazines warned against that. Against allowing your husband to feel neglected and unwanted. Was that what I was doing to Rory?

Hard to ignore him now, though. He lay on the sofa, his head back, snoring loudly. I prodded him in the side.

"Why don't you go to bed?" I suggested.

"I don't want to go to bed," he said, eyes wide open. "I don't need to go to bed. I want to watch *Match of the Day.*"

I sighed. He was so dogmatic when he was drunk.

"Watch what you like, then," I said, "I'm going to bed."

I climbed under the duvet and pulled the pillow around my head. From the room below I could hear Jimmy Hill's voice commentating on the match. I wondered whether Rory was awake or asleep down there.

I nodded off and awoke with a start at two in the morning. The bed beside me was still empty and I sat up in confusion. Then I remembered and wondered whether Rory could possibly be awake downstairs, or whether he had fallen asleep watching TV. Or whether he had gone out. He was quite capable of going out again if he got into a black enough mood.

I pushed the duvet away and padded downstairs.

Rory was stretched across the sofa, still asleep. I turned off the TV and looked at him critically. Did I want him to wake up and come to bed now? His snoring would keep me awake. Better to leave him there. He'd only get narky if I woke him, anyway.

So I went back to bed and, for the first time in my married life, slept alone.

14

April 1986

(US No. 5 – West End Girls – *Pet Shop Boys)*

I stood in the Arrivals building at Dublin Airport and waited for flight EI 875 from Paris. I loved to stand in the terminal building and look at the destinations on the boards – Milan, Rome, New York, Boston, Madrid, Copenhagen – all seething with the excitement of a new place to go, new people to meet. When I drove into the car park and stepped out of the car, I was immediately infected with the desire to get up and go. Anywhere, just to leave my humdrum life behind and escape into the skies. Preferably to somewhere warm and sunny.

It was a miserable day today. The clouds were heavy and low, there was a persistent drizzle and a cool, easterly breeze.

I'd dressed up to go to the airport, much to Rory's amusement. But I didn't want to be put to shame by Lucy's French chic and I didn't want her to walk through the sliding doors and see a fat, frumpy matron waiting for her. I wasn't really fat or frumpy yet but I was very sensitive about my size. I'd begun to talk to my baby too, disconcerted when Rory caught me out, although he always laughed when he did.

Things had improved between us since the night when he'd slept on the sofa. I'd come down the next morning to find him making breakfast and looking sheepish. He'd apologised profusely, promised never to drink and drive again and looked so miserable that I kissed him and told him not to worry, that it was probably my fault as much as his.

Then we'd gone upstairs and made slow, languorous love. Since then, he had gone out of his way to be caring and understanding and I felt much, much better.

But I was still glad that Lucy was coming home because I'd missed her a lot.

The board flickered and "Landed" appeared against her flight. I stood at the barrier and scanned the crowds for her.

She looked great and I felt a pang of envy as I saw her. She was wearing a tight pair of 501s which must have been ironed on to her and a very French navy and white striped T-shirt. Her hair, which she had always worn straight before, fell down her back in a mass of thick, golden curls.

I was very glad that I was wearing a pair of black trousers and a long emerald green jacket which hid my slight bump. I waved vigorously at her and she hurried towards me, almost killing someone with her trolley.

She kissed me, French fashion, on each cheek, then held me by the shoulders and looked at me.

"You look *fantastique,*" she cried. "Absolutely great. You've got a glow about you."

I laughed at her enthusiasm. "You do too," I said. "And a lot more *fantastique* than me. I love your hair."

"Mmm," she said. "I love it myself. I got it done in a salon in Paris. Girl called Genevieve. Brilliant hairstylist. Makes me look like a bit of a blonde bombshell, doesn't it?"

"And how." I looked at her trolley. "Is this all your luggage?"

She nodded. "Not much, is it?" she said. "For four years away."

"Travelling light," I smiled.

She made a face. "I left stuff behind. I couldn't bring it with me." Tears glistened in her eyes and I hugged her.

"Don't worry about me," she said, sniffing. "You know and I know that Eric was not the man for me. I, my dear, am a businesswoman. I don't have boyfriends. Just partners. And escorts."

I smiled at her. "Maybe you'll meet someone here," I said.

"I truly don't care," said Lucy as she pushed the trolley towards the exit. "This new job will keep me very busy. You know, I'm not sure that I was cut out to be married."

I put the money in the automatic parking machine and took our exit ticket.

"Which is strange," continued Lucy, "given that we

spent so much time dreaming about it when we were younger."

"Dreams are always a lot better than reality." I helped her throw her cases into the boot of the car.

She looked at me curiously. "You don't mean that, do you, Jane?" she asked. "I thought you and Rory were very happy."

I smiled brightly at her. "Of course we are," I said. "I didn't mean for a minute that we weren't. I'm merely saying that you think and dream about something, and then it happens and it's not half as good as when you imagined it, that's all."

I started the car and we drove out of the airport and on to the motorway. I liked driving fast and the motorway was the only opportunity I ever got to indulge. Rory had warned me about speeding. He said that there were Garda cars stationed along the road with speed guns to trap unwary motorists, but I didn't care.

"Horrible weather, isn't it?" Lucy peered out of the window.

"What was it like in Paris?" I braked sharply as we reached Whitehall in about three minutes.

"Dry," she said. "But not particularly nice. It will be in a couple of weeks, though."

"Won't you miss it?" I asked.

"Probably," she said. "But you have to decide what you want to do. I didn't want to live in France for the rest of my life. I'm a Dub at heart."

She leaned back in the passenger seat and yawned. "Nice car."

I nodded. "Company car," I told her. "It's great.

We don't have to worry about petrol or maintenance or insurance, the bank looks after it all."

"Sounds wonderful," said Lucy.

"It is," I said.

"How's Rory's job going?"

"Very well," I said. "He's really busy. Remember I told you he got promoted before Christmas? It means he's out a lot, but he enjoys it."

"And how about you, you're still working?"

I nodded and accelerated through the amber lights at Bolton Street.

"Yes, and I'm doing OK. I don't think I'll every be as committed as Rory, though." I shot her a sideways glance. "And I'll be taking a bit of time off this year."

"Time off!" she exclaimed. "Why?"

"Don't be thick," I said. "Why do you think?"

She looked at me in amazement. "Are you pregnant?" she demanded.

"I'm surprised you didn't notice straight away." I laughed.

"Oh, Jane." Lucy hugged me and I almost swerved into a cyclist. He shook his fist angrily at me and we giggled.

"Shit," I said. "I could have killed him."

"No, you couldn't," said Lucy confidently. "Jane, I don't believe you're going to have a baby!"

"Why not?"

"It's such a grown-up thing to do."

I laughed. "I know. I can't believe it myself, really."

"So tell me all about it. When is it due?"

"Around September," I told her. "They're not a hundred percent sure, because my dates are a bit mixed up. But sometime around then."

"Brilliant," said Lucy. "So how have you been? Are you sick or anything?"

I related the tale of the disastrous dinner party at the Hamiltons'. Lucy roared with laughter.

"If you ask me, they could do with someone puking on their carpet," she said. "She sounds like a right bitch."

"Even so." I gestured at an Alfa that had cut in front of me. "I felt terrible about it."

"And poor old Louise Killane serving the food," said Lucy. "Bet she thought she'd poisoned you."

"I know," I grinned at her. "I was so embarrassed. But Karen let Louise know that it was because I was pregnant. Not something I'd want to happen again, though."

"Never mind," said Lucy. "People understand."

I drove on through the city. Lucy kept up a commentary on the changes since her last trip home. The traffic in Terenure was heavy, even though it was Sunday. "Lots of new houses being built around here," I told Lucy. I pointed out the twins' shop. The facade of *"Les Jumelles"* had recently been redecorated and it looked very exclusive. Lucy nodded approvingly at it.

We drove past St Attracta's school. A huge new extension had been built since we'd been there, taking over a chunk of what had once been the nuns garden where they'd grown herbs and neat little rows of flowers. The field past the sports ground had been sold, and a development of red-brick town houses now overlooked the school.

It had changed a lot since we were there, nearly ten years ago. Sometimes it seemed like a whole lifetime and other days I could close my eyes and remember it as though I'd only just left.

"Wonder who the head nun is now?" mused Lucy, as we turned past the school and on to the Riverbrook Estate.

"I don't know. Remember we said that we'd have a reunion five years after we left?" I said. "And we never bothered."

"I think there was a reunion last year," said Lucy, "not just our year, a school reunion. I'm sure Emily mentioned it."

I shrugged. "Going back isn't such a good idea," I said. "I don't really care what happened to most of them."

"Jenny Gibson got married." Lucy told me. "She's living in London."

"Is she?"

"Yes, in Greenwich. Somebody met her, can't remember who. Married an English guy."

"What about the other one of that gang? Camilla McKenzie." I pulled up outside Lucy's house.

"Don't know," said Lucy. "Haven't heard a thing about her. Funny, isn't it, those girls were the absolute bane of our lives and now we don't know a thing about them."

I hadn't seen Mrs McAllister in ages. Her hair was

greyer, but she still looked the same as ever. I smiled at her and she waved at me. Then she ran down the garden path and hugged Lucy fiercely.

"Lovely to see you, Jane," she said, over Lucy's shoulder. "Do you want to come in for a drop of tea?"

I shook my head. I'd better get back home. Rory hated being in the house on his own. I waved good-bye to Lucy, arranged to meet her for lunch on Tuesday and drove back to Rathfarnham.

My husband sat in an armchair, legs over the sides, watching rugby. He had a bowl of crisps beside him and a can of beer in his hand. He was completely relaxed.

I planted a kiss on his head.

"So Lucy is home." He offered me some crisps.

"I'm meeting her for lunch next week." I took a crisp, sniffed it and decided against it. "I'm glad she's back."

I met her for lunch in FXB's the following Tuesday. She had two weeks to herself before starting her new job, and she wanted to go apartment-hunting. Living at home was already driving her demented. Mrs McAllister gave her a lot of stick over my marriage and pregnancy. She thought that Lucy was missing out. I told Lucy to stay free and single as long as she could and my friend grinned and told me she'd do her best.

"Where do you want to live?" I asked her, as we sipped our coffees after lunch.

"I'm half thinking of something the other side of town," said Lucy. "Maybe Clontarf or Howth."

"Oh, don't do that," I protested, "that's miles away."

"I'd like the coast," Lucy mused, "but this side of town is so expensive."

"Why don't you want to be near Terenure?" I asked. "Don't you like it?"

"It's not that," Lucy confided, "but if I was within easy distance of home, then Mam would always be asking me to drop by and I couldn't take it. Easier if I'm a bit further away."

We decided to look at apartments the following Saturday. Lucy was armed with colour brochures and a vague idea of what she wanted.

"They're very small," said Lucy, doubtfully, as we wandered through the first block, a white painted scheme known as "Bayview". The apartments were a lot smaller than the one we had shared at Waterloo Mews. The one bedroom was barely big enough for a wardrobe, there was no chance of putting even a tiny table in the kitchen and the living-room was completely dominated by a round table. There was no spare space whatsoever and Lucy shook her head. "No way," she said.

We drove up and down the coast looking at apartments. Ones that had a view of the sea, today an angry green topped by frothy white waves, were much more expensive than those that didn't. Every floor had a different price. Most of them had maintenance agreements which were expensive. We despaired of finding anything within Lucy's budget.

"It's not as though I'm being a cheapskate," she complained, after yet another block failed to live up to the description in the brochure. "I only want something with a bit of space."

She had been spoiled by the St Just apartment, with its high-ceilinged rooms, shuttered windows and polished wooden floors. The little boxes we were being shown didn't match up to what she had left behind.

"What about this one in Sandymount?" I suggested.

"That's second-hand," said Lucy. "We'll have to make an appointment with the auctioneer."

"Maybe the people would let us have a quick look around," I said, hopefully. "We can always make an appointment for another viewing if you like it."

So more in hope than expectation we drove down the road, over the track at Merrion Gates and towards Sandymount. The apartment actually overlooked the sea, so we expected that it would be too expensive and we weren't very optimistic as we rang the bell.

The disembodied voice of a girl told us to come on up, it was the top floor. This amused us as the block was only two stories high.

A pretty young girl carrying a baby on one hip and holding a toddler by the hand opened the door to the apartment.

"It's chaos at the moment," she said. "Sorry, you won't get a very good impression."

Although the apartment was a mess and needed decoration, it was much bigger than the ones we had looked at and Lucy raised an eyebrow at me. The living area was a big square room, with a dining table in an alcove at the end. There was enough space for a small table in the kitchen, and there were two bedrooms, one double room and one with just enough space for a bed.

"We're moving back to Galway," said the girl, whose name was Anita. "We're both from there, we came here because my husband was working on a long-term contract and this was convenient. But I'm glad to be going back. This place is OK, but it's no place to bring up a couple of kids. The sooner we sell, the better."

Lucy and I agreed with her. Lucy talked about the price of the apartment, Anita said that she hadn't actually considered anything about it, the auctioneer was looking after everything.

We decided that Lucy would contact the auctioneer on Monday.

"What did you think?" she asked, as we got back into the car.

"I liked it," I told her. "It was a lot bigger than some of the ones we looked at. And she wants to be out soon."

It sounded ideal and it wasn't really that far away. Lucy couldn't wait for Monday to contact the agent.

"Why don't we do a bit of shopping before you go home?" she suggested. "Rory isn't expecting you too early, is he?"

I shook my head. "When I told him I wanted the car to go house-hunting with you, he arranged for his pal Niall to pick him up. They've gone golfing out in Royal Dublin. He won't be back for ages."

"Let's go back to Blackrock then, and have a mooch around," said Lucy.

Lucy was a fantastic shopper. She breezed into shops, picked clothes off the racks and carried them all to the changing cubicles. Whenever a sales assistant told her that she could only bring two articles in with her, Lucy fixed her with a withering glare and said that she anticipated buying much more than that if the clothes were up to standard.

Amazingly, most of the assistants gave in. Lucy told me that everybody brought loads of clothes into the changing-rooms in Paris.

"We're far too humble," she said. "You don't buy a skirt or a blouse there, you buy a look. They let you try on everything. And they don't look at you and pretend something suits you if it doesn't. They're brutally frank."

"If you want brutally frank, then you should call into Brenda and Grace," I told her. "Brenda once told me that I looked like a sack of potatoes in a dress I tried on."

"Always known for her tact," laughed Lucy. "We might be a bit late for the twins, though, it's five o'clock."

"They stay open until six," I said. "If you want to go there, we'll go."

So we hurried back to the car. We'd bought nothing in Blackrock, much to the disgust of the sales assistant who was left to hang half a dozen skirts back on the rails. I drove to Terenure. There was a small carpark behind the twins' shop – a luxury in the village. It wasn't a very big shop but the girls had made the most of the space. Clothes were arranged around the walls, hanging in what looked like tall, doorless wardrobes. It looked less like a shop and more like somebody's house.

"Bonjour," said Lucy.

Grace looked up and shrieked in delight. She dropped a bright yellow dress on to the floor. "Shit," she said.

"Is that any way to treat a friend?" asked Lucy as she held out her arms.

Grace hugged her. "I didn't know you were back," she said.

Brenda abandoned her customer and came over to hug Lucy too. "Visiting or home?" she asked.

"Home." Lucy pecked her on each cheek.

I looked around the shop. All the subtle signs of a prospering business were there. The quality of the decor, the designer clothes, an ambience of understated money. Of course, if they were selling clothes to Karen Hamilton's friends, then they must be doing very well.

Lucy told them about the apartment. "I hope I'll get it," she said. "It's me, somehow."

"How's the baby coming along?" Brenda asked me.

"Cooking away." I patted my bump.

"Isn't it amazing that you're the only one of the four of us to get married?" mused Grace. "You'd imagine that we'd have a better hit rate than that."

"I keep having disastrous affairs," laughed Lucy. "If I could find the right man, then maybe I'd be married too."

"And you two are always far too busy," I pointed out. "Besides, how could one of you get married and the other one not?"

"That's one of the things about being a twin," commented Brenda, ruefully. "We can't seem to let go of each other."

"Thank God you managed it anyway, Jane." Grace smiled. "How's the high-flying husband?"

"High-flying on the golf course at the moment," I said. "But otherwise doing well."

"Have you been to Jane's house yet?" Brenda asked Lucy. "It's gorgeous."

Lucy shook her head. "Not yet."

"You can come for tea during the week," I told her.

"Admire what a hardworking husband can provide," laughed Brenda.

"It's not just him," I said, irritated suddenly. "I work too, you know."

There was a moment's uncomfortable silence.

Brenda chewed the bottom of her lip and Grace slotted a few hangers into spaces on the rails. I looked at them.

"I do work," I said. "I know that my job isn't as exciting as Rory's, or as having a shop, or doing whatever it is Lucy has been doing in France, but I do have a job which paid me a bonus of five hundred pounds last year, so please don't scoff at me."

"We weren't scoffing," said Grace. "Honestly, Jane."

I wiped my forehead, ashamed at my outburst. "I know," I said. "I'm sorry."

"Don't worry about it." Grace patted me on the shoulder.

But I did worry about it, I couldn't help it. The twins were completely caught up in the shop, Lucy had a great job and had been offered an incredible salary in her new position and everyone seemed to think that Rory's job was so much more important than mine.

I lived in his shadow. He was a high-profile person and I was only his wife. It wasn't fair. I worked very hard.

When the baby was born they would look at me and say, there's Jane McLoughlin and her baby. I would be linked with the child forever. Nobody would see me as Jane, in my own right, ever again.

"You're very quiet," said Lucy, as I drove her back to her house.

"I'm fine," I said. "It's been a hectic day and I'm feeling a bit tired."

"I'm sorry." Lucy was contrite. "I didn't think. You're probably worn out, Jane. You should have said something."

"I don't really get that worn out," I said. "It comes on me suddenly."

Lucy sat silently beside me. What was she thinking? I wondered. That her friend was a misery and a bore? Mind you, she had always called me a bit of a bore. Yet there had been so many times when we were boring together. When we didn't get Valentine cards, when we panicked about the debs' ball, when we dreaded going to the disco. Those were the days, of course, when Lucy was a fragile china doll and looked shy and demure. Then we became more interesting, got boyfriends, rented our apartment. Lucy had her affair with a married man, then disappeared to France. She'd carried on doing interesting things while I subsided into a sea of domesticity with my husband and my house.

I knew that I was probably over-reacting, I knew that I was being very stupid, but I honestly couldn't help it. It would be OK when the baby was born, I decided. Once I cradled my son or my daughter in my arms, everything else would fall into place. In the meantime, all I had to do was get through the next few months without cracking up.

15

May 1986

(UK No. 15 – A Kind Of Magic – *Queen)*

I whistled under my breath as I waited in the reception area for Rory to descend from the lofty heights of the fifth floor. I'd finished work for the day but he was still trading. The dollar had gone nuts today so the dealers were very busy. I didn't mind sitting in peace, if not in comfort, down at reception. I wasn't comfortable because the leather seats were slung too low and, once I'd lowered myself into one, I found it almost impossible to get back out.

I leafed gently through *The Irish Times,* finished the Simplex and was having a go at the Crosaire when Rory finally emerged from the lift. I smiled at him. He looked distracted – his russet hair stood up in demented spikes on his head.

"Hi, sorry I'm late." He peered over my shoulder at the crossword. "Knave of Hearts," he said. "Nine down."

"I would have worked it out." I folded the paper. "Lift me out of this goddamned chair."

He grinned as he hauled me out of its green leather depths.

"Like taking a hippo out of a mudbath," he commented cheerfully.

"Thanks."

I felt fine these days and had a lot more energy but I wished that I would stop growing. I wasn't eating that much, but I still seemed to bloat a bit more every day. I was terrified that my baby would be so huge that I would never be able to deliver it.

I sat in the passenger seat and fiddled with my skirt. It seemed comfortable that morning when I'd put it on, but now it was irritatingly tight and I couldn't seem to get it to sit properly.

"Stop fidgeting." Rory pulled out of the carpark and into the evening traffic.

He switched on Radio 4 to listen to the news. I would have preferred music. My attention span had shortened dramatically over the past few weeks and I found the news no longer interested me at all. I closed my eyes and ignored the flood of talk as I allowed myself to be lulled by the movement of the car.

Rory swung into the driveway. I jerked into wakefulness and Junkie leapt hysterically on to the wall.

"One day you'll kill him." I got out and rubbed the cat's head. Junkie purred happily as his entire body vibrated with pleasure.

"Too right," said Rory, sourly. He always talked disparagingly about the cat, but I knew that deep down he liked him. Sometimes when I was upstairs, I could hear him talking to Junkie in the affectionate tone he usually only reserved for me.

"Sit down and relax," he said, as we got inside. "I'll make dinner tonight."

This offer was so unexpected that I knew immediately something was wrong. Rory never cooked unless forced into it.

"What have you done?" I asked.

He looked hurt. "Why should I have done anything?"

"Because you never cook otherwise." I sat on the sofa and slid my skirt over my bump, sighing with relief.

"Sit there and I'll bring you a cup of tea," said Rory.

There was definitely something up and I wanted to know what it was. I was useless at waiting for things, I needed to know straight away. But Rory busied himself in the kitchen, clattered cups and saucers and tripped up over the cat. I grinned to myself as I heard him swear. Junkie would have removed himself from Rory's range immediately. The cat always disappeared out of the target zone when Rory fell over him.

"So," he said, as he settled on the sofa beside me and handed me a mug of tea. "How was your day?"

"Fine."

"Tiring?"

"They're all a bit tiring now." I sipped my tea and waited for him to get to the point.

"You'd prefer to be on maternity leave already?" he asked.

"Not exactly." I wriggled my toes. "But a day off would be nice, I suppose."

"How about a week off?"

I regarded him curiously. "No point," I said. "I'd get bored sitting at home and Lucy can't take any time off work at the moment. She's up to her neck."

"And you think I wouldn't take time?" asked Rory, sounding wounded.

"You're busy too," I reminded him. "That bloody dollar."

He beamed at me.

"What?" I demanded. "Stop doing your Cheshire cat impression and tell me what on earth you're going on about."

"How would you like to go to Portugal for a week?"

I looked at him in stunned silence. "Portugal?" I said finally.

He nodded.

"You and me?"

He nodded again. "More or less."

I looked at him intently. "More – or less?" I asked.

"You and me, definitely," he said. "Think about it, whitewashed villa, your own pool, bougainvillaea falling over the walls, warm sun . . . "

"There is a catch to this, Rory McLoughlin," I said. "What is it?"

"My parents," he said, making a face.

"Oh, Rory." I knew I looked horrified. "Not your parents."

I'd never managed to get on with the McLoughlins, which was a pity. I didn't know why I wasn't the girl for their son, but for some reason I felt that they thought he could have done better. Peter McLoughlin was a decent enough man, but he always ignored me; Eleanor McLoughlin didn't really like me at all. I felt that she tolerated me but that she would have liked a more elegant daughter-in-law – and a more pliant one. I knew that she disapproved of the fact that we hadn't tried to have children before now and that she blamed me for that.

Still, if you weighed them up against the idea of a week in the sun, maybe it wasn't too bad a deal. The burgeoning spring had made me long for warmer weather. Portugal in May would be perfect.

Rory watched me anxiously. I knew that he was worried that I didn't get on with his parents. I could see that he was afraid that I wouldn't want to go on holiday with them.

"How come?" I asked finally.

"Week's golfing holiday," Rory told me. "Good deal for four. Dad found out about it and asked if we would like to go."

"Us?" I asked in amazement. "You and me."

Rory had the grace to look abashed. "He asked me originally," he admitted. "But the holiday was for four. Actually, he thought we could get another couple of men, but Mum wouldn't let him go without her. So he suggested you might like to come along."

I'd known all along that Mr McLoughlin wouldn't have thought of me.

"Mum wanted you to come, though," said Rory, hastily.

I smiled. "I'm sure she did."

"Honestly, Jane. She said she didn't want to be stuck on some rotten golfing holiday and that you could probably do with a bit of time off."

I was touched by his mother's concern. Maybe I'd misjudged her.

"So?" said Rory.

"Of course I want to go," I said. "Are you mad? Provided that there isn't a problem about me flying. Provided I can get the time off. When would we go?"

"Saturday week," he said.

I looked at him, my eyes full of excitement. "Really?"

"Really."

"Oh, Rory!" I hugged him. "I love you." I lifted my face so that he could kiss me.

I wasn't quite so keen on him when he woke me at six o'clock on the Saturday morning. I found it hard to sleep through the nights now and I'd fallen into a sound sleep at five. So it was hard to drag myself out of bed even with the promise of the holiday ahead of me.

It wasn't so bad once we were in the airport waiting for our flight to be called. Eleanor McLoughlin sat knitting, oblivious to the excitement around her. She was cool and aloof, completely self-contained.

I fell asleep on the flight, the first time I'd ever managed to sleep on a plane. I missed the breakfast. I opened my eye as they came around but couldn't wake up, so by the time we touched down at Faro I was refreshed and ready for action.

The sun was already high in the sky, washing the

Mediterranean town with brilliant light. The heat was welcome and enticing.

We'd hired a car. A minibus brought us from the airport to the car-hire office a mile down the road. Mr McLoughlin grumbled that the car should be available at the airport and that we shouldn't have to travel anywhere. Rory told him not to be daft. Mrs McLoughlin ignored both of them and took out her knitting again. I couldn't believe that she would come to Portugal and knit. She told me that it was a christening robe for my baby and I felt a chill of horror. I knew that Mam expected that I'd use the family christening robe, the one in which all of the McDermotts had been christened. A row for the future, I thought, glumly.

But I wasn't going to let any of this bother me while we were on holiday. I stood, quite happily, outside the car-hire office and waited for Rory to organise everything while I revelled in the warmth.

Rory emerged from the office with the keys to the Ford Escort, a selection of maps and the keys to the villa. He spread the map out over the bonnet of the car and sketched out the route to Albefuiera.

"It's quite straightforward," said Rory. "Along here, then here. It's easy enough."

"Wouldn't it be better to go this way?" suggested his father, pushing his horn-rimmed glasses up on his nose. A sheen of sweat had broken out on his forehead.

"No, look. This way, then this and this."

"But if we turned here, then – "

"Dad! I'm driving." Rory was irritated. "I'll choose which way we go." He refolded the map.

They loaded the golf clubs into the boot of the car, then couldn't fit in the cases and had to reload and start again. Mrs McLoughlin got into the car and sat there, like an empress.

"Don't forget to drive on the right side of the road," said Mr McLoughlin. Rory didn't deign to reply.

Rory was a good driver. It didn't bother him that he was driving on the opposite side of the road. He put the boot down once we reached the main highway and we sped off into the sunshine.

The sunroof was open and a cool breeze fanned our faces. Rory's mother knitted, the needles clicking in continuous rhythm. Mr McLoughlin kept up a monologue about the last time he had come here golfing, and how well he had done and how good the courses were. He had an irritating voice. I tried to block it out.

I leaned back in the seat and ignored Rory's parents, gazing instead out of the window at the passing scenery. We could have been anywhere because main roads are pretty much the same everywhere, but suddenly we would see a sign saying "Apartmentos" or "Jardimeria" and I knew that we were abroad. Our villa was about three kilometres past the town of Albefueira, so we drove past the supermarkets and shopping centres, bypassed the town and continued along the coast road.

The sea glittered invitingly, showering us with sparkles of sun. The sand, when we could see it, was pale and soft. I felt a thrill of anticipation run through me.

We drove past the turn for the villa, ended up

going another couple of miles too far and had to turn around again. Mr McLoughlin moaned that Rory hadn't read the map properly. Mrs McLoughlin's knitting needles stopped temporarily until the issue was resolved. We turned around and found the turn this time. Our villa was a few hundred metres up a steep hill.

"You won't be able to walk up this hill, Jane." Rory's mother eyed me speculatively.

"Of course I will," I said briskly, "once it's not too hot."

The villa was named "Beach Villa", which had made me imagine some awful seaside resort holiday house. Nothing could have been further from the truth. It was a two-storied whitewashed building with a red roof and a profusion of brightly coloured flowers growing in the very green garden which surrounded it. A couple of almond trees shaded the entrance and Rory used the cover of the trees to protect the car.

We piled out on to the sandy driveway. I exclaimed in delight at the balmy temperature of the air and wandered away immediately to look for the pool.

It was on the other side of the villa, bathed in clear sunlight, blue and beguiling. I could hardly wait to get in. Reluctantly, I went back to the car to unpack.

Rory and I took a bedroom upstairs at the front of the house. His parents took one downstairs near the back. I opened the cases.

Rory had already retrieved his shorts and gone for a swim. When I heard him dive into the water, I decided to abandon the packing and go for a swim myself.

I felt self-conscious in my black maternity swimsuit, but neither of Rory's parents was there to see me and I slipped happily into the water.

"This is divine," I gasped, bobbing around.

"Nice, huh?" Rory swam towards me and grabbed hold of me. "Better than being at home?"

"Much." I turned on to my back and allowed the water to support me. "This is bliss."

"We'll have to get a lounger to fit you," he teased, as he poked me on my bump.

"Sod off," I said lazily. "Although I won't be able to tan my back because I can't lie on my stomach. I'll go home brown at the front and white behind."

Rory chuckled. "As long as you go home relaxed," he said.

I was overcome with love and affection. I kissed him fiercely on the lips. I broke away when I realised his parents were standing at the edge of the pool watching us.

The days passed in a tranquil routine. Every morning Rory and his father would get up at seven-thirty, have breakfast and disappear off to whatever golf course they were playing that day. His mother (do call me Eleanor, dear) got up shortly after they left, had her own breakfast and went for a walk. I got up at about ten, brought my fruit and cake on to the verandah, put on the coffee machine and breakfasted overlooking the pool. That was my favourite part of the day, sitting in the warmth, shaded from the sun, totally at peace.

Wouldn't it be great, I thought, to live like this. To eat papaya and watermelon for breakfast, outdoors in the sun. To spend the day reading books, listening to tapes, occasionally exercising the mind with a crossword. I knew that I'd get bored eventually, but it was a very appealing idea.

The men usually arrived back by about two or three o'clock. Rory would instantly belly-flop into the pool, showering me with icy water, and laugh at my shrieks of horror. Eleanor would get in for a dip too, swimming daintily across the pool in a stylised breaststroke. I preferred to be in the pool by myself although Rory begged me not to get in unless somebody was around – just in case.

"In case what?" I asked him, one day. "If I get into difficulties, I can't see how your mother can help." The idea of Eleanor diving in to save me was ludicrous. Eleanor never dived into the pool, but descended elegantly down the ladder at the side, splashing herself all over with water first. Then she would launch herself across the water, head dipping and rising with each stroke. She always looked uncomfortable, as though she was hating every moment. Once she got out she'd immediately change into a dry bathing costume, rinse the other one out and hang it over the line to dry.

"Wonderful drying here, isn't it, dear," she said, on the third afternoon.

"Yes, it is." I glanced up from my book.

"Of course, if we only got this weather at home, we wouldn't need to come abroad, would we?"

I squinted at her. "No, I suppose not."

"Ireland is such a beautiful country. So green. Such magnificent scenery. Such wonderful places to see. These foreign places are all very well but it's not the same, is it?"

I agreed that, no, it wasn't the same. I wanted to say that if we got this sort of weather at home then we wouldn't have countryside that was so green but I hadn't got the will to argue with her. Besides, she obviously wanted to talk. We hadn't had any conversations up until now. Despite my tentative overtures, she'd stuck her head in magazines and romantic novels or immersed herself in knitting.

"So, Jane." She settled back into her sunlounger and placed a huge straw hat on her head. "When will you resign from your job?"

I looked at her in amazement. "Resign from the bank?" I asked. "I don't plan to."

"When you have the baby I presume you will resign," she said. Her tone implied that I'd no choice in the matter.

I rubbed some factor six on to my arms. "I don't think so Eleanor," I said neutrally. "I like working. Anyway, all women work these days."

She laughed, a short barking laugh. "Don't be silly, Jane, no woman likes working."

I wanted to be fair to her. I'd thought about it quite a bit lately. I was going to take an extra month's unpaid leave after my baby was born, but I'd definitely decided to go back to work afterwards. I liked walking in to the office in the mornings, knowing that there would be problems during the day that it was my responsibility to sort out, that there were schedules to be kept and deadlines to be met and that I could do all of this. I supposed that if we had more children I would feel differently about it, but at the moment Rory was so involved in work that I had to be as well, otherwise I would be crucifyingly lonely. All of my friends worked. I didn't want to be the odd one out. No one gave it up after just one child. Besides, it gave me financial independence. All my life I'd wanted to feel free, if I were to depend on Rory for every penny, I'd be trapped.

"I wouldn't mind giving it up, sometimes," I admitted, finally. "But I don't want to resign yet."

"It's hardly fair on either your husband or your child," said Eleanor, her eyes glinting.

"What's not fair?" I asked. It was none of Eleanor's business what we did.

"Rory has a very difficult job," she said. "He works hard, long hours. You don't seem to realise that. He needs comforting when he comes home, and you don't provide that, do you?"

I looked at her in amazement. "I don't know what you're talking about," I said. "I provide him with love and companionship and I look after our home. What more do you expect?'

"Do you have the dinner ready for him when he comes in?" she demanded. "I always have done for Peter."

"Well, maybe your husband comes in at the same time every night," I snapped. "Unlike your son, who doesn't come in the same time any night."

"Are you accusing him of something?" she asked, a red spot of anger on each cheek.

"Of course not." I tried to keep my temper in check. "I'm just saying that his job doesn't mean he comes home at the same time every evening, that's all. So there's no point in me preparing meals for him. Anyway, he either eats in the canteen or out with clients, so he's not hungry. If he's going out after work then it's up to him to get something to eat. If he's coming home with me, then I'll make something for him."

"And how do you propose to manage when our grandchild is born?" Eleanor asked me. "Farm him out to a baby-minder?"

She spat the word baby-minder as though it was a word of abuse.

I wiped traces of sweat from my brow. I wasn't sure whether it was the heat of the sun or the heat of my anger that had caused it.

"Our baby will be well looked after." I kept my voice as calm as I could. "I will look after him or her to the very best of my ability."

She smiled at me in a sort of pitying way. "It's your ability I worry about, dear," she said.

I resisted the temptation to throw my book at her.

"Why are you concerned about my ability?" I asked.

"It's your attitude. I know you slept with Rory before you married him. I don't think that's the behaviour of a responsible woman."

"What exactly do you mean by that?" I asked. I was shaking.

"I mean that a girl who sleeps around is not exactly ideally suited for motherhood."

"I didn't sleep around," I said, furiously. "I *did* sleep with Rory. He is your son. It was our choice."

"I found some of those things in his pocket, you see," she said. "When I took his suit to the cleaners. Disgusting things."

I wanted to laugh now. The look of horror on her face was hilarious.

"Eleanor," I said gently, "people do sleep with each other before getting married, now. You didn't like me doing it, but I did it with Rory. And I married him. We love each other."

She still didn't look very happy. "I expected it of him, somehow," she said. "But I don't think it's right for girls."

"Even if you don't," I tried to keep the exasperation out of my voice, "it doesn't make me an unfit mother."

"It's everything," she said. "The work thing. You know nothing about being a mother."

"Neither did you!" I exclaimed. "What experience does anyone have?"

"I had younger brothers and sisters," said Eleanor. "I knew how to care for children."

I sighed deeply. "So what?"

"You have no brothers and sisters," she said. "What do you know?"

"Don't be bloody silly," I said. "Not everyone has brothers and sisters, does that make them bad parents?"

"I'd be happy to give you my expertise," she said, as though I hadn't spoken. "I'll be able to stay with you if you like."

I hoped that the shock wasn't too clearly written all over my face.

"I'll manage myself," I said. "Thank you."

She sat back, looking self-satisfied. She had expected me to say this, I realised. She was a weird woman. She watched me, but I'd nothing more to say to her. I didn't want to talk to her. I wanted Rory to come home and rescue me.

Naturally they were late back. I spent the rest of the day feeling irritated both with her and with Rory. When he eventually did arrive back, I hustled him into the bedroom and started crying. I sobbed that his mother hated me, that she wanted (despite hating me) to live with us, that she thought I would be a hopeless mother, that I was a hopeless wife and that, probably, I was a tramp.

Rory comforted me, wiped away my tears and told me not to be silly. I sniffed and told him that his mother was a cow.

"She doesn't mean to be," he said. "She's anxious, that's all."

"I'm anxious too," I said. "But I don't go around slagging other people off."

"Come on, Jane." He put his arm around me. "Don't let her spoil our holiday."

But it had put a damper on it, and I didn't enjoy sitting at the opposite side of the pool from her as she clicked away at her knitting or read her magazines.

She couldn't destroy the glorious weather, though, and the sense of wellbeing that lying in the sun gave. She had a point about not working, I thought, ruefully. It would be easy to slip into an indolent lifestyle.

I walked down to the shop at the bottom of the hill one morning to buy some chocolate milk. I'd developed a craving for it, but we had run out and I couldn't wait until Peter and Rory returned to get it. So I slipped on a pair of espadrilles and took off.

It was very hot, and I half-regretted my impulse. But it was nice to walk along the narrow road, smelling the scent of the flowers and listening to the chirping of the cicadas. It was also nice to be free of the tyrant of the villa. The shop was cool and pleasant, a small corner shop, stocked with over-priced imported foods and very cheap fruit. I bought my chocolate milk, half a kilo of cherries and walked back to the villa.

Eleanor stood under the almond tree looking down the road.

"Where were you?" she demanded.

"I went for a walk." I headed towards the pool.

"A walk." She spat the words at me.

"Yes, you know, one foot in front of the other."

"You went down to that shop, didn't you?"

"Sure I did."

"Rory told you not to."

"Rory told me nothing of the sort. You told me I wouldn't be able to walk up the hill, and you were wrong."

"You're red in the face, you're breathless and it was far too hot to go anywhere," said Eleanor.

She was right about being red in the face and breathless. The last few yards had seemed like a mile and I was tired. But I wasn't going to admit it to her.

"You see," she said triumphantly. "You can't deny it!"

"I don't deny being a bit out of breath," I said. "You'd be out of breath if you'd walked to the shop and back."

"It was a stupid thing to do."

"Oh, give me a break!" I cried. "I stopped on the way down and on the way back. I took my time. I was fine. I'm pregnant, Eleanor, not a bloody invalid!"

"You could have killed my grandchild," she said. "It was a stupid, selfish thing to do."

"Oh, fuck off," I said, tired of listening to her.

Eleanor stared at me in horror. She opened and closed her mouth a couple of times, then turned around and stalked into the villa, slamming the door behind her.

I didn't care. I sat out in the sun and read my book. I drank the chocolate milk and ate a mountain of cherries. It was bliss.

When Rory came back I told him about the *contretemps,* hustling him over to the other side of the pool, out of earshot of the downstairs bedroom.

"She's only doing it because she's concerned," he said, placatingly.

"Concerned to stick her nose in," I retorted. "She's driving me around the bend."

"She had a point," said my husband.

"Oh, come on, Rory," I said. "You'd swear that I was suffering from some awful disease. People in Portugal get pregnant too, you know. They have to walk around in this heat."

"Well, yes, but they're used to it," he said. "You're not."

"I was fine," I said. "But if you feel like that about it, I won't walk down there any more."

"I would feel better about it," admitted Rory. "I'd hate anything to happen to our baby."

Rory always called it "our baby" now. I was amazed at how paternal he had become, reading the books, asking umpteen questions, wanting to find out about everything. I hadn't thought he would be so interested and said so.

"Why shouldn't I be interested?" he asked me.

"I don't see you as the paternal type," I said.

"Jane!" He was shocked. "Why not?"

"Your way of life," I said, suddenly speaking about things that had bothered me for a long time. "Early to work, often late home, golf, football, everything." My voice quavered. I felt tears prickling at the back of my eyes.

"So, you think I'll be a rotten father, do you?" he asked. "Just because I'm out and about a lot. You're as judgmental as my mother."

"I don't mean to be." I felt terrible.

"I'm just surprised you're taking such an interest in the, the finer details."

"I am interested," he said. "This is my first baby."

I turned to look at him. "I should hope so," I said.

He got up and dived into the pool. I sighed. I'd annoyed him and I hadn't meant to. I wasn't handling my husband very well these days.

The mood of the holiday changed. The sun still shone, the sea still sparkled but there was an undercurrent that hadn't been there before. I blamed Eleanor, of course. Stupid, meddling, interfering old bat. Each day I sat on the opposite side of the pool to her, engrossed in my book. Each day she sat in the shade of the verandah, eyeing me speculatively. She hated me. I knew she hated me.

Our final evening was a nightmare. Up until now, we had gone our separate ways at night. We drove to Albefueira together but ate in different restaurants. On the last night, Rory decided that we should all eat together. I could have killed him. Despite the arguments, he obviously didn't realise how deep was the antipathy between his mother and me.

So we went together to the Restaurant Stella Maris (chosen by Eleanor because she liked the name) and we talked uneasily about trivial things. I let the conversation bypass me as I picked at my chicken *piri piri* and gazed out over the sea. It was too dark to see anything other than the reflection of the town's lights, but I could hear the soothing rhythmical thud of the waves breaking on the shore and I allowed them to calm me.

" – when Jane gives up work." His mother's words reached through to me.

"What?" I said, looking up.

"I was talking about how much easier it will be when you give up work." Eleanor smiled at me. It wasn't a real smile, the corners of her lips barely lifted.

"We've talked about this before." I put my knife and fork down carefully on my plate. "I won't be giving up work. Not immediately."

"Of course you'll have maternity leave," said Rory.

"And then I'll be going back to my job," I said. If they could only hear me at the bank, I thought in amusement. Nobody there saw me as a career woman.

The sea breeze wafted towards us and lifted the corner of the paper tablecloth. I fiddled with the piece of plastic that kept it on the table.

"I don't see any reason for you to keep on at that job," said Peter. He took out a packet of cigarettes and lit one. I liked the smell of cigarette smoke in warm air, although I hated it at home. "Our Rory makes enough money for you, doesn't he?"

"It's not a question of that, Peter," I said calmly. "It's a question of earning my own money."

"Rubbish!" Eleanor was tight-lipped.

"It's not rubbish," I said. "I like to earn my own money."

"It's all this wanting everything." Peter inhaled deeply. "Why should you want to work when you don't need to work?"

I found it difficult to believe we were having this argument.

I wished Rory would say something, but he sat there slicing his peppered steak into bite-sized morsels, head down, ignoring his parents.

"Because I spent five years of my life being educated to work," I snapped. "And I'm not going to sit around and vegetate all day."

"It is not vegetating," said Eleanor, her eyes flinty. "I spend my time at home."

"I rest my case," I said, taking a sip of wine.

There was a brittle silence. I almost laughed from sheer terror. Peter and Eleanor looked furious.

"You're not going to sit by and listen to this, are you, Rory?" asked Eleanor. "You're not going to let her insult me."

My husband looked at me, his eyes pleading. "I think you were a bit out of order there, Jane," he said.

Great, I thought. He supports her, not me. I couldn't believe it.

"I think you're wrong, darling," I said, coolly. "Your mother has spent the entire holiday insinuating that I'm not good enough for you, not good enough for our baby and not good enough for my job. I'm more than good enough for all three. I don't intend to give up work. Maybe I'll change my mind, but I don't want you to decide it for me now."

"I don't think Mum meant to insult you," said Rory.

"Don't you?" I asked.

I sipped at my mineral water. My throat was dry and I was close to tears but I was proud of the way that I didn't allow them to fall.

"I think I'll go back to the villa." I pushed my chair back from the table. "I've had enough of this shit."

I stalked off into the dusk, hurrying through the throng of people crowding the narrow streets. The tears were falling now. They slid down my cheeks and dripped from my chin. I pushed past the brightly lit stalls selling handicrafts, roasted almonds and souvenirs.

"Jane! Wait!" Rory caught up with me and held me by the wrist. "Where do you think you're going?"

"Back to the villa. I said so."

"Oh, Jane, this is silly."

We stood face to face.

"Not to me, it isn't," I said.

"Mum didn't mean it the way it sounded," he said. "And you've overreacted."

"Bullshit! She meant every word. And I haven't overreacted. I've listened to her sniping at me at every available opportunity. Trying to tell me what to do. How to live my life. Do you know that she thinks I'm some sort of tramp for sleeping with you before we got married? She doesn't seem to think it's any problem for you, of course. She doesn't like me, she's never liked me and she's a stupid bitch."

"Jane, I won't have you saying things like that about my mother." Rory was angry.

"Why not?" I asked. "She says things like that about me all the time."

"She doesn't, Jane, she doesn't."

"Huh." I wasn't going to be placated. Rory usually did a good job of trying to placate me. I usually listened to him. But I'd had enough of his mother.

"I want to go back to the villa," I said.

"I can't leave them in the restaurant," said Rory. "They're expecting us back there."

"Well, you can go back if you like but I've no intention of sitting around with them."

"I'll drive you back to the villa," said Rory, tiredly. "Let me get the car keys. I left them on the table."

I waited in the town square while he went back, no doubt to explain away my behaviour as hormonal. I sat on a warm stone seat and listened to the sounds around me. Various languages were being spoken, the different bars pumped out music, birds chirped in the trees, fooled by the brightness into thinking it was daytime.

Rory returned with the keys. "Come on," he said, shortly.

I followed him to the car. We drove back to the villa in silence.

"I'm going back to town to bring my parents home," he told me, when I'd opened the door. "I'll see you later."

"Fine," I said.

I sat on the balcony of our bedroom overlooking the pool. It was almost silent, just night-time sounds. I didn't care about what I'd said to Eleanor. I was fed up with her. I was fed up with people telling me what to do. I was twenty-six years old, old enough to live my life without interference from anyone. I supposed that one day I might like to leave work, but that would be when I decided, not Eleanor McLoughlin. I leaned my head against the smooth, white wall. I wished Rory had been more supportive. It was frightening to think that he was, in some way, under his mother's influence. He should have told her to butt out.

I got up from my seat and went back into the bedroom. I sat in front of the dressing-table, scrupulously removed all my make-up and threw the cotton wool across the tiled floor in temper.

The bed wasn't very comfortable and I'd found it difficult to sleep in it. I couldn't sleep now. I lay there, staring at the ceiling.

It was at least an hour later before I heard the villa

door open and the murmur of voices downstairs. The kettle was filled, I could hear Eleanor asking if anyone wanted tea. They must have both said yes because it was ages before Rory came to bed. He tiptoed around the room, swearing softly when he stubbed his toe on the wicker chair in the corner.

I waited for him to put his arm around me as he usually did, but he rolled on to his side immediately and pulled the sheets up around his shoulders.

Be like that, I thought, furiously, anger coursing through me. Be like that.

I didn't sleep that night, I was too angry, too warm, too uncomfortable. As the early morning light filtered through the thin curtains I resolved never to set foot inside his parents' house again. And that my baby wouldn't be christened in Eleanor's christening robe.

16

June 1986

(UK No. 2 – Holding Back The Years – *Simply Red)*

Lucy moved into her apartment in the first week of June. I wanted to help her, but I couldn't lift anything. I'd stopped growing and I was immensely grateful for that, but I still felt huge and I hated not being able to tie the laces on my runners properly. She told me not to worry, that she had somebody to help her. I was glad. I'd felt that I was letting her down in some way.

"It's OK, Jane." She'd rung me at work for a chat and I was glad of the break. "David will help me."

I scanned through my memory to recall someone called David but drew a blank.

"Who's David?" I asked.

There was a silence for a moment and I wondered if I'd insulted Lucy by forgetting someone in her family.

"I met him while you were on holiday, Jane," she said enthusiastically. "He's really nice."

"Oh, Lucy!" I started to laugh. "I remember once

you told me that I fell in love too easily. Do you remember? When we went to Majorca? And look what's happened since then – I've got married and you've fallen in love more times than I can count."

"I said that because you are hopelessly romantic," Lucy told me, firmly. "I don't always fall in love. I might fall in lust occasionally but that's entirely different. I've never met anyone that I thought was the one for ever."

I felt a bit sorry for Lucy. She was doomed to search for perfection. But perfection never happened. I asked her to give me all the details about her new boyfriend, but she said that she'd tell me next week. Would I come over for dinner. She was asking the Quinlan twins as well.

"Do you want me on my own, or Rory and me?" I asked.

"It's a girls' night," she said. "Just the four of us. Like old times."

I was looking forward to it. Sometimes I thought that the best days of my life had been living in the apartment with the girls, doing whatever we liked, having fun, occasionally behaving badly. Now my life was boringly suburban; my greatest social occasion this week had been a trip to the supermarket and then my prenatal class. I hadn't even gone to Lisa O'Toole's departmental transfer booze-up on Friday, because by the end of the week I was shattered.

I was becoming more and more terrified about the baby. I was scared stiff about the birth, despite the kindness of the nurses at the hospital. I couldn't help remembering all those films of women screaming in agony, hair matted, wet from the sweat oozing from every pore. Even though the video they'd shown us portrayed the birth as a peaceful process, I knew that it would hurt. I was terrified of the pain.

Rory came to one of the classes with me, then said he'd seen all he wanted to see and refused to have anything more to do with it. I couldn't blame him. If it hadn't been for the fact that I had to go through it, I wouldn't have wanted to watch either.

Jessica told me not to worry, to ask for the epidural, everything would be fine. I didn't believe her.

I didn't let anyone know how frightened I was. I told myself that women had done this for generations and that I could do it too, but I wondered whether I was really ready for it. I couldn't talk to Mam about it, I was too embarrassed. I wouldn't have dreamt of speaking to Eleanor McLoughlin. She'd already earmarked me as a failure, anyway.

I still hated Eleanor. Since we'd come back from our holiday I hadn't spoken to her, although Rory had been home to see them a couple of times. He'd come back with the christening robe and handed it to me.

"You see, Jane, I told you she cared."

I took the fine knitted garment as though it was a time bomb. "I have a christening robe," I told him. "It's a McDermott family tradition."

I'd already made up my mind to use the McDermott robe. Mam would be very disappointed if I didn't. Eleanor had made me determined to use it anyway, and I didn't care if there was an almighty row. I was still annoyed at Rory for siding with his parents. I was sure I'd heard him murmuring phrases like "highly-strung" and "under pressure" to his mother on the plane as we flew home.

My relationship with Rory had altered subtly. I felt as though he had let me down. Sometimes, in the darkness of the night when his arm lay across me and his slow, steady breathing filled the air, I knew I was being stupid. When he rang my extension to say he'd be leaving late and would I be OK on the bus, I knew that I wasn't. I was a mess of turbulent emotions and I couldn't decide whether it was because of the pregnancy or because I was having a nervous breakdown.

It was a relief to go to Lucy's for dinner. The girls had known me all my life and I could let my hair down with them.

I arrived with a bottle of wine and – as a tribute to my domesticity – a cheesecake which I'd made. I also brought Lucy a house-warming gift, a watercolour of the Arc de Triomphe.

She hadn't done anything to the apartment yet, but it showed signs of her personality. The pine furniture was new – very like the stuff she'd had in Paris. I recognised some of the pictures on the walls.

"Come in," she said, "welcome to my new home."

I sat on the edge of an armchair and looked around.

"I haven't got all my furniture yet," said Lucy. "I know it's still a bit of a mess, but I feel great about it."

"It looks more you already." I handed her the wine and the cheesecake.

She peered under the tinfoil at the cake.

"Oh, lovely," she exclaimed, "Food!"

"It's the only thing I can make," I told her. "I fake being brilliant at home by doing this."

"Looks gorgeous." She sniffed appreciatively at it.

I gave her the watercolour and she tore off the gift wrapping.

"Oh, lovely." She smiled. "I'll put it on the wall straight away."

"You don't have to. Wait till you decide exactly where you want it."

"I want it covering that ugly spot over there." She nodded at the opposite wall. "I'm not sure what happened, but it seems to me like there was a bit of a domestic crisis and she threw something at him and missed. There were a few patches like that – they're hidden behind the ones I've hung up already!"

Lucy rummaged in a cardboard box and produced a hammer and a nail. "Watch how handy around the home I am." She banged the nail into the wall with great enthusiasm.

The picture looked well and it hid the stain.

"So," I said, settling back into the chair, "tell me about your new lover."

"He's not a lover yet," said Lucy wickedly. "But I want him to be. Actually, Jane, he's really nice."

"Nice?" I said.

Lucy shrugged in her Gallic way. "Nice," she repeated. "Comforting. Stable. Caring."

"Sounds perfect," I said wryly. "Is there anything about him that isn't – nice?"

"Sod off, Jane," said Lucy companionably. "He's different to my usual man, that's all."

The doorbell rang. The twins arrived, Lucy kissed them and they, too, proffered bottles of wine and a house-warming present. They had bought her a bagful of scatter cushions. I immediately claimed some to put behind my back.

"Is that chair uncomfortable for you?" asked Lucy, anxiously.

"No, it's fine now," I said. "Honestly, Lucy. I'm OK."

In fact, now that we were all together, I felt like the odd one out. Deep down I was envious of my friends. Lucy, as always, was like a sylph, in tight jeans, a peach-coloured silk blouse and hair cascading around her face. Brenda Quinlan wore a red linen dress which emphasised her hour-glass figure and Grace wore the same dress in jade. All three of my friends looked young, healthy and slim. I was wearing a light, elasticated skirt and a huge T-shirt. I felt like an elephant in a flower garden. At least I still had a dusting of my Algarve tan. It made me look less washed out and dowdy, but I was horribly aware that I hadn't managed to shave my legs in weeks and that little hairs were poking out of my support tights.

"So." Brenda tossed her black hair out of her eyes. "How do you like being back in Dublin, Lucy?"

"It's great," she said. "I'm glad I've got this place, the job's going well – I'm paid far too much for what I have to do – but who's complaining? and I like being home again."

"It's nice to have you back," said Grace. "Isn't it strange to be back together in an apartment again?"

It was. When the twins had come in and sat down

it was, for a brief moment, as though we were back in Waterloo Mews.

"We've come a long way since then." I glanced involuntarily at my bump.

"You certainly have," giggled Brenda.

"You've done more than me," I objected. "With the shop and everything."

"How is the shop?" asked Lucy. "I meant to call in again, but I've been up to my neck moving."

"Doing really well," said Grace. "We've been selling more and more of our own stuff, which is fantastic. We're wondering if, maybe, we should move into town."

"It's more difficult in town," I observed. "The rents are so high."

"That's the problem," agreed Brenda. "We haven't really decided yet."

"Are those your own designs?" asked Lucy, waving at the girls' dresses.

Grace nodded. "Thought we'd try them out today."

"They're lovely," I said warmly. "I wish I could find something nice to wear."

Grace looked sympathetically at me. "There are places that do elegant maternity things," she said and immediately made me feel that I was wearing the wrong sort of clothes.

"Have you ever done anything for a pregnant woman?" I asked her. She shook her head but eyed me speculatively. "Maybe I could try," she said. "What would you like?"

"Oh, just a nice sexy number," I laughed. "Something that would make me look like Jerry Hall."

Hysterical laughter greeted this statement and I stuck my tongue out at them.

"I might be able to do something," mused Grace. "I'll have a try. Why don't you come down to the shop next Saturday?"

"OK," I said.

Lucy went in to the kitchen. I sat back and listened to the twins chatting about the shop and clothes and designs. They were smart and businesslike.

Lucy carried two huge bowls of salad into the room.

"I catered for summer," she said as she plonked them down on the table. "I forgot it was June in Ireland!"

The day wasn't very summery – not exactly cold, just overcast and dull.

Lucy opened the big windows overlooking the sea. Her one disappointment about the apartment was that it didn't have much of a balcony, just a strip of concrete surrounded by a wooden railing, barely enough room for a chair.

"D'you remember the time the nuns invited our year to tea in the convent?" asked Grace, as Lucy poured coffee.

"Could I ever forget!" Lucy laughed.

It had been an exercise in checking our vocations. We were served tea and sandwiches while Sr Elizabeth talked about the "call from God".

I giggled at the memory. "I was terrified I'd actually got the call. For nights afterwards, I dreamed that God had called me and I'd have to go into the convent."

Grace shuddered. "Can you imagine? A little room and a huge crucifix hanging on the wall! That'd terrify anyone."

"None of our year did get the call, did they?" asked Lucy.

We looked at each other blankly.

"Don't think so," said Brenda. "Got lots of other things maybe, but not the call."

"I hated school." Lucy leaned back in her chair and yawned. "People bossing you around all the time and girls like Stephanie and Camilla to make you feel totally inadequate."

"Will you ever forget those discos?" Brenda laughed. "Weren't they absolutely awful? Standing around waiting to be asked to dance." She shook her head at the memory.

"You two were always OK, though," I said to the twins. "You always had each other."

"I'm not sure if that's good or bad," said Brenda. "We can never make up our minds about it, either. You know, I don't know if either of us will ever get married. We're so busy and we never get the time to go out."

"What about you, Lucy?" asked Grace as she speared an ear of baby corn and dropped it into her mouth. "Will you ever get married?"

I was surprised to see the faint stain of colour on Lucy's cheeks.

"I don't know," she said uncomfortably. "I keep thinking I might but I'm never convinced about it. Not like you, Jane."

They all looked at me, the married woman. It was

funny how people thought you changed when you got married. I still felt the same person as I'd been years ago, but the girls now seemed to think that I'd some special, secret knowledge about relationships that they lacked.

"Marriage isn't everything." I blushed, realising that I sounded completely disillusioned. "But it's OK."

"Only OK?" Lucy looked disturbed. "I thought you were very happy."

"Oh, I am!" I nodded my head vigorously. "I am happy. Don't get me wrong. It's just that you become part of a couple and people see you in that light. And there's a whole load of other shit like your in-laws and everything."

I recounted the experience with Eleanor McLoughlin. I hadn't told anyone about it before and it was a relief to tell an audience which was basically on my side.

"The old bitch!" exclaimed Grace, with feeling. "Who does she think she is?"

I shrugged. "I always knew she didn't like me but I never realised that it ran so deep."

"But that's terrible, Jane." Lucy sounded horrified. "Why didn't you get Rory to tell her to butt out?"

"He doesn't know how," I said. "I didn't think so at first but he seems to be a bit in awe of her."

"I wouldn't have put up with it," said Brenda. "Cow."

I smiled at them. They had already made me feel a million times better about it. It wasn't a crime to want to work for a bit longer, although Eleanor acted as though it was.

"But don't keep working if you're exhausted," said Grace. "Give yourself a break."

"I'll work until I feel I should stop." I grinned at her. "After all my talk, I'll probably be knackered straight away!"

Brenda asked me what it was like to be pregnant. I refused to tell them on the grounds that we were about to have dinner and I didn't want to make them sick.

Lucy had prepared *coq au vin* as her tribute to France. She was a great cook.

"Why did you leave?" asked Brenda. "I thought you loved France."

"I did." Lucy handed around some hot bread. "It's a great place to live and my job was wonderful, but when I split up with Eric I couldn't stay there any more."

"It seems a pity to have to change your life completely because of some man," remarked Grace.

Lucy shrugged. "I was probably ready to change, anyway. I know that Eric and I finally broke up because he was seeing someone else, but I'm not sure we had a long-term thing going anyway."

"Why not?" asked Brenda.

"I don't know," Lucy answered. "I loved lots of things about Eric but I'm not sure I really loved him. Just as well, really. I was disappointed about leaving my job because the salary was great and I had a terrific amount of responsibility, but I was lonely. Anyhow, I wanted to come home."

"I wonder do all relationships come to a natural end," said Grace thoughtfully. "You know, ten years and suddenly you've both changed too much. A different partner for different periods of your life."

"Have you felt like that, Jane?" asked Lucy light-heartedly. "Like you've had enough of Rory, that you've outgrown him?"

"Sometimes," I said. "But you get through that. Then sometimes I know that we'll be together forever."

"How lovely," said Brenda, and she meant it. "It must be great to be so confident."

I felt lucky. Lucky that I'd a wonderful husband, a nice home, and would soon have a beautiful child. They might all be happy in their own way, but it wasn't the same. Lucy didn't have anyone to come home to, to share her hopes and her dreams. The twins had each other, but it could never be the same as having someone you could hold in the middle of the night, who you knew loved you.

"So," said Lucy, clearing away the dinner things. "Here we are, nine years since we left school and still friends."

"A major achievement," said Brenda. "I haven't seen anyone else from school since we left."

"Jane met Louise Killane a few months ago," laughed Lucy.

"Did you?" asked Brenda. "How was she?"

I giggled uncontrollably while the twins looked at me in amazement. "Tell them," I choked, looking at Lucy.

She recounted the horror story for them, and they shook with helpless laughter.

"Poor Louise," I said, wiping the tears from my eyes. "I bet Karen gave her hell."

"Do you remember Anne Sutherland sending herself the Valentine card?" said Grace. "She hadn't even disguised her writing."

"I nearly did that once," I admitted. "I was so depressed when all the others had them."

"I've only ever got one card in my whole life," said Lucy. "That was the year we left school. I never found out who sent it."

"The first year we got married, Rory brought me to Paris for Valentine's Day," I said. "Remember, Lucy, we met you in Montparnasse."

She nodded. "He was incredibly romantic," she said.

"Last year he gave me one of those jokey ones," I said. "You know, about loving me even though I was old and wrinkly. How romance lives on."

"I suppose you can't keep being romantic all the time," offered Grace..

"From Paris to a jokey card in four years," I said. "Not bad, huh."

They didn't know whether I was serious or not. Neither did I, really.

"Anyway, Lucy." I got up and walked around to stretch my back. "Tell us about your new love."

The twins looked amazed. "Already!" gasped Brenda.

Lucy made a contorted face at me.

"Very mature," I said. "Very *avant-garde* businesswoman with her own flat."

"Come on, Lucy," said Grace. "Reveal all."

"His name is David Norris," said Lucy. "He's an architect. I met him when I was wandering through one of those tile showrooms. I was looking for something for the bathroom. It needs to be completely redone. Anyhow, I bumped into him beside the discontinued lines."

"Sounds very romantic," observed Grace.

"Lucy McAllister, you are the only person I know who could pick up a man in a tile shop," I said.

"I didn't pick him up," she said primly. "I actually dropped one of the tiles I was looking at and it shattered. Pieces of ceramic all over the place. Very embarrassing. A salesman came racing over and David said it was his fault."

"Wow," breathed Brenda. "Chivalrous."

"He's quite well-known in the shop because he recommends it, so it was no problem," said Lucy. "I asked him for a coffee."

"How do you have the nerve to do things like that?" I asked.

"Easy," she said. "The worst that could have happened was that he would say 'no'. Anyway, we went for coffee and got talking. He asked me out. I said OK. That was all there was to it."

"So where have you been?" I asked.

"The movies, once or twice," she said. "Dinner. Things like that."

"How come you've turned into this *femme fatale* when you were such a drip at school?" I complained. "We were hopeless at getting dates, then. How have you managed to change so much?"

Lucy considered the question. "I think it's because I don't care as much," she said, seriously. "When we were at school I was always afraid of what other people thought. Now I don't give a toss."

"Fair enough," said Brenda.

"So, is this a serious relationship?" asked Grace.

Lucy blushed. "Maybe."

"Lucy!" I looked at her in amazement. "You're having a serious relationship with a nice man."

"Nice?" asked Brenda.

"She called him nice when I arrived," I said.

Lucy grinned. "I know, I know. I've always had relationships with totally unsuitable men which ended up going down the toilet. Cian O'Connor – a disaster. On, off, on, off, hopeless. Nick Clarke." She flicked a look at me. "Jane was right about Nick. Didn't care about me at all, just used me. Then Robert Maher. On the rebound, doomed to failure. Then Eric the frog."

"Lucy!"

"Well, he was a toad," she amended, amid laughter.

It was good to be with the girls again, I thought, listening to the conversation. This was the sort of thing I'd missed in the years of Lucy's absence.

"We should meet regularly," I said suddenly. "Once a month or something."

Lucy nodded. "It's a good idea."

"Will you be able to get out when you've had the baby?" asked Grace.

"Of course," I said. "Rory will be a model father. He told me so."

"Why don't we try and make a regular date?" said Lucy. "Like the first Friday of the month."

"That's your Catholic upbringing," laughed Grace. "First Friday, indeed."

But we decided that it would be a good idea and made a date to meet again. In my house, this time, I suggested. After all, I would be like an even bigger elephant by then, and I mightn't even be able to drive.

I was more nervous behind the wheel these days. Rory had offered to drive me to Lucy's but I wanted to go myself. He was relieved when I returned home and I was touched by the concern in his face.

"You were longer than I thought," he said, as I handed him the car keys.

"Girl talk," I told him as I went upstairs to bed.

17

July 1986

(UK No. 1 – Papa Don't Preach – *Madonna)*

"Have you thought about moving house, lately?" Rory looked up from the *Sunday Times* and pushed his Ray-Bans to the top of his head.

We were sitting in the back garden, soaking up a glorious Sunday afternoon in July. I'd woken up at six that morning to the sound of the birds shouting at each other from the branches and lumbered out of bed to look through the window. Already, the sun spilled over the rooftops opposite and slid across the garden. I stayed out of bed and had an early breakfast as I waited for the sun to come around the house and on to the back garden.

Junkie loved sunny weather. He stretched out in the grass, stomach facing skywards, sleeping peacefully. Occasionally the buzzing of a passing bee would wake him and he'd jump into life, stalk the bee in a frenzied bout of chase and stop around the garden before collapsing in an exhausted heap beneath the cherry blossom tree.

"Where do you want to move to?" I put the magazine supplement to one side.

"Somewhere bigger," said Rory. "In a better area."

"What's wrong with this area?" I asked. "It seems OK to me."

"It's very young," said Rory. "I'd like to live somewhere older and more settled."

"We're young," I told him. "And when this baby grows up he or she is going to want somewhere to play – with kids around the same age. This place is ideal."

Rory sighed. "I'm not suggesting we move into a geriatric ward. I'm merely saying a better area would be a good idea."

I nudged Junkie with my toe. "He won't like it."

"Jane, you're talking about a cat," said Rory. "He'll go where the food is."

Rory had a point. The way to Junkie's heart had always been through his stomach.

"Do you really want to move somewhere else?"

Rory leaned back in his chair. "As senior forex manager, I think I should be living somewhere consistent with my status," he said pompously.

I looked at him in surprise. "Have you been promoted again?" I asked. "Why didn't you tell me before now?"

"It's not official," he admitted. "Bill told me Friday. It has to be ratified."

"Oh, Rory." If I'd been able to leap from my chair I would have. "That's brilliant news."

"I thought you'd be pleased."

"I'm pleased for you," I told him. "I'm thrilled for you."

"Anyway, this means more money and I thought you might prefer to live in something better than a three-bed semi."

Our three-bed semi was a very nice house and I'd felt comfortable there from the moment we moved in. But if there was a chance to move up, then I supposed we should take it.

"Where had you got in mind?" I asked.

"Don't care," said Rory. "Foxrock, maybe."

I made a face. "I don't know Foxrock at all. Couldn't we go somewhere I know?" I liked Rathfarnham. I liked the village and the countryside. It was close enough to my parents without being uncomfortably close.

"Where do you know?" asked Rory.

"Here." I shrugged at him. "Wherever."

"I'd like to be nearer the coast again," he said. "I'm not mad on the mountains. How about Dún Laoghaire or Blackrock?"

"I really don't mind, Rory," I said. "But it depends on what sort of house you're thinking about. Anyway, we can't move until the baby is born."

"I know that," he said. "Give me some credit."

I went into the house, poured some more orange juice for myself and brought out a can of lager for Rory. I hadn't really thought about moving house before, although I'd muttered once or twice that we wouldn't have half enough space when the baby was born.

That was the thing about Rory. I'd make a casual remark and then, one day, before I knew where I was, he'd acted on it. It would be great to have a bigger house, though where I'd find the time or the energy to clean it I couldn't imagine. My energy levels had fallen quite dramatically in the last week, coinciding with another leap forward in the size of my bump. My gynaecologist, Mr Murphy, said that I was cooking up a wonderful baby. I was happy that he was pleased with my progress, but I wished my wonderful baby wouldn't grow so much. Or that it was a bit less active. The baby had started kicking and moving so much now that I felt seasick. I couldn't wait to have my body back again. I was fed up sharing it.

"Rory thinks we should move house," I told Mam the following weekend when I called around for a visit. I was feeling a bit guilty because I hadn't dropped around to her in ages, and the last two times she had called around to see me I'd been out.

"Not right now, surely?" she said as she filled the kettle. "You need your rest, Jane. You look very washed-out."

Why did my mother always have to make me feel under the weather? I was feeling OK. I didn't think I looked washed-out. In fact, I'd brushed Egyptian Wonder over my face simply so that she wouldn't be able to say that I looked washed-out or peaky.

"We weren't thinking of moving straight away," I told her. "But he's been promoted again and he thinks this would be a good time to move."

"He works hard, doesn't he?" said Mam.

"He enjoys it," I replied.

We went into the back garden with our tea. The

weather had stayed warm, although not very sunny. The garden was beautiful. Mam and Dad had grown into gardening in the last few years They lavished loads of care and attention on the flowers and shrubs that had once grown higgledy piggledy around it. Now the various colours complemented each other and the shrubs were neatly trimmed. I liked sitting there. Strange, I thought, I always did feel more relaxed at home now. When I came in the door, I reverted to being my mother's daughter instead of a woman in my own right and, although this usually drove me crazy, I enjoyed it now. Besides, Mam always made me tea, gave me apple tart or fussed over me. If it had been a regular occurrence it would have been tedious, but at the moment it was brilliant.

"I was thinking of buying a car," I said to Mam.

"Really?" She leaned towards me. "What sort?"

"I don't know yet," I said. "I thought I'd ask Dad if they've anything in."

The garage was doing well. Dad was working more, not less, now but they'd been able to hire additional staff and he and Mam had gone on holidays last year for the first time in ages.

"Something small," I said. "I don't need anything too flashy."

I asked him when he arrived home and he scratched his head thoughtfully. There were a couple, he told me, Metros and Fiestas, if I was interested. Why didn't I drop down during the week?

I agreed. "You can bring me home afterwards," I told him.

The following Thursday, Rory left me at the

garage. He was going on to Woodbrook for a game of golf with Bill Hamilton. "Don't get anything silly," he warned me.

"Like what?"

"Like Lucy McAllister."

I laughed. Lucy had bought a little yellow MG which she drove around the city like a lunatic. I supposed the years in France had changed her method of driving. I'd always thought that I drove quickly, and I did, but I drove safely too. Lucy was an erratic driver. She stopped to do her make-up in traffic, ate croissants at the wheel and read the newspapers when in a jam. But she got away with it because other drivers appreciated a blonde in a sports car. They would have blasted me out of it with the horn.

I strolled into the garage, past reception and into the workshop. Dad was looking underneath the bonnet of a Corolla, shaking his head. That meant nothing, Dad shook his head no matter what was wrong with a car. It was something they obviously learned in mechanics' school.

"Terminal, is it?" I teased, kissing him.

"Nothing that I can't fix," he said. "Do you want to see some cars out the back? Be careful you don't trip over anything."

I'd loved coming to the garage when I was small because it was nearly impossible to walk through it without getting covered in oil and grease. Mam had never been able to say anything because, of course, Dad would come home covered in oil and grease too. It was the only time I ever had a legitimate excuse for getting filthy.

The garage was cleaner now and more carefully laid out. I was able to walk into the large yard at the back of the building without once tripping over a hubcap or brushing against an oil drum.

"There's a Micra over there, quite nice," said Dad. "Low mileage, lady owner. And we've two Fiestas. And a Metro."

I looked at them all. Any one of them would have done, they were all ideal second-car material. It would have been nice to say that I wanted a Porsche or an Aston Martin or anything fast and steamy. It was terrible to think that I would have to be so sensible as to buy a neat little one-lady-owner car.

The road was long, and dusty, the red sands sweeping across it. I shifted the car into fifth gear and kept the needle at eighty. It was vital that I made good time. They needed the material and they needed it now. It was no good to say that I'd been delayed. Excuses would not be tolerated. I glanced in the rear-view mirror. The Lotus was catching up, gaining on me. I stamped down firmly on the accelerator and was rewarded by a surge of power from the Mercedes. My car was bigger, more powerful. I could keep ahead of the Lotus. I sensed, rather than heard, the sound of the gunshot. I ducked involuntarily. They were getting closer. Whoever it was, he could drive. I tried to drive still faster, glancing down at the speedometer and watching the needle push further and further along the dial. The road curved suddenly and I hauled the wheel around with a screech of protesting tyres. The Lotus was still behind me. There were fifty miles to go. I would have to deal with the Lotus and deal with it now. I decelerated and allowed it to draw level. I could see him now, dark, sloe-eyed, determined chin. He looked across at me and I half smiled at him. Then I hauled at the steering wheel again and took him broadsides, sending the Lotus careering off the road and down the steep incline to the valley below. I was an excellent field operative. I always had been.

"So what do you think?" asked Dad.

I opened the door of a Fiesta. "I like it," I said. "It looks like the sort of car I need. Not, maybe, the sort of car I'd like."

He laughed in understanding. "I know," he said. "But you've got to compromise."

"Unfortunately." I smiled at him. "Do you want to discuss the sordid aspect of money?"

"You definitely want this one?"

I nodded.

"Sure?"

I nodded again.

"Then it's my present to you."

I stared at him. "I can't accept this," I said. "It's far too much."

"I want to give it to you," said Dad.

I remembered once being pissed off with him because Lucy's father had given her a car and he, the garage owner, hadn't given me one.

"I can afford to buy it, Dad," I said.

"But I'd like to give it to you." His face shone with pleasure. "I know that when you were younger, we really didn't have the money to send you on all the trips you would have liked and we couldn't buy you all the things you wanted, but I can give you this car now. And I'd like to do it. Think of it as a present for the baby."

"Oh, Dad." I hugged him. "Thank you."

"It's my pleasure," he told me. "I love you, Janey. I want you to be happy."

I released him. "I am happy," I said.

"Are you sure?"

"What on earth makes you ask that? Of course I'm happy. Why shouldn't I be? I have a great home, a great husband, I'll soon have a great baby and I now possess a great car. And, of course, I have wonderful parents. What more could a girl ask for?"

Dad puffed a bit. I was surprised at him. We rarely exchanged anything but trivialities, never any innermost feelings, certainly we never got emotional with each other.

"Your mam is a bit worried, that's all," he said gruffly. "We're concerned that you're running yourself around too much."

"Mam is always concerned about me," I told him. "The last time I was at the house she said I looked peaky. I couldn't possibly have looked peaky, I was wearing make-up."

He laughed. "It's just that Rory works so much and he always seems to be out." he said.

I bristled, although I tried not to show it.

"It's because he works so hard that I can afford to buy the car, if I want to. And we can afford this baby and we can probably buy a new house as well," I said. "I can't begrudge him a couple of evenings out playing golf."

"We were afraid you might be lonely."

"Don't be silly, Dad."

I kissed him on the cheek to show him that I hadn't taken offence, but I was shaking inside. Why did my parents think that my life with Rory wasn't as it should be? We'd had difficult times but, overall, it was going well. Why should they think otherwise? I'd never complained to them.

I collected the car at the weekend, drove it home and parked it with a flourish behind the BMW in the driveway. Rory came out to have a look at my acquisition. He peered under the bonnet as though he knew what he was looking for, revved the engine a couple of times and told me that it seemed to be OK. I pointed out to him that my dad did own a garage and that he should know a thing or two about cars. Rory nodded wisely and continued to look it over. I let him, it was easier than arguing with him.

Lucy and David called around at the weekend. I'd rung her earlier in the week to check if they were definitely coming and she'd said of course, they couldn't wait. I couldn't wait to see the man whom she'd seen every day for the past six weeks. This was so totally unlike Lucy that I was intrigued.

"They're here," called Rory, hearing the MG pull up.

I struggled into my baggy trousers and loose-fitting top and hurried downstairs to greet them.

David Norris was a short, slightly overweight man

with fair curly hair and round glasses. I was surprised. Every other man Lucy had gone out with had been very handsome. He was wearing sand-coloured trousers and a slate-grey shirt. He looked very ordinary. I couldn't see what it was that had captivated Lucy.

She looked incredible tonight. Her hair was caught up in a velvet bow and was gathered to one side of her head. She wore a pink and blue dress, short skirt, tight under her buttocks. Her eyes sparkled and her skin glowed. I had never seen her look like this before.

"Come in." I kissed her on the cheek. "Lovely to see you."

"This is David." She introduced him by dragging him by the hand and presenting him to me like a child showing off her best friend.

"Pleased to meet you." I held out my hand. His grip was firm and decisive.

"Come through." I led the way towards the back of the house. "Do you want to sit in the garden for a while?"

We sat outside in the small patio behind the house. It got the best of the afternoon and evening sun and was warm and sheltered. David looked at it approvingly.

"I feel you're weighing up the house," I laughed. "Can I get you a drink or anything?"

"Beer, if you have it," he said.

I brought out cans of beer. Rory and David started to talk about golf.

"You're making a big mistake, dating a golfer." I

laughed at Lucy. "Have you noticed the way they spend hours talking about one single shot? How they drove off superbly, played a wonderful iron shot from the fairway, chipped neatly on to the green and sank a six-foot putt?"

"Jane! I didn't realise you were listening!" Rory laughed. "Another drink, David?"

"I'll get them." I got up and went back to the kitchen.

Lucy followed me. "What d'you think?" she hissed when we were out of earshot.

"He's not like I expected," I admitted.

"What did you expect?"

I wasn't sure what I had expected. Someone more suave, perhaps, more determined. David Norris seemed terribly laid-back. He listened to Rory, allowing him to expound his ideas on golf without ever interrupting him. He didn't impose himself on the company, rather became part of it. I liked him. Living with Rory was like living with a bomb about to go off. I was used to someone who was convinced he was always right, that his opinions were the only possible ones to hold, that life was for living to the utmost all the time. All dealers were like that. They had to be super-confident in their own abilities at work and it rubbed off at home too. It came as something of a shock to realise other men were more relaxed than Rory.

"He's very nice," I told Lucy.

"He's not the best-looking man in the world," she said, waiting for me to contradict her.

I was happy to. Not handsome, I told her, but attractive nonetheless.

"Come on, Jane, we're friends," said Lucy. "He's not good-looking at all. But he's such a decent person. I haven't known a decent bloke in ages."

She sounded so distraught, I hugged her.

"I think he's lovely," I told her. "And he's awfully polite. He's sitting there listening to Rory going on and on and he hasn't clocked him one yet."

"He's not into violence," grinned Lucy. "He's very peace-loving."

"I hope he's not a vegetarian," I told her. "You'd never be able to live with him."

She smiled at me. "No, he's not," she said. "Although he's very concerned about the things that we eat. Not too much red meat, lots of vegetables, things like that."

"How will you cope?" I asked playfully. "Anyhow I'll get good marks, I'm doing Dover sole for dinner."

"How are you eating, yourself?" asked Lucy.

"Fine." I poured some milk into a glass. "I can't eat a lot in one go because I get dreadful heartburn, but I'm not sick or anything. I suppose you can't really be too sick at this stage, you wouldn't be able to lean over the toilet."

"Jane, you're disgusting," said my friend. "Give me some more beer and I'll bring it outside."

We spent a very pleasant hour in the garden until dinner was ready and I told everyone to come back into the house. I'd set the table with care. I'd bought a floral centrepiece, remembering how pretty Karen Hamilton's had looked.

They complimented me and I flushed with pleasure. It was nice to be a foursome, I thought. I was glad that Lucy had found somebody that she cared about.

They were perfect for each other. They were on the same wavelength. They even finished each other's sentences. It was though they had known each other for years.

"Where do you live, David?" I asked, during a lull in the conversation.

"I'm renting a place in Donnybrook at the moment," he said. "I bought a house there and I'm renovating it in my spare time. So I need to be somewhere nearby."

"Do you actually do the work, then?" I asked, in surprise. "I thought that architects only did the drawings."

"Oh, I don't plaster or lay bricks or anything like that," said David. "But I can do a certain amount. I enjoy it."

"What do you actually design?" asked Rory.

"I'm with a company that does corporate work," David told us, "office blocks, that sort of thing."

"Sounds really interesting," I said. "What are you working on now?"

"An office park development out in Sandyford at the moment. You should come and see it."

We said that we would. I was interested in the idea of designing something and seeing it being built. It must, I thought, be very satisfying to see your drawing actually take shape on the ground. Much more satisfying than checking letters of credit, or worrying about the staff holiday rota.

The dinner was a success. Despite Rory's usual attempts to hog the conversation and David's natural reticence, there were no awkward silences or moments when I wondered why on earth I bothered. We played Trivial Pursuit afterwards. Rory and I narrowly beat David and Lucy.

They left about midnight. Lucy hugged me, told me to look after myself and then whispered again "Do you like him?" I gave her the thumbs-up as they got into her car and she roared away down the road.

I wished that Rory would look at me the way David looked at Lucy although, in my current condition, it was asking a bit much. But he'd never looked at me like that, as though I was the only one in the world that mattered. He had a very pragmatic approach to life, see something, want something, get something. He regarded me as his partner and he did care about me, but he didn't show it and I wished he could.

I shook myself, trying to banish the thoughts. Was I envious of Lucy? It didn't make sense. She was in the first flush of another infatuation and I knew that the infatuation stage didn't last very long. I was the one to be envied, I told myself. I was the one who, one day soon, would have it all.

18

August/September 1986

(UK No. 11 – Every Beat Of My Heart – *Rod Stewart)*

I sat in front of my dressing-table mirror and outlined my lips with Rouge Absolut lip colour by drawing a neat line around the contours of my mouth. I blew myself a kiss, then filled in my lips with deep red gloss. I loved red lipstick, it was daring and looked well with my colouring. I leaned my head forward and shook my hair so that it fell in a cloud of copper around my face. Over the last few years the colour had lightened, it was more red-gold than pure carrot now and I liked it. For the first time in my life, my natural riot of curls was fashionable and I luxuriated in the feeling of not having to spend hours in a hair salon to make it look right.

I took the cream knitted suit out of the wardrobe. I'd spent a fortune on it, far more than I should have. It was, after all, a maternity dress. I felt good in it. Not (obviously) thin, but just a little bit sexy. It was so long since I'd felt desirable that it was worth paying the money for that feeling alone.

It was a pity that Rory couldn't be here to see me like this. He'd put up with me dossing around the house in track suits and sweatshirts for months. A pity he couldn't see me looking feminine and alluring now.

He'd gone to New York, a sudden crisis, nobody else could go. I was incandescent with rage.

"Surely there must be somebody!" I yelled at him. "You're not indispensable. What would they do if you dropped dead?"

"That's a completely different scenario, Jane, and you know it," he snapped. "I have to go. It's my job."

I cried and sniffled until my face had gone blotchy and I'd given myself an attack of hiccoughs.

"Here." Rory gave me a glass of water. "Drink this."

I drank the water and set the glass down on the coffee table.

"It's a terrible time for you to be away," I said. "The worst."

"Jane, the baby isn't due until the end of September. You'll probably be late anyway and I'm only going to be away for four days – at the absolute most. If I could get out of it, I would, believe me, but I can't."

"It's not the baby!" I retorted. "You'll be in plenty of time for the baby. It's Lucy's wedding!"

Rory grimaced. "I'm very sorry about Lucy's wedding," he admitted. "I truly would like to go, I know she's your best friend. But I can't, Jane. I just can't."

I sat in the corner of the room and sulked for

almost a day. How could Rory be away for Lucy's wedding? How could he leave me alone on such a day?

Lucy had rung me three weeks after our dinner date. "Guess what?" she said.

"What?" I was fed up with Lucy because she hadn't phoned sooner.

"You'll never guess," she said, a thrill of excitement in her voice.

"If I'll never guess, you'd better tell me." I was annoyed at myself for sounding so ratty. I resolved never to get pregnant again. It didn't suit me at all. I was getting more and more cranky with every passing day.

"David and I are going to get married."

"Lucy!" I dropped the potted plant I'd been holding. "You're joking."

"Why should I be joking?" she demanded.

There was no reason why she should be joking. I was simply stunned at the news. I couldn't believe that she was finally getting married. And to David. Whom she had known only for a few months!

"When?" I asked, wondering whether I would have regained my figure for the big day. Probably if I did all of those exercises, religiously, I could manage.

Lucy cleared her throat. "The end of August," she said. "It was the soonest we could get."

"Lucy!"

"What's the point in delaying it?" she demanded. "We both know we're doing the right thing, we both want it, and there's no need for us to wait. Anyway, I don't want to wait. This is it, Jane! This is the one, I know it."

"I'm delighted, Lucy." I sounded half-hearted and I knew it. What was the matter with me? I should be delighted for my best friend. I should be pleased for her.

"You sound pissed off," she complained. "I thought you'd be pleased for me, Jane."

"Lucy," I said firmly. "I am truly, completely, absolutely thrilled for you. You've just given me a shock and, in my condition, I have to be careful of shocks!" I laughed to prove I was joking.

"That's all right, then." She sounded relieved. "I thought you might give me grief. I've already had that from Mam."

"Doesn't she approve?" I asked curiously. I would have thought that Mrs McAllister would be only too pleased to get Lucy finally married. She had moaned at her daughter about it often enough.

"It's not that she doesn't approve of the marriage, she doesn't approve of the speed," explained Lucy.

"She'll get over it," I said confidently. "But didn't you have to give loads of notice to get married?"

"He asked me the first week we met," she said. "And I said yes and we went to the priest straight away."

"Why didn't you tell me?" I asked.

"Because I was afraid that we were moving too quickly," she answered. "I didn't want to tell anyone until we were going out for more than seven days."

A week! She had agreed to marry him after only a week. How could she have been sure? I hoped she wasn't making a terrible mistake but I kept my thoughts to myself.

"Joan and Emily will be my bridesmaids," she said. "I'd love to ask you, Jane, but they'd be disappointed if I didn't have them."

I expected Lucy's sisters to be bridesmaids and I said so. Besides, I would have looked like a battleship staggering down the aisle behind her.

"Where are you going to get your dress?" I asked.

"I was hoping the twins might make it," she said, "I haven't asked them yet and I know it's not what they usually do, but maybe they wouldn't mind. I'm going to drop down to Les Jumelles today and check them out. I didn't want to go without telling you."

"Thanks," I said.

"Jane, isn't it wonderful to be completely in love?" Lucy was on a cloud of happiness. "Isn't it the most perfect thing?"

I wondered if she thought it would be perfect when her husband expected her to clean the ring around the bath after he had used it. I chided myself for being so cynical. Honestly, I told myself crossly, you can't see the good side of anything.

I was miserable when Rory said he'd be away for the wedding. I drove him to the airport the night before and I didn't bother to go in to the terminal building with him. It was totally unlike me. I knew that he was annoyed and I drove home feeling fragile and unsure of myself. I tried to convince myself that I was over-reacting and that everything would be all right when the baby was born.

But for some reason I sat in front of the TV that night and cried my eyes out, even though *Cheers* was hilarious.

I felt better the next morning. I'd had an amazingly good night's sleep, probably because I could roll all over the bed. I woke up feeling refreshed and looking forward to the wedding.

The twins were driving me to the wedding. I was ready by two, pleased with how I looked and glad that the day was almost warm, though hazy. I looked through photographs of my own wedding day while I waited for them to arrive. I'd changed a lot since then, I thought. I'd looked so young, so innocent.

Innocent my foot, I remembered. There I was in snowy virginal white and I had been having the most erotic sex with Rory. Maybe that was what was wrong with me now, our sex life had dwindled impossibly in the last three months. I'd lost interest in it, and I was terrified that Rory had lost interest in me, because he never pestered me about it.

Oh well, only a few weeks to go. Please God, I prayed, let me be on time. The idea of going a couple of weeks overdue was too awful to contemplate.

The Polo van emblazoned with "Les Jumelles" pulled up outside the house and the twins emerged wearing their latest outfits, the power shoulders, nipped waists and vibrant colours of Versace.

"We've only taken one or two of his lines," explained Grace. "But we thought these would be ideal."

"You look great," I told them, "I thought you'd be wearing something of your own."

"If we'd had time," Grace said. "But we didn't have anything spectacular lined up and Lucy wanted us to do the wedding dress and bridesmaids' dresses. She didn't give us an awful lot of notice, you know."

I hadn't seen Lucy's dress yet. I hadn't wanted to see it in advance.

"I'll bet she looks lovely," I said.

"Lucy is the one person I know that grew up to be more beautiful than she was at school," commented Brenda. "She was pretty then, but too cute. She always looked five years younger than she actually was. But now she's really lovely."

I half-hoped she'd say something complimentary about me, but she didn't. Fortunately Grace told me that my dress looked great.

"Thanks," I said. "I got it in BTs. It cost a fortune."

"Worth every penny," said Grace. "Clothes are so important."

I knew exactly what she meant. The right clothes were like a key to unlock your inner self. Wearing the right thing made you feel confident, wearing the wrong outfit left you unsure. I was confident as we arrived at the church to wait for Lucy.

St David's church was built on land that had once belonged to the religious brothers who had built the boy's school. It had been one of the early modern churches, built a few years after Riverbrook Estate, to cater for the ever-increasing population. It was low and round, rather like a squat cake. I hadn't been in the church since the Christmas after my wedding. It was still the same. It smelled of beeswax and candles and the lingering traces of incense.

Lucy had arranged little floral bouquets at the end of every pew, peach and white posies of carnations. The altar was decked out in peach and white too – it was Lucy's favourite colour combination.

I remembered walking up this aisle myself. The trouble with weddings, any wedding, is that it reminds you of every other one you've ever been to and it reminds you of your own. I wished fiercely that Rory was with me now and that I could slip my hand into his while the two of us remembered, together.

The congregation murmured. The sun shone through the stained-glass windows, scattering coloured light over us. A purple shaft fell on the end of my dress, illuminating it. The organist played softly, background hymns, until suddenly there was a flurry at the back of the church and Lucy began her walk.

I turned to look at her as she approached. She held her father's arm, staring straight ahead, dignified and aloof. Her golden hair was twisted high on to her head, and fell in soft tendrils around her face, which was hidden by the short veil. A diamond band in her hair glittered with a thousand different colours. The dress that the twins had designed was raw silk, slightly off-white, tight at the bodice and flared into a tulip shape in the skirt. She was stunning. Tears of happiness for her welled up in my eyes. Why do I always cry at weddings? I asked myself, surreptitiously fumbling in my sleeve for a tissue. Grace handed me one as a tear rolled down her cheek too.

The wedding Mass started. Grace, Brenda and I were to say the Prayers of the Faithful. I hoped I could say my prayer without stumbling. I felt very difficult about being in the Church since I didn't go to Mass any more. But I was happy to stand up and pray that Lucy and David would have a long and happy life together.

Lucy winked at me as I stepped down from the altar and I had to stifle a giggle. It was like being at school again, when the nuns sat in the congregation and watched us as we prayed. We'd pass the time by whispering jokes to each other. We tried to get somebody caught laughing by Sister Elizabeth, which meant a tongue-lashing in the head nun's office afterwards.

Mrs McAllister and Mrs Norris brought up the offertory gifts. I looked at David's mother with interest. A short, plump woman with a round face. David looked rather like her and I wondered if he would end up a fat little barrel of a man. Don't be horrible, I told myself. He looked great now – black tie suited him.

Then the ceremony was over. The organist swept into the wedding march and Lucy and David strode down the aisle together, smiling broadly. I cried again, of course, but then nearly all of the women were sniffling. We couldn't help it, it was in our nature.

"We cry because we know what she'll have to put up with," said Valerie, David's sister, who was married with three children. I liked Valerie, who was a cheerful no-nonsense sort of person.

"You're very cynical," I told her, and she said rubbish, she was being practical.

"Doesn't Lucy look absolutely heavenly?" said

Mam. "I must go and talk to Mrs McAllister. I do like her hat."

I thought it was terrible myself – a pink and white fondant creation – but parents have different views on appropriate wedding dress.

The reception was in a marquee in the Norris family home, which was in Stillorgan. The wedding was being held at such short notice that Lucy and David hadn't been able to book a hotel they liked. So Lucy had ordered me to ring Karen Hamilton and get Louise Killane's number. Lucy phoned her to see if she could organise the catering. Louise was delighted, her company, "Celebration Cuisine", specialised in weddings, she told Lucy. And she'd be delighted to offer a special discount to an old friend.

The photographer tried to organise us for a group photo. I siezed the opportunity to talk to Lucy, went over to her and hugged her. "You look fantastic."

"Thanks, Jane. Isn't it great?" She beamed at me. She was having a wonderful time.

"I'll talk to you later," I said and melted back into the crowd.

It took about half an hour before we left the church grounds. The priests of St David's never let confetti be used outside the church, so we'd brought rose petals and flung them over the happy couple. Stray petals lay on the tarmac, splashes of pink and yellow against severe black.

Although the Norris family home was relatively small, its corner site meant that the garden was about three times the size of its neighbours. I'd wondered how a marquee could possibly fit into a suburban garden, but there was plenty of room. The red-and-white striped tent took up most of the lawn. A red-and-white striped canopy linked the tent to the house. The only big problem was the mad queue for the loo when we all arrived. Women clustered around the bathroom door in various degrees of need, but thankfully they let me go first.

Only thirty people had been invited for the meal, and they were close family and a very few friends. The twins and I were Lucy's only guests. David had invited a couple of fellow architects but that was all.

Two long trestle tables were set up for the guests, at right angles to the main table. Louise had done great work. The tablecloths were shining white, decorated with fresh flowers and thin swirls of silver and gold ribbon. The cake stood on the top table, not a traditional wedding cake, which Lucy didn't like, but a huge chocolate *Sachertorte* gleaming with rich chocolate icing.

Classical music wafted from the CD player discreetly positioned in the corner of the tent.

Louise excelled herself with the food. Little smoked salmon parcels to start with, arranged temptingly on a bed of iceberg lettuce and topped with a sprinkling of dill; carrot soup (thank God she'd given green soup a miss) served with the most delicious white crusty bread, still warm so that the butter melted into it; lemon chicken for the main course, delicately flavoured with a hint of tarragon, and finally, for dessert, a pyramid of profiteroles and cream.

It was the best wedding meal I'd ever tasted and

the most food I'd eaten at one go in months. Thank God, I thought, that the knitted suit was a dress and jacket and that I didn't have to cope with the waistband of a skirt.

I watched Lucy during the meal. Her face shone with happiness and she looked completely at ease. I hoped that she would be very happy with David. He looked very happy sitting beside her. He smiled and joked, but always turned back to her, checking on her, completely devoted to her. Did Rory ever look at me like that, I wondered? Somehow, I didn't think he ever had the time to look like that any more, eyes soft and caring. Rory was in too much of a hurry.

I asked him, sometimes, of course. "Do you love me?" I'd say, gazing at him, and he would reply, with a hint of exasperation, "Don't be stupid."

Then I would ask again and he'd tell me that of course he loved me and could we get back to watching TV or we'd miss the best part of the movie?

The passion would come back, I promised myself. After the baby.

"Finished?"

I looked up at Louise and nodded. She took the empty plate away from me.

"Wasn't that a fantastic feed?" said Grace. "I didn't realise that Louise was so talented."

"Neither did I. I didn't exactly do her food justice the last time I ate it," I said. "And to set up the company herself. I never thought she had it in her."

"Goes to show," laughed Grace. "St Attracta's girls. Lots of get up and go."

Grace was right about St Attracta's girls. The twins

were becoming more and more successful and Lucy had led a very varied working life. Her present job was earned her a staggering salary which shocked me when she told me. Louise's catering company was obviously thriving. And me – well, I had a good job too, I supposed, and a successful husband. But, as I looked at the others, I wished I'd done a bit more with my life. That I hadn't rushed into marrying Rory. Not because I didn't love him, but because being married to him was such hard work.

I got up from my seat and made my way to the bathroom. I locked myself inside and sat on the edge of the bath. I was worried about myself and the way I always seemed to criticise my own life. In my childhood, Mam would have slapped me across the back of the legs and told me to go out and play if I got into a mood like this. Mam didn't have time for introspection.

I redid my make-up and went back to the marquee. They had begun the speeches, Mr McAllister welcomed David into the family.

David's own speech was short and eloquent. He told us that he had known the very moment he had met Lucy, that very first second when she had, he said, thrown a ceramic tile at him, that they were meant to be together. She captivated him in that instant and he would remain captivated for the rest of his life.

Lucy blushed but we could see the pleasure in her face. Mrs McAllister beamed at her new son-in-law.

The speeches over, we went to the bar which had been set up in the conservatory at the side of the house. The evening was warmer than the day had been; the sun suddenly broke through the layer of cloud that had covered the sky earlier. People murmured in pleasure at the warmth of the conservatory and crushed together to get their drinks.

"Hello, Jane." Michael McAllister bumped into me.

"Michael, how are you?"

He smiled. "Great. And you? No need to ask, I suppose."

I looked down at my stomach and made a face. "Getting bigger every day." I laughed.

"When are you due?"

"Three and a half weeks," I said. "They think. I can't wait for this to end."

He nodded. "Ulrike was overdue with our first," he told me. "We thought young Karl would never make his appearance. But she was exactly on time with Helena."

"I'd like to be early rather than late," I commented. "But everybody is different. Is this Karl?"

A small boy who looked irritated at being dressed in a pair of green velvet shorts and green velvet jacket tugged at Michael. He was an attractive child, fair, like both his parents, with Lucy's clear complexion.

"Dad, can I wear my jeans now?" he asked.

"No," said Michael.

"Why?"

"Because I said so."

Karl wandered off, scuffing his feet along the ground.

"You do your best," sighed Michael. "But they

never appreciate it. I'd better find Ulrike, he's going to give her hell."

She deserves it, I thought, dressing up the poor boy in a velvet suit. He probably felt a right idiot.

I met Louise and apologised to her in person for my awful behaviour at Karen's dinner party. Louise laughed it off, although she admitted that she had nearly thrown up herself when she realised that one of the guests had puked all over the living-room floor.

"Green soup," I told her. "Never serve green soup."

She laughed with me and said that it was popular. "But if I ever do any catering for you, I'll remember."

Eventually I got talking to Lucy, who had been flitting around her guests like a butterfly.

"I hope you're really happy," I said. "You're having a great day, anyway."

"Thanks, Jane. It's good fun, isn't it? I'm sorry Rory couldn't make it."

"So am I," I said dolefully. "It's not quite the same being at a wedding on your own. He's sorry to miss it. He told me to give you a kiss for him, but I think I'll pass that message on to David."

"Don't you think I'm incredibly lucky?" asked Lucy. "I mean, isn't he perfect?"

I grinned at her. "Perfect," I said seriously.

"We'll stay close friends," said Lucy. "Both of us being married won't change that."

"Of course it won't." I was shocked at the thought.

"Good," she said. "Look, I'd better go and talk to

Aunt Marjorie. She gets fidgety if she's left on her own."

I glanced at my watch. Nearly seven. People would soon arrive for the evening entertainment. My parents, who hadn't come to the meal, would be along. A friend of David's was DJ for the night – Lucy promised that he was good. I wondered if Rory would be available if I rang the New York office. I desperately wanted to speak to him. I saw Mrs Norris, and asked her if I could make the call. I'd pay her, I assured her. David's mother told me I could call Australia, if I wanted. She was too happy to care. There was an extension in the bedroom, if I wanted some privacy.

I dialled the number of the bank.

"Dealers." The voice sounded as though it could be in the next room.

"Could I speak to Rory McLoughlin?" I asked.

"Hold the line a moment."

Thirty seconds ticked away before he came to the phone. I watched the second hand sweep across the face of the clock.

"McLoughlin."

"Hi," I said.

"Jane? Are you all right?" I was glad to hear the concern in his voice.

"Of course I'm all right," I said. "I simply thought I'd give you a call to say hello."

"Jane, this is not a good time. I'm very busy."

I bit my lip. "I'm sorry," I said. "It's just that I miss you."

I could hear the sigh coming across the Atlantic.

"And I you," he said perfunctorily. "But I'm up to my neck, Jane."

"I won't delay you. I'll see you soon."

"Jane – Jane, take care of yourself."

"Yeah, sure."

I replaced the receiver. In the middle of all the romance, Rory's distracted indifference was hard to take.

David's friend was a good DJ. He played a lot of old seventies numbers, especially for Lucy and David, he said. To recapture their youth. It was strange to think that some of the songs which were so fresh in my mind were now over ten years old. It didn't seem that long since we were dancing to them in the cricket club.

"Knowing me, knowing you
There is nothing we can do
Knowing me, knowing you
We just have to face it, this time we're through."

People poured into the marquee.

"Do you know where you're going to?
Do you like the things that life is showing you?
Where are you going to, do you know?"

I wished he'd stop playing ballads. Something with a bit of go in it would be better. He'd depress us all if he stuck with the sad songs. They were just an excuse for David and Lucy to hold each other tightly in the middle of the dance floor.

My parents arrived and waved at me from the opposite side of the tent.

Emily McAllister, Lucy's twenty-three-year-old sister, looking almost as lovely as Lucy in her peaches-and-cream bridesmaid's dress, danced with David's brother, the best man. They gazed into each other's eyes. What were the odds, I wondered, on another sister marrying into the Norris family?

Mrs McAllister took off her hat and left it on a chair. I couldn't see it lasting the night.

Mr McAllister danced with his other daughter, Joan.

Michael and Ulrike danced with their children.

The DJ speeded up the music and the floor was crammed with people. I wished I could dance, but I didn't have the energy.

Lucy took off her veil. Her hair had begun to come down but she didn't care.

The tent was very warm and the air was stuffy. The smell of the canvas was very strong. I went outside and walked in the night air for a while, sipping my orange juice. After my baby was born, I was never going to drink orange juice again.

"What are you doing out here?" David Norris came around behind the marquee. I almost spilled my drink.

"Having a break," I told him. "It's so warm in there."

"Lucy couldn't see you and she was worried that you mightn't be feeling well," he explained.

"I'm fine," I said. "A little bit tired, that's all. It's been a super day."

"Hasn't it?" He smiled at me. "Thanks for your present, by the way."

"It was nothing." We'd bought them a video. Rory got it at a discount from one of his clients.

"Coming back inside?" asked David.

"In a few minutes," I said. "I'm fine, David, really."

It was peaceful in the garden. When we moved house, I was going to tell Rory I wanted one with a huge garden like this. Without the marquee taking up so much space, it would have been fantastic. Probably need a lot of looking after, I supposed, but worth it in the end.

Jane O'Sullivan, I thought, how middle-aged. Thinking about gardens. You're only in your twenties. I still called myself by my maiden name when I talked to myself – it came more naturally.

I went back inside the tent. The atmosphere had hotted up, the dancing was more frantic and it was extremely warm. I took off the knitted jacket and sat down on one of the folding chairs.

The music was Glenn Miller and my parents were jiving. I shook my head at them in amusement. Mam had always been a great dancer.

David's brother was dancing with Joan. Brenda and Grace were talking about fabrics. Lucy was dancing with Mr Norris.

I wanted to dance myself. I would, for the last dance.

"Come on, Jane, a quick one for the girls!"

Lucy pulled us on to the dance floor, Brenda, Grace and myself. We stood together, like old times.

"Don't love me for fun, girl, let me be the one, girl
Love me for a reason, let the reason be love."

We sang together, holding hands high above the crowd. We hugged each other again.

"Got to go and change," murmured Lucy.

They were going to Crete for their honeymoon, leaving in the morning. They'd refused to say where they were spending the night but we guessed they were going to the airport hotel. The flight was at eight in the morning and, as Lucy was not a morning person, she'd like to be as near as possible to the airport.

She returned wearing a ecru linen jacket over a pair of red culottes. She had taken down her hair and had tied it back into a ponytail. She looked about fifteen.

"So let's make a tunnel of love for the happy couple!" cried the DJ.

We formed an archway with our arms and Lucy and David ran under it while the DJ played *Congratulations!* over and over again. When they reached the end, Lucy turned and threw her bouquet into the crowd. If I hadn't jumped out of the way, I would have caught it. As it was, Emily pounced on it, squealing with pleasure.

Lucy and David disappeared. The marquee buzzed with animated conversation.

I was chatting to Brenda when a white-hot pain seared through me. She didn't notice anything, she was still laughing about some incident. I could feel the tent revolve around me and then the pain hit me again, as though someone was driving a skewer through me. I grabbed my stomach and gasped. In slow motion, I could see Brenda stare at me in horror. The pain ripped through me again and I think I screamed. I looked down and saw that my beautiful cream knitted dress was stained bright red with blood. I sank, slowly, agonisingly, to the floor.

19

September 1986

(US No. 4 – Take My Breath Away – *Berlin)*

I heard the siren of the ambulance as it raced up the road. The sound broke through the fog that surrounded my brain. Other guests at the wedding had gathered around me, then Mam rushed to me and I felt her cradling my head in her arms, murmuring words of comfort to me. The pain cleaved its way through me, hot and sharp.

I was afraid. Afraid for me and afraid for my baby. Strange how I'd regarded it as something of an encumbrance but now, when I knew that I might lose it, I felt closer to it than ever. I tried to communicate with the baby, to say that it would be all right, that I would stay alive, that we would both survive. But with every stab of pain I felt even more terrified.

The ambulance men got me on to a stretcher and into the vehicle more quickly than I would have believed possible. Mam climbed into the ambulance with them. I closed my eyes. My breath echoed around my head, rasping in my ears. I tried to regulate my heartbeat, to calm myself, to do my breathing exercises. I wondered whether those damned breathing exercises helped when you were losing your baby.

I didn't want to lose it. I didn't want to die.

They were ready for me at the hospital and rushed me through the corridors to the theatre, where Mr Murphy was waiting.

I opened my eyes to see him standing over me.

"Hello, Jane," he said, gently. "Things not going exactly to plan, are they? But don't worry. You'll be fine."

"My baby," I croaked.

"Don't worry about your baby, Jane. We'll look after your baby."

"I don't want to lose my baby," I said as I tried to focus on him. "Make my baby be OK."

"We'll look after you," he repeated as he moved away from me.

I stared upwards. The blinding white lights of the theatre made my eyes water.

"You'll just feel this for a moment." The doctor injected me. My eyes blurred. I knew that he was there, I could sense him but I couldn't see him. I had to stay awake to protect my baby. It was important to stay awake.

"This is my daughter."

"What a beautiful girl."

"Yes, isn't she?"

"So pretty."

"And talented. She's top of her class in school, you know."

"Really?"

"Oh, yes. Very clever."

Then the teacher came over to us.

"Get away from that child."

"But she's my daughter."

"She's not your daughter. She's Mrs Norris's daughter."

"Lucy's child. No. She's not Lucy's child."

"She's not your child."

"She is! She must be! She's my daughter."

I fought with them. I raised my hand as they tried to take her away from me and cried "No!!"

My eyes snapped open. The wall in front of me was pastel pink. I thought I saw my mother's face leaning over me, but I wasn't certain. My eyes fluttered closed again.

Where was I? I couldn't remember exactly what had happened. The fragments were all over the place. Something had gone wrong but I couldn't remember . . . I opened my eyes again. I remembered, now.

"How are you, Jane?" Mam's face, clouded with anxiety, looked into mine again.

"I think I'm all right," I said. Then, with trepidation, "My baby."

"She's fine." Mam's eyes were full of tears. "She's beautiful."

"Where is she?"

"They have her in an incubator at the moment," Mam said. "But they don't think she'll be there for long. She's lovely."

"What happened?" I looked at her in bewilderment. "What went wrong?"

"I don't know, exactly," said Mam. "But Mr Murphy was wonderful. He says you'll be fine, Jane."

"Good," I said, and fell asleep.

It was bright when I woke up again. Mam was dozing in the chair beside me. I moved my arm and the drip dragged. I lay still, trying to assess the damage to my body. My stomach ached. It was strange not to feel the baby inside. My baby was born, it was somewhere in the hospital. No, she was somewhere in the hospital. I remembered Mam saying that "she" was all right.

I cleared my throat. Mam jerked into wakefulness. I smiled at her.

"How are you feeling now?" she asked.

"I'm OK," I said, more strongly. "I think I'm OK."

She got up and kissed me. "I'll get a nurse," she said.

I didn't care about me. I only wanted to know about my baby.

"Your daughter is still in the incubator," said Mr Murphy. "But not for long. You'll be able to see her soon. You're doing well."

"Has anybody called Rory?" I asked, suddenly. "Does he know?"

"We phoned him last night," said Mam. "He'll be here later."

I wanted to see my husband and I wanted to see my baby. I didn't feel as though I'd had a baby. I wasn't sure she really existed.

They brought me down after a while. I looked at her, in the perspex container and I wanted to reach in and take her in my arms. She looked so tiny and so vulnerable, although actually she was pretty big for a premature baby. The nurses said it was just as well she'd come early. She would have been huge, otherwise.

Rory arrived that night, looking dishevelled and with stubble on his face. He burst into my room, startling me.

"Jane!" He put his arm around me. "Jane, I'm so sorry I wasn't here. Are you OK?"

I nodded.

"What happened?" asked Rory.

"I don't know." I shook my head. "One minute I was fine – dancing with the girls – the next – "

"Dancing! Jane, really!"

"I wasn't doing anything very energetic," I protested. "It couldn't have been the dancing."

"I'm going to find a doctor and ask exactly what happened," said Rory. "They should have warned you."

"It doesn't matter," I said. "Not now."

"Of course it matters." Rory walked around my bed. "Look at you!"

"I"m OK now," I said, trying to placate him. I was feeling tired. I was fed up having the drip attached to me, my arm was sore and so was my stomach. I was afraid to look at my stomach.

"Have you seen our baby yet?" I moved gingerly in the bed.

He shook his head. "I came straight here."

"Ask one of the nurses to bring you down," I told him. "She's lovely, Rory."

He came back, beaming all over his face. "She's gorgeous!" he exclaimed. "A beautiful baby." He put his arm around me. "You're a clever girl."

Clever wasn't exactly the word I would use. I'd nearly ruined Lucy's wedding. They had delayed their flight until the following day to be sure that I was all right. Lucy had phoned her mother the next morning and Mrs McAllister had told her about me. I was annoyed with Mrs McAllister, she should have let Lucy go on her honeymoon without fussing. The delay meant that they had to fly to London and then to Crete. They'd sent me a huge congratulations card from the airport.

Rory and I fell asleep together, he in the chair, holding my hand. I felt closer to him than I had for ages.

They brought my daughter to me the following day and I took her in my arms for the first time. She was so tiny, I thought, and so wonderful. I looked at her smooth, soft skin, her blue eyes and the covering of downy red-gold hair. I picked up her tiny hands, with their perfect fingers. It was hard to believe that I'd once been this small myself.

We hadn't decided on a name. We'd thrown a few around but hadn't yet found one that we both liked. Then, as I looked at her, one of them came back to me. Clodagh. My daughter Clodagh.

I told Rory when he came in later that day. He made a face at first but then walked around the room saying "Clodagh McLoughlin" over and over until he proclaimed himself happy with it.

"How would you like Eleanor as a second name?" he asked.

"You must be joking," I said.

Eleanor and Peter came in that evening to see me. I could see that Eleanor thought I was totally inadequate. Her own daughter, Sandra, had produced three perfectly healthy children without any problems whatsoever. Three eight-pounders, all born after short labours.

Eleanor peeped into the crib beside me, and sniffed.

"She'll be a carrot-top like you," she said.

"I know." I wasn't going to let Eleanor upset me.

Peter pulled back the blanket a little. "She's a dote," he said, and I smiled at him.

They sat uncomfortably in the room, unable to think of anything to say but not willing to leave. I would have made conversation but I couldn't think of anything to say either.

"That the mother-in-law?" asked one of the nurses, after they left. I nodded. "You can always tell the mothers-in-law," she said as she took my temperature.

Rory looked uncomfortable when he came in the next day. He brought me a selection of magazines, the knitting I'd been attempting, and my Walkman.

"Hope that's enough to keep you occupied," he said.

I was occupied enough, I told him. There were so many things I could do besides simply lie there. I had to learn how to bath my baby, how to change her, how to feed her. I hadn't got the hang of feeding her yet. Then there were "parenting" classes. I would go to one tomorrow, right now I was still confined to bed.

"Wish I was in bed," said Rory, robbing a grape from the bunch Eleanor had left me.

"How are you getting on at home?" I asked.

He shifted uneasily in the seat. "Fine," he said. His tone was unconvincing.

"What's the matter?" I asked. I knew that there was something wrong, something he didn't want to tell me.

"I've got to go back to the States," he said. "I'm sorry, Jane, I'll be back in a couple of days."

I looked at him in horror. "You can't do that!" I exclaimed. "What about us?" Clodagh lay in her crib, totally unconcerned.

"I'll be back before you're out," said Rory. "It is, literally, a couple of days. The nurses said you'd be here until the weekend."

I could feel myself want to cry. "But, Rory," I wailed. "You'll be leaving us on our own."

"Hardly on your own," said my husband. "Be reasonable, Jane. You're in a hospital with hundreds of other people. This is probably the best time I could have had to go to New York."

He had a point but I didn't want to concede it.

"It's not fair," I grumbled. "Everyone else will have husbands visiting them every day and I'll be on my own."

"Don't be silly," he said. "Your mother is in every day. Your aunts are in every day, I met Grace and Brenda Quinlan as I arrived. You're hardly on your own."

"It's not the same," I said mutinously.

We were silent. Clodagh sighed deeply and Rory

went over to peer in at her. He stroked the side of her cheek. He loved the baby, I could see that. His eyes crinkled into tenderness whenever he looked at her. Suddenly I felt selfish and mean. It wasn't his fault he had to go to the States. Probably he would have preferred to be at home. I was only making things harder for him.

"I'm sorry," I said. "Of course you must go."

He sat on the edge of the bed and kissed me on the forehead. "I don't want to, Jane, you must understand that. I'd much prefer to be at home lounging in front of the TV."

"I know," I said, although Rory hardly ever lounged in front of the TV. "When would you fly out?"

"Tonight," he said. "I'll be back by Friday, Jane. Honestly."

He looked like a child, begging me.

"All right, all right," I smiled. "I believe you."

"You're a wonderful wife," he murmured. "And I'm very proud of you."

I was proud of myself. Not many women would be as understanding as me, I thought later as I flicked through *Cosmopolitan*. We had a truly adult marriage. I didn't need Rory beside me every moment of the day to know that he loved me.

All the same, Mam and Dad were horrified that he had to go away. Mam thought it was dreadful and that he should have told the bank that he couldn't go. I made the point that it was as well he went now, that at least I was in hospital being looked after. Better now, in fact, than next week when I was at home. Besides, he was going to get time off next week.

Dad didn't say anything, but he looked worried all the same. I wished that people would stop looking at me as though I was some piece of china that would break. I was fine now, the doctors all said so.

But I was miserable the next day. It was very lonely knowing that Rory was in the States, that no-one would be coming in to see me until later, and that my stomach felt as though it had been trampled on by a herd of wild buffalo.

I lay back on my pillows and tried to read my magazine, but I was tired, and sore and fed up. I couldn't even pick up my baby because I still couldn't move properly and I didn't have the strength to take her out of her crib. I felt absolutely hopeless. I closed my eyes and a tear trickled down my cheek.

"How is my most favourite girl in the whole world?" The door to my room burst open and I opened my eyes in surprise, scuffling underneath my pillows for a tissue to dry them.

All I could see was a huge flower arrangement hiding the man who carried it.

"Sorry I couldn't get in earlier, but I only got back to Dublin today. How are you feeling?"

The flower arrangement moved towards the shelf and I watched it with interest. He put the bouquet down and looked at me.

"Oh, my God!" he said, "I'm terribly sorry. I've got the wrong person."

He was tall and thin. He looked underfed. His soft brown hair was unfashionably long, tousled and unkempt. His eyes were brown too, huge in his lean face. He wored faded denim jeans and a lumberjack shirt. He looked shocked.

"Who were you looking for?" I asked, horribly aware that my cheeks were streaked with tears. Maybe he wouldn't notice, I thought; probably women who had just given birth cried all the time anyway. He'd think, hopefully, that they were tears of joy.

"My sister," he said falteringly. "I thought she was in here." He broke off to look at me intently. "Have you been crying?" he asked, abruptly. "Have I butted in at an awful time?"

I shook my head vigorously. "No, no, I'm fine." I said, wiping under my eyes quickly. "Absolutely fine. No problems at all. Everything's fine."

"That's good," he said uneasily. "I thought maybe you weren't fine. It happens, doesn't it? Sometimes you think it's going to be the best experience of your life, and of course it's not!"

"It was the best experience of my life," I said firmly.

"Really?" he asked. "I always thought it was very painful."

I smiled faintly. "I don't know, exactly. They knocked me out."

"The best way," he told me. "Great idea."

"Not in tune with modern thought," I said. "Not in tune with the birth experience."

He laughed. He had a rich, deep laugh which seemed to come from deep within him.

Clodagh started to whimper.

"Oh, Lord," he said contritely. "I've woken your baby. I'm terribly sorry."

"Do you think you could hand her over to me?" I asked. "It's just that I can't actually get out of bed yet."

"Of course," he said, hurriedly. "Don't worry."

As he walked to the crib, I was filled with a sudden sense of foreboding. What if he was one of these people who try to kidnap babies? If he took my baby and ran out of the room, would anyone be able to stop him? Would anyone notice? My heart raced fearfully as he bent to pick up Clodagh.

"What a gorgeous baby," he breathed as he lifted her carefully in his arms. "Isn't she wonderful?"

"I think so," I said. "Can you give her to me, please?"

He handed my baby to me, nestling her carefully into my arms. Clodagh pursed her lips and opened her clear, blue eyes, looking straight into mine.

"Hello," I said. "Howyah doing?"

She blinked at me and yawned.

"I'd better be going," the man said. "I'll leave you to it, shall I?"

I smiled at him. "Thanks," I told him. "Don't forget your flowers."

"Gosh, yes," he said. "There'd be war if I forgot the flowers." He picked up the bouquet and took out a yellow rose.

"Here," he said, proffering it to me. "For you."

I raised my eyebrows at him. "For me?"

"Of course," he said. "For my intrusion. I'm sorry again."

"No problem," I said as I watched him walk out of the room. "No problem."

I got out of bed the next day and had a bath. The water seeped its way into every pore of my body, cleansing me. I felt a million times better after it. Mam had been to the house and had brought me more nighties and some make-up. I told her that I hardly intended getting made up in hospital, but she said it was for the day I left so that I'd look nice in the photographs.

I half expected Peter and Eleanor to show up together, but they didn't. Jessica called in though, her face clouded with concern. She cooed over baby Clodagh and asked probing questions about my health, which I dismissed. She told me to take every second of maternity leave that I could, and to take the month's unpaid leave I was entitled to as well.

Much to my surprise, Karen Hamilton also dropped in, looking radiantly beautiful in her lime-coloured Escada jacket over a Lagerfeld skirt. Rory would be pleased when I told him she'd called. He liked the idea of being good friends with the boss's wife. Karen told me to join a gym once I got out of hospital to get my figure back in shape. I didn't like to say that it had never actually been in shape in the first place.

"It's the only way," she said as she flicked back her mane of black hair. "Otherwise, you'll simply let yourself go. Those little wads of flesh won't disappear of their own accord. You have to work at it."

I told her I would think about it and promptly forgot about her.

I was tired by the evening. Mam and Dad called in but I wasn't in the mood for casual conversation and they left after a short while. I could hear them talking to each other in low voices outside the room. I'm sure Mam was worried about me.

I wished so much that Rory was with me. It had seemed such an easy thing to say that it was all right if he went away, but I missed him hugely. This was a point in our lives when he should have been there. It wasn't fair. I hated his job.

There was a tap at the door, and a head poked around it. I looked up. It was the man from yesterday.

"Hi," he said. "Mind if I come in?"

"Not at all." I was curious. What did he want?

"I thought I got you at a bad time yesterday and I wanted to see how you were today," he said. "Are you OK?"

"Why does everyone seem to think there's something wrong with me?" I exploded. "I've had a baby! Millions of women have babies! Why should there be anything wrong?"

He shrugged, his brown eyes direct. "No reason," he said equably. "I thought you were upset yesterday, that's all. And I wondered if there was anything I could do to help?"

"I really don't see that it's any of your business," I said icily. "If I want to burst into paroxysms of tears, then surely that is my prerogative."

"Absolutely," he said. "Without a doubt. I'm terribly sorry. I seem to have made things worse. Janet says I do it all the time."

"Janet?"

"My sister. The girl next door. She's always complaining that I keep putting my foot in it. I can't help it, it's my nature."

He looked so hangdog and contrite that I couldn't help laughing.

"You didn't put your foot in it," I said. "You just got the wrong end of the stick."

"Good." He sat on the edge of the bed. "How's the baby?"

"She's great," I said enthusiastically. "Feeding like a horse."

"That's good." He peeped in at her. "Aren't they superb like that?" he asked. "So tiny and dependent?" His voice softened. "So much promise. They could grow up to be anything they choose."

"So." He sat back on the bed again. "Where's her dad?"

"That's a very impertinent question," I said as I leaned back against my pillows. "What business is it of yours?"

"None whatsoever," he admitted cheerfully. "I just wondered what Dad looked like."

"Do you think I'm an unmarried mother or something?" I asked. My wedding and engagement rings were in the ashtray on the bedside locker.

"Not at all!" He looked surprised. "I wouldn't have imagined you to be unmarried at all. Not that there's anything wrong with it if you are," he added hastily.

"Her father is in New York," I told him. "He'll be back the day after tomorrow."

"Good," he said. "Because I'm sure you wish he was here."

"Of course I do," I said. "But he's very busy at work just now and he's taking next week off to look after us, so I can't exactly begrudge him two days away now."

"I suppose not," said the man, "but I bet he hates to be away from you right now."

"I know he does." I looked him straight in the eye. He met my glare without flinching.

"Have you decided on a name for your baby yet?" he asked.

"Clodagh," I said, and wondered as I did so why I was even bothering to talk to him.

"Lovely name," he said. He glanced at his watch and exclaimed in horror. "Look, I'd better be going. Got to see the sister. Take care of yourself."

He disappeared as quickly as he had come and I shook my head. Maybe tomorrow I would knock on the door of the next room and see his sister. Janet. I wondered what his own name was, surprised we hadn't got around to such pleasantries yet. We seemed to have got around to so much else! Actually, although I pretended to be annoyed with him for dropping in, I was quite pleased to see him. It was great to talk to somebody different for a change and it was nice to have such an attractive man visit me. And he was attractive. In other circumstances, like if I wasn't married and hadn't just had a baby, I would have found him extremely attractive. I shook my head as I thought about him. I was losing my marbles.

When I peeped around the door of the next-door room the following day, his sister had already left.

Gone home, the nurse had told me, lovely girl, beautiful baby, easy delivery.

Easy delivery! While mine had been a disaster. I still couldn't rid myself of my feelings of inadequacy about Clodagh's birth. Probably if it had all gone wrong at home, privately, I wouldn't have minded so much. But it had been so spectacular. I grew hot with embarrassment as I remembered keeling over at the wedding. All those people watching me. It was horrible.

He popped his head around the door again later that day.

"Your sister has gone home." I looked up from my magazine.

"I know," he told me, "but I was driving by and I thought I'd see how you were."

"There's nothing wrong with me," I said impatiently. "And I don't see why you have to keep calling in here. I don't even know who you are!"

"Oh!" He looked surprised. "My name is Hugh McLean," he said, as though that explained everything.

"Should it ring a bell?" I asked. "Are you famous?"

"No."

"Are you a doctor?" I asked, suddenly realising that this could account for his turning up again at the hospital.

"No."

"So why are you here?"

"I don't know." He walked into the room. "I know it's awfully cheeky of me but I'm interested in you."

"How dare you!" I was really angry.

He flushed, the colour staining his sallow cheeks. "Not that sort of interested," he said. "Interested that you were OK. That's all."

I looked at him carefully. "It's a bit strange," I said. "Don't you think? You wander in here by mistake and I can't get rid of you and now you tell me it's because you're interested in me. I find that terribly offensive."

He didn't seem to be the sort of person to take offence. "It sounds awful, doesn't it," he agreed. "But I was concerned."

"Why?" I couldn't understand him.

"Because you were bawling your eyes out when I came in and I thought you might do something terrible."

I put my head to one side. "You mean – like I might top myself or something?" I asked.

He looked embarrassed. "Something like that."

I laughed, suddenly, the first real laugh in months. "I'm not that sort of person."

"That's a relief." He did look relieved. As though he'd actually believed it.

"So you don't have to worry."

"Good," he said, simply. "Because I was worried." He scratched his chin thoughtfully. "Do you mind telling me why you were crying?"

His cheek was incredible.

"Of course I do," I said. "It was a private moment."

"A sad private moment?"

"Look!" I exclaimed. "Are you some kind of psychiatrist or something? Has somebody sent you in here to make a not-so-subtle appraisal of me? Does my family think I'm off my rocker?"

He bit his upper lip to stop smiling. "No."

"Well, do you mind telling me what bloody concern is it of yours whether I weep into a bucket, kill myself, or not?"

"I don't know," he said.

I sighed. "You're very kind," I said. "At least, I think you probably are. But really, none of this is any of your business. I was unhappy. And it was because my husband had to go away. That's all. But I'm going home on Friday, he'll be back to collect me and everything is going to be fine. So it's really decent of you to care but there's no need."

He walked around the bed and looked out of the window at the jigsaw of rooftops and chimneys. He thrust his hands into the pockets of his jeans and turned to look at me.

"I don't know what came over me," he said. "I really don't. I've been dreadfully intrusive and I know, don't tell me, that you're probably very vulnerable right now."

"I'm not a bit vulnerable," I interrupted him.

"Oh."

I grinned. "Actually you have cheered me up immensely," I said. "So you can believe that you've done some good. Are you a trainee Samaritan or something?"

"No," he said. "Just an idiot."

"Well, idiot," I said. "Thanks for looking out for me, but there really was no need. I'm miles better now."

He exhaled deeply. "Good."

"So please don't feel the need to call in again. It's

not a great idea. If you bump into any of my family they'll think I'm having an affair."

He shook his head. "I don't think so," he said.

I laughed. "Maybe not. Anyway, please don't call in again. I'm not at my best entertaining men when I've just given birth."

"Nice seeing you, though," he said, walking towards the door.

"And you," I told him.

I thought about him after he had left. Such a strange person. Interesting, though. Why had he continued to call in and see me? Did he really think I might do something dreadful? I smiled inwardly at the thought. How could I even consider anything like that with the most beautiful baby in the world sleeping right beside me?

It was great having my own baby. A part of me, I could see that she was a part of me. I loved the way her eyes squeezed closed in sleep and the way she clenched her tiny fists. I loved the touch of her peachy soft skin and the silky feeling of her hair. I loved when she nestled close to me. I loved her, completely and entirely.

Rory arrived home on Friday morning and came straight to the hospital from the airport. The week had been a bit chaotic. We hadn't expected Clodagh's arrival to be quite so sudden so we hadn't bought the cot and the pram and the car seat and the changing mat and all the other paraphernalia that babies need. Mam and Dad had done the running around, buying whatever we thought of.

I was ready now, though. I'd showered and

washed my hair and had dressed in my favourite maternity trousers which didn't look too bad at all with a new, white blouse worn over them. The blissful part was that they were now too big for me. There was buckets of room in them. Hah! I thought. Jane regains control of her body, at last!

I used the make-up that Mam had brought in, carefully applied the foundation, the eyeshadow, the blusher and the lipstick. I clipped on my huge gold earrings and my bracelets and I pulled my hair back from my head with a velvet ribbon. I was delighted at how I looked.

So was Rory. He'd been so used to my indifference about my appearance over the past few months that I must have seemed like a butterfly emerging from a chrysalis to him. He kissed me deeply on the lips, told me that he loved me and gave me a bottle of Dior's *Poison.*

I bundled blankets around our daughter, who looked like a doll in her pink sleeping-suit, and picked her up confidently. Already I'd grown used to her. I couldn't imagine what life would be like without her. In the last week, she had become much more a part of my life than she ever had when she had been inside me.

She snuggled down into the blankets and closed her eyes tightly. She was so lovely, I almost cried again. But I'd made a resolve not to cry any more. It could be misconstrued.

One of the nurses took a photograph of us before we left. She told Rory that he had a wonderful wife and a beautiful daughter and Rory agreed with her as he put his arm around me.

I was glad to get home again. The house was my cradle, my comfort. I was happy to see my own bed, to have my own things around me again. I settled Clodagh into her Moses basket and made sure that she was well wrapped up. Then I went upstairs and threw all my washing into the laundry basket. Rory's suitcase was on the bed, but I hadn't the energy to unpack for him too. Anyway, I was absolutely dying for a cup of tea.

So I threw my own case into the back of the spare cupboard and closed the door on it. I'd already forgotten about the shrivelled yellow rose which still lay inside.

20

April 1990

(UK No. 1 – Vogue – *Madonna)*

The shrill ring of the telephone woke me. I rolled over in the bed and reached out for the receiver as I blinked in the watery morning sunlight.

"Hello." My voice still heavy with sleep.

"Good morning," said Rory. "Happy birthday."

I blinked again and looked at the clock. Seven o'clock. "Good morning," I said. "How are you? How are things in Frankfurt?"

"Busy."

"Too busy?" I pulled myself up in the bed, waking up properly.

"Not too busy," he said. "I'll be home in time, I told you that."

"That'll be a first." I tried to sound as though I was joking.

"I wouldn't miss your party," he said. "I organised it, didn't I?"

"Of course you did," I said. "I'm looking forward to it."

"I'll see you later then," said Rory. "Enjoy your day."

"Thanks." But he'd already replaced the receiver.

I stretched in the double bed. The door opened and my daughter walked in.

Clodagh was wearing her Care Bear pyjamas and carrying her blue teddy.

"Can I get in?" she asked.

I held out my arms and she ran at the bed, jumped on to it and burrowed under the duvet.

"I'll go to sleep," she said as she squeezed her eyes closed and stuck her thumb into her mouth. Clodagh was a chip off the old block when it came to bed. She enjoyed her sleep. Other mothers I knew were exasperated by the fact that their children woke up at the crack of dawn every morning. Usually I had to wake Clodagh, even at weekends.

She curled into the crook of my body and slept. Her long eyelashes fluttered over her creamy skin and her strawberry-blonde hair curled around her face.

People said that she looked like me, but I couldn't see it. I thought that she was the image of Rory. She had the same determined features, even in sleep, the same high forehead and the same bright blue eyes. She had my colouring, but even then she would be lucky enough never to be called "carrots" at school, her hair was too fair for that. She was not exactly a pretty child but she was striking and, naturally, I thought she was very intelligent. She had Rory's quick brain. She was good at numbers, she asked sensible questions and she was incredibly self-possessed. But I liked her best like this, curled up against me, needing me. She was like a little angel.

"Get a grip," I muttered to myself as I slid carefully out of the bed so as not to disturb her.

I sat in front of my dressing-table and looked at myself in the mirror. I was thirty years old. How had that happened? I couldn't believe I was thirty! When, during the previous week, I sat back and thought about my impending birthday, I wondered where on earth my twenties had disappeared to. I could still clearly remember leaving school, that part of my life hadn't dissolved into the mists of time as I thought it would. I could visualise the teachers, the students, Sr Elizabeth, all as precisely as the day I left. If somebody had insisted that I write down a list of all the girls in my class, I was sure I could have done it. And yet here I was, thirty years old. Thirteen years since I left school. Married for eight years. A mother of a three-and-a-half-year-old girl. It seemed utterly impossible.

I peered into the mirror to check my hair. At Christmas, I'd noticed that the occasional grey hairs were becoming more noticeable and now they seemed to be growing geometrically, every day another couple, to annoy me. It seemed ludicrous to have grey hairs on my head when I felt so young. At seventeen, thirty had seemed an absolute lifetime away. Now that I'd reached it, I knew that it was nothing.

All the same, my birthday present to myself was a morning at the hairdresser's, getting a decent colour to hide the unwanted grey streaks.

I stood up and looked at myself full length. I was in better shape now than I'd ever been, my work-outs at the gym had seen to that. The bulge of my stomach had flattened and I had a waist again. I wasn't perfect, of course, but leaner and fitter. Strange that, as I got older, I should acquire the shape I wanted when I was a teenager. I went to the gym three times a week now, and it made a huge difference. I'd decided against Karen Hamilton's gym, though, because I really didn't want to see her every day. She kept asking me to go to lunches with her, or help to organise charity functions. It wasn't that I didn't care about the charities, but Karen was so overwhelming that I could only take her in small doses. I was in her good books at the moment because I'd helped her organise a dinner last week which had raised twice as much as she'd originally hoped. The down side of that success was, I knew, the chance that she'd try and get me to help with the next event too. Karen was not the sort of person to take no for an answer easily and of course Rory always tried to get me to do whatever Karen wanted. If it kept her happy, it kept Bill happy, he said. And Bill was still the Group Treasurer.

Triona Bannister arrived at eight o'clock. She was Clodagh's nanny, although perhaps nanny was exaggerating slightly. She came every second week to look after Clodagh. The arrangement suited us perfectly because Triona had another part-time job and I wasn't out and about enough to need someone to look after her all the time. Triona lived about a mile away. I'd met her in the library when she was looking at the "Wanted" notices. She had four younger brothers and sisters, she'd baby-sat as a teenager and she was looking to continue baby-sitting as much as possible. That way she could study, work and earn money at the same time, she said. In addition to her part-time jobs, she was going to college at night. I didn't know where she got the energy. She had lots of references, including one from one of my neighbours, and so I'd given her a trial. Clodagh loved her. Unfortunately, Triona was going to the States to work from June to September. I'd be sorry when she left us, especially as I was thinking of going back to work full-time myself. I was fed up with doing bits and pieces with Karen Hamilton. Last month, I'd told Rory that I was going to get a job. "Outside the home," I put it.

"You're what!" he exclaimed, looking at me as though I was subnormal.

"I want to work again, Rory," I said. "I need to have something to do."

"But Clodagh will be going to school next year," he said. "Surely you can wait until then."

At first that was what I'd thought myself. After all the tantrums I'd thrown when I was pregnant about not giving up work, I'd been forced to stop after Clodagh was born because I'd managed to end up in hospital again two months after her birth, this time with appendicitis. When I got out of hospital I resigned from the bank. I couldn't cope with both work and Clodagh, I just couldn't.

I didn't mind looking after Clodagh at first. She was a very alert baby, always looking for someone to play with her. I enjoyed taking her for walks, to the mother-and-baby swim, playing silly games with her, acting idiotically. It was fun.

Then the lunches with Karen were organised, I joined the gym and took up art classes. So I needed someone to look after Clodagh, at least some of the time. Triona was the answer to a prayer and I was able to fit in the things I wanted to do while she minded Clodagh.

The only problem was that I was bored. I didn't want to work with Karen Hamilton. I wanted to earn my own money again. I enjoyed being with Clodagh, but I couldn't be with her every minute of the day. I was starting to go mad. The afternoon that I found myself standing in the supermarket in front of the vegetable display with no real idea of why I went there in the first place, I knew that I had to get back to work.

Rory didn't agree with me. I didn't know why he was so set against it, although I supposed his mother might have had something to do with it. He insisted that there was no need for me to work and that I should be at home with Clodagh.

"None of the other girls work," he said. "Why should you?"

"Because I'll go barmy if I don't," I told him.

"That's ridiculous," said Rory. "Karen Hamilton isn't barmy."

"If that's what you believe," I said bitterly. She'd driven me nuts that day. She'd got into a flap about whether the tablecloths for a lunch should be pink or green. I couldn't see that it mattered either way and said so. She'd told me that I just didn't understand.

Eventually, after heated discussion, Rory and I decided that I would get a job once we'd arranged something suitable for Clodagh.

I wanted her to go to a kindergarten of some sort. I'd been to a kindergarten myself when I was a kid and I thought it would be better for her than being on her own. Rory was sure that she would be better off at home and that we should get someone in to mind her. I said that I would check things out and let him know but I didn't want her to be on her own in the house with someone. I was determined that it would be a crèche or a kindergarten.

When I started to look for a job, I didn't realise how difficult it would be. I supposed I'd been lucky when I was younger – I'd waltzed into the bank with no real effort. But there were lots of people looking these days. I wanted to get any job, just to get out and start working again, but Rory told me that I should get a suitable job. His idea of a suitable job was one where I'd have plenty of time to be at home whenever he wanted. We argued about it, but he won. He told me that the bank would be looking for temporary workers later in the summer and if I could hold out until then, he knew that they'd offer me something.

It wasn't exactly what I'd imagined, but it was better than nothing and, deep down, I was glad that I would be working at something that was even a little bit familiar. After nearly four years out of the business world, my confidence was a little shaky.

"I'm going to get my hair done this morning," I told Triona, as she hung her coat in the cloakroom. "I'll be back by lunch-time."

"OK, Jane," she said. "Is Clodagh awake yet?"

"What do you think?" I called as I put on the kettle. "It's about time you got the little madam up."

I waited until Clodagh had run downstairs in her bare feet to kiss me before I left the house. The traffic into town was busy. I parked my Honda Civic in the Setanta Centre and walked across to the Royal Hibernian Way where my current hairdresser worked. Practised, I supposed, was a better way of putting it. ZhaZha's Hair Sculpture was more like an operating room than a hairdressing salon. It was hi-tec all the way, everything in grey and chrome and no chintzy bits to make the austere atmosphere more homely. But I rather liked it that way. I hated salons where the junior who washed my hair made inane conversation about my probable holidays or the state of the weather. In ZhaZha's they didn't speak unless they were spoken to. It made everything much more peaceful.

But today I would have liked something a bit friendlier. I pointed out the grey hairs to Sabrina who peered through the rest of my hair disdainfully, pulled up lengths of it and looked disappointed. She was thinking "another old bat" and wondering how to tell me that they really only wanted young, trendy people in her salon. I felt out of place in the grey and chrome, suddenly too old for it.

Was this how it was going to be from now on? I wondered, frantically. Always feeling too old? Soon I would be as bad as my parents, hankering after the good old days.

God, I was like that already. As I sat in front of the

mirror and watched Sabrina snipping away at my locks, I realised that I didn't recognise any of the songs that were being played in the background. I was an old fogey. I shuddered at the thought.

Sabrina used an all-over colour on my hair. "They're not too obvious, anyway," she said patronisingly, "you're lucky you're not very dark."

I paid by credit card and left. Why should I feel bad about it? Karen Hamilton had her hair done here, so did Lorraine. They were both dark – and no way could it be natural. So snotty Sabrina must have her quota of greying women. I couldn't be the only one. But I knew that I'd never go back to ZhaZha's again.

I drove back to our house in Dún Laoghaire. From now on I would get my hair done here. Somewhere cosy in the town centre which would be a damn sight more convenient anyway.

Our house was one of five, built half a mile outside the town. It was new when we bought it, a couple of months after I had my appendix out. It still looked new, although the saplings that I'd planted in the front garden had begun to grow and were now covered in spring-green leaves. Each house was slightly different although all were redbrick and all had a built-in garage. They weren't anything spectacular from the front, but they were big houses with plenty of room and a reasonably-sized south-facing garden with a conservatory.

It was the conservatory that had persuaded me, even though I'd no interest at all in moving house at the time. But the sun shone warmly through the glass, and I could see myself sitting in a room which was as much part of the garden as the house, and I agreed.

Rory employed a gardener to landscape the back garden, which was a good idea because I would never have made it so pretty. It had colour all year round, although summer was my favourite time when the Californian lilac and the fuschia and the roses were all in bloom.

I liked my house, but I'd preferred our home in Rathfarnham.

Triona and Clodagh were in the garden when I got in.

"Oh Jane, I do like your hair!" cried Triona.

"Really?" I was pleased that she'd noticed.

"It's lovely. The colour really suits you."

"Is it that different? I want it to look natural," I said.

"It does," said Triona, "but the colour hides those few grey ones."

Ouch, I thought. I hadn't realised that Triona had noticed the grey. I'd fondly believed that only I'd seen them.

"You haven't forgotten about tonight?" I asked her.

"Oh no, of course not," she smiled. "I left my overnight bag upstairs."

Rory had organised a big birthday dinner for me in The Copper Beech restaurant. He'd invited twenty guests. I was really looking forward to it. I was forever going to dinner parties with him, but I'd never been to one which was for me. Most of our dinner parties were work. Tonight would be for fun.

Well, almost for fun. I put my foot down when I

realised that half of the guests were to be either Rory's bosses or his clients. "I can put it on expenses that way," he told me. "Bill thinks it's a great idea."

I threw a fit. My birthday was not some marketing exercise, it was my birthday. If he only wanted to bring people that he worked with, then he could cancel it. I wasn't interested. He sighed, exaggeratedly, and told me that he had also invited Lucy and David Norris, Brenda and Grace Quinlan, and Jessica and Neil Dawson. I was afraid that Lucy, Brenda and Grace would feel intimidated by the number of bank people present, but there wasn't much I could do about it.

Lucy was delighted anyway. "I hardly ever get out," she said. "I'm looking forward to it."

David Norris had set up his own company two years earlier and Lucy was working for him. They were, she said, only now starting to make money and it was a great treat to know that they could go and feed their faces at someone else's expense.

Brenda and Grace, whose boutique was now absolutely booming, were also delighted to be invited out. "We never have time, usually," said Brenda. "And anything we ever go to is tiny little *hors d'oeuvres* carried away before you eat them. Because of the models, of course, you can't tempt them with real food."

I was looking forward to a bit of time with the girls. We hadn't got together since Christmas.

I was in great form that evening when I put on my black trousers and body and my multicoloured Frank Usher sequinned jacket. I left my hair loose in a cloud of copper unsullied by any grey.

"You look fantastic," Triona told me as I came downstairs.

"Lift me, lift me," cried Clodagh, so I did, hoping that she wouldn't try and pick all the sequins off the jacket.

It was half past seven. The restaurant was booked for eight. Rory's plane had been due in at six-thirty, but I'd phoned the airport and it had been delayed. It had landed at seven, they told me cheerfully.

I wasn't sure whether or not I should go to The Copper Beech and be there in case the guests arrived on time. I was pretty sure none of them would, they were notoriously late for everything, but it would be awful for someone to show and for neither Rory nor myself to be there. And by the time he got back, had a shower and changed, it would be half eight at least.

If only he didn't always put me in these situations. Nothing with Rory was ever cut and dried. There was always some moment of high drama to mess things up. But if I went to the restaurant now, before Rory, he'd probably get on his high horse and ask me why I hadn't waited.

I made my decision. I'd go.

It was just as well I did. Lucy and David were arriving as my taxi pulled in front of the mews building. I called to them as I handed over my fare.

"Jane!" cried Lucy. "It's great to see you. Happy birthday!" She threw her arms around me. "Now you know what it's like," she said. I'd sent Lucy a card for her birthday and enclosed tickets for the theatre. She'd phoned me one day when I was out and left a message on the answering machine to say that she would speak to me when she had got over the trauma of her new age.

"Hello, Jane." David kissed me on the cheek. "Where's Rory?"

"On his way," I said hopefully. "He was in Frankfurt all week, only got back this evening. I decided I'd better come on ahead."

I led the way inside. They had reserved the upstairs dining area for us, the tables arranged side by side.

The Copper Beech was the in-restaurant of the moment and it was patronised by what Lucy called the "glitterati". It wasn't a very big restaurant but it was tastefully decorated, bare walls covered in murals, natural wood tables and an uneven stone floor.

"I've never been here before," said Lucy. "Nice, isn't it?"

I nodded. "Rory does buckets of entertaining here," I told her. "It's like the staff canteen to him."

"Nice canteen your husband has," said David. "We must set up something like this at home, Lucy."

"Our canteen is the kitchen," she said. "Beans on toast my speciality."

"How's business?" I asked.

"Pretty good," said David. "Busy, thank God."

"How do you like working for him?" I asked Lucy.

She squeezed me by the elbow. "He's the best boss I ever had an affair with," she whispered.

We sat down at the tables and the waiter brought us drinks. I hoped that Rory wouldn't be too late, it would be so embarrassing if people I barely knew arrived. I'd met all of the clients he had invited before, but I still felt that he had a bit of a nerve turning my birthday into a works outing. I turned around when I heard footsteps on the iron stairway, hoping it would be him.

Bill and Karen walked in. I was surprised to see that they were on time. Karen looked simply stunning, as always. She wore a tight lycra dress and a long red jacket. Her black hair had been cut into a shorter, softer style.

"Happy birthday," she cooed, kissing me on the cheek. "Welcome to the thirties club."

"Thanks." I accepted the perfectly-wrapped present she handed me. "I'm so glad you could come."

"Where's the husband?" asked Bill. "Hiding somewhere?"

"He'll be along shortly," I told them. "He only got back from Frankfurt tonight."

Bill nodded and lit a cigar.

More people arrived, bank people I knew. They were served with drinks while I fluttered around greeting them, wondering where the hell Rory was. I was tense and, so far, not having a good time.

Then he swept into the room, looking handsome and relaxed, and managing to embrace everyone in his welcome. He shook hands with the husbands and kissed the wives and eventually made his way over to me.

"Sorry I'm late," he whispered, "the bloody traffic was terrible."

Now that he was here I was able to relax, and I

stopped feeling as though I had to look after Bill or Karen or Graham or Suki. I joined Lucy and David who were sitting in the corner.

"I would have preferred a little party of my own." I waved apologetically at the gathering in front of us. "But Rory was organising something for the bank anyway, and he felt that this was as good an occasion as any."

"You must do it for me, darling," said Lucy. "A big meal and line up all your builders."

We laughed.

"I love your hair," said Lucy. "You've coloured it, haven't you?"

I told her about the grey and she nodded in understanding. "Happens to us all." She ran her fingers through her own hair.

"At least you can't see yours," I told her.

"Nothing like a good colour." She winked.

Then the Quinlans arrived, followed by Jessica and Neil. The conversations buzzed around the room as people grouped themselves in little bunches.

Finally the waiter appeared, sat us down and handed us the little menus that said "Happy Birthday, Jane" on the front.

I felt very important. It was good to be the guest of honour for a change. I looked around at everyone. Although I still classed Lucy and the twins as my closest friends, I kept in touch with Jessica and I did see a lot of the other wives. Some of them used the same gym as me and, of course, I often met them at Karen's charity lunches or at one of the bank's corporate hospitality functions.

They were not the sort of people I could get very close to. I wanted to fit in with them, but for some reason I never felt on the same wavelength. I didn't understand why, unless it was that I was never convinced that I, Jane, was the sort of person who could spend a fortune on a dress or a pair of shoes and still have enough money for a facial or a hairdo afterwards. The O'Sullivan household had been frugal. Money was never wasted. Although I'd always thought I would enjoy spending it, I felt guilty every single time I did. Especially because I still considered it to be Rory's money. Maybe I wouldn't feel so bad when I was earning, myself.

"So where are you going on your summer holidays this year?" asked Grace, leaning across the table. The twins were dressed in their own creations tonight and they looked great.

"I don't know." I shrugged. "It depends on my husband."

Rory turned towards me. "What depends on me?" he asked.

"Our holidays," I told him. Last year we'd gone to the South of France and stayed in a *gîte* a couple of miles from the coast. We'd talked about the States this year. Rory wanted to bring Clodagh to Orlando.

"The way work is going, we'll be lucky to get away at all," said Rory. "Isn't that right, Graham?"

Graham nodded and said that Rory was the hardest-working individual on the team.

"By the way," he asked my husband, "did you clear the outing with Jane?"

"What outing?" I asked.

Rory looked daggers at Graham. Whatever the outing, he didn't want to ask me about it now.

"Trip to Edinburgh the week after next," said Graham. "Golfing. Just the lads. A bit of a laugh."

"He didn't mention it," I said cheerfully, "but I never stop him going anywhere."

Beside me, Rory breathed a sigh of relief. He didn't know that I would kill him when I got him home. We'd planned to go for a few days down the country ourselves the week after next. I was looking forward to it. Not just the break, but the opportunity to spend some time alone with Rory. We hadn't spent time alone in so long, I sometimes felt that we were two separate people who shared the same house. When we talked, we never seemed to talk about our hopes and our dreams but about the plumbing or the car or Clodagh. I knew that I couldn't expect romance all the time, but a little bit would have been nice. When he'd told me about the birthday dinner, I thought that was very romantic until I realised that half the bank would be there. Now it was no different to the millions of other functions we attended, except for the fact that everyone had been forced to buy me a present, which was very embarrassing.

"You and Rory must come to dinner with us soon," said Lucy. "We haven't been out together in ages."

"You and I must go out to dinner together ourselves," I told her. "I haven't had a decent girls' night out in I don't know when."

"Great idea," said Brenda, who had overheard. "How long is it since the four of us went out?"

I shook my head. "Months."

"Exactly," said Brenda. "Months. And we're supposed to be friends."

"We did well for a while but we've let it slip lately," agreed Lucy. "And I keep meaning to ring people, but I don't."

"I know," I said. "But I'm always afraid you'll be too busy."

"I'd never be too busy to go out with the girls," retorted Lucy.

The food in The Copper Beech was delicious. I felt absolutely stuffed by the time dessert was finished, a lovely strawberry and cream pie. Then the waiters returned with bottles of champagne and Rory stood up and proposed a toast to me.

My cheeks flushed with embarrassment as he called me his "beloved wife" but I was glad he used the words and glad that he felt he could say them in front of other people.

"To Jane!" he said, raising his glass.

We drank champagne and liqueurs and people swapped seats and talked to each other. It turned into a very pleasant party. Jessica came and chatted to me about children, she was now pregnant with her third. She wanted to know when I'd have another one. I grinned and said never. I presumed that this was because of the trauma of Clodagh's birth, but I felt terribly guilty about it because I remembered how much I'd longed for a brother or sister when I'd been young. But the thought of being pregnant again, sick and fat, which was exactly how I'd felt for the entire time, was too horrible to contemplate. Linda Sherry joined us and I allowed Jessica to talk baby talk with her while I kept half an ear on their conversation and watched the other people at the party.

Everyone seemed to be having a good time. People sat around in relaxed groups and chatted to each other, while the waiters whizzed around making sure that everyone had enough to drink. I looked around for Rory. He was talking to a girl who had been introduced to me as Amanda Ferry, the new corporate treasury dealer. I wondered over and over how the women put up with the chauvinistic ethos that dominated most dealing rooms. It was still a male preserve, all about money and power and egos. I imagined there'd been a few sharp intakes of breath when Amanda had joined the dealing room. She was tall and very striking, with auburn hair, almond-shaped grey eyes and sallow skin. She had a fantastic bust. I wondered who would be the first to take her out. They'd probably put bets on it among themselves. She'd sat between Graham and Bernard during the meal and they'd vied for her attention. I'd noticed her talking to Leo and then Bill and then one or two other men whom I didn't know very well, and now she was talking to Rory. She laughed suddenly and leaned towards him. Rory smiled at her and squeezed her arm. He caught me looking at him and jumped back like a child caught with his hand in a sweet jar.

I waved at him and he came over to me. "Enjoying yourself?" I asked.

He nodded. "It's going well, don't you think?"

It was going well. People were having a good time. I nodded.

"Have you met Amanda?" He gestured towards her. She'd turned away from us and was talking to David Norris.

"You introduced us earlier," I said. "Nice girl."

"Very bright," said Rory. "Sharp."

"Good," I said.

We looked at each other for a moment.

"Do you want another drink?" he asked.

"Any more champagne?"

He smiled at me. "Sure." He kissed me fleetingly on the lips and disappeared to get more champagne. I grinned to myself.

Lucy came over and kicked off her high-heeled shoes.

"God, I can never wear these," she sighed. "And I do so like to look tall."

"Nice shoes," I said.

"Ancient," Lucy told me. "About five years old. I can't afford anything new at the moment."

I stared at her. "Money problems?"

She shook her head. "Not really, Jane. It's simply getting the business going. It's taking all our spare cash. It'll all work out in the end, I'm sure of that, but we're a bit strapped at the moment. And there's our own house, of course. Every additional spare bit of cash goes on that."

They'd bought a lovely old house in Howth, but it needed a lot of repair work to make it habitable.

"How is the work going?" I asked.

"Slowly," groaned Lucy. "I'd love to be able to walk into the kitchen and not have a piece of the ceiling fall in on top of me."

"It'll be worth it in the end," I said. "Your house will be much nicer than mine when you've finished."

"Oh, Jane, your house is lovely," protested Lucy.

"But it's new and doesn't have much character," I said. "It's a good family house, but not a beautiful one."

"Character is all very well but I'd adore an en suite bathroom," laughed my friend. "You really will have to come out and see me, Jane. Not you and Rory, just you."

I looked at her suspiciously. "Why not Rory?"

"You said earlier we girls didn't get together enough any more. Well, you and I are even greater friends than we were with the twins. We need to keep in touch."

"I know," I said. "To be honest, I suppose I've felt that maybe you'd be bored with my company now, Lucy. After all, I'm not doing anything much and all I'd do is natter on about Clodagh and the cat."

"I like hearing about my goddaughter," said Lucy. "She's a lovely baby."

"Not a baby now," I said. "An *enfant terrible.*"

"Bring her with you," said Lucy.

"Don't you want to have a baby of your own?" I asked, curiously.

"Not yet," she laughed. "Not after your experiences."

"You get over it," I said. "Almost."

Rory and David came over with glasses of champagne for us. Rory told stories about his flight back from Frankfurt, David told tales of architects' nightmares and then Grace and Brenda came and talked about horrible customers.

"Huge, fat, blobby women trying to get into our size twelves," giggled Grace. We all laughed. I was merry with drink. It was ages since I'd drunk more than a glass of wine, tonight I'd had at least three, and champagne as well. I was light-headed and everything seemed fantastically funny. I staggered over to talk to Karen for a while, then back to Lucy, then more people joined us; David had disappeared, Grace and Brenda looked a bit drunk and we started swapping old school stories. It was a long time since I'd had such a good time.

It was past midnight before people started to disperse. I slipped downstairs to the Ladies to repair the ravages of the night. I didn't look thirty, I decided as I squinted at myself in the mirror. I still looked young.

"Well, I don't think they can possibly be happy." David's voice carried into the Ladies, and I stopped, my lipstick halfway to my mouth.

"Of course they are." Lucy sounded abrupt. "You just don't like Rory, do you?"

"No, I don't. He's pompous and self-centred. I would never organise a birthday party for you and then invite all my clients."

"Maybe you would," said Lucy and pushed open the door. She looked surprised to see me, and a little worried.

"Hi," she said. "I didn't know you were here."

"Running repairs," I said lightly. She disappeared into a cubicle and I hurried upstairs again.

"There you are!" Rory put his arm around me. "We're going down Leeson Street."

"Who's we?"

"The gang. Bill and the lads, their wives, Amanda."

I looked around for the twins. "Are you coming?" I asked.

Brenda shook her head. "I'd love to," she said, "but we've a busy day tomorrow and I can't go to the shop feeling like death. We'd better give it a miss."

"You two used to be great clubbers," I protested.

Brenda laughed. "Before we got sense." She gathered up her bag. "We'd better go, Jane. Give us a call. Happy birthday."

I gave her and Grace a hug and then Lucy appeared at the top of the stairs.

"Going clubbing?" I asked. She looked over at David, who had preceded her. He shook his head almost imperceptibly.

"Guess not," said Lucy. "Busy day tomorrow."

Why did they all think they had such busy days? Tomorrow was Friday. The dealers would all be at their desks at eight, however late they stayed out tonight. I was disappointed in my friends. Jessica had left earlier, unable to stay awake because of her pregnancy.

So I said good-bye to the twins and Lucy and David and went to Buck Whaley's with a dozen of the guests, where I drank myself silly and passed out in the corner. I only vaguely remembered Rory carrying me upstairs to bed at half past three in the morning.

21

May 1990

(UK No. 17 – I Still Haven't Found What I'm Looking For – *Chimes)*

I sat in the conservatory, legs tucked underneath me, Junkie curled up at my feet and my book open on my lap. The scent of lemon thyme floated in the air and a gentle breeze from the open skylight stirred the fronds of the potted ferns. There weren't many flowers in the conservatory. I preferred it as a place to sit in the sun than as somewhere to grow plants. It was sunny outside but the wind was from the north-east and cool, so the conservatory was the nicest place to be that afternoon. I loved being there, curled up in the wicker chair, on my own.

Soon, Triona would be back with Clodagh. My daughter would run into the room and throw herself at me and the fragile quiet of the day would be shattered. Of course I'd be glad to see her, I missed her when she was away. But in the meantime, the silence of the conservatory was very peaceful.

I stared out at the garden and watched the wrens

hop across the lawn. The birds fed nervously in our garden, aware that it was cat territory and always keeping an eye out for Junkie.

His tail switched lazily as it hung down from the chair, and his nose twitched. I wondered what he was dreaming about. I glanced at my watch, my birthday present from Rory. Time seemed to be passing so slowly today. Surely I should be up and doing something? I wondered what time Rory would be home this evening.

Last night there'd been a terrible row. He was late home, not drunk, just late, and I screamed that I was fed up with him treating our home like a hotel and me like an unpaid servant. He roared back at me, listing all the things he'd ever done for me, as he dragged me around the house and showed me what a beautiful home he'd provided. Then Clodagh woke up and started crying which upset me and upset Rory.

But we didn't make up and slept back to back, rigid in the bed. I didn't fall asleep for ages. I lay there, tears dripping on to the pillow, as I wondered why we couldn't appreciate each other any more.

Of course, David Norris was to blame. His careless words to Lucy were still clearly etched in my mind. David thought my husband was self-centred and pompous. And sometimes I did, too. I kept asking myself over and over "does it matter?" So what if he was those things, he was a also good and loving husband and father? The trouble was that I couldn't decide whether he was a good and loving husband and father any more. He was good to us. He adored

Clodagh. He loved me. There was just something not quite right and I was frightened.

Tears welled up in my eyes again but I wouldn't let them fall. I was a stupid, selfish woman. I lived in some damned dream world that wanted everything to be like a fairytale. Life wasn't like that. It was hard. And a lot harder for most people than it was for me.

When Triona and Clodagh returned I was scratching Junkie under the chin. Clodagh showed me the stones she'd gathered on the beach and Triona offered to make coffee. We sat around the island worktop in the kitchen while they told me about their day and I listened to Clodagh's happy chatter. She pushed her hair out of her eyes as she displayed her stones, laying them out carefully in neat rows in front of me.

"She's very bright," Triona told me. "She talks a lot and she talks a lot of sense."

I hoped that she hadn't talked to Triona about last night's row. She'd clung to my leg, her eyes wide and terrified as I'd hissed malevolent words at Rory and she'd cried when he stormed into the bedroom and slammed the door behind him.

For her sake we mustn't have any more rows like that.

He arrived home early and walked straight upstairs. Clodagh and I were sitting together in the living room playing *SuperMario*. I listened to his footsteps overhead as he walked across the bedroom. I tried to guess his mood from his tread, but it was impossible.

When he came downstairs he was wearing his track suit. He flopped down on to the bed and allowed Clodagh to jump on to him, tickling her until she squealed for mercy.

"I left something on the table for you," he told me shortly.

My heart was thumping as I went into the kitchen. I didn't know what he might have left me. It was an envelope containing reservations for a weekend in the Park Hotel in Kenmare for two people. Our weekend away, delayed because of his golfing trip to Edinburgh. I hadn't said a thing to him about it, even when he'd packed a bag on the Thursday evening and told me he'd be back by Sunday. I walked back into the living-room.

"Is this for me and you?" I asked.

"Naturally," he said. "I said we'd go away, and we're going."

I looked deep into his eyes. "Thank you," I said as I sat down beside him. He hugged me briefly and turned on the TV.

We went the following weekend, leaving Clodagh with Rory's parents. I hated leaving her with Peter and Eleanor. I still didn't get on with them very well, and I didn't like the way they tried to influence Clodagh. But they'd offered to take her and I couldn't very well turn them down.

Clodagh didn't mind because Eleanor and Peter's house was full of toys that they kept for all their grandchildren. "We'll be back on Sunday night," promised Rory as he kissed her goodbye.

I settled into the leather seats of the Mercedes and slid a CD into the deck.

Dire Straits filled the air and I closed my eyes. Rory was a good, dependable driver and I trusted him completely. The Mercedes was a great car to snooze in.

We drove as far as Matt the Thresher's almost without speaking, but it was a relaxed silence without the tensions of recent weeks.

We had French Onion Soup and crusty rolls in Matt's, followed by a coffee for me and a pint for Rory. "And I'm only having one pint, so don't get your knickers in a twist," he told me as he ordered it.

"I wasn't going to." I sipped my coffee.

The drive from Limerick to Kenmare was tortuous. Lots of traffic and, once we had reached Killarney, long and twisting roads through the mountains.

Eventually we reached Kenmare, strung out at the beginning of the peninsula. Rory drove through the main street, swearing softly at the parked cars in the middle of the road. Finally he swung in through the gates of the hotel and pulled up outside the door.

A porter helped us with our cases. The room was beautiful, L-shaped with a small sofa, table and TV in one part and two beds side by side in the other. I flopped down on the sofa and yawned widely.

"What do you want to do tonight?" asked Rory as he sat on the edge of the bed and slid off his shoes.

I put my arms behind my head. "I don't mind. Eat, drink and be merry?"

"Do you want to have a shower before we go down to dinner?" he asked.

I nodded, and sat upright. "Oh, yes. I'm sticky from the drive down."

The water in the shower was hot and powerful. I massaged shower gel into my body and turned around under the spray. The bathroom door opened and Rory appeared. "Mind if I join you?"

I shook my head and he got into the shower. Rory's body had changed over the last few years. Business lunches, dinners, entertainment had all added a few pounds around his waist. I poked his more rounded belly with my finger. He caught my hand and pulled me towards him.

It was a long time since we'd showered together. When we were married first, we shared the shower every weekend. I liked it – the warmth, the closeness, the water cascading over us. Sometimes we'd make love, sometimes not, but it was always a supremely sensuous experience. Now Rory massaged shower gel over me, his hands gliding expertly around my body. I quivered with pleasure and kissed him on the chest.

We made love in the shower and then again on the bed. Rory was strong and passionate. I loved the passion, but it was the togetherness that made me happiest, the knowledge that he wanted me.

He held me tightly to him afterwards, cradling me in his arms as he rocked gently back and forwards. We dozed together, at peace. I woke with a start about twenty minutes later and wriggled out of Rory's arms to dry my hair. The hum of the dryer woke him, and he dressed while I wrestled with my hairstyle.

He wore casual trousers and a cotton shirt. I put on a light pair of blue trousers and white blouse and draped myself with jewellery. We looked good together as we walked into the dining-room.

"Do you still want to go back to work?" Rory asked, as he sipped his glass of Pinot Noir.

I nodded. "Funny, I wasn't that keen on it when I started and then I got interested. When I left, I missed it like mad. I still miss it."

"I can't understand you," said Rory. "I'd have thought that most girls would like to be able to swan around and do what they liked."

"You'd think that until it happens to you," I told him. "But I need to feel that I'm doing something."

"Having a good time is doing something," he objected.

"Not worthwhile, though." I poured myself some more wine. "Even though it might be boring work, it's still something I'm doing for myself."

"Don't you think that rearing Clodagh should be enough?"

"You sound like your mother." I laughed. "I love her, but, all day, Rory. Can you imagine what it would be like to talk to a three-year-old all day?"

He laughed, too. "I suppose so. Here, fill your glass."

We lingered over the food and talked to each other for what seemed like the first time in months. Then we went to the lounge and sank into the low armchairs, drinks in our hands.

There was a fair number of people sitting in the lounge already, in couples and in groups. Rory knew one of the couples, Kieran and Antonia Woods. Kieran was the treasurer of a company which dealt with the bank. I sighed deeply as my husband went over to talk to him. Abandoned again.

My gaze roamed around the room and out into the hallway where more people were arriving. I swirled my Bailey's, watching the liquid adhere to the side of the glass, allowing the ice cubes to clink against each other.

When I looked up again, I was surprised to find the man standing at the bar looked vaguely familiar. He was tall, rangy and his business suit looked as though he had put it on by mistake. He wore tortoiseshell glasses perched on the edge of his nose, and carried a jacket and very battered briefcase. He was out of place in the refined elegance of the Park Hotel and yet very attractive in a dishevelled sort of way. He moved out of my line of vision and I frowned. I knew that I knew him, but I couldn't remember where I'd seen him before.

Rory returned, Kieran and Antonia in tow. "Kieran was wondering if I'd like to go golfing with him tomorrow," he said, as they sat down beside me. "But I told him you wouldn't let me bring my gear."

"I'm sorry, Kieran," I said. "But it's a get-away-from-it-all weekend. We couldn't do that if he brought it all with him."

"You should take up golf yourself," said Kieran, "I'd say you've got a lovely little swing."

"The last time I came home late, she had a great little swing," laughed Rory. "She got me on the edge of the head."

The all laughed. "You must teach me that move," said Antonia. "I could do with it myself."

We spent the evening with them. At first, I was aggrieved that Rory had brought someone over to join us but Kieran and Antonia were entertaining company, and I didn't feel as if talking to them was hard work.

Antonia had a son around the same age as Clodagh so we chattered about our children, sharing gossip and tips. Antonia was a beautician who ran a salon from her house in Rathgar.

"I must call in to you sometime," I said.

"Any time." She smiled. "You have great bone structure."

"Thanks," I said, even though I knew that she was just being kind.

We stayed in the bar until nearly midnight. My eyes were closing as we walked up the stairs to our room.

We pushed the beds together to make an enormous and comfortable double bed. We fell in beside each other, kissed perfunctorily and then both fell instantly asleep.

The following day was glorious. The sun blazed out of the blue sky, dotted with fluffy white clouds. The air was warm and balmy and the countryside green. We went for a walk through the town and across the bridge, stopping to watch the river speeding its way to the sea.

"Isn't it beautiful?" asked Rory. I nodded in agreement. I could see why people lived in the country. The pace of life seemed to have slowed already, local people nodded in greeting to us as though we were already known to them, and the air was clear and sweet.

I was starving by lunch-time so we went into a pub and ordered soup and sandwiches. Then we went back for the car and drove through the winding countryside to Sneem. I bought a toy woollen lamb for Clodagh, an Aran jumper for Mam and a blackthorn walking-stick for Dad. Rory laughed at me for buying presents to take back to Dublin.

We didn't eat in the hotel that evening, but in a local restaurant where the food was plentiful and full of flavour and where nothing was too much trouble for the owners.

"Don't you feel that you could live like this all the time?" said Rory, as we strolled arm-in-arm back to the hotel.

"You're joking!" I glanced at him and saw that he was smiling. "You'd never be able to live somewhere like this," I told him. "It's far too tranquil for you."

"I suppose you're right," he said. "But I wonder. Maybe in a few years, when I earn enough money, we could retire."

"You'll never retire," I said, positively. "No matter how much money you earn. You like it too much."

"I don't know," he said, as we turned up the gravel driveway. "We burn out, you know."

"Oh, yeah! And if you burn out from foreign exchange trading, you'll still probably want to do something like it."

"You hate my job, don't you?" said Rory.

"Not hate it," I told him. "I resent it."

"Why?" he asked. "It pays the bill, it gives us a good life and – at the moment, anyway – I enjoy it."

"I know you enjoy it," I said. "You enjoy it too much, I think. You'd prefer to be at the desk than at home."

He made a face. "Not really. But when I'm dealing, it's the most important thing in the world. I can't think of anything else. All the same, have you noticed me giving a damn about exchange rates this weekend ?"

"Since they can't move at weekends, it's hardly relevant," I retorted.

"I didn't look at today's papers for yesterday's closing prices," he protested and I leaned my head against his shoulder and told him that he was a wonderful person.

We sat in the lounge again and sipped our drinks. I felt perfectly in tune with Rory as we sat there. When he went to the Gents, I got up and went over to the bar to order again.

"A pint of Heineken and a Bailey's," I said as I leaned against the bar counter.

"Hello again."

I turned around, recognising his voice. Of course, I thought, looking at him. He was wearing jeans and a denim shirt tonight and that made him easier to identify, even though the haircut was so much tidier and the glasses changed the shape of his face.

"What are you doing here?" I asked abruptly.

"That's a wonderful greeting." He smiled and pushed the glasses up on his nose.

"I'm sorry." Why was I rude to him? "I'm simply surprised to see you."

"I'm surprised to see you," said Hugh McLean. "How's your daughter?"

My tone softened. "Clodagh is lovely," I told him. "A beautiful child."

"She was a lovely baby," he said. "Really lovely."

I smiled. "All babies are lovely," I said. "How is your – niece, nephew?"

"Niece," he said. "Cliona."

"Do you see her often?" I asked, making conversation.

"Quite a bit," said Hugh. "I'm her godfather."

"Do you have any children of your own?"

He threw back his head and laughed. "Not that I know of," he said, wiping his eyes. "I certainly hope not."

I looked embarrassed. "You married?"

"Not at all." He looked incredibly cheerful. "No one will have me."

"Why?" I asked. "You talk too much?"

"Not at all." He sounded wounded. "You know I hardly ever open my mouth."

I grinned at him. "You never shut up every day I saw you."

"But I cheered you up," he told me. "Come on, I did cheer you up."

We looked at each other for a moment. His eyes were soft. I turned away and picked up the drinks. "It was nice seeing you again," I said. "I'd better get back with these."

I felt his eyes follow me across the room. I wondered why on earth he disturbed me so much. Why he seemed to be able to see right through me, to my soul.

You're being fanciful, I told myself, taking a gulp out of the Bailey's.

Rory returned and sat beside me.

"I was thinking of converting the garage," he said.

"What?" My mind was on other things.

"The garage. I thought we could convert it."

I stared at him. "Into what?"

"Another room, Jane. What did you think?"

"Don't be daft, Rory. We've four bedrooms, a living-room, a dining-room, a kitchen and your study. We've also got a utility room and a conservatory. What on earth do you want more rooms for?"

"When the family grows a bit." He winked at me.

I made a face at him. "I'm going back to work, darling. The family can wait a little longer."

"Don't you think it would be nice to have another room downstairs?"

I shrugged. Rory loved talking about changing the house. It was part of his nature to want to change things all the time. He was never content to leave them as they were.

He continued to talk about the extension and I half-listened to him as I tried not to look in Hugh McLean's direction.

A girl came into the bar, looked around and joined him. I observed them from beneath my eyelashes.

She was average height, quite attractive in an understated sort of way, in a charcoal-grey suit and smart red shoes. She carried a folder which she opened out and gave to Hugh. They looked through it, pointing out items of interest to each other. Hugh nodded from time to time.

So, a business acquaintance and not a girlfriend, I decided. Although he might be attracted to her. When he wasn't reading through the folder he was watching her. Maybe they were down on business but he was hoping to get her into bed, I thought. Maybe he was already dreaming of the moment when they would slide into those very comfortable beds together and he would put his arms around her.

Jane! I was horrified at myself. What on earth was I doing, thinking about the man like this? I hardly knew him. I didn't have any right to make up his life for him. Besides, she might be happily married and completely uninterested in him.

He looked up then. I wasn't quick enough to drag my eyes away so I pretended that I wasn't looking at him, but past him. I yawned exaggeratedly. The faintest trace of a smile hovered around his lips and he bent his head to the folder again. I felt my face redden with embarrassment.

"Do you know them?" asked Rory, suddenly.

"Sorry?"

"Those people over there? Do you know them?"

"Why?"

"Because you're staring at them, Jane."

I turned around in the sofa until I was practically facing Rory. "No, I don't know them," I said, keeping my voice level. "But he looks vaguely familiar to me. I thought he might have been somebody from the bank."

I was a good liar. I could keep my voice neutral and unexcited.

"He was staring at you, too," said Rory.

I shrugged. "Probably because he noticed me looking at him. Anyway, they're definitely not from the bank. You'd recognise them, wouldn't you?"

He nodded. "No, I don't know them. Oh, who cares! Do you want to go to bed?"

I nodded. "Isn't amazing how sleepy you get in the country?" I said.

"God knows why, we haven't done anything all day," said Rory.

"Good for you." I grinned and followed him out of the bar. I didn't look back at Hugh although I was sure that he was watching me.

We made love that night again, doing immense good to our averages, which had slipped alarmingly of late. It was great to be desired and wanted by Rory. I loved holding him, being held by him, being close to him.

I stood by the window, looking out on to the bay. He came up behind me, softly, so that I jumped at the touch of his hands on my shoulders.

"You look lovely," he whispered, kissing me on the cheek.

"For you," I breathed. "It's easy to be lovely for you."

"I want you so much," he said.

"I want you too."

He began to slide the clothes from my body. My linen jacket, my silk blouse, my cotton skirt, until I was naked before him. I hadn't turned around while he did this, enjoying the anonymity of it. I could feel his skin close to mine, the warmth of his body.

"Oh Rory," I whispered, turning finally to face him.

The face was not Rory's but Hugh's, smiling down at me in silent mockery. I screamed, but no sound came from my throat. I put my hands up to protect myself, but he caught them and then forced his face down on mine to kiss me.

I struggled against him and shouted "No!"

"Jane! Jane! Wake up!" Rory was shaking me. The sheets were wrapped around me and I couldn't free myself.

"You're OK! Don't worry!"

I looked at him and remembered who I was and where I was.

"Sorry," I mumbled. "Nightmare."

"Eating too much rich food," he snorted. "Are you OK?"

I nodded.

He yawned. "It's only half three," he said. "Let's get a bit more sleep."

I rolled over in the bed, shaking. The dream had been very vivid. I didn't know why it had come to me like that, but it seemed so real that it frightened me. So unfair on Hugh McLean too, I thought, as I pulled the sheets around me again. He wasn't the type to force himself on anyone.

My sleep was dreamless and sound after that. I woke up when I felt Rory slip out of the bed to have his shower. I lay there, cocooned in its warmth. It was great to know that I could lie there and that Clodagh wouldn't come running in at any moment. I lay there half awake, half asleep, revelling in my laziness until Rory switched on the hairdryer and startled me into full wakefulness.

We planned to leave after breakfast so that we wouldn't be too late arriving at his parents' house to collect Clodagh.

I strolled into the dining-room while Rory bought

the morning papers from reception. I chose a seat near the window at the opposite side of the room from Hugh McLean, who was reading a book at a table on his own.

He looked up as I walked by and nodded to me as I sat down. I smiled very briefly at him, the memory of my previous night's dream very clear in my mind. I couldn't understand why he had invaded my dreams like that. He was very attractive but not really my type. That scruffy, academic look was not for me. But his face was arresting. You couldn't help being drawn to him.

I ignored him and then Rory entered the room and sat down in front of me, blocking my view of Hugh. I was relieved. We ate our breakfast, chatted and went up to our room to collect our bags.

Hugh and his girlfriend walked past as we settled our bill.

"Nice to see you again." He waved at me.

I opened and closed my mouth, unsure what to say.

"Meet you in another few years, perhaps," he said as he opened the door.

Rory didn't hear the exchange. He was signing the credit card voucher.

It was six o'clock when we finally arrived back at the McLoughlin family home.

Clodagh squealed with excitement when we walked in and ran the length of the hall to me. I picked her up and swung her in the air.

"Be careful with the child, she's only just finished her tea." Eleanor came into the hallway, her lips pursed.

"Did you have a nice tea?" I asked Clodagh, who immediately made a face and said no.

Eleanor looked annoyed and I stifled a giggle. Good girl, Clodagh, I muttered under my breath, annoy the old bat.

We stayed for almost an hour. Peter wanted to show Rory their new alarm system and security lighting. Peter was paranoid about being burgled and the house was protected like a fortress. I often wondered how they would ever get *out* in an emergency.

I always enjoyed coming home, even if I'd only been away for a couple of days. Clodagh ran upstairs to check on her toys and I unpacked our bags.

It had been a lovely weekend, I mused, as I unfolded our clothes. If only we could have more of them, maybe we could be closer to each other. The romance of our relationship had long since disappeared under the day-to-day living of our lives and sometimes it seemed as if we were just two people sharing the same house. But we had been lovers at the weekend, doing simple things for each other, finding pleasure in each other's pleasure. I loved Rory. I was going to make more time for us. It was up to me to make sure that we were as happy as we deserved to be.

I went to bed that night on a cloud of happiness and dreamed of my husband and my child.

22

June 1990

(UK No. 14 – Nessun Dorma *– Luciano Pavarotti)*

The country had gone World Cup crazy and so had everyone in the bank. They'd organised various different trips to see Ireland playing in Italy and Rory had gone on almost every one. It wasn't something I felt I could complain about. Everyone I knew wanted to go to the matches. All the same I was sick to the back teeth of football and, even though I wanted Ireland to win as much as anyone else, I was relieved when we were finally beaten and our lives got back to normal.

I sat in the living-room on the last Friday in June and spread out holiday snaps in front of me. Our holiday plans had been entirely disrupted by the World Cup. I'd suggested to Rory that maybe I could go with him to a match and stay on in Italy. He'd looked so horrified that I hadn't pressed matters, but I still wanted a holiday. I'd enjoyed the weekend away with Rory so much that I thought two weeks with him and Clodagh would be magic.

I still hadn't started working yet although I'd gone

for an interview with the bank and they'd assured me that they would get back to me soon. That was nearly three weeks before and I presumed that the World Cup had disrupted the recruitment programme as it had disrupted everything else. When Rory was home we had some fierce battles. I wanted to watch Wimbledon and he wanted to watch soccer. Our second TV, in the bedroom, was black and white and neither of us wanted to give way and be the one to retire upstairs. Rory pointed out that it was easier to tell which tennis player was which because they were on different sides of the net; soccer players, he said, were all over the pitch, it was much harder to follow the game in black and white.

He had a point and so I was the one who usually ended up in the bedroom. He'd bring in a gang of his mates and they would sit in front of the TV, drinking cans of beer and eating microwave popcorn as they screamed abuse at the players.

Clodagh loved watching the football and would scream at the TV as much as Rory, to his great amusement.

"She's a great little girl," he said to me one night as we curled up in bed. "Maybe it's time for her to have a brother or sister."

His words chilled me to the core.

"Not yet." I ran my fingers up his chest. "But one day."

"You should have another baby soon," he said. "Clodagh will be at school before it's born and you don't want too much of an age gap. It wouldn't be fair on either of them."

"I'm not ready," I said.

"Oh, come on," said Rory. "You were fine the last time. A little hiccough at the end but you came out of it OK, didn't you?"

"I nearly died," I told him.

"Don't exaggerate."

"You weren't there." I rolled over so that my back was to him. "It wasn't my finest hour."

"But you can't put it off forever," he objected. "And we agreed that we should have a couple of kids."

"I know, I know," I said. "And we will. Just not yet."

He sighed and lay on his back. I pulled the pillow around my face. I wasn't ready to be responsible for another person around the house. It would stop me from going back to work too. I knew Rory didn't want me to go back but I had to do something. Mam had always worked and I was used to the idea. It hadn't done me any harm, after all.

So I wasn't going to have a baby yet, whatever Rory said. Maybe in another couple of years.

I woke up the next morning with a runny nose and scratchy throat and wondered why I always managed to get colds in the summer. I spent the day being irritable at Clodagh and then guilty at my irritation. Her eyes filled with tears as I told her that no, she couldn't have another bar of chocolate. I shouldn't have given her one in the first place. I was trying to be the sort of mother whose children preferred fruit as a treat, not sweets.

In the end I did something which was probably

even worse and brought her to MacDonald's where she had a great time eating burgers and chips and almost exploded trying to suck up her strawberry triple thick milk shake.

I called in to the chemist on the way home and bought some lozenges for my throat and Night Nurse for my cold.

I met my next door neighbour as I arrived home. Claire Haughton worked in a stockbroking company and I rarely saw her, but today her black Mazda MX3 was parked in the driveway and she was eyeing her garden with some concern.

"Hello." I nodded at her.

"Hi," she said.

Claire and her husband Martin had lived next door for a year and a half but we had very little contact with them. The last time I'd spoken to Claire was in the pub at Christmas when we'd bumped into them, all four of us a little the worse for drink.

"Nice day." I fumbled in my bag for the house keys.

"Huh." She put her head on one side. "Do you know much about gardening, Jane?"

"Not a lot." I grinned at her. "When we moved in, Rory got a friend of a friend to do our garden. All I'm supposed to do it take up the daffodils in the summer and plant them again later in the year. I usually forget. But I did manage to get a nice display of pansies in a few pots on the patio."

"I took the day off because I thought I might do something with this." She indicated her garden with a broad sweep of the hand. "But I don't know what to do, really."

"Why don't you get someone to do it for you," I suggested. "Then all you have to do is pay the bills."

"It seems a bit of a cheat," said Claire. "I know that it's a good idea but my parents have a lovely garden and they do it all themselves. I really would feel so ashamed to say that I couldn't."

She looked so distraught that I laughed at her.

"Why don't you come in for a coffee and you can look at mine and see if it gives you any ideas?" I offered.

She smiled at me. "Love to."

We took our coffee into the conservatory while Clodagh ran out into the garden and started kicking a football around the lawn.

"We needed grass for her to play on," I said. "Given the choice, I might have paved it all over but a bit of green is nice."

"I'd no interest at all until recently," said Claire, "then I went home and my folks' place looked so lovely that I realised that I'd neglected mine shamefully."

"You don't have time to do it, though, do you?" I asked. "You leave early in the morning and it's usually late when you get back."

Claire sighed. "I know. I'd love to have a job where I didn't have to get in to the office until ten o'clock and I could leave at four. When I was at school they used to tell us that computers would make our lives easier and we'd all have much more leisure time. All computers have done is connect everybody in the world so that if someone in the States is awake, I have to be awake too! Madness!

Sometimes I wonder if we've made any progress at all."

"But you must like it surely?" I asked her. "Otherwise why would you do it?"

"I do like it." Her face lit up. "Only it doesn't exactly leave you with time to do things like the garden. I'm always entertaining clients or going to company presentations and things like that."

"You sound like Rory," I said unsympathetically. "He's always complaining that he has to spend hours in the office, but he loves it really."

"He works in foreign exchange doesn't he?" asked Claire.

I nodded.

"Those guys are lunatics," said Claire. "I don't know how they do it."

"Neither do I," I told her. "And I don't know how I put up with it either."

She laughed at me. "What did you do before you had your baby?" she asked. "I'm sorry, but I've forgotten her name."

"Clodagh," I supplied. "Oh, I worked in the same bank as Rory."

"An inter-office romance." Claire chuckled. "How lovely."

"What about you?" I asked, "how did you meet Martin?"

"He works in one of the companies I research," she told me. "I met him at a presentation."

"So," I said, "they're worth going to after all."

"Sometimes." Claire drained her cup and stood up. "Can I go outside?" she asked.

"Of course."

We wandered around the garden. I told her the names of some of the shrubs and the flowers. It *did* look very appealing, especially compared to Claire's which was just a square of lawn dotted with weeds. Junkie eyed us with interest from his perch on top of the garden shed.

Claire kept up a stream of idle conversation. It was nice to talk to someone new, I was sorry that I hadn't ever talked to her before. You could hardly count Christmas, people never talked at Christmas, just came out with a stream of seasonal clichés.

"Come to the garden centre with me," she suggested. "You can help me pick out a few plants."

"You should have the garden ready for them," I told her. "Have your sites prepared."

"All I want to do is to chuck down a few colourful flowers," she said. "I'll leave the long term stuff until I've done a bit of work. But a few bright things would be nice, liven up the front and back a bit."

"OK." I was pleased that she'd asked me

"I'll go and get my bag," said Claire. "Will we go in my car?"

"I have to bring Clodagh," I reminded her. "So it'll have to be mine, is that all right?"

"Sure."

I swept *Mr Men* books and fluffy toys out of Claire's way as she got into the car. "It's a run-around," I explained apologetically. "Not really a car for adults."

"It's fine," she said. "It'll get us there."

She wasn't used to a car that was used for children. I could see her looking at the boxes of tissues, the moist wipes and all the various bits and pieces that I needed if I brought Clodagh anywhere.

"It must be a bit of a job for you," she remarked as I unbuckled my daughter from the baby-seat.

"What?" I asked.

"Bringing her places."

"It's not so bad now." I lifted Clodagh out and set her down on the gravel outside the garden centre. "When she was a baby it was an absolute nightmare. Everywhere we went we had to bring stuff to feed her and change her and keep her warm. It used to take hours to get her organised. Now I can simply strap her in. Mind you," I added as I grabbed a hold of her and removed the gravel from her hand, "she's at an awful age now. She wants to be in absolutely everything. You know, they say you need eyes in the back of your head – well, you need eyes all around your head with her."

Claire laughed. "She's lovely."

We spent a very pleasant half-hour as we strolled around the centre and picked out some plants for Claire's garden. I enjoyed myself immensely. I was surprised at how much I knew about gardening after all. I managed to steer her away from high maintenance plants and get her to buy stuff that didn't need much looking after.

Eventually she made her purchases and we loaded up the car with a selection of bedding plants and a few shrubs.

"It must be wonderful having time to do this," said Claire, as we unloaded her purchases and carried them through to her back garden.

"It's OK," I said. "But you get bored after a while."

"Are you bored?" she asked as she placed the little pots in a row across her patio.

"I want to go back to work," I told her. "I was never particularly fond of it, but I do enjoy meeting people and it's very difficult being at home all the time."

She nodded. "I can imagine."

"Working life isn't designed around women with children," I said. "Despite the fact that hordes of married women work."

"Companies are making the effort," said Claire.

"Some are." I picked a few leaves off the privet hedge. "But you're really a second-class citizen if you're a working mother. You know the way a company expects you to give your time whenever it wants. It's so difficult if you've got a kid. They get sick at the most inconvenient times, you have to put them first. If you try and do that at work there's always going to be a conflict."

"I suppose so," said Claire. "Sometimes I think I'd like a kid myself but every time I do I get into a panic." She smiled. "We've been married three years so I feel as if I should. I don't think I'm ready yet, though. But my biological clock is ringing alarm bells all over the place."

"How old are you?" I asked.

"Thirty-three," she said.

I was surprised. I'd assumed that she was younger than me. She certainly looked it.

"It's great having a child," I told her. "But it does change your life completely. Anyway, you've loads of time." I glanced down at my watch. "I'd better go back home," I said. "I promised Rory I'd make him a meal this evening and I'll have to get started."

"Of course," she said. "I'll get on with this. Maybe we could have a chat again some time."

"Love to," I told her. "Come on Clodagh." I dragged my daughter away from the flowerbeds. She'd managed to get clay all over her.

"See you again," said Claire.

I washed Clodagh's face and hands and changed her into a pair of cotton jeans. She looked positively angelic with her hair caught back in a tiny ponytail and her face scrubbed clean and glowing. She sat in a corner of the kitchen and teased Junkie. The cat put up with an incredible amount from Clodagh without ever scratching her. When he had enough, he simply got up, stalked upstairs, hid under one of the beds and went asleep.

I was roasting a chicken for Rory's dinner. He'd complained when he rang earlier that he hadn't been out to lunch once this week and that I hadn't made him anything to eat in the evening either. He was wasting away. I told him that it would be good for him to lose a pound or two, but he said that he was perfectly proportioned.

Over the last year or two I'd improved my cooking skills and now I quite enjoyed chopping and slicing in the kitchen. I was going to rub the chicken with garlic and do a lemon sauce to go with it. Rory liked roast chicken.

The aroma of cooking filled the house. I loved the smell of roasting from the oven especially when it was liberally laced with garlic. I took my book into the conservatory and read it while the dinner cooked.

Rory said that he'd be home by six, but I knew that he'd almost certainly be late. He rarely got home before half-past, so I'd timed dinner for about a quarter to seven. When he hadn't arrived home by seven I was annoyed.

I didn't get *madly* annoyed until eight o'clock. I hadn't realised that it was so late because the evening was bright and sunny and I'd been so absorbed in my book that I hadn't noticed the time going by.

"Where are you?" I looked at the phone. "Why haven't you called?"

That was his other bad habit. If he knew he was going to be late, he didn't ring until the very last minute.

The chicken smelled gorgeous and I was starving. Clodagh had fallen asleep on the sofa, her thumb stuffed into her mouth. I carried her up to bed and undressed her without waking her.

There was no point in getting into a rage with Rory. I went back downstairs, carved myself a couple of slices of chicken, took a couple of roast potatoes and sat down in front of the TV.

It stayed bright until past ten o'clock. I varnished my nails, pillar box red, and sat with my hands outstretched in front of me as I waited for them to dry.

What pub had he gone to? I wondered. Larry Murphy's? Searson's? Where was his latest haunt? I hadn't a clue. I thought about ringing one of the pubs to find out if he was there. I actually took out the phone book and looked up the numbers but I didn't have the nerve to phone. I'd always despised women who rang their husbands or their boyfriends in pubs. Especially as the men concerned would so often shake their heads at the barman and refuse to take the call. No, I would wait for Rory to come home in his own good time.

He hadn't returned by midnight but I wasn't worried because closing time was half past eleven and he wouldn't leave the pub until twelve. I tried to recall his exact words that morning. "Home by six," he'd said. "Nothing planned. Do something nice for tea, there's a love, I'm dying for a bit of good grub."

So I'd done something nice for him to eat but he had failed to make an appearance. Typical, I thought, as I went upstairs to bed.

My mother had never slept when I was out late at night and I found it hard to sleep when Rory was. Even when I knew that he was out on business, I could never fully relax and fall into a deep sleep. Usually I dozed, waking at every noise, expecting him to come in at any moment.

I dozed on and off until two o'clock in the morning. By then I was worried. What if he'd had an accident? The last time I'd worried like this was before we'd married and he hadn't shown up for a date at all. But that was different. Now he was my husband.

I rolled over in the bed. What if he'd had a crash? I could see him lolling in the driver's seat of a car which had careered into a lamppost. If he'd gone to a club, surely he would have called. I whimpered with worry and with rage.

Dawn was breaking when I heard the sound of his key in the door. He stumbled on the stairs and I heard him swearing softly. He pushed open the bedroom door.

I pretended to be asleep. I heard him undress, his shoes fall to the floor with a thud. I could sense that he had simply stepped out of his clothes and left them lying on the floor.

He smelled of stale cigarette smoke and alcohol. I couldn't stay quiet any longer. I turned towards him.

"Where the hell were you?" I asked.

"Out," he said.

"Out where?"

"Met some people." He closed his eyes.

"Rory!" I shook him, but to no avail. He snored gently.

He got up for work at seven o'clock as usual. I'd fallen asleep at six, listening to the dawn chorus and the hum of the milk-float as it had driven down the road. I heard him shuffle into the en suite, banging the door.

I was sitting up in bed when he emerged, rubbing his hair with a towel.

"What happened to you last night?" I demanded.

He looked at me, still unable to focus his eyes properly. He yawned.

"Nothing."

"Something must have happened," I told him. "You were meant to be home at six."

"I was," he smirked. "I didn't say six pm"

The smile annoyed me even more. "Rory, where the hell were you? You didn't call, you didn't tell me you'd be late. What happened?"

"Nothing," he said again. "We had to go out with some clients. They came to a meeting at four and we went for a drink with them. Then Andrew suggested we had a bite to eat. We couldn't refuse them, so we went for a Chinese. Everybody was in good form so we went to a club afterwards."

"For God's sake!" I exploded. "You went to a nightclub?"

"Why not?" asked Rory. "We were having a good time."

"You're pathetic," I snapped. "Nightclubs. You're a married man, Rory McLoughlin, you shouldn't be spending your time in nightclubs."

"Why not?" he asked. "At least they're a bit of fun."

"Sugar daddies go to nightclubs," I said.

He laughed at me. "What would you know about them? You won't ever go."

"I went to Buck Whaley's for my birthday," I protested.

He picked up his suit from the floor and hung it up. "Once or twice a year you might go into a club," he said. "It just so happens that I have to go as part of my job. There's nothing I can do about it. It doesn't make me a sugar daddy."

"Well, what do you call a bunch of men who stand around in a nightclub?" I demanded, "eyeing up the women."

"There were some lovely girls there all right." He took a clean shirt out of the chest of drawers. "Some really lovely girls."

I knew he was trying to annoy me and he was succeeding.

"So you had a good time then?" I asked. "Your boys' night out?"

"It wasn't just boys," he said. "Two of their girls came along and so did Amanda."

"Well I hope they had a good time too." I felt a total frump at the thought of my husband in a nightclub with three women and an indeterminate number of men.

"It wasn't anything," he said. "Only fun."

"So you had fun while I sat in with your daughter," I said bitterly.

"What would you have done if I'd come home?" asked Rory. "Sat in with me."

He was right but I couldn't see what difference that made.

"I'm late." He straightened his tie. "And I'll have to get the DART in to work."

"Do you want a lift to the station?"

"No," he said. "I need the walk."

He left the house, slamming the front door behind him.

The bedroom door opened and Clodagh slid into the room.

"Where's Daddy?" she asked, her eyes big and wide.

"Gone to work," I said.

"He didn't come in and kiss me." Her bottom lip trembled.

Rory always kissed her goodbye. That was her signal to come into the bedroom for her morning cuddle.

"He was late," I said. "Come on in."

She wriggled into the bed beside me. "I don't like it when he doesn't come in and kiss me," she said.

"Neither do I," I told her, cuddling her close.

We lay together in the bed, our eyes closed. I hoped that Rory had an absolutely massive hangover. I hoped that his head was pounding and that he would have a very busy day and that he would lose money. He hated losing money.

Clodagh and I slept for nearly two hours. We spent the day cleaning the house and then I let her play computer games for as long as she liked. This was a real treat for her, usually she was restricted to half an hour. But I didn't have the energy or the inclination to tell her to stop.

I removed my nail varnish and fed half of the chicken to Junkie who loved the garlic and mewed for more.

Rory arrived home at half past five. I heard the roar of the car in the driveway and stood, motionless, at the sink where I'd been filling the kettle.

He came into the house and went upstairs immediately. When he came into the kitchen he'd changed into a pair of jeans.

"Home early," I said.

"Couldn't stay the pace," said Rory. "Any food left?"

I turned to look at him.

"You mean yesterday's dinner?" I asked.

He sighed. "Yes, yesterday's dinner," he said.

"There's some."

"Look," he said, "I really want to go to bed and get some sleep but I decided that I'd better come in here and face the music first. So will you just get on with it and chew me out and then I can go to bed."

"What do you want me to say?" I asked.

"The usual stuff," he said. "About how hurt you are that I didn't call, how foolish I am to go on the piss, how inconsiderate I am to come home drunk."

"It hardly seems worth the effort now, does it?" I asked.

"No, but you might as well say it because it'll make you feel better."

"What would make me feel better," I tried to keep my voice steady, "would be if you behaved like any normal husband and came home after work."

"I did come home after work," he said triumphantly. "Unfortunately my work meant having to stay out late."

"Overtime?" I murmured.

"Exactly," he said. "I'm sorry I was late. Now is that OK?"

"Not really," I told him. "Why didn't you phone?"

"I knew you'd ask that," he said. "I didn't phone because no one else was phoning. I didn't see the point. You'd guess what had happened and you did guess, didn't you?"

"Of course I guessed." I walked into the living-room. "But I'd prefer to be told by you."

I waited for him to follow me, but he didn't. I heard him filling a glass with water.

Was I being unreasonable? I wondered. Did Martin, next door, arrive home in the middle of the night and expect Claire to guess where he had been? Maybe it was Claire who arrived home in the middle of the night in that relationship, though. Did Lucy's husband do it? I doubted that very much. I didn't think that David Norris was the type to go to a nightclub at all. How did Karen or Linda or Lorraine or Fiona react when their husbands rolled in as the birds were beginning to sing in the trees? Did they simply say "had a nice time darling?" and go back asleep, or were there rows in their households too? Was I the only one who objected?

I went back into the kitchen. Rory was staring out the window into the back garden watching Junkie roll in the grass.

"It doesn't matter." I put my arms around him.

"That's my girl." He smiled and kissed me on the forehead. "I am sorry, you know."

"Sure." I leaned my head against him.

We stayed like that for a moment, then he held me away from him. "I'm going to bed if that's all right with you," he said. "I didn't get much sleep last night."

"I guess not."

"So – goodnight."

"You'd better say goodnight to Clodagh," I said.

He went in and kissed her too, then went up to bed. I could hear the sounds of his snores drifting down the stairs so I closed the bedroom door and sat down in the living room with Clodagh.

"Is Daddy sick?" she asked, her voice full of concern.

"A little under the weather," I said.

"What does under the weather mean?" she asked.

"He's sick," I said.

"Read me a story," said Clodagh, dismissing Rory and his possible illness.

So I sat and read *Cinderella* and wondered whether or not the Prince had ever gone on the lash after their marriage and what Cinderella would have done in the circumstances.

23

July 1990

(US No. 18 – You Can't Deny It – *Lisa Stansfield)*

St Stephen's Green was crowded. Hordes of people sat on the grass in a multicoloured display of bright summer clothes against the manicured green lawns. The fountains played in the summer sun and the sparkling drops turned into miniature rainbows. Children leaned into the water and floated plastic boats across the fountains. Ducks quacked furiously on the ponds as they fought for the crusts of bread that were thrown to them. The music from the lunch-time band recital floated across the park, cheerful and spirited.

I walked through the Green. I loved it when it was crowded like this. Once lunch-time had ended, it would be quiet. The men and the boys would put shirts on to backs which had been exposed to the sun and girls would pull their skirts down from the hitched-up position on their thighs.

I was meeting Lucy for lunch in Captain America's.

It was ages since either of us had been there. Because of the sun and the clear blue sky, I wore a T-shirt and a short skirt and revelled in feeling good.

Lucy waited for me in Grafton Street, sunglasses pushed into her hair. I felt sorry for her; she was wearing a smart business suit and blouse, which looked very stylish but was not necessarily the most comfortable dress for the scorchingly hot day.

"Hello there," I said.

"Hi, Jane. Gosh, you look cool." She looked wistfully at my T-shirt and skirt.

It was hot inside Captain America's, too.

"Any chance of a window seat?" asked Lucy hopefully.

"You're lucky," the waitress told her. "Someone's just leaving."

We were shown to a table near the open window where we could look out on to the bustling street below. A juggler stood on the pavement surrounded by a knot of people as he threw silver clubs into the air. The waitress left us with the huge laminated menus and disappeared.

"What are you having?" I asked Lucy.

"Plain burger and chips," she said. "I feel that in this weather I should be having a salad, but I'm absolutely starving."

"Two plain burgers, two chips," I ordered when the waitress returned. "And could I have a glass of milk, please?"

"Coke for me." Lucy handed over her menu and leaned back in her chair.

"How was your meeting?" I asked.

She'd been meeting the bank manager to discuss the affairs of David's company.

"Not bad," she said. "We've renegotiated our loans at a better rate and that'll help the cash flow."

"How's the business going?"

"Quite well," she said. "It's still a bit knife-edge and I'm worried that it won't work out, but I think it will. David has a lot of contracts and he's very good."

"I'm glad," I said. "How do you like working with him?"

Her eyes lit up. I'd never in my life seen anyone as much in love as Lucy Norris. Her marriage hadn't lost the sparkle that had been there at the start. It was strange, I thought, that a girl like Lucy, who could have had any man she wanted, had chosen the very plain David to be her husband. And that they were so mad about each other.

"He's great to work with," she said. "We don't live in each other's pockets. I do all the administration and he does everything else. He sits in his office, I answer the phones so I don't see him all the time, but it's great. People say that husbands and wives find it difficult to work together, but it's perfect for us."

"That's wonderful," I said.

"We just seem to match so well," she said. "He complements me and I complement him."

"Lucky you."

"He never loses his temper, he's always appreciative of whatever I do."

"What a paragon," I murmured.

"Jane!" She looked at me quizzically. "Are you being a touch sarcastic?"

I blushed. "I suppose so," I said. "Sorry."

The waitress returned with our drinks, which saved me from having to explain myself to Lucy straight away. When the girl had left Lucy looked at me, hurt in her eyes.

"So why be nasty?" she asked.

I didn't meet her gaze. I looked out the window at the juggler who was now throwing flaming torches. I was fighting with myself, not knowing exactly what I wanted to say to my friend.

"Jane?"

I looked across at her and picked at my nails, a habit I'd never managed to break.

"I think Rory and I are going through a bit of a difficult patch," I said finally. It was the first time I'd admitted this, even to myself. I was horrified to find that my voice was shaking.

Lucy didn't say anything to me. She took a sip of her Coke and regarded me thoughtfully. I pulled the petals off the carnation in the little vase on the table.

"How difficult?" she asked finally.

I twirled a lock of hair around my fingers. I was afraid to speak in case I would cry.

Our burgers arrived. I loaded some mayonnaise on to the side of my plate and shook salt and vinegar liberally onto my chips.

Lucy was silent, waiting for me to speak. I coughed a couple of times.

"Not too difficult," I said eventually. "But it's getting to me a bit."

Lucy popped a chip into her mouth. "It's hot," she

gasped, her eyes watering. "What exactly is the problem?"

"He's out a lot," I said. Then it all came flooding out. He enjoyed being at work more than being at home, he loved going for a pint with the lads, he spent nearly every Saturday playing golf, he'd spent half the summer in Italy watching football. I was a drudge, a bore, a dullard. We'd spent a great weekend away in Kenmare a couple of months ago, but it had been downhill all the way from then.

"Why do you think this has happened?" asked Lucy.

I wiped the tear from my eye. "I don't know."

"Maybe it's a temporary thing," said Lucy. "You know, like the seven-year itch."

"We've been married for eight years," I said bitterly. "Oh, Lucy, I don't know what's wrong, exactly."

"Has everything always been OK until now?" she asked.

I chewed the inside of my lip. "Sort of."

"What d'you mean, 'sort of?"

"We had a bit of a dodgy run when I was pregnant," I told her. "But once Clodagh was born, everything seemed to get back to normal again. I don't think it's deliberate, Lucy; I think he just feels that once he brings home the money, then that's enough."

"It's not enough," said Lucy.

"You've never liked him, have you?" I asked.

There was an uncomfortable silence while Lucy debated what she should say to me. She had never criticised him in front of me before, but I knew that David and she must have talked about him. I could still hear David's comments of the night of my birthday.

"I think he's very self-centred," said Lucy. "Maybe not intentionally, but self-centred all the same."

I didn't like to hear this from her. I wanted her to say that her marriage was the same as mine and that there was nothing even slightly strange about Rory's behaviour. That all men were self-centred. But she didn't. She just looked uncomfortable.

"I'm probably a bad person to ask," she said. "I'm so bloody happy with David that it colours my judgement."

"What about Eric?" I asked. "How did you feel when it started to go wrong with Eric?"

"Eric was different," Lucy told me. "I never really loved Eric."

She'd lived with him for over two years. She must have loved him.

"Come on, Lucy," I said.

"Seriously," she said. "I didn't love him. I fancied him like crazy; you know I always have had a thing about French men since Étienne, and I was certainly besotted by Eric, but I don't think I ever loved him. Not in the way I love David."

I sighed. "So, what made you decide to split up with Eric?"

"Well, because of Chantalle," Lucy reminded me. "He was two-timing me."

I wondered if it could be possible that Rory was two-timing me. I didn't think so, he wouldn't have the time. I was pretty sure that he told me the truth about where he was most of the time, and I never got the impression that there was another woman. He was far too interested in blokeish things. No, whatever else Rory was doing, he wasn't having an affair with someone else.

"What about going back to work?" asked Lucy. "You've been thinking about that for a while. Have you got any further with it?"

I told her about the interview with the bank. I'd expected to hear back from them before now and their silence was ominous. I supposed that I was out of date for working with a bank now, that things had changed dramatically over the last few years and that it would take too long to retrain me.

"Besides," I continued to Lucy, "Rory keeps harping on about another baby."

"Jesus, Jane," said Lucy, "what do you think about that?"

"You know how I feel," I said. "I don't want one yet. I know that women are meant to get over the pain instantly, but I can't get over the terror I felt and I'm not ready. Some day, I hope. Really, I do – I'd like Clodagh to have a brother or sister, but not yet."

"Have you talked to Rory about it?"

"I don't talk to Rory about anything," I said abruptly. "We talk about things but neither of us is listening to the other one." I sighed deeply. "I suppose I'm as much to blame, Lucy, I don't try to understand him."

Lucy looked doubtful. "Maybe he's not the understandable type," she said.

I dipped a chip into some mayonnaise and ate it slowly. "Why doesn't it work out like you expect?" I asked. "All I ever really wanted was to be married and have a family and live happily ever after. Nothing more than that. I expected to have a job, because we always had jobs in our family. I expected that my job wouldn't be as exciting as my husband's but that I'd enjoy it, anyway. I thought I'd have a couple of children and that childbirth would be simple. I thought I'd lead a normal life, Lucy."

"You probably are leading a normal life," said Lucy. "How many women are truly happy?"

"You're truly happy." I made it sound like an accusation.

She looked abashed. "I know," she said. "And I'm really lucky. But then I was happy when I didn't have boyfriends either, Jane. I enjoyed myself a lot as a single person. Actually, the only times I was truly unhappy was when Nick told me his wife was pregnant and when I caught Eric cooing to Chantalle on the phone."

I laughed. Lucy smiled at me. "I'm glad to see you laugh, anyway."

"You've cheered me up," I said. "I guess I'm going through a phase. Not exactly happy with everything, but a damn sight luckier than most."

"It's funny, isn't it," said Lucy, "how women only gauge their happiness by how well their relationship is going. Men can be happy no matter what, but with most women it's different."

"Except for you," I pointed out.

"I'm a lot happier now than I was before I met

David," said Lucy. "It's a whole different plane of happiness."

"You're a happy sort of person," I said. "You were always the optimistic one. I think I'm the sort of person who thinks the glass is half empty, not half full."

"You need to get out and have a good time," Lucy told me. "And I know what we should do."

"What?" I asked.

"We'll go to a fortune-teller," said Lucy. "Then you'll be able to see the light at the end of the tunnel."

I'd never been to a fortune-teller before, and I didn't think it was a very good idea. What if she told me something absolutely dreadful?

"It's a bit of fun," said Lucy. "We used to do it all the time in France. There was this girl, Simone, she was brilliant. It was on her advice I took the job back in Dublin."

I couldn't believe that Lucy would do anything as important as changing jobs simply on the say-so of a fortune-teller. I looked at her in blank amazement.

"I didn't think you believed in that sort of rubbish," I said sternly.

"I don't." Lucy spooned more mayonnaise on to her plate. "Well, not exactly. Sometimes they tell you useful things but mostly it's for a laugh."

"And do you know one here?"

She nodded. "I've gone to her. I went before my wedding. She's a Belgian woman who lives in Sutton. She's very good."

"Oh, Lucy!"

"Seriously, Jane. She told me that I'd have a long and happy marriage with the man of my dreams."

"Oh, for goodness sake!"

"I've been married for nearly four years and it is happy," said Lucy. "So she was right."

"Did she also tell you that the man of your dreams would be tall, dark and handsome?" I teased.

Lucy grinned. "No, but she said that he would build me my home."

Lucy and David's house in Howth was still under construction.

"How long was this supposed to last?" I asked.

"Unfortunately she didn't give a deadline," sighed Lucy, "but she was right."

I was still doubtful about going to a fortune-teller. I was afraid that my future would hold something terrible and I felt that I could cope with it better if I didn't know about it. I could see Lucy's charlatan making up some horrible story that would actually come true. How could anyone who had been educated by the nuns believe in fortune-telling? Anyway, the Belgians were hardly the sort of people who were fortune-tellers, I thought. If Lucy had said that this woman was Romanian or Hungarian I might have had more faith in the enterprise.

All the same, I agreed to go and see her. Lucy arranged appointments for us the following week and I told Rory that he'd have to be home early, because I was going out with Lucy and somebody had to mind Clodagh.

"You're always going out with that bloody woman," said Rory. I could hear the buzz of the dealing room behind him, someone was shouting "at thirty, at thirty," at the top of his voice. "Hold on," Rory said. I heard him shout, "ten done," and then he was back to me. "I'm very busy," he told me. "I'm not sure what time I can make it."

"I'm meeting Lucy at seven o'clock," I told him firmly. "You'll have to be home by half past six. Surely you're not so indispensable that you can't make it home early one day out of five?"

He gave in, with ill-grace, but gave in all the same. I was in a frenzy, worrying whether or not he would really make it home on time because I didn't trust him not to decide to go for a pint anyway, but I heard the car pull into the driveway at twenty-five to seven and I breathed a sigh of relief.

Clodagh was already bathed and in her pyjamas. She looked good as gold with her hair and skin gleaming and clutching her Enid Blyton book for Rory to read to her.

He swung her into the air and told her that she was wonderful, then asked me what I'd made for dinner.

I hadn't done anything, I told him, but there were plenty of microwave meals in the freezer and all he had to do was heat one up. He looked at me as though I'd lost my head, but just told me to have a good time and not be too late home. His comments reminded me of my mother. I told him I'd be a good girl and then kissed him on the head. His hairline was receding, I noticed. A few years ago, that kiss would have been planted in his hair, now his forehead was much higher. I'd only noticed tonight how much his hair was thinning.

Lucy's house was just before Howth, overlooking the sea. The entire house had fallen into total disrepair before the Norrises had bought it, and it was currently held together by scaffolding and plastic sheeting. I parked carefully in the driveway, out of range of falling masonry, and tooted the horn. Lucy came to the doorway.

"Come on in," she called, "it's perfectly safe."

I didn't like to disagree and picked my way carefully across the garden.

"It's perfectly safe," repeated Lucy. "We wouldn't be living in it if it wasn't."

The only habitable rooms were the kitchen, David's office and the bedroom. I looked around at the half-built walls and didn't envy them.

David was sitting at the kitchen table, architect's drawings open in front of him.

"Hi, Jane," he said absentmindedly.

"Hello, David." This man disapproved of my husband. I liked him very much but it was hard for me to be civil to him.

"Have a good time," said David, as he looked up at Lucy.

"Thanks, darling." She gave him a kiss on the lips and he responded to her. I turned away and gazed out at the garden.

Lucy and David had a much longer garden than Rory and I. The lawn stretched back towards the sea and was bathed in evening sunlight. It would look lovely when the house was completely renovated and the garden cultivated.

"The garden is the last on my list," said Lucy when I told her this. "What I want is to be able to go from room to room without finding bits of plaster in my hair."

I drove to Mrs Vermuelen's house, directed by Lucy. I still had no faith in the ability of a Belgian woman to divine my future.

"She's very strict about her clientele," Lucy told me. "She sees people only by appointment and only through personal referrals."

"Who referred you?" I asked.

"The personnel manager in my last company," said Lucy.

It seemed extraordinary to me that such a range of people went to fortune-tellers.

"What does she do?" I enquired. "Palms, tea-leaves, cards?"

"Tarot cards," said Lucy.

"I don't see how cards can tell you anything," I said. "It's pure chance which card turns up."

"Exactly," said Lucy. "Chance and fate."

We rang the doorbell. I was surprised to feel my heart thumping in my chest. Would this woman have anything worthwhile to tell me? She'd probably get it all wrong, anyway. I'd taken off my wedding and engagement rings and left them at home. I wasn't going to give her any clues.

A girl aged about seventeen opened the door.

"Have you come for fortunes?" she asked in a bored voice.

Lucy nodded and the girl showed us into a waiting-room. "She's the daughter," Lucy explained. I grunted. The daughter obviously thought we were idiots.

There was another woman sitting in the waiting-room, reading a magazine, for all the world as though she was sitting in a dentist's surgery.

I picked up a copy of *Hello!* and skimmed through the pages, examining pictures of Princess Diana looking absolutely miserable, Jane Seymour showing off her home and the latest Valentino fashions.

Lucy went in first. I continued to read the magazines and wondered what on earth Mrs Vermuelen could have to tell me. It'll all be mindless mumbo-jumbo, I thought. I should have stayed at home and saved my money.

Finally Lucy emerged, smiling, and told me to go ahead in. I shook my head in disbelief at myself and walked through the doorway.

I'd expected that the room would be dark and that there would be astrological pictures all over the place. But, in fact, it was a very ordinary room with a pale blue carpet, cream walls and blue curtains. The only concession to the paranormal was a beautiful chart of the Zodiac which hung on one of the walls.

"Hello," said Mrs Vermuelen as she looked searchingly at me.

She was about fifty, a dumpy, matronly woman with salt-and-pepper hair and bright green eyes. She didn't look in the slightest bit like a psychic. I smiled at her. Even if she was going to take my money under false pretences, it was difficult not to warm to her.

She stared at me in silence for a while, keeping her hands on her cards. Then she smiled.

"What is your name?" she asked.

"I thought you were working that out," I said facetiously.

"No," she said.

"It's Jane," I told her. I wasn't impressed. I didn't think she'd need to know my name.

"OK, then, Jane," she said. "I will do a reading for you. I want you to shuffle the cards."

I stifled the urge to giggle. It was all so silly. I shuffled the cards and handed them back to the fortune-teller. I couldn't believe I was doing this.

She began turning them over, talking to me in a matter-of-fact voice.

"You are an only child," she said. I looked at her in surprise. "You come from a happy home." Well, yes, I suppose I did. "You are married." So far it was probably all good guesswork, although I wondered how she knew I had no brothers or sisters.

She touched another card. "Your husband is a professional man. He works hard." She looked at me intently. "He neglects you." I shifted uncomfortably in my seat. "You are concerned mostly with your home and your husband," she said. "And with money. You are well-off." Oh, come on, I thought, this is ridiculous. She's telling me stuff that applies to practically anyone. Lucy and I had already decided that women were concerned mostly with their relationships, and she could tell I was well-off by the fact that I was wearing a rather nice Mondi suit. I should have worn tatty old jeans.

She smiled at me. "You are at a crossroads in your life." I looked down at the cards in front of her. They were very pretty, with pictures of events on them. I tried to see the one she was looking at now. It said "The Fool". I nodded my head. That's exactly what I was, I thought.

"You will soon embark on a new chapter of your life," she said. "A totally new situation for you." She touched another card. It showed a tower being struck by lightening. "There will be sudden changes." She looked up at me. "Not necessarily ones you will like. A complete alteration in your life."

Perhaps she meant I would get a job and go back to work. That would be a complete alteration in my life.

She smiled at me. "There are a lot of people in your life," she said. "Mostly helpful to you. But I would advise you to look out for a dark woman. A professional woman. She means you no harm, but she may disrupt your life."

I thought about it. I didn't know any dark, professional women. I knew dark, unprofessional women like Karen and Lorraine, but I didn't think that these were the sort of people Mrs Vermuelen was advising me against.

"A man will feature in your life," she said. "Important. Not your husband."

I shot her a glance. "What way will he feature?" I asked. "Romantically?" These fortune-tellers always expected you to want to know about romance. I bet they thought that once they mentioned a mysterious dark stranger, everyone believed them.

She shook her head. "I do not think so. Not in this reading. But he is there and he is important. Maybe you can encourage him to be romantically involved."

I blushed. "I don't think so," I said. "What sort of man is he?"

She pointed at a card, the King of Cups. "He is warm-hearted, friendly. A cheerful man," she said. "Pleasant. Not interested in money. Loving."

Definitely not Rory, I thought. I welcomed the idea that there was a romantic warm man in my future. Maybe I would have an affair myself. I clamped down on the thought. I was being silly. That was the problem with having a fortune told. You went and looked for things to make it come true. Imagine if I tried to get off with some casual male acquaintance, just because this woman had said a man would be important in my life!

"You will have decisions to make," said Mrs Vermuelen. "You will doubt your ability to make the correct one, but you will. This will change your life and its direction. Things will not continue as they are. There will be some unpleasantness."

"None of this is very encouraging," I said gloomily.

"You will find happiness," she told me resolutely. "You will be pleased with the choices you have made and they will be the right ones. You must not let yourself be swayed by monetary matters."

Easy for her to say, I thought. God knows how much she's raking in every day.

"So I'm not going to win the lottery!"

"There is no great money in your cards," said Mrs Vermuelen. "Although you will not want for anything.

There is a time of reflection, of contemplation. You must re-evaluate things."

I was doing that already, I thought. She was saying all the things I often said to myself.

"There will be a short holiday," she told me. "And a visit to a hospital, but nothing serious."

I wondered did they always tell you about holidays and illness. This was a dreadful waste of money.

"You need to reach into your heart, Jane," she said, intently. "You must decide what it is that you want from life. You cannot afford to settle for second-best."

I smiled at her. "I don't."

"You must find your own happiness," she told me. "There is nothing wrong with wanting to be happy."

For no reason, I felt the sting of tears in my eyes and I swallowed deeply. "And will I be happy?"

"You can be," she said. "The ingredients are there. You must make the correct choices. Not, perhaps, the ones you think you should make."

She told me more, but I forgot it almost as soon as she said it. I was thinking of her words. There's nothing wrong with wanting to be happy. It sounded like something a psychiatrist would say.

Lucy was waiting for me when I came out.

"Well?" she asked.

"I am allowed to be happy," I told her. "I have to beware of a dark woman. I'm going on a short holiday. I've to watch out for a visit to hospital that won't be serious, and there's a warm and romantic man in my life. Oh, and there are going to be dramatic changes which will all work out for the best."

"Wow!" said Lucy. "Sounds OK."

"Do you think so?" I asked. "I'll tell you how I see it. Some dark woman barges into me on the street, knocks me in front of a car. I spend a couple of days in hospital, but return feeling OK. The dramatic change is that I go back to work and my warm-hearted boss gives me the sack."

"Unbeliever," said Lucy. "I, my dear, am a cool-headed business woman who will reach the dizzy heights of success aided by my loving partner. I too will be going on a short holiday, from which I will return refreshed and with new ideas which will earn me a lot of money."

"My fortune showed money to be conspicuously absent," I told her.

"Probably because you're well-off already," said Jane. "Come on, do you want to pop in to the Marine for a drink?"

We drove to the Marine Hotel and took our drinks out on to the back lawn which stretched down to the sea. There was a wedding reception and a bridal couple stood in the middle of the lawn holding hands while friends took photographs of them. They looked radiantly happy. Her dress was traditional, long and pure white, and she wore an equally traditional long white veil. He was in morning suit. They gazed into each other's eyes.

Rory and I had looked into each other's eyes like that on our wedding day. I hadn't been able to keep my eyes off him and he hadn't been able to keep his hands off me.

We stayed until the sun had slipped down behind the water and then I drove Lucy home.

"Off you go and earn lots of money with your dazzlingly brilliant husband." I smiled at her.

"Off you go and pursue happiness," she smiled back.

"Meet you for lunch again in a couple of weeks?" I asked.

She nodded. "Give me a call. We'll see how Mrs Vermuelen's predictions have worked out."

She got out of the car and let herself into the house. I drove back to Dún Laoghaire, across the tollbridge and along the coast. I thought about my fortune and laughed nervously to myself because, even though I didn't believe it, I was worried about the sudden changes that Mrs Vermuelen predicted. Changes I might not like? I thought of all the changes I might not like but couldn't think of anything awful. And this dark, professional woman. Was that Claire Haughton, I wondered, and, if so, why would she harm me? And what about a holiday? Maybe Rory would bring me for a surprise weekend away. Paris, perhaps, or Rome. He'd done that a couple of times when we were first married. The hospital bit was worrying. I was a bit of a hypochondriac, although living with Rory had half-cured me. I realised that men never got colds, they got flu, and they never got indigestion, they had heart attacks. Listening to him complain had made me realise that occasional twinges meant nothing. All the same, I didn't like the idea of having to visit a hospital. I hated hospitals. But she said it wouldn't be serious. I shook my head. It was all gibberish! A loving stranger would be nice, all the same, I thought wistfully, as I turned into the driveway. But I didn't need a loving stranger, I had a husband. And I was going to make sure he knew I loved him tonight. I shook back my hair, straightened my shoulders and went inside the house. Rory had fallen asleep on the sofa, a tin of beer on the floor beside him and the newspaper on his head.

I sighed deeply. Romance doesn't last forever, I told myself as I tidied up around him. And he'd probably had a hard day.

24

August 1990

(US No. 2 – If Wishes Came True – *Sweet Sensation)*

I was spraying the roses in the back garden when Claire Haughton peered over the top of the dividing wall. I jumped back in shock. I was wearing my Walkman and singing along to *Queen's Greatest Hits* so I didn't notice her until I casually looked up. I switched off the tape and slipped the earphones from my ears.

"You scared the life out of me," I said.

"Sorry about that," said Claire. "Are you busy, can I pop in for a second?"

"Of course." I expected her to come around to the front door. Instead, there was a scrabbling sound and Claire swung her leg on to the wall. She pulled herself into a sitting position on top of it and then dropped lightly into my garden.

"Good God," I said, "that was very athletic."

"I work out in the gym," said Claire. "It's the least I can do."

"I work out, too," I told her, "but I haven't put it to such practical use." I put down my bottle of rose spray. "What can I do for you?"

Claire tossed her hair out of her eyes. "I'm hoping it's more what I can do for you," she said. "Once you don't think I'm imposing."

"Not at all." I was curious to hear what she wanted.

"The last time I was talking to you, you said that you were interested in getting back to work," said Claire. "I was wondering if you'd got a job yet?"

I shook my head. "The bank I went to phoned me up and offered me two weeks' contract work which might or might not have been renewed," I said. "Two weeks is no good to me. I'd have to make alternative arrangements for Clodagh, and it would cost me as much as I'd earn. It's not worth my while. I need something longer-term."

"What exactly is your experience?" asked Claire.

I gave her a résumé of my career. It didn't sound much condensed for someone's benefit, and I supposed that it wasn't much really, but I tried to make it sound more interesting. After all, I'd spent a lot of time on the phone to banks all around the world, surely I could make that sound important when I told people about it.

"So you had a reasonable amount of responsibility," said Claire.

"I suppose so," I said.

"But you can't type or anything, can you?" she asked.

I laughed a little. "Actually, I can. But the thing in

the bank – at least when I was there – was to deny that you could, because then you were sent off to the more mundane jobs. Nowadays I suppose it's OK, because computers are so much a part of everything and people need to be able to use them, but when I started, if you said you could type you were thrown into a typing pool and it was bloody difficult to ever get out."

"So you can use a keyboard."

"I'd be a bit rusty but I suppose it wouldn't take long to get up to speed," I said. I looked at her curiously. "Is there a point to all this, Claire?"

"Of course," she said. She rubbed her nose as though undecided about what she should say.

"Look," I said, "if you know of a job, please tell me about it. I won't say that it's anything to do with you, and if I don't get it there won't be any hard feelings."

She smiled at me. "It's not like that at all." She made her decision. "A few of us are leaving the company where I work, to set up on our own. We'll be providing private and corporate financial services. We need an office manager, someone who can organise us, organise the office, do the paperwork, that sort of thing. If you have computer experience, that would be great."

I looked at her on a rising tide of excitement. This would be ideal. I couldn't think of anything I'd rather do more. But I hadn't any computer experience, not the sort Claire meant, anyway. I was good at computer games but it wasn't exactly the same thing.

"I'd be very, very interested," I told her, trying to sound enthusiastic without sounding desperate. "It would be perfect for me. If I had a full-time job, I would organise something for Clodagh and I'd be able to give my time to the job." I decided that I'd have to come clean about the computer skills. "But I've never used a personal computer," I told her. "I'd need to learn."

She made a face. "It's a drawback, Jane."

"I learn very quickly."

"It wouldn't be a great salary."

"I don't care."

"Never say you don't care, Jane," she told me. "Say that it should be commensurate with experience." She rubbed her nose again. "How about I have a chat with the others and see what they say? I can't guarantee anything, honestly, I can't, but I'll certainly get back to you by next week."

"Claire, that would be brilliant," I said. "I appreciate you thinking about me."

"Oh, we need someone who won't cost the earth," said Claire bluntly. "We can't afford to pay anything great, yet." She glanced at her watch. "I'd better go. I've got a few calls to make." She grasped the top of the wall again and hauled herself upwards. "I'll be in touch," she said and swung back to the other side.

I kept our conversation to myself. I didn't want to tell Rory, in case nothing came of it and he laughed at me for getting my hopes up. I'd asked him to check with the bank again and see if anything was likely to come up, but he'd said that there was nothing yet. It didn't bother me quite as much in the summer, because it was great to be able to be outdoors whenever the weather was fine, but I wanted to have something definite before the end of the year. It seemed to me that time was simply racing by and I hadn't managed to achieve anything yet.

I spent the week in a state of suppressed excitement, which was something I hadn't experienced in years. Every time the phone rang, I hoped it was Claire to tell me that they wanted me to work for them. It was only when I was waiting for a call that I realised how often it did ring. Usually Rory would answer it, because it was normally for him. Now we were practically tripping over each other to pick it up. He looked at me very strangely as I tried to grab the receiver one evening.

"Are you expecting someone to call?" he asked. "You've made a dive for the phone each time it's rung tonight."

"No," I replied nonchalantly. "It does ring a lot, though, doesn't it?"

"People are always looking for me," he said. "The currency markets don't stop moving, you know."

I yawned. I was fed up with the currency markets. I half listened to his conversation as I watched the news.

"No – no – I can't. Well, of course, I'd – yes – yes – you know I do. No – no – absolutely not. Naturally. Yes – yes – yes. Don't be silly. Yes." A laugh. "Yes – no – yes – maybe."

"Funny conversation to be having about the dollar," I said idly when he had replaced the receiver. He looked at me angrily. "Are you eavesdropping on my phone conversations?" he asked.

"No, I'm not," I retorted. "I couldn't help hearing

you. All I said was it was a funny conversation to be having about the dollar. God, you're sensitive."

I flounced out of the room and ran upstairs to check on Clodagh. She was lying in bed, her red-gold hair fanned out on the pillow, her face completely composed, an arm flung out over the bedclothes. I retrieved her blue teddy bear which had fallen out of the bed and tucked it in beside her. She stirred and sighed softly.

Rory was behind me. He put his hands on my shoulders and led me out of the room and into the bedroom. He kissed me, fiercely, on the lips. I was surprised at his passion and excited by it. He slowly undid the buttons on my cotton shirt and eased it from my shoulders. I stood in front of him, glad that I was wearing one of my snow-white bras and not one of the bunch that had gone a murky blue since I'd washed them with a couple of pairs of Rory's navy socks by mistake.

He undid the bra and removed it. I watched him intently. There was a desire in his eyes that I hadn't seen in months. I opened his shirt and ran my fingers through the hair on his chest. He groaned softly and pushed me on to the bed.

Our lovemaking was urgent and demanding. Because we had left our bedroom door and the door to Clodagh's room both open, I'd a feeling of illicit excitement about it and I had to restrain myself from crying out when most I wanted to. We lay there together for a moment, then he kissed me tenderly on the throat.

"You're a wonderful wife."

"I love you," I said.

He closed his eyes and lay across me. He was a bit heavy, but I wasn't complaining.

Claire phoned at lunch-time the next day. I hurried in from the garden when I heard the shrill ring echoing from the house.

"Can you come to an interview?" asked Claire.

"When?" I asked.

"This evening, if possible."

"What time?"

"Five – six?"

I thought about it for a moment. If Rory could be home in time, then I could make six o'clock.

"Where do you want me?"

"Our office is in Merrion Square," she told me. "Could you make it there?"

"By six o'clock," I said. "Sure."

She gave me directions. I would be meeting one of the other partners, a man called Stephen Reynolds. Claire told me that he was very demanding but very fair. She told me not to try and mislead him in any way. She'd given him details of my career, but could I bring a CV along with me?

I was dismayed by that because I didn't have one. I didn't tell her that, of course, but I spent half the afternoon meticulously typing a CV, trying to keep it honest while emphasing all the good things about my career.

I rang Rory and asked him to be home early. He told me that it wasn't possible, that he was supposed to be meeting clients after work. I explained about the interview but he was unsympathetic.

"I'm not trying to belittle you in any way," he said. "But the fact is that I'm earning the money here and you're only doing it for fun. I have to meet the clients, I can't put it off."

"But Rory, this is important to me."

"You'll have to come up with something else," he said. "I can't get home before eight o'clock."

I was furious with him. He was always meeting clients. I couldn't see any reason why he wouldn't defer one meeting once. Or why he couldn't send somebody else. In the early years of our marriage, he told me that he had to go to all the meetings because Graham or Bill couldn't go, and he wanted to do anything they wanted so that he would be noticed and get promotion. Now he was a senior member of the dealing-room staff, but he was still the one who met the clients.

I didn't know what to do about Clodagh. It wouldn't do to turn up at an important interview carrying my daughter. I rang home, but Mam was obviously at work and the number rang and rang without anyone answering. I thought about Lucy but I couldn't ask her to look after Clodagh, she was working herself even if she was at home.

Finally I rang Triona's house. I remembered that she had a younger sister and, even though it was a complete off chance, thought she might be able to help. Triona was so good and so competent, I thought that any sister of hers would be good enough for me. Her mother answered the phone and said that Pat would be home in half an hour and she'd get her to give me a ring. It would have to do, I thought. If the worst came to the worst I would turn up with Clodagh, although I couldn't see that it would help my chances of getting the job.

When the phone rang at half past four I raced to answer it.

"This is Pat," said Triona's sister. "I believe you're looking for a baby-sitter."

I told her the situation, that I would need her for a couple of hours. I'd pay her the flat rate, I said, all she had to do was keep an eye on Clodagh. She said it was no problem, she'd be here by five. I thanked her profusely, delighted that I was out of a mess.

The next half-hour passed in a frenzy of anticipation. I badly wanted to get the job. I stood in front of the wardrobe, surveyed my clothes and tried to pick something suitable for an interview. Something that made me look confident and reliable. I wasn't sure about a lot of my clothes. They were very expensive, but they were either casual or very formal. I didn't have much in the way of business suits and I felt that wearing a suit would be the best way of looking quietly competent. In the end I decided to mix and match, wearing a navy jacket and beige skirt. I kept my jewellery to a minimum, a simple gold chain, tiny earrings and my wedding ring. Looking at myself in the mirror I decided that I looked the part of an office manager. Not too flashy, not too frumpy. My hands were sweating by the time the doorbell rang and Pat arrived.

My first instinct was to tell Pat that the interview had been cancelled. She didn't look to me the type that could look after herself, let alone my precious daughter. In fact, she reminded me a little of my cousin Declan's one-time girlfriend Ruth. Pat was dressed all in black as Ruth used to, although Pat emphasised the darkness of her clothes by wearing very pale make-up and blood-red lipstick. Her skirt was long, almost sweeping the ground, and she wore black lace-up boots. Worst of all, as far as I was concerned, were the four earrings she wore in each ear and the diamond earring on the side of her nose.

"Hi," she said. "I'm Pat Bannister."

I looked at her without speaking. If I told her to go away, I would be reinforcing my prejudice. She could be a perfectly nice girl. She probably was a perfectly nice girl. But could she be trusted to look after Clodagh?

At that moment Clodagh herself ran into the hallway. She stood beside me for a moment, looked at Pat and said, "Why has that girl got a ring in her nose?" loudly and distinctly.

I couldn't help laughing and Pat joined in.

"Why have you got a ring in your nose?" I asked, as she stepped into the hallway.

"I like it," she said. "It gives me character."

Not the sort of character I was used to, but she was a nice girl. Why did she have to ruin her appearance like that? I kicked myself for becoming so middle-aged so quickly.

"Have you baby-sat before?" I asked.

"Lots of times," said Pat, confidently. "Don't worry, Mrs McLoughlin, I'll take good care of her. Won't I?" She looked at Clodagh, who was staring at her with undisguised interest.

"I should be home by seven," I told her. "My husband isn't expected back until eight but don't be surprised if he does show up. I've left some food in the fridge for Clodagh. If you want anything yourself, feel free. There's some ham there if you want to make a sandwich."

"Thanks," said Pat, "but I've already eaten. I'm a vegetarian, anyway."

Probably accounts for the waif-like looks, I thought, although the pale face was definitely more make-up than natural. Oh God, I thought, please let this girl know what she's doing. I didn't want to leave my daughter in the hands of some loony teenager. But despite the make-up, Pat Bannister's voice was confident and assured and I felt that she had common sense and judgement. At least, I hoped she had.

"Do you know how to use the video?" I asked. "She's got loads of tapes and things if you want to keep her amused."

"We'll be fine, Mrs McLoughlin," said Pat. "It's only for a couple of hours. I can cope. Please don't worry."

"How old are you?" I asked.

"Fifteen," said Pat. "But I'm a very mature fifteen."

I smiled. I remembered being fifteen, too. God, I thought, I'm twice as old as this girl. She probably sees me in the same light as her own mother. I shivered at the thought.

I got into the Civic and backed carefully out of the driveway. I had the address and phone number of Claire's offices in my bag. I hoped that I would be on time.

I was almost twenty-five minutes early. I wondered

should I go into the office straight away, but dismissed the idea. It would look too keen, I thought. So I sat in the car until five to six, listening to 98 FM and practising being interviewed.

The offices were in the basement of a Georgian building. There was no name-plate or distinguishing feature outside and I hoped that I'd got the right place. I was very tense. I took a deep breath and rubbed the palms of my hands against my skirt. I rang the bell.

Claire herself opened the door. I was glad to see a familiar face. She showed me to a small office off the hallway and told me to wait. Stephen would be in to see me in a couple of minutes, she said. I sat in the office, gazing around me, nervously clearing my throat from time to time. It was very quiet. I could hear the occasional murmur of voices and, once, the shrill of the telephone but otherwise it was silent. I coughed and the noise seemed to echo around the room, bouncing off the walls back to me. Why am I doing this, I wondered? I didn't need this job. I didn't need to put myself through this. I desperately wanted them to like me, to think me good enough, but it wouldn't be the end of the world if they didn't. Would it?

The door opened and Stephen Reynolds walked in. He was a huge man – tall, broad-shouldered and heavy. His face was slightly pudgy, with a double chin. But his eyes were clear and direct and looked straight at me.

"Mrs McLoughlin," he said. "Pleased to meet you."

I took his proffered hand nervously, afraid that my

clammy handshake would put him off. But he didn't seem to notice. His grip was firm and determined.

"Come into my office," he said and I followed him meekly along the hallway up some stairs and into another room. Stephen's office was at ground level. It was a small, utilitarian room. The walls were beige, without any pictures or charts and the only furniture was a pine desk, a swivel chair and a couple of computer monitors. He looked around, then went outside and brought back a chair for me.

"Sorry," he said, "we're not up to strength on the equipment yet."

I smiled tentatively.

"Did you bring a CV?" he asked.

I handed it to him. He read through it carefully, taking his time, looking up at me occasionally.

"So you left work after the birth of your child," he said. I thought that there was accusation in his tone.

"I was very sick," I said. "My baby was born early."

For a moment he looked sympathetic. "But you're ready to get back into the workforce again, Claire tells me."

I nodded enthusiastically. "Absolutely. I've enjoyed being at home, but I'm ready to work again."

I was sure he wanted to ask me whether I was going to get pregnant again but I'd read somewhere that it was discriminatory to ask women that. He didn't risk it.

"You don't have PC experience," he said.

"No. But I'm ready to learn," I told him.

He leaned back in his chair and looked at me. "I'm sure you are, Mrs McLoughlin. But I can get plenty of school-leavers who are already computer literate."

I took a deep breath. "I'm sure you can, Mr Reynolds," I said. "And I know that there are hundreds of people looking for a job. But I'm ready to work hard to help this company do well. I'm experienced at dealing with people, and I have got mainframe computer experience, so I'm not entirely computer illiterate. I think I could be an asset to you, if you'll give me the chance."

I was proud of the way I managed to say all this without letting my voice quiver with the timidity I felt.

"That's very ambitious of you," he said.

"I'm not ambitious in the sense that I want someone else's job," I said. "But I'm a quick learner and I know I can do this. I'm prepared to go on a computer course to learn enough to be able to cope. I'm prepared to do that in my own time."

"At your own expense?" He lifted an eyebrow.

I thought about it for a moment. "I'll pay for the course if you reimburse me after six months' work," I said. "If I haven't worked out by then, well, I'll never work out. If I have, then it would be only fair to pay for the course."

He laughed then. "You seem shrewd enough, anyway. If we offer you a job, when can you start?"

"I have to organise something for my child," I said. "I haven't done that yet, but I suppose it would only take a couple of weeks. Anyway, if you want me to do anything in the evenings I'd be happy to take work home until I can start here."

"What do you think is a fair wage?" he asked.

I didn't know what to say to that. I mentioned my last salary at the bank, wondering whether that was incredibly high or incredibly low. It was higher than they were prepared to offer me, but not much. When I thought about it a bit more, I realised that my salary was exactly one fifth of what Rory had earned last year. Not including his bonus.

Stephen Reynolds stood up. "I'll send you a letter confirming what we've said," he told me. "I'd like you to start the first week of September. That should give you enough time to organise yourself. If there's anything I need you to do in the meantime, I'll give you a call. If you can organise yourself to attend a computer course, then do it. I don't think it need take you that long. One or two days usually does it." He extended his hand again. "Welcome to Renham Financial."

"Thank you," I said. I was dizzy with the speed of it all. When I'd gone for an interview with the bank for my first job it had been weeks before I'd heard back from them, and that was to tell me that I was on a panel from which vacancies would be filled. This man had just offered me a job on the strength of my cobbled-together CV and a fifteen-minute interview.

I walked on air to the door. I didn't see Claire Haughton but I wanted to hug her. What a wonderful person, I thought, floating back to the car. Imagine, one little conversation with her had changed my whole life.

Suddenly the fortune-teller's words came back to me. That there would be changes in my life, not necessarily pleasant, but necessary. The interview hadn't been particularly pleasant but it had been necessary. And I'd done well at it. I was so pleased with myself. All this time, I'd been scared of trying to get a job again because I knew that things had changed and I was afraid that my qualifications were out of date. But they weren't. And once I'd done a computer course, I'd be back on top in no time.

I didn't even care that the traffic around Merrion Square was so awful that it took me nearly forty minutes to get home.

Pat and Clodagh were playing in the garden when I let myself in. There was no sign of Rory yet but it was only seven o'clock. I walked out to join the girls.

"Guess what," said Clodagh. "We're playing princesses."

"Are you?" I waved at the hair-band made of tinfoil in her hair. "Is this your crown?"

"No," she said, derisively. "It's my tiara."

I stifled a giggle and turned to Pat. "I hope she behaved herself."

"Oh, she was an angel," said Pat, who was flushed under her white make-up. "She did exactly what she was told all the time, didn't you, my little princess!"

"Of course. Because I'm good," stated Clodagh.

"You're very good," I said. "But now it's time for you to have your bath and go to bed."

"I don't want a bath. I want to play with Pat."

"Pat has to go home now," I told her. "You have to have your bath."

She looked mutinous but gave in. I paid Pat and thanked her for coming at such short notice.

"No problem," she said. "Any time. She's a great kid."

Rory's Mercedes turned into the driveway as Pat walked down it. He got out of the car, briefcase in his hand and looked at her in amazement. She smiled at him, waved at me and walked down the road.

"Who on earth was that?" he asked, as he stepped into the hallway.

"Pat Bannister," I told him. "Triona's younger sister. She was baby-sitting."

"Baby-sitting?" he queried. "Why should she be baby-sitting? How come you let a girl like that look after Clodagh?"

I looked at him in exasperation. Surely he could remember that I'd been to an interview. I'd assumed that he was home a bit early because he was interested. Obviously, I was wrong.

"She minded Clodagh while I went to my interview. And she's not 'a girl like that'! She seems to be a very nice, capable young lady," I said.

"Looked like a total spacer to me," he said. "Is she on drugs or anything, do you think?"

I held my temper. "Don't be stupid," I said. "Why are you home already? You're early."

"Clients didn't turn up." He sat down on the sofa and turned to the TV page in the newspaper. I nearly screamed with annoyance.

"So you could have been home at five, after all?"

"I didn't know they hadn't turned up until a few minutes ago," he said. "I wouldn't have been able to leave earlier. What's for dinner?"

I stared at him in disbelief. "I haven't had time to

do anything yet," I said. "I didn't know if you'd want dinner or not. You could have been eating with your bloody clients. And how could I make dinner when I was out getting a job?"

He stopped looking at the paper and looked up at me instead.

"You got a job?" he asked, amazement in his voice.

"Don't sound so surprised," I said. "Why shouldn't I have got a job?"

He didn't answer that part. "So what about Clodagh?" he asked.

"Maybe you'll have to give up your job to mind her," I retorted.

He laughed. "Why, what are they paying you?"

I told him and he laughed again. "You won't have enough to cover her child-care expenses."

"She's going to school next year," I said. "That's not the point."

"You'll still have to get someone to look after her in the meantime. And school will finish much earlier than you, I suppose. I think you're being very silly, Jane."

"I'm not being silly," I said. "I'm doing something I've wanted to do ever since I left work."

"I just don't understand you," Rory sighed. "You never particularly liked the bank when you were there, but as soon as you gave it up you'd swear that it was the most important thing in your life. Well, I have to remind you that your child is the most important thing in your life, and you should be a bit more responsive to her needs."

I looked at him wordlessly. I couldn't think of anything to say.

"It's not as though you need the money," he continued. "You have everything you could possibly want. I never scrimp or tell you that there isn't enough. So I can't see why you can't be like Karen or Lorraine and be content with what you have."

"Because I wasn't brought up like that," I said, perilously close to tears. "Because I want to earn my own way, like my own friends."

"Like Lucy and those dyke twins," said Rory.

"Brenda and Grace are not dykes," I snapped.

"Bit odd, don't you think?" said Rory. "Both of them over thirty and unmarried. From what you say, hardly ever a boyfriend."

"They've had boyfriends," I said. "But they're twins. And even if they were dykes," I added, "that's no reason to be snotty about them. Karen and Lorraine buy things in their shop."

"Karen and Lorraine are lovely girls," said Rory. "But sometimes they take friendship a bit far."

"They don't shop in Les Jumelles because of me," I shouted. "They shopped there before they knew us. So it's nothing to do with us or you or me."

I flounced out of the living-room, slamming the door behind me. There was a crash and a tinkle as a pane of glass fell out of the frame.

"Oh, fuck!" I cried.

Rory opened the door and put his head around it. "Temper, temper," he said. "D'you need help to clear it up?"

"No," I snapped as I picked up the pieces of glass. I wanted Rory to understand, but he wouldn't. I wanted time to be me again and not just his wife or

Clodagh's mother. I wanted to be able to say that I was going out for a drink with people from work, even if I never actually went. Surely he could understand that.

"Tell me about your job," he said, in bed that night. So I told him about the interview, about Stephen and Claire and about having to do a computer course.

"And you said you'd pay for it?" he asked, incredulously.

"They'll reimburse me," I said. "Once I'm in the job a while."

He sighed into the darkness. "You're awfully naive," he said. "They'll use you until they can stand on their feet and then they'll get someone else."

I couldn't see the point in them doing that and said so. But Rory only sighed again and rolled over in the bed. I lay beside his sleeping body, unable to sleep myself. They weren't going to use me, I wouldn't let them. Besides, I would be good at this job and I would make myself indispensable. Working at home all day made you good at prioritising things and it made you organised. I would be the very best office manager they could have, and in six months, not only would they pay for my computer course, they would offer me a raise.

I smiled to myself. Maybe I wasn't such a pessimist, after all. And maybe I was ambitious, too. Already I could see myself as some sort of director. I snuggled down beside Rory and tried to sleep, but my dreams were of huge computers, blank screens and the awful feeling that I hadn't a clue what I was doing.

25

September 1990

(UK No. 16 – Listen To Your Heart – *Roxette)*

It took me only a week to settle into my new routine. I enrolled Clodagh in a playschool which she absolutely loved. I was very relieved that she liked it, because the first day I left her I was so utterly racked with doubts that I almost rang Renham Financial and told them that it was all off, that I couldn't possibly leave my child. But she walked into the bright, sunny room and stood there, mesmerised by the coloured drawings and the child-sized tables and chairs, and she was instantly ready to join in. In fact, I was slightly put out at how quickly she adapted. I'd steeled myself for some tears and a wobbling chin. But it was me who felt bereft leaving her, not the other way around.

I felt bad about Triona Bannister, because I would have to find somebody to look after Clodagh each weekday after school and Triona couldn't do that. But she said not to worry, that she could do her other job full-time now if she wanted and that she knew somebody ideal. Audrey Bannister, Pat and Triona's mother, was the new childminder, and she collected Clodagh after school and brought her back to the Bannister house. There were another three Bannister children: Toby, Caroline and Donie, aged ten, eight and five respectively. Audrey adored children, she told me, and was only sorry that she hadn't been lucky enough to have a few more. But (and she whispered confidentially to me) her body had decided that Donie would be the last. She chatted to me non-stop when I was there and I liked her a lot. I was perfectly happy for Clodagh to be looked after by her, especially as she was used to Triona and Pat already. Clodagh loved the Bannister's home as much as she loved the playschool. She liked having other children around her and she was adored by Caroline, who followed her around the house like a mother hen.

"Caroline has Ninja Turtles," Clodagh informed me, one evening. "And she doesn't have to put her crayons in a box."

I was relieved that Clodagh was happy. It helped to ease my guilt.

I told myself that the new arrangement was better for both Clodagh and me. And in a lot of ways it was, because when I was with her I enjoyed her company so much more. Because I wasn't playing with her all day, I was much more prepared to play when I came home at night, even though I was often tired.

The tiredness came from the fact that everything was so new. I'd done a two-day intensive computer course, learned how to use the new products and was pretty pleased at how quickly I picked things up. But it was very different going into the office and looking at a heap of files and hoping that I'd managed to input them correctly into the computer. I didn't have too many disasters, although one day Stephen came in and spilled something on the keyboard which jammed it and I couldn't save any of the work I'd done that afternoon. He didn't want me to leave the machine switched on in case anybody came in and accessed the files, so he insisted in switching it off there and then. I felt sure that there must have been a better way, but I didn't know one at the time and so the following day, when the keyboard had cleared itself, I had to do the work all over again.

Claire was wonderful to work for. She treated me with courtesy and understanding and never made me feel that I owed her anything for finding me a job. She was incredibly efficient and superb with clients. I was awed when I listened to her on the phone. One day, I promised myself, I would be that confident.

My work was mostly administrative, keeping files up to date, making appointments, phoning suppliers, that sort of thing. I didn't have to give any information over the phone although, as I listened to the others, I began to pick up bits and pieces which I stored away in my mind for future reference.

Rory was amused by my work, but grateful for it too. Because I wasn't at home all day, more or less waiting for him to come home, I didn't snap at him or hound him and so I suddenly found that we were having fewer arguments over what time he came home at and where he had been. He was right about one thing, though, by the time I'd paid for Clodagh's school and Audrey Bannister, I hardly had any money left for myself. But at least it was my money, earned by my own efforts, and I was proud of that.

We were sitting watching TV one night – Clodagh had been put to bed – when Rory announced that he was going to the States the following week.

"What for?" I asked.

"Golfing," he said, looking sideways at me to see how I would react.

I wasn't sure how to react. I hated it when Rory went golfing. It was a great holiday for him, but I was left behind to run the house while he had fun.

"Who are you going with?" I asked.

"Usual gang," said Rory. "The lads."

I picked at my nail varnish and managed to peel off an entire strip of red colouring. I sucked my finger and went to get some nail varnish remover.

"When are you going?"

"Sunday."

"I'm surprised the bank can do without you."

Rory leaned over and put his arm around me. "Come on, Janey," he said persuasively. "You don't mind, do you?"

I wriggled out of his armlock and stood up. "What about our holiday this year?"

"We can't go anywhere while you're working," he pointed out. "I did say this before, you know."

I made a face. "I know."

"So you don't mind, do you?"

"I mind," I said. "But I won't try and stop you, if

that's what you mean. Nothing I could say would stop you anyway, would it?"

"If you threw enough of a tantrum," said Rory. "Then you might stop me."

"Really?"

He looked worried.

"Don't look like that," I said. "I won't throw enough of a tantrum. Go ahead, I don't mind."

I didn't mind as much as I thought I would. A week with Rory away would give me time to relax in the evenings without feeling that I had to cook for him or do things for him. When he was there, I always felt I should be providing something for him, but I never quite knew what. It would be nice to do my own thing for a week.

So Clodagh and I dropped him out to the airport on Sunday morning and even carried his clubs into the terminal building. I didn't see any of the others, but Rory said that they'd probably checked in already and were, undoubtedly, propping up the bar.

"Do you want to have a drink before you go through?" I asked, holding Clodagh tightly by the hand to stop her running off into the throng of people.

"If you like," said Rory indifferently.

I scrunched up my nose. "Probably not," I decided. "She's dying to run around the place and we'd never get to sit down in peace."

"All right, then." Rory nodded. "I'll go along through to Departures."

"Come on, Clodagh," I said. "Let's see Daddy going to the plane."

We walked with him as far as we could and then he kissed me lightly on the cheek. "I'll be back in a week," he said. "You have the name of the hotel, in case you need me." He swung Clodagh into the air and she squealed with pleasure. "Be a good girl," he said. "You never know what Daddy might bring home if you're a good girl."

"A present?" she asked, eyes shining.

"Only if Mummy tells me you've been good. I won't bring anything back to people who aren't good."

"I'm very good," said Clodagh very definitely.

We laughed and Rory walked down to the departure gates while Clodagh and I stood at the huge windows and looked out at the aeroplanes. I still loved airports and I loved looking at the planes.

I stepped down from the aircraft. The heat wrapped itself around me as I stood on the tarmac. The silver-grey Rolls Royce slid across the ground towards me. A chauffeur got out of the car and opened the rear door. The man who emerged from the car was tall and dark although there was a sprinkling of grey in his hair, but it was distinguished and not ageing. He was immaculately dressed, an Armani suit and tie, Gucci shoes, Ralph Lauren sunglasses. We stood motionless for a moment and then he ran towards me, abandoning formality as he clasped me in his arms and hugged me.

"I've missed you, Jane," he said.

"And I you."

"How could you stay away so long?" he asked.

"I didn't want to."

I was protected in the circle of his arms. He led me to the car and we sat inside, cocooned from the outside world by the opaque windows. The car sped through the highways, through the streets, to the house.

Whitewashed – they were always whitewashed in this corner of the world. Welcoming, because it was not a mansion, only a small house.

The chauffeur left us and we sat together on the terrace, overlooking the pool.

"Don't every leave me again," he said, taking off the Armani jacket.

"Never," I whispered as I unbuttoned his shirt.

"Mummy, I want to go to the toilet," wailed Clodagh as she tugged at my skirt.

I shook my head and the dream dissolved. What was I at, I wondered in disgust, dreaming ridiculous dreams at my age. Who was this strange man in the Armani suit? At least my taste was changing. When I was younger, my dream men were fishermen's sons. Now they were business tycoons.

This is reality, I thought, unbuttoning Clodagh's jump suit. More useful than unbuttoning imaginary men's shirts.

We visited Mam and Dad on the way back from the airport. Mam was forever complaining that she didn't see enough of us and so she was delighted when we arrived on the doorstep, Clodagh holding a bunch of flowers for her.

Dad was sitting in front of the TV watching *Star Trek*. Mam and Dad had bought a video at Christmas, and Dad was actually very good at using it. Unlike me. I normally managed to record speedway racing when I meant to video a romantic movie. Dad had an impressive library of films he had recorded perfectly. But he'd bought the *Star Trek* video. Being a Trekkie was his secret vice, something that he had never admitted to before. Now he'd come clean and had bought every video of every episode, and drove poor Mam around the bend because he watched them whenever he could.

I curled up on the sofa beside him while Mam and Clodagh went into the kitchen to arrange the flowers.

My parents were a happy couple. Their marriage had grown stronger over the years, they were in tune with each other. They must have had their share of rows, although I didn't remember them.

They didn't seem to need other people, they were perfectly happy in each other's company. Dad still went to the pub on Saturdays to watch football; Mam was content to work in the supermarket, although she said that she would be retiring soon. She wanted to spend more time in the garden.

I enjoyed being at home with them. Clodagh went for a walk with Mam while I watched *Star Trek* with Dad. I'd loved watching it with him when I was small. I'd wanted to do my hair like one of the girls – in an intricate weave on the top of my head. I'd cried when Mam told me she couldn't do it.

Captain Kirk saved the planet and I made a cup of tea. There were milk chocolate mallows in the biscuit barrel and I took one, eating all the chocolate first, then the mallow then the biscuit as I'd always done.

"That's a perfectly disgusting way of eating a biscuit," observed Dad, who bit his straight through.

"Nonsense," I said happily.

"So tell me, where is Rory playing golf?" Dad wanted to know.

"Florida," I said. "Lucky sod."

"Why didn't you go, too?" he asked.

"Because it's a men-only trip," I said. "And besides, I'm at work now."

He looked at me curiously. "Why did you want to go back to work?" he asked. "I thought you were happy."

"Not you, too." I sighed. "Why does everyone think there's something wrong with me because I want to do something for myself? I couldn't stay at home all the time, that's all. I know I should have baked cakes and done domestic things, but I was never much good at it. I missed work when I left."

"Your Mam was the same," said Dad. "Always out working. But there was a difference. We needed the money."

I nodded. "I know it's not like we need the money. But that's not the point. I wanted to earn some of my own, anyway. It's probably very silly."

"You're putting yourself under a lot of pressure," he said. "Having to get up and get Clodagh out and then race home to collect her again."

"She'll be going to primary school next year and I'll have to run around then, anyway," I told him. "Besides, I'm very organised about it."

"Organised about what?" Mam pushed open the door. Clodagh bounded in, her hands full of stones.

"Look what I collected," she said proudly. "Stones."

"Well done." I took one from her.

"Organised about what?" asked Mam again.

"Getting Clodagh out to playschool," I said. "Clodagh, put the stones down on the fireplace before you drop them."

"You don't need to work," said Mam.

"You sound like Rory," I said dryly.

There was an awkward silence, the sort when everybody is afraid to speak for fear of saying the wrong thing. Mam patted her hair and fiddled with her necklace while Dad rewound the tape on the video machine. Clodagh dropped the stones on to the fireplace and they clattered against the marble.

"Be careful," I said sharply. "You'll break something."

She recoiled at the tone of my voice.

"I'm going to work because I need to do something for myself," I said. "Not really because we need the money. Rory understands."

My parents said nothing. Clodagh and I left soon afterwards and, although I kissed Mam and Dad good bye, I was annoyed with them.

We were very busy in the office the following week. Claire had secured a couple of new clients, Stephen was at meetings all week and I spent nearly all my time answering the phone and producing statements. Although there were lots of set-up costs that still had to be taken into account, it looked as if the company had made a profit for the month which pleased everybody enormously. We were in high spirits, joking about being rich, when the phone rang on Thursday afternoon.

"Renham Financial," I said in my best telephone manner.

"Is that you, Jane?" the voice was distorted and faint, the line crackled.

"Yes, Jane speaking," I said. "Who's that?"

"Jane, it's Audrey Bannister."

Audrey! I felt my heart pound. If Audrey was ringing, then there must be something wrong. What could have happened?

"What's the matter?" I asked jerkily.

"Don't panic, Jane," she said. "Everything will be all right. Clodagh had a bit of an accident, that's all. I'm ringing from the hospital."

Hospital. I moistened my lips and felt sick. "What happened?"

"She was playing in the garden and she slipped and banged her head. She's OK, Jane, but she was a bit dazed and she cut herself on the edge of the paving slabs."

"Oh, my God," I said. "Is she conscious?"

"Of course she is," said Audrey. "Honestly, she's fine. But she wants you and I said I'd call."

"I'll be there as soon as I can," I promised. "Tell her I'm on my way."

My hands were shaking as I replaced the receiver. This was my worst nightmare. The others looked at me in concern.

"Is everything all right?" asked Claire.

I looked at the mounds of paper on my desk waiting to be processed and filed. Rory told me that this would happen one day, that I would have to leave the office because of my responsibilities, and he was right.

"Clodagh has cut her head and she's been taken to hospital," I said, shakily. "I have to be with her, Claire."

"Of course you do." She looked at me sympathetically. "Don't worry, we'll tidy up for you."

"I'm terribly sorry," I said. "I know it doesn't look good to rush out like this but – "

"Will you stop worrying and go," ordered Stephen. "There's nothing here that can't wait for a day. Go on, Jane."

I looked at them gratefully and gathered up my bits and pieces. It was a blustery day and my hair whipped around my face as I hurried across the square to my car. Please let her be OK, I begged, turning the key in the lock. Please let her not be frightened. The car misfired and cut out. I tried to calm myself and started it again.

I bobbed and weaved in and out of the traffic, and caused one irate motorist to bang the horn and gesticulate rudely at me as I cut in front of him. I didn't care. It only took fifteen minutes to get to the hospital.

Clodagh had already been stitched when I arrived, and she was sitting on a trolley holding a teddy bear in her hand. When I saw her I wanted to cry, she looked so small and vulnerable. There was a huge bump on her head and the skin was angry and sore. They had shaved a section of her hair so that she looked like a surprised scarecrow.

I ran to her and hugged her. She whimpered a little and a tear slid down her cheek.

"She'll be fine, Mrs McLoughlin," said the nurse. "She was very brave."

"Were you?" I was almost in tears myself.

"Of course she was," said Audrey, who was standing beside the nurse.

"Can she come home now?" I asked.

The nurse said yes, they had checked her X-ray and she was fine. She rubbed Clodagh on the back and told her again how brave she was.

"I'm terribly sorry," said Audrey, as we walked back to the cars. I carried Clodagh who was quietly sucking her thumb. "They were playing chasing and one thing led to another. Before I knew what had happened, she had gone over with a thump. I brought her to the hospital straight away."

"It wasn't your fault." I hastened to reassure her. "It could as easily have happened at home."

"I feel responsible," said Audrey. "She was in my care."

"Don't be daft." Audrey looked so worried that I felt sorry for her. "It was one of those things. She'll be proud of the scars."

"They said that you won't notice it too much once her hair grows back," Audrey told me. "I'm sure they're right. It wasn't such a big cut, just deep."

"Please don't blame yourself," I said. "What did you do with your own children?" I looked around as though they should be in the hospital grounds somewhere.

"Left them next door with Nancy," sighed Audrey, "with strict instructions to sit still and do absolutely nothing."

I laughed. Audrey's children were not the sort to sit still for very long. "You'd better retrieve them," I said. "I'll bring Clodagh home and we can sit down and watch TV together. Can't we, Clodagh?"

She nodded, still sucking her thumb.

"Phone me later and let me know how she is," said Audrey.

Clodagh and I sat together on the sofa watching *The Den.* She still looked very pale. I was worried sick about her. Everyone knew that hospitals were madly understaffed these days. What if she was really concussed or something? I resolved to watch her like a hawk.

Of course, the nagging voice inside my head told me, this would never have happened if you hadn't insisted on going back to work. Clodagh was in the Bannisters' instead of at home that afternoon because of my job. Otherwise, she would have been playing safely in her own back garden. I leant back on the sofa, arms around Clodagh, and closed my eyes. What was the best thing to do now? Should I give up work because it was unfair on Clodagh? Should I pretend that I wasn't overcome with guilt?

The doorbell rang at nine o'clock. Claire stood there, a box of Jelly Tots in her hands.

"I brought these for the invalid," she said as she stepped inside. "How is she?"

Clodagh was still sitting on the sofa but she looked a lot brighter. She perked up immensely when Claire gave her the Jelly Tots.

"My goodness!" exclaimed Claire, "you do look as though you've been in the wars."

"They had to cut off my hair," said Clodagh, proudly "And I've stitches."

"Really?" marvelled Claire.

"And everyone says I'm brave."

"You certainly are," said Claire. She turned to me.

"You'd better take tomorrow off, I suppose," she said. "We can manage for one day."

I looked at her gratefully. "Thanks," I said. "Would you like a cup of tea or anything?"

She nodded and I went into the kitchen to put the kettle on. How would I tell her that I'd probably have to give up work? I couldn't do it straight away, of course, I would have to give them time to find someone else. I felt terrible.

"Do you feel that this is all your fault?" asked Claire as I handed her the cup.

"Sort of," I said.

"It's not," Claire told me. "She would have been playing, no matter what."

"I know," I said. "But, Claire, I should have been there for her. If it had happened at home, then *I* would have brought her to hospital and none of it would have been so terrible for her."

"She seems to have got over it quickly enough," remarked Claire.

"I know," I said again. "But I still feel that it's my fault."

"I hope it doesn't affect how you feel about working for us." Claire put her cup gently on to the saucer. "We like you, Jane. Stephen thinks you're extremely good. We wouldn't like to lose you."

I flushed at the compliment. "Thanks."

"I'd better be going," said Claire. "I'll see you in the office on Monday."

"OK," I walked to the door with her.

By Sunday, when Rory was due home, the bump on

Clodagh's head had subsided. She still had a peculiar lopsided look because of her hair and the plaster, but she had recovered from her experience and she was proud of her injuries. She insisted on going to the Bannisters on Saturday afternoon to show them her wounds, much to my relief and amusement. I'd been afraid that she wouldn't step inside their house again. But she proudly brought me to the spot where she had fallen, looking for bloodstains, and finding them on the paving-stones.

The Bannister children were awed by her plaster and her hairdo. Caroline promised to mind her when she next came over. Toby insisted on showing her his appendix scar, and Donie told her that he'd once nearly had stitches but didn't. He'd love stitches, he said enviously.

"Will you be leaving her again on Monday?" asked Audrey anxiously.

I nodded. "I'm not sure about going on working," I confided. "But certainly for another couple of weeks."

"I'll be delighted to have her," Audrey assured me.

I dressed Clodagh in her favourite jeans and sweatshirt on Sunday to go and meet Rory. I brushed her hair until it shone and tied it back with a velvet ribbon. She preened in front of the mirror, still proud of her scars.

"Come on, Madam," I said, "we'll be late."

I drove Rory's car to the airport because he hated travelling in the Civic. I think he felt that a car littered with childish debris was beneath him.

The arrivals hall was crowded with people but I

saw Rory instantly, standing at a meeting point as he waited for me. Clodagh ran to him immediately and he picked her up and held her high in the air.

"What in God's name happened?" he asked, as he looked in shock at her head.

I explained and he was furious.

"What was that woman doing, letting them play somewhere dangerous?" he demanded. "Clodagh could have been seriously hurt."

"It was an accident," I said, able to be calm myself now. "They were horseplaying, Rory, you know how kids are."

"I know how other kids are," he said. "Rough."

"Don't be silly." I didn't want him to argue about it in front of Clodagh. "Come on, let's go home, we can talk about it then."

I slid a tape into the deck and listened to Clannad. The haunting music soothed me.

I drove steadily. Rory wasn't a good passenger, and he'd draw sharp breaths if I overtook other cars or cut in front of someone. I knew that he was a better driver than I was, so I never tried to compete.

There was a sailing ship on the river near the tollbridge, its white sails neatly furled around the masts, proud and majestic on the water. It was lovely to see, a pleasant change from the usual grey or white painted boats.

I pointed it out to Clodagh who looked at it in awe. "It's a pirate ship," she said, her eyes wide. "Prob'ly pirates on it."

I loved the drive once we reached the coast. I loved to watch the sun on the water and the curve of the bay stretching out into the distance.

When we got home, Rory left his case on the bed while he went for a shower. He said he was exhausted and jet-lagged and that the shower might wake him up. I unpacked his bag while he showered, and wondered why on earth he couldn't learn to fold shirts properly.

Then I went downstairs and made some tea, while Clodagh hopped from foot to foot and asked about her presents.

"You'll have to wait until Daddy comes downstairs again," I said. "I don't know what he's brought us."

He'd bought a baseball shirt and cap for her and she was entranced by them. Predictably, he had bought me a bottle of perfume, *Paloma Picasso,* in its distinctive round bottle.

"Thanks, darling," I said, kissing him.

"No problem," he said.

He asked Clodagh about her accident, but she was getting bored with it by now and her answers were perfunctory. He waited until she had gone to bed later that evening, before quizzing me further about it. There was nothing more to tell, I said to him, she was playing, she fell, she cut her head. There was nothing Audrey could have done to stop it happening, it was one of those things.

He didn't look convinced. "And what about Friday?" he asked. "Did you go to work?"

"Of course not," I said. "Claire said it would be OK to take the day off. Anyway, Clodagh's fine now."

"It wouldn't have happened if you'd been here," said Rory, obstinately. "I still think you should have been."

"Rory McLoughlin, I cannot understand you!" I

cried. "What is so wonderful about having me stuck at home? Besides, Clodagh loves the playschool and she loves Audrey's children and it has to be miles better for her than being stuck here with me. So don't give me that sort of crap."

I could see he wasn't happy but he said nothing. He was besotted with Clodagh, of course. She was the most important thing in his life, and the idea of her being hurt in any way was almost too much for him to bear. But he would have to get used to it; she wouldn't go through life without being hurt. Physically or emotionally. Women are, I thought, as we got ready for bed. For some reason, we always manage to be hurt in some way or another. And being female meant physical pain. I knew, I'd had dreadful stomach cramps all day.

So I was glad that Rory didn't want to make love that night but simply pulled the duvet around him and burrowed under it. The jet-lag had definitely caught up with him. He was snoring before his head even touched the pillow.

I lay on my side of the bed and closed my eyes. Suddenly, I remembered that Mrs Vermuelen had predicted a short hospital visit. Was this it? I wondered, my eyes snapping open in amazement. Had she been right after all? I shivered with fear. If she was right about this, then what else could she have been right about? She'd predicted changes in my life and I'd got a job. She'd predicted a hospital visit, and I'd had one. I shivered and pulled the duvet around me. I was scared and I didn't know why.

26

October 1990

(UK No. 19 – From A Distance *– Cliff Richard)*

The weather had taken a turn for the worse. A screeching wind howled around the office, forced its way through the gaps beneath the doors and wound its way around my legs. We didn't have any central heating in our part of the Georgian building – one of the reasons why the rent was reasonable. Stephen had bought an electric heater but, although it warmed the air, it was no protection against the icy blasts of wind. I shivered as I sat at my desk. My feet were cold, the tips of my fingers were cold and my nose was freezing. I'd forgotten, until I went in to the office that day, what a cold person I actually was.

I blew on my hands to warm them and my fingers flew over the keyboard as quickly as accuracy would permit. I would allow myself a cup of coffee, my third of the morning, when I finished this report for Claire. I was drinking far too much coffee, but it helped to keep me warm.

The phone rang, startling me. It had been a quiet morning so far and its strident tone shattered the peace.

"Renham Financial," I said.

"Hi, it's me."

It was a couple of weeks since I'd heard from Lucy, and I should have called her before now. But I'd been so busy that, every evening after I made dinner, I simply flopped in front of the TV, unable to move. Rory had nicknamed me Couch, as in couch potato, but I didn't care. He wasn't much better, I told him, as he channel-hopped with the remote control.

"How are you, Lucy?" I held the phone between my ear and my shoulder and tapped away at the keys. I was adept at this by now.

"Great," she said. "There's a hole in the kitchen wall, the wind is howling around the house and the plumber has left us with no heating. Otherwise, it's wonderful."

I laughed. "I'm freezing, too," I said. "Our heaters are not exactly the furnaces of hell."

"How would you like to get away from it all this weekend?"

A lovely thought, since it was Monday. "Where to?"

"Barcelona," she said smugly.

"Lucy! Are you going there?" I asked. "You lucky devil!"

"We can both go if you like," she said. "It's only for two days. David is doing a presentation next week for a building he's hoping to design. He wants some samples of a particular ceramic tile and it's manufactured in a factory near Barcelona. It would be possible to get them sent over, but David is terrified they won't arrive in time and he'd like someone to meet the manufacturers, anyway. He can't go because he's meeting people on Friday night and he can't get out of it. So he asked me, and the airline is doing a two-for-the-price-of-one fare over, so I thought maybe you'd like to come."

"Oh Lucy, how utterly fantastic," I said. "I love the way you ask me to go away on unexpected holidays with you."

"This is not a holiday," she said sternly. "This is a business trip. I am an important businesswoman and I expect you to treat me like one. Besides," she added, "my fortune said that I'd be going on a brief holiday – and so did yours. I just thought I'd help it come true for you."

Those damned fortunes! I thought angrily. I'd almost forgotten about them again, now Lucy was reminding me. All the same, it was a great opportunity. Anything to get out of the icebox that was Dublin.

The office seemed to warm up instantly. We chatted for a while longer and then I hung up. I didn't like to spend too long on the phone, and I hated it if Claire or Stephen walked in when I was on a personal call.

They were very relaxed about calls. Claire had casually told me that there was no problem about making them, but that she assumed I wouldn't abuse the privilege. I hated the thought of her even suspecting that I might abuse anything to do with Renham, and I made as few calls as I could.

And I didn't like taking too many incoming calls, either.

I didn't get that many. It wasn't like when I first worked in the bank. Then, friends from other departments, or Lucy or the twins, rang nearly every day.

I hadn't seen the twins in ages. I was getting very remiss about my friends, I thought. I would make a trip to Les Jumelles next week, I could probably do with getting a couple of new outfits for Christmas.

Christmas. I sighed. Once you were halfway through October, you couldn't help thinking of the festive season ahead. Rory had already given me a couple of dates for my diary. The bank always had a variety of functions at Christmas, and wives were expected at some of them.

"I don't suppose you'll be doing that much entertaining in your office," he teased, as I wrote the dates in my diary.

Nobody had said anything about it yet but I didn't suppose we would. Our clients were mainly private individuals although we did have a few companies. I guessed that we would probably send a few bottles of wine or brandy to our best customers. The office party would be a riot, I mused. Claire, Stephen and me. A far cry from the hundreds that made up the bank's office party. Of course, there had been a whole range of events then – the official party, the department party, the section party, the occasional boozy lunch. I sighed for my lost sense of irresponsibility.

Still, a weekend in Barcelona sounded romantically

irresponsible. I hoped that Rory wouldn't get too uptight about it. He hated me going away anywhere without him. It didn't happen very often, certainly not as often as he disappeared golfing, or on business trips, but when I'd spent a weekend in London with Mam the previous year he'd been completely lost on his own. He'd been so unsure of how to cope with Clodagh that he'd spent the weekend at his parents' house.

I managed to get home reasonably early and cooked a chicken stir-fry which I knew he liked, so that he would be in a properly receptive mood when I told him. He tucked into his food happily and then stretched out on the sofa. Once he was perfectly relaxed, I casually mentioned that Lucy had asked me to go to Barcelona with her for the weekend.

He sat bolt upright and stared at me. "Barcelona!" he said. "What the hell do you want to go there for?"

"Because it's a foreign city." I beamed at him. "Because Lucy asked me and because I don't even have to pay for the air fare."

"When would you go?"

"We can get a flight out on Friday evening through London," I told him. "I'll go straight from work. The return flight is Sunday afternoon."

"It hardly seems worth the effort," he said.

I explained about the ceramic tiles and he nodded. "I suppose it's a nice opportunity. Even if you will be rushing around like a mad thing."

"It'll be a break," I said. "I haven't been away at all this year."

"Whose fault is that?" asked Rory, but at least he

had the grace to flush slightly. I didn't even need to mention the World Cup, it went without saying.

Clodagh was wide-eyed when I said that Daddy would be collecting her from Audrey's on Friday, because I would be away until Sunday. She nodded wisely but I don't think that she actually understood. But I wasn't worried about her, because she was so adaptable. It wouldn't bother her in the slightest if I went missing for a couple of days.

Friday was cold but bright. The sky was a watery blue and the wind was still icy. According to the weather forecast, the weather in Barcelona wasn't hugely better, it was 11°. I packed a couple of heavy jumpers in my small case and, full of hope, a couple of long-sleeved T-shirts. I'd arranged to meet Lucy at the airport and leave my car in the long-term carpark.

She was waiting for me as I hurried into the building. I was wearing a pair of black velvet leggings, a creamy-white jumper, black ankle boots and a black leather jacket. Lucy wore jeans, desert boots, a chunky angora jumper and a russet coloured suede jacket. We both looked as if we were in our twenties. Well, Lucy certainly did and I hoped that I did too.

I wasn't scared of flying any more, although I always tensed when the plane started its race along the runway and held my breath for those few moments when it seemed that it would never quite make it off the ground. I leaned my head against the window and watched the lights of the city fall away beneath us before settling back in my seat.

Lucy took out a map of the city. "This is where

we're staying," she said, circling an area of the map. "We'll have to get a taxi out to the factory, it's a few kilometres outside the city. Our appointment with Señor Casals is at ten o'clock tomorrow."

"Is the factory open on Saturday?" I asked in surprise.

"Not to manufacture," Lucy told me, "but he'll be there to show me the tiles. And he'll have our samples ready, I hope."

"Sounds OK," I said. "It'll be something different at any rate."

"You sound as though you long for something different," remarked Lucy.

I shrugged. "You know how it is. Everyday living is so boring. Especially in the winter. Up in the dark, home in the dark, can't get outside."

"You wanted to go to work," Lucy reminded me.

"I know," I said. "And I'm very glad I did. But I'd love something exciting to happen to me, for once. I lead a very predictable life."

"You know the old saying," said Lucy. "Be careful of what you wish for, you might get it."

I laughed. "All I want is a tiny little bit of excitement," I said. "And I'm getting it right now, by going on this trip."

We sat back in our seats, drank our coffee and read through our magazines. The flight to Heathrow was exactly on time, and so was our flight to Barcelona. We'd checked our luggage straight through, so we didn't have to hang around waiting for it in London.

"What's the betting it ends up in Madrid?" asked

Lucy as we fastened the seat belts on the Iberia flight.

I already felt as though I was in a foreign country. The air hostesses offered us Spanish newspapers, and there was a different atmosphere in the plane, a slice of Spain sitting on the tarmac.

We flew uneventfully through the blackness of the evening. When we felt the plane begin to descend, I looked out of the window and saw the pattern of the city below us. We flew in over the buildings and then out over the inky sea to make our final approach.

Barcelona airport was much prettier than Heathrow. It was light and airy with polished marble tiles and a sophisticated decor. As usual, our cases were the last to appear. I'd already begun to panic, assuming that they had, at the very least, been left behind in Dublin.

"Here we are," said Lucy, as her case bounced out, closely followed by mine. "Let's go."

It was surprisingly warm outside. Not the intense humidity of summer, but a balmy evening breeze fluttered through the air. It was definitely a million times warmer than the temperature we'd left behind. We got a taxi outside the airport. If it hadn't been getting late, Lucy would have insisted on the bus or the metro – she didn't believe in getting taxis if public transport would do – but we were both tired and the taxi was a welcome luxury.

"Hotel Galina," Lucy instructed him. *"Avenguida del Paral-lel."*

She couldn't speak much Spanish but she could get by. My own command of the language went as far as *"Dos San Miguel"* (essential for any holiday) and *"Gracias"*. I really should learn to speak foreign languages, I thought, but I didn't have the ear for them that Lucy had.

The *Avenguida del Paral-lel* was one of the long streets that dissected Barcelona. It stretched from the beautiful *Plaza d'Espana* at one end down to the port and the *Paseo de Colon* at the other. It was not one of Barcelona's expensive streets but, according to Lucy who was reading her guidebook, it was a night-time street with clubs and shows.

"I don't especially want to go to a club or show," I said.

"Don't be boring, Jane," said Lucy. "You'll go to whatever we can!"

The Hotel Galina was near the end of the street, a few minutes walk from the port. It was a small hotel, aimed at the business traveller who doesn't want to spend too much money. The concierge handed us the key to our room and waved us in the general direction of the lift.

Our room was a very ordinary, a couple of twin beds, TV, minibar and a small bathroom. The decor was cream and brown and not exactly inspiring, but it was immaculately clean and bigger than we'd expected.

I opened the curtains and looked out of the window. There was a small balcony outside, so I pushed open the patio door and walked out. It was still pleasantly warm. I sighed with pleasure as I felt the heat. There was no view from the balcony as we backed on to a jumble of apartments, and all I could see were shuttered windows and oblongs of light. The sounds of TVs and the occasional roar of a motor-bike broke the stillness of the night.

When we'd unpacked, we went downstairs to the tiny bar in the hotel. There was no one else sitting there, but we ordered a couple of drinks and sat chatting inconsequentially to each other. It was great to be away with Lucy again. At midnight we went to bed, much to the relief of the barman who was probably afraid that he would be left with two drunk women on his hands.

Lucy had set the alarm clock for eight o'clock the following morning and I groaned as it buzzed me into wakefulness. Lucy groaned too, neither of us were morning people. I stepped out on to the balcony while Lucy had a shower. It was still quite warm, although the sky was overcast. Probably rain, I thought, glumly. I hadn't brought an umbrella.

But by the time we had both showered and had a breakfast of croissants and coffee, the clouds had disappeared and the sky was a radiant blue. We stood on the pavement outside the hotel and gasped with pleasure at the real heat in the sun.

"My goodness," I said, "I thought it would only be mildly warm. This is positively hot." I slipped my jacket from my shoulders. "I'll be too warm if I wear this."

But we carried our jackets anyway, unable to believe that it would stay so pleasant.

The factory was, as Lucy said, outside the city. We had to take a taxi. It would have looked very odd to arrive on a bus.

Señor Casals was waiting for us. I'd imagined a much older man, I hissed to Lucy, as he left his office for a moment to get coffee. He was young, in his early thirties, I guessed, and very, very good-looking. He wasn't tall, but he had smooth, tanned skin and thick black hair with only the faintest sprinkling of grey at the temples. He had brown eyes which turned even darker when he talked. I knew that I was looking at him like a teenager at a pop star, but I couldn't help it. He was the most attractive man I'd ever set eyes on. His voice was deep and fluid, his foreign pronunciation of English words adding to its charm.

He showed us around the factory, pointed out the various processes of making the tiles and said that he hoped his designs would be the ones that David Norris chose. Lucy talked about prices and consignments and deliveries to him, and I admired her business acumen. I would have given him the contract simply to see him again.

Really, Jane, I told myself as I watched him, you are behaving like a schoolgirl. But I couldn't help it, there was a magnetism about him which made me want to forget that I was a married woman with a three-year-old daughter.

"This is your first visit to Barcelona?" he asked Lucy, as she finished the meeting with him and took the heavy box of tiles from his desk.

"Yes," she said. "It seems a lovely city."

"Oh, but it is," he said. "We think, the most beautiful city in Catalonia. And in all of Spain, of course."

I knew, vaguely, that the Catalans considered themselves to be completely different from other Spaniards. That they spoke a different type of Spanish and that there had been trouble when they tried to establish themselves as a separate entity from Spain.

"That will not happen," said Señor Casals when I mentioned it. "But it is important for us to be different. Our people are different, our culture is different, our language is different." He smiled. "You must allow me to take you to dinner tonight," he said to us. "It would be a very great honour."

Lucy and I exchanged glances. "That would be lovely," said Lucy, a shade too quickly. I wondered if she found him as desirable as I did.

"I will meet you at your hotel," he said. "I will book a restaurant for us. For nine o'clock."

Lucy's face fell and I grinned. She was still fond of her food – nine o'clock was far too late for her.

"We eat late in Barcelona," he told her, reading her face correctly. "But perhaps you would prefer earlier? Eight o'clock, maybe?"

"That would be fine," said Lucy. "We look forward to seeing you." She dazzled him with a smile. "May we telephone for a taxi from here?"

"Oh, please do not trouble yourselves with a taxi," he said, consternation in his voice. "I will drive you myself."

"Don't trouble yourself, Señor," said Lucy. "We will be happy to get a taxi."

But he would have none of it, and of course we were delighted to be driven back to the hotel by him.

We sat back in the soft leather seats of his car and listened while he pointed out sights of the city to us.

"You will go sightseeing?" he asked.

"Yes," I said, although I knew that Lucy wanted to go shopping.

"You must see the *Sagrada Familia*," he told us. "One day, perhaps, it will be finished, but it is strange to see a cathedral which is so beautiful and so old. And look at our buildings, they are very fine."

He pulled up outside the Hotel Galina. "I will be here for you at seven-thirty," he said. "We can go for an *aperitif* before dinner."

"Wonderful," said Lucy as we scrambled out of the car.

She said nothing until we got back to the room and she put the box of tiles safely at the bottom of the wardrobe.

"Isn't he absolutely gorgeous," she said dreamily. "Wouldn't you run off with him?"

I nodded. "And his voice." I sighed. "Pure poetry."

We sat and drooled for a while and then I told her that we should do some sightseeing, so we changed into our jeans and I pulled on the long-sleeved T-shirt and tied a sweatshirt around my waist. It was actually hot outside now. The sun washed down on to the streets, reflected off the buildings and brightened the pavements. Lucy took out her guidebook and we worked out our route to the *Sagrada Familia* Cathedral.

It was an incredible building, like a sandcastle that was being washed away by the tide. Designed by Gaudi, the four turrets built in his time reached for the sky, topped by their coloured gilt crosses. The other side of the cathedral, where work still continued, mirrored those turrets but in a more modern style. The effect was startling.

We queued up to go inside. We were both amazed when we went through the doors because there was nothing at all inside, only the space which should have been the centre of the cathedral but where no work had yet been done. We walked up the stone spiral staircase inside the turrets to the very top of the building. Twice I nearly fainted with vertigo, but we finally reached as high as we could and stared out over the city.

"How absolutely fantastic," I breathed. Lucy said nothing, equally fascinated by the view.

Lucy wanted to go shopping and so we took the metro back to the shops. She bought some shoes in delicate soft leather which, I informed her, would be totally impractical at home; and a long linen skirt which emphasised her tiny waist. She bought a book on Spanish architecture for David. Fortunately it was English, but she didn't check that until she had already paid for it. "It wouldn't have mattered," she said. "The pictures are enough."

I bought myself another leather jacket, this time in a pale silver grey, and a Barcelona FC football shirt for Rory. I bought a doll and a pretty yellow dress for Clodagh and a box of rich chocolates for my parents.

We strolled along another of the long, wide streets, so that Lucy could take photographs of the incredible wavy buildings that were so much a feature of the city.

"They must have all been on drugs when they were designing them," I said, looking up at a particularly crazy one.

"Probably," agreed Lucy, "but aren't they brilliant?"

The city was timeless. Modern and old, jumbled together in a delightful cohabitation. We strolled down the Ramblas and stopped for a drink, just for the pleasure of sitting at a pavement bar in the middle of October in the warmth of the sun. Cars fought their way either side of the pavement area, hooting impatiently at each other. I couldn't understand why the drivers weren't more relaxed. If I lived somewhere as beautiful as this, I thought, I would never get annoyed.

There were other things I wanted to see, but Lucy started to moan that she had a blister on her foot and so we caught a metro back to the *Paral-lel* and the Hotel Galina.

We had coffee at another pavement bar there, like children unable to give up a special treat.

"Isn't is wonderful?" sighed Lucy. "Can you imagine sitting out in the middle of O'Connell Street trying to drink a cup of coffee now?"

"Not any time," I said. "You'd be killed by the fumes before you froze to death."

Both of us took an age to get ready for dinner. Lucy washed her hair again and gelled it, so that she could plait it into a neat braid which fell to her shoulders. She was a mixture of innocence and sophistication. Her eyes gleamed softly out of her perfectly complexioned face. She wore a black Quinlan Lycra dress which hugged her figure like clingfilm and made me madly envious of a body which had not been subjected to the rigours of pregnancy.

I wore a pale green skirt and matching shirt. It was a pretty outfit, but not as alluring as Lucy's. I brushed my hair into a loose cloud of curls and went a bit heavy on the lip gloss.

We are both being very silly, I thought, as I blew kisses to myself in the mirror.

I looked down at my hands. The diamond of my engagement ring sparkled in the light and the gold of my wedding band glowed warmly. I hadn't thought about Rory all day.

Ferdinand Casals called for us at exactly seven-thirty. A chauffeur was driving him and Lucy and I exchanged surprised glances as it pulled up outside the hotel. Obviously the tile business was doing well, Lucy murmured.

"Did you come to this part of the city earlier?" he asked, when the driver stopped in the old quarter.

Lucy nodded. "We looked around. It's very – ancient."

He laughed. "It is the oldest *barrio* of the city," he said. "There is a restaurant here which I think you will like. But first we will have our *aperitif*."

He led us to a small bar in a sidestreet. It had marble-topped tables with wrought-iron legs.

"What can I get you to drink?" he asked.

We both ordered gin and tonics and he went up to the bar to get them. We looked at him as he stood there in his charcoal suit, impeccably dressed.

"I wish David could look like that," sighed Lucy.

"But every time he wears a suit, he looks like he found it at the bottom of the wardrobe."

"Rory has some very expensive suits," I mused. "But they don't sit on him like they do on this man. God, he's attractive."

We giggled again.

He came back with the drinks and talked about Barcelona and the tile business and his family. He talked in a completely uninhibited way, telling us that he was divorced which was a shame on him and his family. He did look unhappy about it and I felt I should ask him more.

"We were married very young," he said. "I was twenty-one and she was twenty. We changed too much."

"Do you have any children?" asked Lucy.

His eyes light up. "A son," he said. "Andreas. A fine boy."

"I have a daughter," I told him. "She is three years old."

"You look far too young to have a daughter." He lied beautifully. "You look hardly old enough to be unchaperoned."

Lucy and I broke into a fit of giggles which I thought was terribly childish of us, but we couldn't help it.

"It is true," he protested. "You are two lovely ladies."

"Thanks," said Lucy, wiping her eyes. "And you are a charmer."

"Sorry?"

"You try to charm us like birds off trees," she smiled. "And you are succeeding very well."

"I'm glad," he laughed. "I'm having a good time. It's not often I go to dinner with two ladies who are not from my family."

"I'd say you go to dinner a lot with single ladies," I told him. "A man like you must have many girlfriends."

He shook his head. "I have no time," he said. "My business takes so much of it. I wonder which is right, to spend time working or to spend time in leisure? What do you think?"

"If you have money, then you don't have to worry about working," said Lucy, "and it can be leisure."

"But it's nice to do something with your time," I said. "You can't sit around doing nothing."

He nodded vigorously. "And I like to be busy," he said. "It is probably what destroyed my marriage. However," he put his glass on the table, "let us not worry about these things now, but go and have a wonderful meal in La Cocina."

We followed him out of the restaurant and back into the streets, Lucy on one side of him, me on the other. We linked arms with him and I shivered at the warmth of his body close to mine. I didn't recognise the scent of his aftershave. You are an awful idiot, I told myself, as I hurried to keep in step with him.

The restaurant was tucked away behind the town hall, in an old stone building. The proprietor greeted Señor Casals like an old friend, which he was. He used this restaurant a lot, he told us, the cooking was superb.

I don't remember much about the meal. Ferdinand – we were on first-name terms by now – ordered for us, traditional cooking which was heavy and full of flavour. He ordered Spanish Rioja to accompany the food and it was rich and warming. He told us about the city and the people, how they always asked if you were a Catalan and not a Spaniard. His voice was hypnotic and the words spilled comfortably between us.

I wanted to go to bed with him. I'd never felt that about anyone since I'd met Rory. The attraction I felt now for Ferdinand was exactly the same as I'd felt for Rory when I'd first known him. I was ashamed of feeling like this, but I couldn't help it. Lucy was attracted to him too, I could see it in her eyes. Every so often we would glance at each other and a look of complete understanding would pass between us. Inside me, feelings that had lain dormant for years stirred uncomfortably.

I shivered. What had I come to that I was having thoughts like this about a man I'd only just met? Who was nothing to do with me and who I would never meet again? I shouldn't feel like this, I told myself, I should be moved by his attractiveness but I shouldn't feel this slow, burning longing to throw myself at him. And it wasn't love, of course, it was simply physical desire. I understood, briefly, how men could be tempted when they were away on business. I wondered, not for the first time but with a lot more concern, whether Rory had ever felt like this when he was away.

I was sorry I thought of Rory. That made me think of Clodagh, too. Both of them would be sitting in front of the TV. Rory – if he thought of me at all – secure in the knowledge that I would come home from this break having enjoyed myself with my girlfriend of nearly seventeen years. He certainly wouldn't imagine that I was having erotic fantasies about Ferdinand Casals who was, I realised, flirting outrageously with us.

It was great to feel desirable again, though, and that was why I encouraged him. I didn't feel desirable with Rory any more. It wasn't his fault, of course. Time had muted the mad passion but I was amazed that I could still feel the way I did. It was a heady experience.

He brought us back to the hotel and kissed us both on the cheeks. I felt his lips burn against me as though he were branding me. It was hard to break away from him. I wanted to hold him and be held by him.

"I think he fancied you," said Lucy as we undressed for bed that night.

I sat in front of the mirror and removed my make-up carefully.

"Don't be daft," I said. "He flirted with both of us."

"But it was you he concentrated on," she said. "I could tell, Jane. There was a rapport between you."

"There was nothing between us," I said as I relived his final, casual kiss. I touched my cheek I spoke, still sensing him. "But he was some operator."

"He was devastatingly attractive." She slipped out of her dress and folded it neatly before putting it into her case. "Men like that aren't safe to be let out alone."

"He didn't try anything, though." I brushed my hair.

"No," said Lucy. "Just as well."

"Do you think David will like the tiles?" I asked.

"The what?"

"The tiles. The reason we came here."

"I'd forgotten about the tiles," admitted Lucy. "My mind is still full of Ferdinand." She shook her head. "Yes, I think the tiles are fine. But I'd better get David to come over the next time, I wouldn't be responsible for my actions with a man like that if I was on my own. I mean, I'm mad about David but Ferdinand has such a physical presence . . . "

"Just as well I came, then," I said virtuously. "I was able to protect you."

She eyed me dubiously. "Oh yes," she said. "And who will protect the protector?"

I dreamed of Ferdinand that night, a hotchpotch of a dream that included all the men I'd ever known, even Jesse, my first boyfriend. Jesse stood in front of me telling me that I was a wanton woman and that he was going to divorce me, while Rory was the solicitor I engaged to look after my interests. I was disturbed by the dream, it preyed on my mind even the next day as we boarded our flight and left Barcelona behind us.

I was glad to get home to a takeaway pizza which Rory had ordered and to sit beside him on the sofa eating it and watching Inspector Morse on TV.

"Did you have a good time?" he asked, as I cut myself a triangle of pizza.

"Fine."

"Did Lucy get her tiles?"

I nodded, my mouth full. "What did you do?" I asked, when I'd swallowed the food.

"Nothing much. I was out last night, I left Clodagh with my mum. She enjoyed it."

"Where did you go?"

"Nowhere special. Few drinks, that sort of thing."

It must have been nice for him to go out and know he didn't have to face my wrath if he came home pissed.

"Did you miss me?" I snuggled up to him.

"Of course," he said. "Jane! I can't eat pizza with your head in the way."

I sat up again. He was right, of course.

27

November/December 1990

(UK No. 6 – We Want The Same Thing – *Belinda Carlisle)*

November was the month I hated most. Dark, dreary, cold and usually grey, it settled on me like a cloud. The days were still getting shorter, the weather bleaker. I never had any energy in November, everything was a chore. I often wondered what it was like in Barcelona in November, whether the air was still vaguely warm and whether the sun still shone on the crazy buildings. I thought about Barcelona a lot, not about Ferdinand Casals who had been relegated to the back of my mind along with my other schoolgirl crushes, like Bryan Ferry and Eric Clapton, but about the light of the sun, the gaiety of the people, the buzz of the city. It contrasted all too starkly with the driving rain and the huddled bodies of Dublin.

Rory gave up drink in November. Not on a permanent basis, merely to give his body a rest before the ravages of December. The dealers spent

December in a virtual haze of alcohol, with business lunches almost every day and business dinners or drinks almost every night. Usually that meant I saw more of him in November, but this year was particularly busy and he never seemed to make it home before eight in the evening. Then he'd throw himself down on the sofa and close his eyes.

I thought that maybe he was becoming burnt out. They said it happened to dealers. Living on the edge all the time suddenly became too much to handle, and they couldn't keep going. Rory had been living on the edge now for ten years and I felt that it was too long. Even though he'd been promoted, he still traded. Often, when people were promoted they became backroom people, or administrators, but Rory didn't want that. I wondered now if he wouldn't prefer it to constantly trying to outguess what was going to happen in the increasingly volatile currency markets.

I wanted to talk to him about it, but I couldn't. There was something off-key about Rory in November. He came home, sat down, watched TV or fell asleep. He played with Clodagh and he talked to me, but as though he were really somewhere else. I felt our relationship slipping through my fingers, like water in a cupped hand, but I didn't know what to do about it. We were two people living in the same house, each with a private agenda that the other knew nothing about.

We'd have to confront it, I knew, but not now. Not until after Christmas and the New Year. So I struggled though the dank and dreary days of November in a half-world of happiness and misery that I couldn't do anything about.

The bank's annual Christmas party was the first Friday of December. This was not the staff party, but a dinner for the bank's clients which the more senior staff and wives attended. I usually enjoyed it. It was the one bank function that was fun and Rory was always in good form. This year it was in the Berkeley Court and so, the Saturday beforehand, I drove across to Les Jumelles to see if the twins had anything in stock that would turn me into a sex siren for the night.

I brought Clodagh because Rory was playing squash with Bill Hamilton. I remarked sourly that Bill would probably have a heart attack on the squash court – he was just the right age for it and getting heavier all the time. Rory laughed and said that if Bill did keel over he, Rory, was next in line for the job, so maybe it was would be killing two birds with one stone. I liked it when Rory joked with me, it was rare these days. So I didn't mind when he drove off laden down with his kit-bag to beat Bill.

Clodagh was in a dreadful mood, wriggly and contrary. She didn't want to get into her car seat and cried that she wanted to go with Daddy. Her current personality was obstinate. No matter what we wanted her to do, she wanted to do the opposite. She wasn't happy about anything. Her favourite word was "No". I hoped that she wouldn't try to pull Brenda or Grace's beautiful clothes off the hangers or throw a screaming fit in the middle of the shop.

Les Jumelles wasn't the sort of shop where women

brought three-year-olds. It was an exclusive shop, with breathtaking prices which most women seemed quite prepared to pay.

I turned into the carpark of the shop and switched off the engine. Clodagh refused to get out of her carseat.

"Come on," I said, impatiently. "I'll bring you to MacDonald's on the way home if you're good now."

The books didn't agree with bribery, but it was my only weapon. Clodagh got out of the car.

The shop was full. Well-dressed women clustered around the rails of silks and satins, swooped on the best designs and carried them off to the changing rooms.

"Hi, Jane!" Brenda pushed her hair out of her eyes. "It's a bit manic in here today. The party season, you know." She dropped to her knees and smiled at Clodagh. "How's my favourite little girl?"

Her favourite little girl clung to my leg and buried her face in my skirt. I shook my head at Brenda. "She's not in a good mood today. Temper tantrums. Little devil."

Brenda laughed at me. "She's lovely," she said. "Why don't I bring her into the office and she can play with some of the materials? Would you like that, Clodagh?"

My daughter nodded, trotted off with Brenda and left me to rummage through the rails in search of the perfect dress.

"You should have rung and said you were coming." Grace appeared by my side. "I would have put some things aside for you."

"I wasn't going to come today," I said. "I thought I'd another week before the bank do, but I realised this morning that it was next Friday. Anyway, I like milling around like this, it whips up the buying frenzy."

"Anything in particular you'd like?" asked Grace. "Do you have anything in mind?"

I shook my head. "Once I look thin and gorgeous, that's all that matters."

"No problem," grinned Grace. "Let's have a look at the thin and gorgeous rail."

She selected a few different dresses for me, all beautiful and all horrifically expensive. She chose my favourite colours, purple, green and royal blue. But she also included a gold lamé dress with a matching jacket that was different to anything I normally wore. I fingered the material and held it against me.

"I'm not sure it'll go with my hair," I said as I carried it into a changing room.

"Trust me," said Grace.

The dress fitted perfectly and it looked great with my hair. I preened in front of the mirror as I turned around to check how I looked from every angle.

"It's lovely." Brenda peeked in at me.

"I know," I said. "It's so completely different from what I usually wear that I feel odd."

"Buy it," she said.

"Is that your expert boutique manager advice?"

"Absolutely."

I bought the jacket and dress and stood at the desk while Brenda wrapped it in tissue paper and slid it into the exclusive dark green Les Jumelles carrier bag.

"You'll look fantastic at the party," she promised me.

"Thanks." I signed the credit card slip. "We must get together some time soon, we haven't been out in an age."

"After Christmas." said Brenda, "We're up to our necks now. Open on Sundays from next week."

They worked hard for their money, I thought, as I collected Clodagh from their office.

"I'll give you a buzz after Christmas," I told them. Brenda nodded. She was already attending to another customer. Grace called a "goodbye" after me as I led Clodagh out of the shop.

"MacDonald's," said my daughter immediately.

I sighed. "Soon," I promised. "I'm going to buy some shoes first."

Clodagh started to cry. "MacDonald's," she sniffled. "You said."

So I drove back to Dún Laoghaire, joined the throng of people queuing at the counter and bought her a burger and chips. She ate like a horse when she wanted to, but every day her tastes changed and so food that was perfectly acceptable on Monday was hated on Friday. MacDonald's was a constant, though. I was starving myself so we both tucked in to Big Macs and chips.

When we'd finished, I dragged her across to the shopping centre where I managed to buy a pair of shoes and a bag. I was sure that I would look good on Friday. Last year, Karen Hamilton had worn a long multicoloured dress with a deep slit down the cleavage and a deeper slit up the side. All of the men, both from the bank and their clients, had spent the night looking at her. Whenever she took to the dance floor or walked up to the bar, their gaze followed her. Rory had tried to pretend that he didn't even notice her, but I saw his eyes almost pop out of his head when she brushed past him at one point.

My dress would not have that effect, but it was pretty and it suited me. I'd look like a corporate wife.

Pat Bannister baby-sat for us on party night. She arrived at seven, as I was putting the finishing touches to my make-up and Rory was pacing around the bedroom begging me to hurry up. He was meant to be there early because he had to greet his clients. I ignored him and continued to outline my lips with lip pencil before colouring them in with lipstick.

"Why don't you just slap it on?" he demanded, as I blotted it on a tissue.

"Because it lasts longer this way," I told him, filling in the colour again. He sighed in an exaggerated fashion and looked pointedly at his watch.

"All right, all right," I grumbled. I sprayed myself liberally with Dune. "I'll be ready in a minute."

I looked in to Clodagh's room. She was already asleep, tired by her day out, her eyes squeezed shut and her teddy bear grasped in her hand. She was such an angel when she was asleep, I thought, a lump in my throat as I looked at her. I kissed her on the forehead and she sighed gently. I pulled her quilt over her and tiptoed out of the room.

Pat was sitting in front of the TV reading *Hard Times*.

"Still forcing you to read that dreadful book?" I remembered how much I'd hated it at school myself.

"I quite like Dickens," said Pat. "Although I'm not mad about this one myself. I loved *Great Expectations,* though."

"Enjoy it, then," I said. "Although I preferred Arthur Hailey, myself. You know where we are if you need us. There's plenty of food in the fridge if you get hungry. We'll be back about two."

"That's fine." Pat looked up from the book again. "I'll probably go to bed around midnight."

"OK, then," I said. "Goodnight."

I hurried out into the driveway where Rory was already impatiently revving the engine of the car.

"We're late," he said sourly.

"They won't even notice," I said.

The Berkeley Court was crowded with people. Most of them were in dress suits and were with the bank; the bar was crowded, and people thronged around the foyer too. The women were like tropical birds strutting around the hotel in their party clothes. Brightly-coloured dresses stood out among the tuxedos and the black cocktail numbers. I felt gaudy but striking in the gold lamé. I'd been to the hairdressers that day and had my hair pulled into an impressive chignon on the back of my head, secured by a diamanté clip in the side. My height was always an advantage at dressy occasions, I could carry the extravagant outfits well.

"Jane, how wonderful to see you." Bill grasped me by the hand. "We thought you'd never get here."

"Sorry," I said, "my fault. Gilding the lily."

"You look super," he said. "What can I get you?"

"I think Rory has gone to get me a drink," I said. "Perhaps later, Bill."

Not that it mattered. The entire night was paid for by the bank, which meant a free bar for the evening. I was driving home, of course. Rory would drink tonight but I wouldn't. I'd allow myself a gin and tonic before the meal and a glass of wine with it and then I'd switch to Ballygowan. It would have been nice to get blazingly drunk at one of Rory's parties, but I knew that I never would.

"Hi, Jane." Karen Hamilton, looking fabulous in cerise velvet, wandered over and took Bill's arm. "I rather think there's a man over there you want to talk to," she murmured to him and he left us alone. "How's Clodagh?"

"She's fine," I said. "And Gary?"

"He started college this year. Amazing how time flies."

"Isn't it?" I said.

"Clodagh must be staring school soon," said Karen idly.

"Next year," I said. "She's going to playschool at the moment."

"Bill tells me you're working again."

"A financial company," I said. "Small. Nothing special."

"Rather you than me," said Karen.

"I enjoy it."

We made desultory conversation for a little longer, then we were joined by Bill again and a couple of the bank's clients. I looked around for Rory who was chatting to a rounded, bald man who looked as if he might explode out of his tux at any minute. This was the part of the night that I disliked. Rory always abandoned me to talk to someone else and, although I understood his motives, I hated being left with people I didn't particularly like.

Luckily, we moved fairly quickly into the banqueting room. It was wonderfully decorated in silver and gold. A huge Christmas tree sparkled with thousands of fairy lights at the top of the room. Rory steered me towards our table. I sat down at my place and looked at the name beside me. I opened my eyes wide in surprise and checked it again. There was no sign of any of our guests yet, so I asked Rory if they were all particular clients of his.

"We share them around," he told me. "Conor Donnelly will be at my table, he's one of my better clients. I've got Richard Dennison as well, that should keep you happy. And Kieran Woods and Antonia."

I nodded. "And this one?"

"Some credit client. I'm not sure who. He accepted at the last minute and they put him at my table."

At that point Richard Dennison and his wife, Susan, arrived and we shook hands with them. I knew them quite well by now, we had gone to dinner with them a number of times. I liked Susan. She was in her mid-twenties and taught French. Richard was fifteen years older than her, and absolutely besotted by her. They had a daughter a couple of months younger than Clodagh.

We kissed, continental fashion, on each cheek. But with Susan it was a genuine greeting.

"You look great," she said, sitting down. "Love the dress. Where did you get it?"

"Les Jumelles."

"That's where I picked this up," said Susan. "But – I'll let you into a secret here – last January, in their sale. They always have a fantastic sale."

"I know," I said. "I bought some stuff last January myself. But I wasn't smart enough to buy a cocktail dress."

"That is really pretty." Susan looked admiringly at my dress. "Distinctive."

"I'm never sure that's a good idea," I said. "Distinctive sounds like it should be nice but it's a major disaster."

"No, it's nice," said Susan. "Are we terribly early or is there a reason that there's nobody else at this table?"

"I don't know." I fiddled with the cutlery. "I hope they sit down soon. I'm starving."

A crush of people walked into the room, checking the table plan at the doorway and making their way to the tables. Conor Donnelly and his wife, Lisa, joined us, followed by a man introduced to us as Fergal Slattery and his wife, whose name I didn't catch. The final guests arrived a few moments later.

"I'm terribly sorry," said Hugh McLean. "Were you waiting for us?"

"Not at all." Rory stood up and extended his hand. "Rory McLoughlin. I'm with the Treasury team."

"Hugh McLean," he said, shaking hands. "And this is Denise."

Denise was a pretty girl who couldn't have been

more than twenty. She had soft brown hair, brown eyes and a flawless complexion.

"My wife, Jane," said Rory.

I held my breath as he took my hand. "Delighted to meet you," he said. He smiled, a tiny smile that only barely turned up the corners of his lips.

We sat down and the managing director of the bank made a brief speech of welcome. Then the food was served.

No matter how wonderful, the food at a Christmas party is always predictable. The first parties you attend are always such novelties that you don't mind turkey and ham, followed by pudding. After a few years of the same food every year, I'd grown blasé about it. But I was hungry and I tucked in to the paté with enthusiasm.

Susan Donnelly chatted away to me, talking about her daughter and asking me questions about discipline which, given Clodagh's current form, I felt ill-equipped to answer. I replied to her but with only half a mind on the conversation. I was too much aware of Hugh McLean sitting in the seat beside me.

How on earth had he managed to get here? Rory had never mentioned him as a client of the bank and obviously didn't know him anyway. Why did this man keep turning up? He had a power to disturb me for reasons I didn't understand.

He was attractive, but I'd grown out of his sort of attraction. He seemed interesting, but not especially to me. He was kind. I suppose he'd been kind to me. I shook my head, recalling those few days after Clodagh's birth, when Hugh had breezed into my room every day. A most peculiar man, I'd thought then.

I shot surreptitious glances at him as I ate, careful to look at him only when his attention was directed at his companion. I wondered whether she was his wife or his girlfriend. I thought they were talking rather too much for her to be his wife. She wasn't the same girl I'd seen him with at the Park. He hadn't been married, then. No one would have him, he'd said. He looked quite different tonight. He'd abandoned the run-down look for a far more groomed appearance. His shirt was crispy white with a winged collar over a thin black bow tie. His dress suit was brand new, with impeccable creases. The tortoiseshell glasses gave him a slightly distracted look, just enough to stop him looking completely in control.

He caught my eye as the waiters cleared away the soup bowls. I flushed slightly and tried to glance away, but it was too late. He cleared his throat and spoke to me.

"How is your daughter?" he asked.

"You're always asking about my daughter." I folded and refolded my napkin. "She's fine."

"Then how are you?" he asked.

"Fine."

"And your husband is fine too, I suppose?" he said.

"Of course."

"Did you enjoy your stay at the Park?" he asked.

"It was – "

"Fine?" he supplied.

"Very enjoyable," I said. "A lovely hotel."

I picked at a fingernail and looked at the table. I

really didn't know what to say to him. It was like meeting someone with whom you'd an affair. Or so I imagined. But I hadn't had an affair with Hugh, I'd hardly even spoken to him. Why did I immediately feel guilty when I saw him?

The girl, Denise, tapped him on the arm. He turned away from me and talked to her, leaving me sitting staring into space. Susan talked to Rory. I watched the waiters bustling around the room, choreographed by the head waiter. It must be difficult to cater for a huge party like this, I thought, as I played with my name card. There were about two hundred people here tonight.

"Penny for them," said Hugh.

I turned to look at him. "I was thinking that there's a lot of hard work involved in catering," I said.

"I'm sure there is."

I was convinced that he was laughing at me. I didn't know why.

"How is it that you were invited tonight?" I asked bluntly. I supposed I should have been more polite to someone who was obviously a good client of the bank, only good clients were invited to the party, but I didn't see him like that.

"We're clients," said Hugh, simply.

"I guessed that," I said. "I wondered in what capacity."

"In the borrowing capacity."

I nodded. "Rory said you were a client of the credit department," I said. "What do you do?"

He relented. "I own a bookshop. Well, a few

bookshops. I've amalgamated them into a chain. You may have noticed. CityBooks."

"Oh yes." I'd seen one of the shops in Dún Laoghaire. It looked very inviting, period facade and a huge display of books attractively placed in the window.

"We've three shops now," said Hugh. "Dún Laoghaire, Sutton and Rathmines. We're hoping to open more at some point. The bank has lent us the money to do the refits and make sure that the design is the same in them all. Give them the corporate look."

"I've seen the one in Dún Laoghaire, although I haven't been in it," I said. "It looks very attractive."

"Obviously not attractive enough if you haven't bought anything yet," he said.

"I buy magazines more than books." I told him. I felt a complete philistine.

Denise attracted his attention again and he turned away from me. I wished that dinner was over and that the dancing would start. It was very difficult to be trapped beside someone like this. Susan spoke to me and I turned to her gratefully, keeping the conversation going with her throughout the main course and right through the dessert as well. It was easy enough to do, because Susan could talk for ages about the students she taught or about her daughter. All I had to do was to ask the right question and she would be off and running, leaving me to nod and agree with her whenever necessary.

Rory didn't talk to me at all during the meal, but I didn't expect him to. He was working, after all. He swapped golfing stories with Conor, Kieran and Richard which kept them all amused. Sometimes they made a fourball together, so they were close as friends as well as clients.

It seemed forever before the tables were cleared and the band got up to play. They started with some sixties music which had a lot of people up dancing straight away. Rory looked at me and raised an eyebrow in silent query and I got up and started dancing with him.

"Who's the guy beside you?" he asked me as we twisted on the dance floor.

"His name's McLean," I said breathlessly. "He owns some bookshops. He's apparently just got a loan from the bank for refurbishment."

Rory nodded. "I can place him now. Did we meet him before? He looks familiar."

"He was at the Park last Easter when we went down," I said. "You accused me of knowing him."

Remembrance dawned in Rory's eyes. "And did you?" he asked.

"Don't be silly." I spun around him in a flurry of gold.

We sat down after a few minutes and Rory asked Antonia to dance. Hugh danced with Denise, and they laughed happily together.

The band was good. Most people got up and danced. Rory got up with another client's wife. I tapped my foot under the table, even though I was sitting down. Then Richard asked me to dance, then Conor, then finally I sat down again and drank some Ballygowan.

I smothered a yawn guiltily with the back of my hand, then glanced at my watch. Midnight already.

They played some slow music. Rory and his pals were propping up the bar as they smoked cigars and drank brandy. He looked over at me and I smiled at him.

"Would you like to dance with me?" Hugh stood beside me.

"I don't think so," I said.

"Why ever not?"

"I'm tired."

"Why do I get the feeling you don't like me?" he asked.

I looked up at him. "I don't know," I said honestly. "I don't dislike you. You make me uncomfortable."

"Why?"

I looked down at my lap. "I'm not sure."

"Come and dance with me and we can talk about it," he suggested. "I don't like to think that I'm making someone uncomfortable."

"What about your girlfriend?" I asked.

"Denise is my sister," said Hugh. "She's my partner in the bookshops."

I felt silly. He was a client, after all. I stood up.

"I love your dress," he said.

"Thank you."

His hand was on the base of my spine, hot through the thin fabric. Only hot in my mind, because his other hand, in mine for the waltz, was cool and dry. He was a good dancer. I moved with him around the floor.

"So why do I make you uncomfortable?" he asked again.

"Because you met me when I was feeling down," I told him. "And seeing you reminds me of that time. It embarrasses me."

"I'm truly sorry," said Hugh sincerely. "I didn't mean to upset you then. It seemed like a good idea at the time."

"Oh, I was upset anyway," I said. "And you did cheer me up. But I suppose people don't like being reminded of difficult times."

He spun me around. "Why was it difficult?"

"You know why. I told you then. Rory was away, I'd had a difficult birth, I felt – lonely."

"You looked it," he said. "That's why I kept coming in."

"I know. And thank you."

"It was nothing. Denise always says that I like interfering in other people's lives. Sorry if I interfered in yours."

"You didn't," I said. "You were very kind."

He made a face. "I don't want to be known as kind," he said. "I want to be known as a daredevil, risk-taker."

"That's my husband," I told him gently.

"Ah." He looked searchingly into my eyes. "And how is the husband?"

"You asked me that already," I said. "And I answered you. He's fine."

"So tell me about your daughter, then," he said. "Since everything is OK in the husband department."

So I told him about Clodagh and chatted about my

life and he was very easy to talk to. He didn't judge but simply listened. I found myself telling him stupid things, about how I felt going back to work, about my envy of Lucy and the Quinlans, but he didn't tell me that I was foolish or selfish, he merely held me as we danced and nodded encouragingly from time to time.

When the band changed the tempo of the music, I thanked him and went to refresh my make-up. Lisa was in the Ladies and asked me about Hugh.

"A credit customer," I told her. "Nice guy."

"Very attractive," she said, "in a laid-back sort of way."

"He owns a few bookshops," I said. "I don't think he's very, well, businessman type."

"You get tired of the suits after a while," she said. "I long to meet someone who isn't turned on by a balance sheet."

I laughed at this but knew what she meant. I told her about Ferdinand Casals. "There's a man you would have liked," I said. "Businessman with a difference."

"Not really," she told me. "They're all the same, really. It's a power thing."

I supposed she was right, which was disappointing. Would Ferdinand have been half as attractive to me if he was a farmer in an olive grove? Probably not.

Rory was dancing with Amanda Ferry from the dealing room when I got back. They were doing some very vigorous jumping about. I'd have to warn him about the danger of having a heart attack. He was the right age.

The music seemed very loud. I wondered would

anyone notice if I sloped off to the foyer for a while. There was nobody at our table anyway, they were all dancing.

I went outside and sat in one of the deep sofas. It was blissfully quiet.

He sat down beside me five minutes later. "Are you all right?" he asked, concern in his voice.

"Are you following me?" I opened my eyes.

"Of course not," said Hugh, "I went to the Gents. Saw you sitting here. Thought you might be feeling unwell."

I sighed. "You're always thinking I'm unwell."

"Sorry," he said.

"And you're always apologising."

"Always is a little strong," he said. "We don't meet that often."

"I know." I hung my head. "Forget it."

"Forget what?"

I shrugged. "I don't know. You're very difficult." My voice rose. "You're different to other men I've known."

"I'm so glad," he murmured.

I looked at him. "Why?"

"You know lots of people that I don't particularly like," he said. "I'm glad I'm different."

"There's nothing wrong with commerce," I said sharply. "You mightn't like the bankers or the accountants or the solicitors but they're the people who make life tick. No doubt you think it's immoral to earn money."

"Not at all," said Hugh. "I don't run my shops for charity."

I was deflated. "I suppose not. You get me at dodgy moments in my life. I'm the one who should apologise to you."

"Don't worry," he said. "It's water off a duck's back to me. I don't get involved. I interfere but it's harmless, really."

I gazed at him. "Why do you interfere with me?"

"I don't know," he said again. "I can't help it."

"Why?"

"You always look as though something dreadful is about to happen," he said. "As though some awful event is waiting to destroy you. You have this hunted look about you."

I was shocked. "I do not."

"You do," he said. "And that's interesting."

"Well, you're not very good at expressions." I stood up. "Rory is probably hunting for me as we speak. I'd better get back inside."

"Sure," he said. "It's a good party."

In fact, Rory was dancing with Amanda again. They'd been joined by a gang of the dealers and their girlfriends. I joined in, kicking up my heels and shaking my head until the clip in my hair flew off and nearly took Rory's eye out.

"Good party," he said that night when we were in bed.

"Very good." I pulled the duvet around me.

"I'm sorry I didn't get much opportunity to dance with you," he said. "You were brilliant at the end there."

"I'm always brilliant," I said, tiredly, as I closed my eyes.

He pulled me towards him in the bed, rubbed his hand on my stomach and allowed it to slip into the warmth between my legs.

"Too tired," I mumbled.

"Oh, come on, Jane."

"Really, Rory. I'm exhausted."

"It's not too much to ask, is it?"

"In the morning."

"Great," said my husband and rolled over. He was snoring within thirty seconds.

28

January 1991

(UK No. 10 – You've Lost That Lovin' Feeling
– *Righteous Brothers)*

It was a busy week. The Civic packed up on Monday, and Dad couldn't send anyone around to pick it up until Tuesday. He told me that there was something wrong with the clutch and that he wouldn't have whatever the part was until the end of the week. I was in a perpetual rush then, getting Clodagh off to playschool, getting in to work and then hurrying out on the dot of five to pick her up again. I was sort of pleased when Rory announced that he'd got to go to London on Thursday, because it meant that I'd have the Mercedes. He was getting the early morning flight, so I told him I'd drop him at the airport, bring Clodagh to school and go in to work myself afterwards. Rory was unusually pissed off about going to London. He said he was far too busy in work to be losing a day wandering around the City. He'd be back some time on Friday, he'd give me a call.

Thursday was hectic. It was pouring with rain at six in the morning, Clodagh didn't want to get out of bed and Rory was grumpy. He'd been late home the previous night, but he hadn't been in a pub – there were no stale smells of tobacco and alcohol clinging to his suit, but his eyes were red from staring at the Reuters screens so late.

We didn't talk on the way to the airport. Rory drove because he reckoned we'd get there faster that way, Clodagh fell asleep again and I wondered whether I'd ever get the nerve to talk to Rory about the state of our marriage.

We had to talk, no question. I just wasn't sure what to say. That I knew something must be wrong? That I knew that Rory was fed up with me? That I still loved him but that I couldn't go on like this? That he would have to choose between his career and me? I didn't want to ask the last question. I was afraid he'd choose his career.

I left him at the set-down point. He kissed me prefunctorily on the cheek, said he'd ring and then disappeared along with all of the other men in business suits. I slid into the driver's seat and headed back across town.

The rain sloshed against the windscreen of the car, and I needed the wipers on at full speed to cope with the torrent of water. I hurried Clodagh into school, holding my coat over her and cursing the weather. I was still wet by the time I got in to work. Fortunately, the mad scramble ended in the office and, amazingly, it was quiet that day. I'd managed to get up to date on all of the day-to-day stuff, Claire was in meetings most of the day and Stephen was in the States. Claire popped her head around her office door at about four o'clock and told me to go home if I wasn't busy. "No need to hang around," she said. "I'll be here for a while and I'll answer the phones, if you like."

"Great." I tidied my desk. It was nice to get off early for once. I ran across the street to the car. It was still pouring with rain.

I cursed when I realised that I'd got a ticket, but then remembered that it was Rory's car and that he could probably get the bank to pay for it. I crumpled the pink and white paper and put it into the glove compartment. Rory was madly untidy. The compartment was a jumble of tapes and CDs, half-opened packets of mints and miniature bottles of aftershave. There were a couple of other parking tickets in there, too. With a bit of luck he wouldn't notice this one. I pushed it in towards the back and felt the soft, yielding material. More rubbish, I thought, as I pulled it out. It was a stocking. A black silk stocking.

I was sick on to the passenger seat. I couldn't help it. A sudden heave over which I had no control brought my food racing back up my throat, burning it. I couldn't do anything to stop myself and the foetid pool landed on the empty leather seat beside me. After it happened, I didn't know what to do. I sat in the driver's seat, shivering with the cold and the shock. My face was wet but I didn't know whether it was with sweat from being sick or with tears. And the smell clung to me. I didn't know what to do about the vomit. There wasn't anything to clean it with. My car always had plenty of tissues for emergencies, but Rory's hadn't. I looked around in confusion. The smell was so awful I knew that I would have to do something. If I stayed in the car, with that, I would be sick again.

So, in the end, I used the evidence to clean up. I stretched the sheer black stocking between my hands and used it to scrape the mess out of the car. I didn't know what to do with the stocking afterwards. Part of me wanted to keep it, to confront Rory with it, maybe even to throttle him with it. But I couldn't keep it, and eventually I dumped it out of the window.

I don't remember the drive home. I remember that, at some point, the rain eased off but I left the wipers racing across the windscreen in a frenzy. I remember that, as I waited for the railway gates to lift at merrion, *Unchained Melody* played on the car radio. I also remember that, despite the temperature outside, I was very hot, that a rivulet of sweat ran from my temple to my chin and that my hands were clammy on the steering wheel. But I don't really remember the details of my drive. One minute I was in Merrion Square then, suddenly, I was at home, fumbling for my house keys.

I sat in the kitchen and cried. I cried until my eyes were so sore that I couldn't stand the salt tears, until my cheeks were swollen and until I felt positively sick again. I leaned forward in the chair and rocked with my grief, with the shock of Rory's betrayal and with the knowledge that I was a fool. I buried my head in my arms and sobbed like a child.

I cried because I knew that Rory was having an

affair, and that the affair was the only thing that could explain all the late nights, and the whispered phone conversations, and the fact that he didn't seem to care that we hadn't made love since before Christmas. I didn't know whether to hate him or to hate me for driving him to it. I was a useless wife, a hopeless mother. I wasn't there for him when he needed me.

How long had it being going on? I wiped the tears from my eyes and went into his den to search for more evidence. At the back of my mind lingered the very faint hope that there could be a rational excuse for Rory having a sheer black stocking in the glove compartment of his car. I vaguely remembered Dad once saying that stockings had been used as emergency fan belts on cars. I couldn't imagine that a slinky 7-denier would be much good as a fan belt and I wasn't sure that the Mercedes even *had* a fan belt, but it was the only hope I had.

Rory's den was as messy as the car. It wasn't really an office, more a place where he kept all his bits and pieces. His golf clubs were propped up in the corner, against the small filing cabinet. There was nothing in the filing cabinet, just American Express dockets and old copies of the *Financial Times.* There was a desk in the office, too. The top drawer of the desk was locked and I pushed and pulled at it frantically. I was convinced that there was evidence in the desk. I searched the den for the keys as tears fell down my cheeks. The keys of the desk were in the filing cabinet. My hands shook as I opened the drawer. It was empty, except for an electric razor. I scrabbled around in the drawer. It didn't make sense to lock it if there was nothing in it, but I couldn't find anything. I pressed against the side of it, looking for secret panels. Suddenly I realised that I was making a complete idiot of myself. This was an ordinary desk, there couldn't be secret panels in it.

I sat down in the swivel chair and closed my eyes. Maybe I was wrong after all. Maybe there was a perfectly rational explanation for the stocking.

The phone rang and I jumped in fright.

"Jane, are you coming to collect Clodagh?" It was Audrey Bannister. I looked at my watch. Half past six. I'd been in a daze, hadn't realised it was so late. I told her I'd be around straight away.

"Are you all right?" she asked, as she opened the door. I'd splashed cold water on my face and run a brush through my hair, but I knew that my eyes were still red and that my cheeks were blotchy.

"Upset stomach," I said.

"You poor thing." She looked anxiously at me. "Will you be OK? You look wretched."

"I'll be fine," I said. "I just need to lie down for a while. I think I ate something dodgy at lunch-time."

"Rory can keep an eye on Clodagh," said Audrey. "You should go to bed."

I nodded tiredly. Clodagh knew that something was wrong. She sniffed the air in the car. "It smells of sick," she said. I'd have to do something about it. I couldn't let Rory know I'd thrown up in his precious Mercedes.

"Don't be silly," I said.

"Well, it does." Clodagh was adamant. "Sick, sick, sick."

"Be quiet," I said, but I could hear her muttering under her breath, sick, sick, sick.

I made her something to eat and then parked her in front of the TV without even checking to see what was on. I went back into Rory's den and opened the filing cabinet again.

The American Express dockets were jumbled together in a red folder. His business card was Amex, so there was every reason for him to have lots of receipts. There were loads of them. For Dobbin's and Gilbaud's and The Copper Beech. For petrol. For flights to London and Frankfurt. For the theatre. For the flower shop. I looked at the flower shop ones more closely. Flowers? To whom? Why? I was beginning to shake again. Was this it? Was this the evidence?

I looked at the dates on the restaurant receipts, but they didn't mean an awful lot. He could have been on business, it could have been anything else. Same with any of the others. How could I tell?

There was nothing else in the den. I don't know what sort of evidence I'd expected. Had I thought that, just by looking, I could have identified the receipts documenting his infidelity? It wasn't as easy as that. But the flowers. The flowers still bothered me. Every Friday since October. That was an awful lot of flowers.

I put Clodagh to bed and the phone rang again.

"Hi, Jane," said Lucy. "How are things?"

I really didn't want to talk to Lucy then. She'd guess there was something wrong.

"Fine." I spoke carefully.

"I know it's a bit late but d'you want to go to the cinema tonight?" she asked. "David and I were going and I've booked the tickets on my credit card, but now he can't. So I'm looking for another victim."

"Sorry, Lucy," I said. "But Rory's in London and I can't get anyone to mind Clodagh at this hour."

"That's a pity. Oh, well, never mind. Another time, maybe."

"Sure."

"Are you all right?" she asked. "You sound a bit funny."

"Headache," I muttered. "All day."

"You poor thing." Lucy was sympathetic. "And here's me asking you to go to the movies. Probably the last thing you want to do."

"I'll be fine," I said. "I'll take a few Hedex or something."

"Well, look after yourself."

"I will, Lucy. I'll give you a call. Maybe we can go to the cinema next week?"

"That'd be great. See you, Jane."

"See you." I replaced the receiver. I felt sick again.

I didn't sleep that night. I turned over and over again in the big five-foot bed and wondered what I should do. How could I confront Rory? What should I say to him? I was useless at arguing with him. He always managed to make me end up apologising to him. But this was his fault. His. I wished that I'd kept the stocking. He could hardly bluff his way out of that.

I wondered about the owner. What was she like? Where had he met her? How long had he known her?

Who the hell was she? Was she a client, perhaps? Or somebody from the bank? Did everyone except me know about it? Was it true that the wife was always the last to know?

The worst question, the absolutely earthshattering question, was – what had they been doing in the car and why was her stocking in the glove compartment?

Pictures of the unknown woman swam into my mind. Tall, blonde, willowy. Eminently sexual. A thin woman. Without a stomach. Or maybe Rory would go for someone dark. He liked dark women. Not fat, though. Not with hips or anything. Was it because of Clodagh? I wondered. Was it because my body was different? God, it couldn't be that, my original shape wasn't as good as my body now. I still went to the gym once, sometimes twice, a week. I thought I was in good shape. Relatively speaking. But I didn't think I was unattractive. Obviously I was wrong.

It was hard to get through the next day, but somehow I managed to get myself under control. I worked like a demon in the office, chivvying Claire and Stephen to make appointments, phone clients, do things they'd put off doing. I even tidied up Stephen's office which usually resembled a battle zone. When Rory called, unexpectedly, I was surprised at how calm I suddenly was.

"I'll be home tomorrow," he told me. "Sorry, Jane, I thought I might get back tonight but it'll have to be tomorrow."

"No problem," I said. "Easier to pick you up tomorrow." I wondered if his mistress was with him now, if it was all an excuse and if they were lying together on some hotel bed, revelling in each other. Was she tracing her finger along his chest as I usually did? Was she kissing him behind the ear, which he absolutely loved? Was she – I couldn't bear to think of what else they might be doing. I felt my stomach churn, but I hadn't eaten since yesterday so I knew that I couldn't be sick again.

"See you tomorrow, then," he said.

"Sure." The tears were welling up again.

The question of how to confront him remained. Maybe I *had* made a terrible mistake. Maybe there was a perfectly rational explanation for the stocking. I sat on the sofa with my legs curled beneath me, rocking gently back and forward, and tried to think of a perfectly rational explanation. I couldn't.

Lucy called again that evening. "How's the headache?" she asked. "You sounded terrible last night so I thought I'd ring and check."

"Better." I looked at my still-puffy eyes in the mirror. "I think it was a bug of some sort."

"Why?"

"Because I still feel a bit shaky. I was sick last night," I said.

"Is it something you ate?"

"I'm not sure, Lucy. Might be a touch of flu. I think I've a bit of a temperature, snuffly nose, sore throat, that sort of thing."

"When is Rory back?" she asked.

"Tomorrow, sometime."

"OK, then. Take care of yourself Jane, you still sound rotten. Talk to you next week."

I couldn't talk to Lucy about it yet. When I knew

for sure, then I would talk to her, but not now. I couldn't share this pain with anyone, I held it close to me. I got through the evening somehow, but every so often, my thoughts and my grief fizzed together in my head so that tears suddenly welled up again and I'd scrub frantically at my eyes.

I practised meeting Rory. "Hi, darling, how are you? You bastard!"

"Rory! Your girlfriend called. Can she see you in the car later?"

I'd spent ages getting the passenger seat clean. It smelled of disinfectant now. "Rory, my love, I've missed you. By the way, did your girlfriend lose her stocking in your car? You bastard!"

Being angry helped, it meant I could block out some of the pain. But how would I feel when I met Rory face to face? The thought made my head swim. I didn't know how I would cope. Should I try and get more information first? Be absolutely, one hundred per cent certain?

I was baking a cake when he phoned on Saturday morning. I don't know why on earth I was baking, it was something I did so rarely that Clodagh watched me with great interest. I gave her some pastry to play with and she was rolling it into a long, doughy snake when the phone rang.

"I'll be in at two," said Rory. "Will you be there to pick me up?"

"Sure."

"Everything OK?"

"Yes."

"Clodagh OK?"

"Of course."

"Do you want anything in the duty-free?"

"No."

"See you at two."

"We'll be there."

I was trembling as I replaced the receiver. I put the cake in the oven, set the timer and told Clodagh that we had to go and pick up Daddy.

We stood in the arrivals area and waited for him. Clodagh jumped up and down to see him. My mouth was dry. He came into the arrivals hall, looking tired, and my heart leapt at the sight of him. Why? It made no sense. This morning I'd hated him, and now I'd give anything to make everything all right between us. He pecked me on the cheek and I wanted to recoil from him but he was my husband, I couldn't. At that moment, I wanted to bury my head in his shoulder and tell him that I loved him and that it was probably all my fault and that it didn't matter what he had done but now would he leave whoever she was alone and come back to Clodagh and me, be my husband again. I could make it all right I knew I could.

We walked out to the carpark together. He talked about the London trip. It must have been business, he couldn't have made up all of the stories.

"Accident?" he asked, sniffing the disinfectant as he got into the car.

"The usual." I maligned Clodagh, who occasionally had bladder problems.

"Maybe we should take her to a doctor."

"She'll be OK," I said as I pulled out of the parking bay.

I didn't confront him. Not that evening, nor even the next day. I couldn't bring myself to do it. I still didn't know what to say, but I was alert now for clues and I found them. Not tangible clues, but his behaviour gave him away. So did the faint, lingering traces of *Samsara* which clung to him some nights when he had been working late.

I said nothing. I had to wait until I was ready. It helped that we didn't talk to each other very much any more. He didn't have to lie to me very often. Every night, as we lay together side by side, the tears would slide down my cheeks and saturate my pillow so that I would have to turn it over. But he never heard me cry and he never knew that I knew.

On Friday, two weeks later, he told me that he was going out to dinner. Meeting clients. The Copper Beech, he said. He wouldn't be too late. Would I come in to town with him and take the car so that he could get a taxi home? No sense in risking being done for drink-driving. He'd become very serious about drink-driving since one of the dealers had been breathalysed on Baggot Street after a long lunch and had been prosecuted. I told him that it was no problem, I'd be happy to drive him in to town. It was a lot safer than risking his licence, I agreed. He came home and showered and changed. He looked good in his Hugo Boss suit, even though his slight paunch had got a little bigger since Christmas.

"Who are the clients?" I asked, as we pulled out of the driveway. I sniffed the air. The faint aroma of disinfectant still lingered.

"The usual," said Rory. "Couple of guys from Hamburg. Boring, really."

If it were true, then it could be boring. But I didn't know now whether he ever ate with clients or whether it was always with his . . . his what? Mistress. The word made me retch.

"Poor darling," I said unfeelingly. "What time will you be home?"

"We're having a drink beforehand, dinner at eight. Maybe a drink afterwards. Back by midnight, I suppose."

"That's fine," I said. "I might go over to Lucy. She wanted to go to the cinema last week but I didn't go. Pat can stay on and baby-sit."

"Good idea," he said. "Tell her I was asking for her."

I knew then that he must be meeting his mistress. He never thought it was a good idea for me to meet Lucy. He still didn't like her.

He got out at Searson's and I thought of all the times we'd met there ourselves in the past, as I watched him walk inside. I wondered whether she was there, waiting for him. Perhaps she was sitting back in one of the seats, long legs crossed, elegantly waiting for him. She'd look at the door each time it opened, expecting to see him come in. Did she worry that I would ever find out? Did she care that maybe, some day, I would know about them and create a scene? I laughed to myself. I never created scenes, I wasn't the type.

Once, in school, our geography teacher, Miss Hennessy, had accused me of copying my homework.

I told her I hadn't but she didn't believe me and she ranted and raved at me for ages, telling me that it was useless to copy other people's work and that I would never amount to much if I didn't put the effort in myself. And I let her shout at me because I couldn't think of anything to say to defend myself and it was easier to take the blame rather than to try and argue my corner. I didn't like causing trouble then and I didn't like causing trouble now. I didn't like people looking at me and whispering about me. The thought that people like Karen and Lorraine might know about Rory's girlfriend made me shiver.

I was shaking again. I spent a lot of time shaking. I wished he hadn't taken her to The Copper Beech. Where he had taken me for my birthday. How could he do this to me? I drove home feeling utterly exhausted.

Pat was sitting on the sofa watching a video, Clodagh on her lap.

"I've got to go out again, Pat," I told her. "Can you stay until a bit later?"

"No problem," she said. "I'll just phone my mother."

I left her to phone while I went upstairs and had a shower. I turned the heat up as high as I could and let the steaming hot water scald its way through my hair and to my scalp. I massaged shampoo into my hair until it foamed and lathered so much that the soapsuds ran into my eyes and stung them. I scrubbed myself with a loofah until my skin was raw and sore. I let the needles of water hit me on the chest, leaving red weals on my breast, and then I wrapped myself in a huge bath-towel and padded into the bedroom.

"Where are you going, Mum?" asked Clodagh, who had followed me upstairs.

"Out," I told her.

"Out where?"

"Just out."

"I want to go, too."

"Don't be silly. Here." I handed her an old lipstick. "You can get made up with me, if you want."

We sat in front of the dressing-table and turned ourselves into creatures of the night.

Clodagh was beautiful. Glossy red-gold hair, big blue eyes, clear, bright skin. I loved her fiercely. I hugged her suddenly, strongly, and she wriggled away from me.

"You'll mess me up," she complained.

I finished my preparations and went downstairs again. Pat was sitting in the living-room in front of the roaring gas fire, her homework spread around her.

"You look stunning, Mrs Mac," said Pat, looking up and eyeing me appreciatively.

"Thanks," I said. "One has to make the effort from time to time."

"Where are you going?"

"Just out for a drink," I said. "I won't be that long, Pat."

"A boyfriend," she giggled. "You wouldn't bother looking like that for Mr Mac."

I gave her a withering glance and she dug me in the ribs. "Only joking!" But I knew that she was wondering, her eyes gave her away.

"Mr McLoughlin is in The Copper Beech," I told her. "The number is on the notice-board. I'm not sure where I'll be, so if you need anything, ring him."

I knew she wouldn't. Pat was the most capable person I had ever met. She'd changed her look since the first time she had come to the house. Now her hair had reverted to its natural nut-brown, and she didn't wear the pale make-up any more but brushed her cheeks with Body Shop beads.

I slipped into the car and drove back into town. It was cold now, the air temperature was way down and the stars glittered grimly in the black velvet sky.

I hadn't been to The Copper Beech since my birthday. Cars were lined up outside, obviously it was still doing well and still pulling in the business trade. Rory liked it because they knew him, deferred to him and called him by his name. Since the party, they'd been especially nice to him. They kept a good wine cellar, he'd say sometimes, sounding particularly pompous. Once, when he'd said something like that, I'd have hit him and we'd both laugh. "But they do," he'd say, defensively.

The doorman stood outside the rough stoned building. He smiled at me as I crunched along the gravel courtyard and clicked up the granite steps. I was another woman meeting her date.

The foyer of The Copper Beech was separated from the main restaurant by folding screens. A woman sat behind a high old lectern, a book of reservations in front of her. A pot of ink and a quill pen stood on top of the desk. A pair of half-glasses hung on a chain around her neck. She hadn't been there the night of my birthday party, I would have remembered her.

"Hi," I smiled. "Is Mr McLoughlin here yet?"

She looked at me in surprise and glanced down at her book. "Mr McLoughlin?"

"Rory McLoughlin. I think the reservation was for eight o'clock."

She was definitely put out by my question. I looked at her carefully.

"He may have only made the reservation for two," I said casually.

She smiled in partial relief. "Well, yes," she said. "His companion is with him."

With those words my world disintegrated. I'd kept a faint hope that I was wrong, deep inside me. I'd hoped that maybe I'd arrive here, and Rory would be with clients from Hamburg, and I would have made a huge mistake. In my heart, I'd known that I was wrong but I couldn't help hoping. For a split second, I thought I was going to faint, then I became aware of the receptionist watching me. She looked worried. I wondered if they were used to confrontations in this restaurant. I wasn't going to confront Rory, she needn't have worried. I was going to walk up to him and say hello and walk away again. That way, he would know that I knew and he'd have to talk to me about it.

"I'm just here to give him something," I said. "Don't worry. He's expecting me"

"He's at table five," she told me. "Behind the yucca plant."

I looked around the screen.

My husband and his mistress were sitting opposite each other. He had his back to me so I couldn't see his expression, but she watched him, her eyes soft. I knew those emotions, I had looked at him like that once. As I stood there, she reached out and touched his hand.

Rage, hot and furious coursed through me. Until that moment I'd still half-hoped that I was making a terrible mistake. That maybe there was an explanation and I just hadn't managed to find it. That Rory could not have been unfaithful to me. Maybe he brought girls out, but on a purely platonic basis. Maybe it *was* business. Maybe the stocking – well, I couldn't come up with a reason for the stocking, but it was always possible that there was something I hadn't thought of. But Amanda Ferry was looking into his eyes and there wasn't an innocent reason why she should look at him like this. The bile rose in my throat as I looked at them.

Neither of them had seen me yet, I was still screened by the yucca plant. I breathed carefully, trying to stay calm.

Time was suspended as I walked across the granite floor towards them. It was as though I was walking through a tunnel. I couldn't see to the right or to the left of me. I was oblivious to the other diners, I couldn't hear the hum of their conversation. I stood beside them.

Amanda looked up and an expression of sheer horror crossed her face. Rory's own mouth had dropped open. He stared at me, dressed in my expensive purple velvet dress, my choker of pearls, my drop earrings and my hair, scooped into a plait at the back of my head and secured by a matching velvet ribbon.

We looked at each other in silence. I wondered, fleetingly, whether anyone in the restaurant was watching us. But they wouldn't know that there was anything wrong. To them, it might be a perfectly normal scene.

"Do close your mouth, Rory," I said calmly. "You'll be left like that." I remembered hearing that line delivered in a movie years ago. I had thought it very effective then and it made me feel good to use it now. I was still shaking inside, but my hands were still and my voice was steady.

"Mushroom soup?" I inclined my head towards the bowl on the table.

He nodded, speechlessly.

"I hope you enjoy it," I said. I picked up the bowl and emptied its contents over his head. "You fucking bastard!"

I watched the contents of the bowl adhere to his hair and drip solemnly down his face. He cried out in shock. Amanda gasped in horror. I looked at her coldly. "Bitch," I said, although I almost felt sorry for her.

The restaurant was silent. It was the first time in my life that I'd ever created a scene, but I'd created one now.

A waiter hurried over and grabbed me by the arm.

"I'll have to ask you to leave," he said.

I started to laugh; maybe there was a touch of hysteria in it.

"Of course I'll leave," I said. "There's no reason for me to stay here."

We walked side by side through the hushed restaurant. My high heels clattered on the stone floor. I sensed rather than saw the eyes of the other diners follow me. From the flurrying behind me, I knew that another waiter had brought a towel over to Rory.

I pulled my coat closer to me as I walked back to the car. The waiter and the doorman both watched me as I left.

The car was cold and I was shaking as I sat in the driver's seat. I thought that I might be sick again but I managed to take deep breaths and stay calm. I closed my eyes and visualised them again. I'd thought over and over about the sort of girls that Rory might choose to have an affair with, but I wasn't sure exactly what sort of person his choice would be. Given his feelings about me working, I wouldn't have imagined a committed career woman, but that was what Amanda was. He'd talked about her at home from time to time, in a casual way. She was good, he'd said. Strong. She didn't take any shit from anyone. She got on well with the clients. I'd thought that Amanda sounded a decent sort of person.

I started up the engine and drove home. I parked a few streets away from the house and sat in silence.

If I'd wanted to destroy my marriage, I'd probably done it now, all right. What were the chances of Rory ever forgiving me for making such a fool of him? And in a restaurant where he was well-known? The folly of my action was coming home to me and I felt that I had made a terrible mistake. But I couldn't help it. When I saw them there, I wanted to do something to hurt him. To humiliate him the way he'd humiliated me. And it had been wonderful at the time. I'd had a sense of power and excitement and rage as I dumped the soup over him. It had been a fantastic moment. But the wrong thing to do. The thing to do, surely, was to have sat down and talked to him and been rational about it. We could have worked something out. It wasn't entirely his fault. Bitter tears rolled down my cheeks as I leaned my head against the steering wheel.

I cried for a while and then dried my tears. I would go home now, at any rate. I was freezing in the car.

"Did you have a nice evening?" asked Pat, as I walked into the living-room. She looked at me curiously. "Are you OK, Mrs McLoughlin?"

"Of course I am." I rummaged in my bag for her money and handed it to her. "Will you be all right getting home on your own?" I asked.

"Sure I will." She pocketed the notes but still looked at me strangely. "See you again, then."

"I'll give you a call," I said.

When she'd gone, I went upstairs and sat in front of the mirror. I knew now why Pat had asked me if I was all right: my mascara had streaked across my face and I looked as though someone had given me a black eye.

I smeared cleansing cream over my face and then removed it gently with cotton wool. I looked awful. I slipped out of my clothes and into my dressing-gown, then went downstairs and took a couple of Hedex. My head was pounding now. I wondered should I have a drink as well. Maybe a few drinks. Maybe I should take all the tablets and a bottle of whiskey. That would give Rory a shock.

In the end, I made myself a cup of tea and brought it up to bed. At eleven o'clock, I turned out the light. I wondered when – if – Rory would come home.

I slept fitfully, dozing and then suddenly waking up with a startled jump. I waited for the sound of a taxi to pull up outside the house or the sound of Rory's key in the front door. Each time there was an unexpected sound, I was wide awake again.

The hum of the electric milk float woke me at seven o'clock. I blinked a couple of times as I looked at the gentle green glow of the alarm clock. The bed beside me was still empty. Rory had not come home. I suppose, deep down, I hadn't expected him to. I sat up in the bed, knowing that I wouldn't go back to sleep, knowing that I had irrevocably changed everything.

I hugged my knees to my chest. Oh, God, I thought, through another flood of tears, what have I done?

29

January 1994

(UK No. 7 – The Perfect Year – *Dina Carroll)*

"Happy New Year!" Lucy turned to me and flung her arms around me as the chimes of her carriage clock finished ringing in 1994. I hugged her, and then everybody at Lucy and David's New Year's Eve party hugged each other.

It was a great evening. We arrived about nine and Lucy handed around bowls of steaming hot chilli and crusty garlic bread. David played his *Hits of the Seventies* CD, and followed it up with Queen, Status Quo and (for the girls, he said) Abba. It was great fun. Lucy cracked open the bottles of champagne to toast the new year, and I sipped mine as I leaned my head against the French windows and gazed out into the darkness of Lucy's garden.

January was always difficult for me. It wasn't that I still felt anguished, although I didn't think the hurt would ever completely disappear, but it was hard not to think back and wonder how things might have been.

The scene was clear and vivid. I could recall every moment as though it were on videotape, running it in slow motion through my head.

Rory had arrived home at five o'clock on the day after I'd dumped the soup on his head at The Copper Beech. I'd sat around the house all day, afraid to move in case the phone would ring, not knowing where to ring myself or even who to ring, and wondered where on earth Rory had got to. I supposed that he was with Amanda and the thought chilled me. Was she comforting him about the fact that he had a deranged wife? Or did either of them care? Was he revelling in my lunacy in having made a show of him? Or was he humiliated beyond belief? Would he ever come home again? Or had I driven him away forever?

Every so often I'd go upstairs and check to see if all his clothes were still there. There was no reason why they shouldn't be, but I needed to check all the same. The Hugo Boss and Armani suits nestled in the wardrobe and his shoes gleamed on the shoe-rack at the bottom. I fingered the fabric of his suits, held his ties to my face and shook with nerves.

I was sitting on our bed when I heard the sound of his key turning in the lock. I moistened my lips and tried to steady the thump of my heart as it hammered against my chest.

I heard Clodagh run from the living-room into the hall, and Rory pick her up and talk to her. Then the measured tread of his footsteps up the stairs and into the bedroom.

He was wearing the trousers from his suit and a woollen jumper which I didn't recognise. He didn't speak as he walked over to the wardrobe and looked inside. Then he took a suitcase from the top shelf and opened it on the bed.

"What are you doing?" I asked nervously.

He didn't answer. He took trousers from hangers and laid them neatly into the suitcase.

"Where are you going?"

He continued to fold his clothes.

"How long will you be away?"

He ignored me completely.

This had always been his way when we had a row. Freeze me out. I had to make him talk. I didn't want our marriage to end. I didn't want him to walk out on me. I could and I would forgive him for Amanda Ferry.

"Rory, can't we work something out?" I pleaded.

He looked at me as though I was an insect. "I hardly think we have anything left to say to each other."

"Of course we have," I said. "We have to talk about this."

"You think there's anything to talk about?" he hissed at me. "You humiliated me in a place where I have a reputation to maintain. I do a lot of corporate entertaining in that restaurant. You humiliated me in front of a fellow colleague. You made a spectacle of me and of yourself, and you think that there's something left for us to talk about. Don't make me laugh, Jane."

"And what about you?" I asked him. "What about

you and Amanda Ferry? Don't you think we have something to talk about there?"

He gazed at me. "Not really."

Suddenly I was shaking again. "Why 'not really'?" I asked. "What were you doing with her?"

"Having dinner," he said.

"Oh yeah?"

It was like talking to a brick wall. He didn't want to discuss it, he wouldn't discuss it. He went on packing.

"Where are you going?" I asked.

"I haven't decided yet," he said. "But anywhere is better than here."

"Why?" I asked. "Why, Rory?"

"Why not?"

"Didn't we have a good marriage?" I said, even though I'd wondered about that so often myself. "Did you hate it? Do you hate it?"

"We're different," he said, as though that explained everything. "We want different things, Jane."

"But I thought we wanted the same sort of things," I said, helplessly. "I thought we wanted a good life and to be together."

"Being together isn't enough," said Rory. "You have to work to make life together a good thing."

"But I did!" I cried. "I tried. I thought you were happy, Rory. I never stopped you from playing golf or going for drinks or doing any of the things you wanted to do. What more could you ask from me?"

"You always looked down on me," he said. "From your lofty idealistic heights. You wanted to be well-off, but you never tried to get on with Bill or Karen or

Graham or Suki. You never tried to be friendly to the girls, invite them over for lunch or anything like that. You went to the functions, but you never really wanted to go."

"So you have an affair with someone in your office because I wouldn't ask Karen Hamilton over for lunch and because I thought all those things she dragged me to were crashingly boring. Makes sense, Rory."

"Who says I was having an affair?" he demanded. "Where did you get that information?"

"I didn't need to get that information anywhere," I said. "It was patently obvious to me when I saw you. Anyway, I found her stocking. In the car."

"Her stocking." He looked guilty.

"Yes." All the spirit suddenly evaporated from me. "Yes, Rory, you left it in the fucking glove compartment."

We looked at each other silently. For a moment, I thought our marriage would be OK. Rory would hold me and I would forgive him, he'd understand how I felt and then everything would be all right again.

It seemed a bit daft to want our marriage to be saved. After all, he'd been having an affair. He'd consistently, persistently deceived me. He had come home to me having spent an evening with her, and he had lied over and over again. And yet, right then, if he had said that he was sorry and that it had been a mistake, I would have believed him and I would have tried again. I'd have been different too. I'd have given up work if that made any difference, because my marriage was more important than anything else. I'd have tried really hard to be a good wife to him and to ensure that there would be no reason for him to have an affair. Because there must have been a reason, and I must have been part of it.

"I'm going to live with Amanda," he said.

I looked at him, aghast. "You can't."

"I can," said Rory. "And that's what I'm going to do."

"Do you love her?" I demanded. "Do you?"

He shrugged lightly. "Maybe."

"You fucking bastard!" I cried. "You don't give a toss for me or for Clodagh. What about her? You're just going to leave us, are you?"

"Jane, you made a show of me. Now, I admit that I should have told you about Amanda before now, and I know that it must have been a shock to you, but these things happen. There was no need for you to behave the way you did. We can't put it back together, Jane, and I don't want to. It never really worked, did it?"

We'd been married for ten years and he'd decided that it had never really worked. I couldn't believe it. I knew that there had been times when I was miserable in our marriage, when I wondered whether I'd done the right thing. But I knew that I loved Rory and that, even if everything wasn't exactly perfect, it was probably as good as it was going to get. I didn't believe in fairytales, after all.

I watched him pack and then sat in the bedroom while he drove away, and I couldn't believe that it had actually happened.

"Are you all right, Jane?" Lucy stood beside me, a

glass of Ballygowan in her hand. Lucy was expecting her first baby in March. Once again she was on a cloud of happiness. She looked great, too. No morning sickness, heartburn or constant backache for Lucy. She continued on as though there was nothing different about her. Even her bump was a neat, round thing which she carried well.

I turned around to her. "I'm fine," I said. "Just thinking."

"Don't think," said Lucy. "Just have a good time."

"I am having a good time," I told her. "Honestly, Lucy. This is a great party."

"I hate it when I see you looking melancholy." She squeezed my arm.

"Don't be silly," I said. "I'm reminiscing, I suppose, but I'm not melancholy."

And I wasn't. Not any more. For six months after Rory left, I barely functioned. I kept expecting him to come back. I couldn't believe that I wouldn't hear the car pull into the driveway, and that he wouldn't come in. No matter how late. I hated sleeping in the big bed on my own; when I stretched into the empty space where Rory should have been, I would gasp with the pain of losing him.

Clodagh couldn't understand it. Every day she asked where Rory was. I told her that he'd had to go away to work and she accepted that for a while, but I knew I'd have to tell her the truth.

"Daddy's living somewhere else at the moment," I said eventually.

She looked solemnly at me and pulled at her ponytail.

"Why?"

"Because he needs to live away from us."

"Why?"

"Daddy and me – " This was awful. What the hell do you say? "Daddy and me are not getting on together just now. You know, we're not friends at the moment."

"You're not meant to be friends," she said scornfully. "You're Mammy and Daddy."

She sat in a corner and drew pictures of him which she stuck on her bedroom wall.

I hated telling people about it. I didn't want them to know. I didn't cry when I told Audrey and Claire, but I broke down completely when I met Lucy.

"Oh, Jane," she said, and put her arms around me. "The bastard."

I told her the entire story. I couldn't bring myself to tell anyone else.

"I'd have throttled him with the fucking stocking," she said. "He never deserved you, Jane, never!"

The twins *looked* shocked, but I didn't think they really *were* shocked. They called him a bastard, too.

But the real trauma was telling my parents. Mam didn't believe it.

"Can't you patch things up?" she asked, over and over again. "For the sake of Clodagh, at least?"

I hadn't told her about the stocking. I couldn't.

"There's nothing to patch up," I said.

"But surely – "

"No. He's seeing someone else."

She stared at me. This was something that happened to other people, not us.

"Who?"

I shrugged. "A girl from the office."

Dad wanted to kill him. "Nobody treats my daughter like that," he muttered. "Nobody."

I felt as though I was a permanent topic of conversation with everyone I knew, as though they were pointing me out and saying, "Look, there's Jane McLoughlin, her husband left her." I would have liked to have said that I threw him out, but he hadn't even allowed me to do that. I resented that. I should have been the one to say leave, not the one who wanted him to stay. I despised myself.

"Come over and join the rest of us," said Lucy. "Don't stay here on your own."

I smiled at her. "I'm fine on my own, Lucy, I like it."

That was true. I was used to being on my own now and I could cope with it. I didn't need anyone any more. Clodagh and I were a good partnership together, we understood each other.

When he first left, we found it difficult. I was in shock. I got up every day, went to work, came home, argued with Clodagh and went to bed. She kept asking for Rory, I kept saying that he was at work. Rory and I didn't speak for a month, and then he rang me and said that we had to talk.

He told me that he wanted to sell the house, that he'd give me half of the sale price. He'd continue paying maintenance for Clodagh. He was efficient and cool and seemed to have totally forgotten that we had shared a house and a life for ten years. Claire

Haughton told me to get a good solicitor and squeeze the bastard for every penny but I couldn't do that. I still felt that somehow it was all my fault.

Every night I cried myself to sleep. Every night I wrapped my hurt and my pain to me. Every night I asked myself why this had happened to me. All I'd ever wanted was to get married and to live happily ever after. It wasn't too much to ask, was it?

The pain and the hurt was always there, in the background, no matter what I was doing. I would be standing in line at the supermarket checkout and suddenly longing for my husband and my marriage would well up inside me and I would almost cry out in my unhappiness.

Then, one day, it didn't hurt so much any more. Clodagh and I were in St Stephen's Green and she was throwing bread to the ducks, squealing with laughter and enjoyment every time one of them pecked at the bread. A warm breeze carried the scent of newly-mown grass and the sun was warm on our backs. Quite suddenly, it was good to be alive. I picked up my daughter and swung her around and she wrapped her arms around my neck and told me she loved me.

I explored my feelings from time to time. Like a person who's had a tooth out, I poked around at the gap in my life, always expecting it to hurt and being surprised when it didn't. Every so often, I would conjure up a picture of Rory and Amanda and it didn't send the dagger through my heart that it had done a few months earlier. It was more a dull ache, and I could cope with a dull ache.

We sold the house. It wasn't as much of a wrench as it might have been, because I'd never felt as happy in the Dún Laoghaire house as I'd done in the Rathfarnham one. With my half of the money, plus a mortgage which I took out, I bought a small town house nearer my parents. The house was nothing special, two bedrooms, a small living-room and a kitchen/dining-room. It was about half the size of our previous house, but it was mine and I was happy. Rory and I divided the furniture between us. It was a horrible time, doling out chairs and sofas, lamps and pictures. Some of the pieces that I wanted looked awful in the new house so I stored them in the attic out of sight. I told him he could have the bed but he said that Amanda already had one and I bit my lip but bought a new one for myself. Now the house had a feminine personality. There were no golf clubs in the hallway, or grubby football jerseys in the laundry basket, or Kung Fu videos lying around the TV. It was weird at first, but we got used to it.

Clodagh wanted to know if Rory was dead. She'd heard about death at playschool. I told her that he was busy but that he was still alive and still loved her. It was hard not to rubbish him in front of her, to tell her that he was an unfaithful bastard and that he couldn't possibly love her, otherwise he'd never have left us. I wanted so much to say it, but I didn't. Then, when we had managed to be civilised to each other, he came and visited Clodagh and took her to MacDonald's.

"Why can't you stay?" she cried, as he put his jacket on to leave the house again. "I don't want you to go, Daddy!" She sat on the bottom stair and howled. I was crying too and Rory looked anguished.

"Why don't you stay?" I asked, as I swallowed the lump in my throat. "We need you."

"It wouldn't work, Jane," he said. "It couldn't work. I'm sorry."

So I was left with a screaming child who wouldn't be placated and cried over and over again for her Daddy, until I felt like bringing her to Amanda's flat and dumping her on the doorstep.

That was my low point. If Clodagh didn't love me, didn't want me, than who could? I poured myself a brandy, then another and another and got pissed out of my brains curled up on the sofa. I passed out, Clodagh on my knee, and woke up at three o'clock in the morning freezing cold and with a stiff neck. I carried Clodagh to bed and crawled in beneath the duvet, both of us still dressed. It was a nightmare.

The next morning I woke up to hailstones drumming against the bedroom window and a hangover drumming against the back of my eye. I had to call in sick to the office. There was no way I could have made it through the day.

"I think I've got the flu," I told Claire, not caring that I was lying to her.

"We need you back by next Monday," she said firmly. "I need somebody I can depend on, Jane." The warning in her voice was very clear. I flushed with embarrassment. "I'll be there," I said. "Tomorrow, if I can."

But I took the next day off and used the rest of the weekend to pull myself together. He's not worth going to pieces over, I told myself over and over. And Clodagh depends on you. She does need you.

"We're going to play charades." Lucy broke into my thoughts again. "Come on, Jane, you can be on my team."

I was good at charades, I could think laterally. Lucy was hopeless. The Quinlans were brilliant, and we had to split them on to different teams because Brenda could guess Grace's mimes instantly.

We fell around the room laughing and got drunk. After the charades, Lucy made coffee and most of the guests left. The twins and I were staying overnight, because we'd have had to drive across town and we were way over the limit.

"I'm going to bed," said David, at about four am. "If you girls want to sit up and gossip please feel free, but I can't keep my eyes open."

"You must be exhausted, Lucy," I said. "You've organised all this, you've been awake all night. Surely you want to go to sleep."

She shook her head. "I was asleep from three o'clock this afternoon until eight. I'm grand now. Not a bother. Anyway, I like staying up until I'm so tired I just pass out on the pillow. Otherwise it's so bloody uncomfortable I can't stand it."

I nodded. "When you can't lie on your side properly, it's awful."

"I sleep on my stomach, usually," said Lucy. "I'm destroyed."

We laughed at the picture of Lucy lying on her stomach now.

"You look great," said Brenda. "You hardly look pregnant at all."

"Bitch," I said. "I looked like an elephant after seven months."

"And you only managed eight months," said Grace.

I shivered at the memory. "Never again."

"Really?" asked Lucy. "Or are you just saying that?"

"Well it would be a bit difficult for me to have another child in my current celibate lifestyle," I said. "And I can't see that changing in the near future. So it looks highly unlikely, but it doesn't bother me that much. I feel sorry for Clodagh, though, she'd love a brother or sister."

"Maybe you will find someone," said Grace. "You're only thirty-three, Jane."

I looked at her, disbelief in my eyes. "Yeah," I said. "And Prince Charming will come along and sweep me off my feet. Me and my seven-year-old daughter. I can just see it, can't you?"

"Why not?" argued Brenda. "You're still an attractive girl, Jane."

I laughed. "Thank you," I said. "But I'm a woman, not a girl, now and nobody wants a woman and a child. Besides," I added truthfully, "I'm perfectly happy as I am. I don't want anybody else."

The three of them looked at me, not sure whether to believe me or not.

"Truly," I said. "I know I nearly cracked up when Rory left me."

"The fucking bastard," they said in unison. It was a

standing joke with us that, whenever I mentioned his name, they added the next statement.

"But I can cope now. I can more than cope." I took a sip from my glass of wine. "I know it sounds corny, but I'm happier now than I ever was before. I've got a lovely daughter – who is hopefully sleeping peacefully in her grandparents' house tonight – parents who are very supportive, a good job, and – " I looked around me, "brilliant friends. So I don't actually need someone to come in and reorganise my life and try to mess things up for me."

"But don't you miss having someone?" asked Brenda.

"Why?" I asked. "Do you?"

The twins were still single. They both doubted that they'd ever get married, now.

"It's not the same," said Grace. "I know people think we're weird, but neither of us has ever met someone special. We have separate friends and occasional boyfriends, but we haven't been lucky – or unlucky – enough to meet someone to marry. But if you've been married, I can't help feeling that you'd always want someone."

"Rubbish," I said, spiritedly. "Rory McLoughlin sapped me of all of my confidence. His horrible parents hated me. He spent all his time working, in the pub, on the golf course or bonking his fucking girlfriend. I never knew where I stood with him. I was always rearranging my schedule to fit in with his. Now I only have to worry about Clodagh, and I don't actually have to worry about her. She's great. We plan things, we do them, we have fun. Nobody messes around with us. I don't need someone and I don't want someone."

The amazing thing was that what I'd said was almost completely true. All my life, I'd believed that I needed a boyfriend or a lover or a husband to make me a complete person, to give me a sense of worth. Now I knew that I could stand on my own two feet and that I didn't need anyone else. It was an exhilarating feeling. I tried not to let the thought (occasionally, at the back of my mind) that Rory was still my husband, and that he was still part of my life, ever bother me.

"I understand how you feel," said Lucy quietly, "but I'd be miserable without David."

"You have a marriage made in heaven," I told her sincerely. "And if I'd been lucky enough to marry someone like David, I'd be miserable without him too."

And that was true, too. David Norris was almost too good to be true. He was the New Man personified.

"Wait until the baby is born," said Lucy darkly, when I said this. "New Man, I don't think! If there's one thing about David, it's that he loves his sleep. I can't see him getting up in the middle of the night to see how junior is getting on. Chances are, he won't wake up at all!"

"Clodagh was a demon," I said, remembering. "She howled for the first three months. I thought I'd never get to sleep again. And then, of course, I was sick."

"Poor thing." Brenda stretched out her long legs. "When we went to visit you in hospital after your appendix operation, you looked so miserable."

"I was," I said, feeling. "It's funny how quickly you recover from things, although I felt absolutely exhausted for ages."

"I feel perfectly fine and then suddenly I want to collapse," Lucy sighed. "It's like all my energy disappears at once."

"Mine is disappearing now," yawned Grace. "Thank God we're not opening the shop tomorrow. This idea of opening all the hours God sends is dreadful."

"When does your sale start?" asked Lucy. "I might go in and buy a few things. For life after the bump."

"That's a terrible way to refer to your child," grinned Brenda. "We don't start our sale until the fourth."

"I'll call in myself," I told them. "I need some new blouses for work."

"Do you know who was in the other day?" asked Brenda, looking at me. "Karen Hamilton. She hadn't been in for ages."

"I haven't seen her in years," I said. "How does she look?"

"Wonderful," said Grace glumly. "She seems to get younger all the time."

"Surgery," I said, confidently. "Nobody could look as good as her naturally. Her son must be – gosh, he must be twenty-one or twenty-two, by now!" I looked around at them, horrified. "Imagine knowing people with adult children! It's creepy."

We laughed, but it was. I couldn't believe that I was thirty-three. It had been bad enough to be thirty! And still, inside, I felt about seventeen. I hadn't changed all that much.

"This will crack you up," said Brenda, as she curled her legs under her knees and looked for all the world like a schoolgirl herself. "Stephanie McMenamin's kid is in secondary school."

We shivered with the horror. To me, Stephanie – the most beautiful girl in our class in school – was frozen in time as a teenager.

"We're like a crowd of senile old women gibbering away," said Grace. "As though we were ancient old crones. We're only thirtysomething, after all!"

"Would you do anything different?" I asked Lucy. "If you were only a teenager again?"

She wrinkled her brow. "It's hard to know," she said. "I wouldn't have worried so much about bloody exams, for a start."

"You'd probably have to worry twice as much now," I said.

"But so much worrying," she said. "And it didn't make a blind bit of difference to me, in the end. There are so much more important things."

"What about you?" I asked Grace.

"Nothing," she said, simply. "I'm happy."

"Me too," said Brenda. "I suppose there's loads of things that you might do differently but I think my life has worked out pretty well. And you, Jane? What would you have done?"

I sighed. "I suppose I wouldn't have married Rory, but that's hindsight," I said. "And if I didn't marry Rory then I wouldn't have Clodagh, so that's all wrong. I don't know, really."

"So what's your New Year's resolution?" asked Lucy, standing up and rubbing her spine.

"To diet," said Grace and Brenda, simultaneously.

"To grow my nails," I said, stretching out my hands in front of me. I didn't bite them any more, but I would have loved long nails.

"Why don't you just get them stuck on?" said Lucy. "There are loads of places for that."

"I did, once," I said. "Sculptured nails. Then I wanted to take them off and I had to buy a bottle of acetone to soak them in. While I was doing that, the doorbell rang and I jumped up and knocked over the little bowl it was in. The stuff spilled all over the table and over Rory's scientific, extremely expensive programmable calculator. It melted all the keys and they stuck together so that he couldn't use it any more. He went absolutely berserk!"

The girls laughed. "You may laugh now," I said, giggling myself. "But he was absolutely furious with me. And, of course, I laughed when it happened, which made it worse. So long nails, naturally grown, for me. Also, I'm going to make a definite effort to improve my painting."

I'd taken up art classes again the previous September in the local vocational school. I was quite good at it now, and was sneakingly proud of some of my watercolours. I harboured a very private dream that one day I would actually sell one, although I couldn't quite see anyone being daft enough to spend money on one. Still, it was a lovely thought.

"Girls, I'm going to bed," yawned Lucy. "It's been a great evening but my eyes are closing and I'll fall asleep here if I don't go upstairs."

We all got up.

"Happy New Year," I said again as I drained my glass.

"Happy New Year," they echoed. We hugged each other before going upstairs to bed.

30

February 1994

(UK No. 1 – Without You – *Mariah Carey)*

I met Rory for lunch in the National Gallery. I didn't want to meet him but he said that he needed to talk to me and he sounded so urgent that I agreed. I didn't like meeting him in public places. I always felt that people looking at us would know that we were a separated couple (although I knew that I was being ridiculous) and that they would be watching us curiously, wondering why we were together. I preferred meeting Rory in my house, when he came to pick up Clodagh. I was always in control in my house.

I liked the National Gallery. Quite often I would walk down Merrion Square and go in there at lunchtime, not to eat in the restaurant but to gaze at the paintings. I loved the portraits, people's expressions captured on the canvas since the eighteenth century. Had they ever dreamed that their pictures would end up in a public gallery rather than in the grand houses where they once lived?

My favourite was a painting of a nun. Among the dark oils of the gallery this was a bright painting, full of light and colour. The nun stood in a flower garden, her white veil perched on her head in a complicated continental arrangement that looked rather like a kite. I thought she might be a postulant because she was dressed completely in white whereas the nuns in the background were in white and black. She held a prayerbook and was gazing towards something outside the frame. She looked so peaceful that she made me feel peaceful too. I often wondered whether she was a real nun, or whether the painter – William Leech – had conjured her up from his imagination. The painting was called *"A Convent Garden, Brittany"*. I had a copy of it at home in the kitchen but it wasn't the same as the real thing.

Rory was already at the gallery when I arrived. He was standing in the foyer, stamping his feet to warm them. It was freezing outside, bright and sunny but with a biting northerly wind. I handed in my coat and pulled my woollen hat from my head.

"I like your hair," said Rory.

"Thank you." We were always polite to each other.

"It suits you like that." This was going beyond the call of duty, I thought although I was pleased that he noticed. My hair was shorter now, just above my shoulders instead of rampaging down my back, and it was cut in a neat bob. The curls had relaxed a bit over the last couple of years and I could wear it shorter without feeling silly.

"Do you want to go and eat?" he asked.

"It's why we're here," I said calmly.

He didn't have the power to upset me any more. I didn't need to try and score points off him, which I'd done when we first split up and which I was never any good at anyway.

The restaurant was already full of people. We took our trays and joined the end of the queue. I was starving.

I had chicken and a salad while Rory chose beef casserole. He picked up a couple of individual-sized bottles of wine and put one on my tray.

"I don't want any wine, thanks," I said as I replaced the bottle. "I'm busy this afternoon and wine at lunch-time makes me sleepy."

"It's only a small bottle, for God's sake!" he said. "It won't kill you."

"I didn't say it would," I told him. "I just don't want any. A glass of water is fine."

He sighed exaggeratedly. "Whatever you like."

We took our food to a table and sat down. He had bags under his eyes, I noticed, and he looked tired. His hair was streaked with grey and it was thinning out even more on top.

"So, what do you want?" I jabbed a cherry tomato with my fork and squirted juice in his direction. It missed him by a whisker.

"Be careful," he said sharply. "You nearly got me that time."

"Sorry," I grinned. "Accident."

"Huh."

I took a sip of water.

"Amanda and I are going on holiday this year,"

said Rory. "We're going to Florida and then to the Bahamas. We want to take Clodagh with us."

I put down my knife and fork and looked at him. My heart pounded. One of the rules was that Clodagh didn't actually ever stay with Amanda and Rory. It was probably very stupid of me, but I couldn't stand the idea of my daughter sleeping under the same roof as the girl who had robbed my husband. Robbed? Another stupid statement. I knew she had done nothing of the sort. Rory had allowed her to rob him, an entirely different thing. But I still didn't want her as a surrogate mother to my child.

"You know our arrangement," I said.

"Of course I know our arrangement," said Rory, impatiently. "That's why I'm meeting you today. I want to change it."

"No," I said.

"Great," said Rory. "I'm offering our daughter the opportunity of a lifetime and you don't even give her a chance. You just say no. How do you think she'll feel when she hears she had the chance to go to Disneyworld and you didn't let her?"

"Thank you," I said. "I'm so glad to be cast in the role of wicked mother."

"Oh, come on, Jane," he said. "I want to take her. I haven't had her for even a weekend since we broke up."

"Since you left," I reminded him tartly. I didn't want to behave like this but I couldn't help myself.

"I knew you'd be like this," said Rory. "You don't want me to have access to her at all."

"That's not true," I replied half-heartedly. "I don't

mind in the least you seeing her. I just don't want her to stay with you. Not when Amanda is there."

"There's nothing wrong with Amanda," said Rory. "You'd swear that she was some evil monster, the way you carry on."

I shrugged. "Sorry," I said. "I can't help it."

We ate in silence for a while. I thought about Rory's request. I should really let her go. Rory was right. But, for her to be with them – as though they were a family unit. The thought made me tremble. People would think that Amanda was her mother! It was too much to take. I couldn't let her go, I just couldn't.

"You always were a selfish bitch." Rory drained his glass of wine.

"Oh, come on, Rory," I said impatiently. "I'm not being selfish."

"Yes, you are," he said. "You don't want her to go, so you say no. You don't care about what Clodagh wants."

"Of course she'll want to go," I said. "I'm not stupid."

"Then think about it," he pleaded. "It's only for two weeks."

Two weeks without her. I'd never been parted from her for that long, before. But Rory looked so unhappy. He did love Clodagh, I knew that. He had always been mad about her. I sighed and bent over my food to hide the tears in my eyes.

"I'll think about it," I said, finally. "When do you want to go?"

"Easter," Rory told me. "But she needs a passport and a visa."

I nodded. "She'll need it quickly, then," I said.

"Thanks," he said.

"I only said I'll think about it," I reminded him. "I'm not promising anything."

"Thanks for thinking about it, at least," he said. He took my hand and squeezed it. I jumped at the touch.

"Do you hate me that much?" he asked.

"No," I said. "I don't hate you at all any more."

He smiled wryly. "I'm glad."

I removed my hand from his and looked at my watch.

"Better be getting back soon," I said.

He nodded. "Sure."

We walked slowly through the gallery together.

"I'm just going to the Ladies," I said. "I'll talk to you soon, Rory."

"OK," he said. "Thanks."

I watched him leave the building, pull his wool coat around him and stride purposefully out on to the street. I didn't go to the Ladies but walked back into the gallery.

What should I do? I stared blankly at the canvases around me. What was the best, the fairest thing to do? To let her go, I supposed, but it was hard to make that decision. I didn't want to let her go.

I stood in front of the painting of the nun again. What would you recommend? I asked her, silently. You should know, you're a nun. Should I let my daughter stay with my husband and his mistress?

It was unfair to call her his mistress. They'd been together for three years.

"I thought it was you." I recognised his voice instantly and turned around. Strangely, I wasn't surprised to see him. He hadn't changed at all. A few extra lines on his face, maybe, but still the same glasses, the same tousled look, the same boyish grin.

"Hello," I said. "Where did you spring from?"

"Come here for lunch quite a bit. And you?"

"So do I."

He looked around. "Have you eaten yet?" he asked, "or are you waiting for someone?"

"I've eaten," I told him.

"Pity," said Hugh.

"Why?"

"I'd have treated you, of course."

"Aren't you meeting anyone yourself?"

He shook his head. "Not today."

"So you come here on your own?"

"Nice place to be," he said. He looked at the picture. "It's one of my favourites."

"Mine too." I smiled at him. "I often wonder what she was like."

"The nun?"

I nodded.

"She was a princess," he said. "A beautiful princess, obviously, since all the best princesses were beautiful. She was engaged to be married to a prince. And he wasn't exactly her choice. She was in love with somebody else. But she was promised to him and so she met him because she always did what she was told. She told her lover that she could never see him again because she was engaged to be married to the prince. Then she realised that she couldn't go through with it. But her lover had already killed himself because she had rejected him. So she joined the convent."

"You made that up," I said, accusingly.

"Perfectly true," he told me.

"I don't believe a word of it," I said. "She looks far to serene to be the sort of girl who has locked herself in a convent because she didn't want to get married. A girl who did that would look more – bottled up."

"Actually, she's the painter's wife," said Hugh.

"Really?"

He nodded.

"Not a nun then." I smiled slightly.

"No." He turned to me. "They split up eventually."

I turned away from the picture and began to walk back to the entrance.

"Oh, look, sorry." He walked after me. "Jane, I'm sorry if I spoiled it for you. I didn't mean it."

I turned back to him. "You didn't spoil it," I said. "I have my own thoughts about her anyway."

"What are they?"

"Secret," I said.

We stood beside each other. "Where are you going?" he asked.

"Back to work."

"Where?"

"Merrion Square. Five minutes away."

"I'm going to Baggot Street," he said. "I'll walk with you."

"If you like." I collected my coat and hat, pulled the collar high around my neck and the hat low over my head.

"You look like a pixie," he said.

"You're a nutter," I told him.

The wind was icy and whirled down the street, catching dust and litter as it went. I shivered.

"How is your little girl?" asked Hugh.

"Getting bigger," I said.

"She must be at school by now," Hugh mused.

"For the past few years. She's seven."

"My God," he said. "I wouldn't have believed it."

"Same age as your niece," I told him.

"I can't believe she's seven, either," he said despairingly. "It only seems like last year she was born."

I nodded. "I know."

"And your husband?" he asked.

My teeth chattered with the cold. "What about him?"

"How is he?"

I shrugged and said nothing. Neither did Hugh. We walked in silence as far as Renham Financial.

"This is where I work," I said. "Nice seeing you again."

"And you," said Hugh.

"Maybe in another few years," I said, lightly.

"That's my line," he said. "See you, Jane." He turned and was gone. I hurried down the steps to the office, feeling strangely alone. I tried to forget that Hugh McLean always turned up when I least expected him to. Well, of course, I never expected him to turn up. He wasn't part of my life, how could he be?

And yet – seven years. I'd know him that long. I remembered him as he barged into the room in the maternity hospital, carrying the bunch of flowers for his sister and going red to the roots with embarrassment when he saw me crying in bed. I smiled at the memory.

Some people just bobbed in and out of your life. Hugh certainly seemed to bob in and out of mine.

I thought about Rory's request for nearly a week. Eventually I decided to ask Mam what she thought, although that was a mistake. I called into the house to pick up Clodagh, who was now attending St Attracta's primary school. I'd never gone to the primary school, it hadn't been built until I was ten and Mam hadn't wanted to move me then. It gave me the shivers when I thought that my child would one day attend my old school, sit in a classroom where perhaps I'd once sat myself. I wondered whether or not the same desks were there, and if she'd ever sit at the one that said *Jane O'Sullivan was bored here 1975.* She'd look out the classroom windows, but instead of seeing the rolling fields that had surrounded the school when I was there, she'd see rows of houses which had been built on the surrounding land, crawling halfway up the mountains in an ever-advancing army.

Our routine was simple. In the mornings I'd drop Clodagh at my parents' house, where she'd have tea and toast before walking to school. Then I'd pick her up on my way home in the evenings. Usually she'd be looking out the window waiting for me so that I didn't have to go into the house every day. She'd run out, banging the front door behind her and streak down the front path, a leggy, coltish thing, long hair flying behind her, her bag bumping against her legs.

Clodagh hated when I came in to the house, because it always took me at least half an hour to leave. Mam would ask me how I was, tell me that I was working too hard and suggest that I buy a tonic. "You're looking peaky," was still her favourite expression.

I helped Mam dry some dishes while Clodagh watched *Blockbusters* and told her about Rory's request.

"And I hope you said no," she said firmly.

I made a face.

"Oh, Jane, you must have refused."

I sighed. "I wanted to, of course," I told her. "But it was very difficult to dismiss it outright. I'm sure Clodagh would love to go."

"That's hardly the point, is it?" asked Mam. "You can't possibly let her go."

"That's how I feel," I admitted, "but I'm not sure it's the right way to feel."

"He's asking you to let a seven-year-old girl go on holidays with him and his – his – fancy piece."

I smothered a smile. In Mam's eyes, Amanda Ferry was a trollop.

"I know," I said. "But he's very good to Clodagh, and I'm sure that he'd give her a wonderful holiday."

"My foot," snapped Mam. "I don't think you should expose her to that sort of thing."

"It's hardly any sort of thing."

"I don't think that girl should be in contact with your daughter," said Mam. "And that's that!"

"It's not fair to call her 'that girl'," I protested, mildly. "She's probably a very nice person."

"Oh, really," said Mam. "Then why did she steal your husband?"

"She didn't steal him." I wondered myself why on earth I was defending Amanda when I absolutely detested her. "Rory let her steal him, which is a very different thing."

"If that girl hadn't got her talons into him, then he'd never have left you," said Mam.

I shrugged. "Maybe not. So, maybe she did me a favour."

"Jane!" Mam was shocked.

"Well, maybe she did. He was driving me around the bend before he left. Maybe it's just as well."

Mam flapped the tea towel in the air. Her face was red with effort. I stacked the dishes neatly in the cupboard. They were new cupboards. Mam and Dad had bought a complete new kitchen a year ago and Mam loved her new pine and glass fitted look.

"I still think it's a bad thing for Clodagh to see the sort of goings-on that would happen on holiday with that pair," she said.

"I don't think she'll see any goings-on, as you put it," I said. "They've been living together for three years. I'm sure they'll be able to restrain themselves in front of the child."

Mam blushed; she hated referring, even obliquely, to sex. The idea that Rory and Amanda might be sleeping together was absolutely abhorrent to her.

"Well, you know my views," said Mam. "I'll let you make up your own mind, I won't interfere."

I hugged her. Since Clodagh was born I felt much

closer to her, I thought that I understood her better. I certainly understood how much she'd had to put up with when I was a child.

"Come on, Clodagh," I called. "Put your coat on, it's time to go home."

In bed that night I made my decision. I would let her go. I didn't want to, but I couldn't always do exactly what I wanted. And I knew that Rory would look after her. He adored her.

He was thrilled when I phoned and told him, promised that he'd take very good care of her and that he wouldn't allow her to do things that I didn't let her do and that he'd make her eat all her greens. I told him that I never made her eat all her greens but he was welcome to try.

I told Clodagh the next day because we had to go and get her photograph taken and fill out her passport and visa applications. Her face lit up and I felt a heel for even thinking of not letting her go.

"Where will we be staying?" she demanded.

"I don't know," I said. "Daddy will tell you."

At first, she thought that I was coming too and, when she realised that I wasn't, she said she didn't want to go. Secretly that pleased me, but I told her not to be silly, that she'd have a great time and that she wouldn't miss me one little bit. So she went around in a frenzy of excitement and couldn't wait until her Easter holidays. She marked off every day with a big red crayon, standing on the three-legged stool to reach the calendar and sticking her tongue out of the corner of her mouth as she ticked off the days.

In the meantime, the office was very busy. Claire was giving a presentation to a group of investors in a week's time and I had to prepare the documents, make slides and charts and organise the venue. So I was absolutely up to my neck. It was strange but, whenever the office was busy, it was manically busy and the phones never stopped ringing. We'd bought a new desktop publishing package, too, and I hadn't quite got the hang of it yet so that I kept having to look up the manual to see if I was doing things properly, which made it all twice as complicated as it should have been. Each time I had the document nearly right, the phone would buzz and I'd forget what I was doing and have to start all over again. Claire and Stephen loved it when the phones were hopping like this, because it meant lots of business. But today, particularly, it was driving me around the bend.

"Renham Financial," I said as I cradled the earpiece between my ear and my shoulder and tried to point the computer mouse at the right icon on the screen in front of me.

"Could I speak to Jane, please?" asked the disembodied voice.

"Speaking." I used my pleasant telephone voice.

"Hi, Jane, it's Hugh."

I almost dropped the phone and I double-clicked the mouse on the wrong icon.

"Hugh!" I cleared my throat. "How can I help you?"

"How can you help me?" he laughed, that rich deep laugh. "You can help me by coming to lunch with me today."

I stared at the phone as though I could actually see Hugh McLean's face on it. "Lunch?" I asked.

"Yes," he said. "I'm going to the National Gallery for lunch and I thought you might like to join me."

"That's very nice of you," I said, in confusion. "But I can't do that."

"Why not?" he asked.

"Well, because – I just can't."

There was silence at the other end of the phone. I could hear the crackle of static on the line.

"I'm sorry," I said. "I'll have to go. I'm very busy." I hung up, my heart thumping.

Had Hugh asked me for a date? Hardly. Lunch wasn't exactly a date. And he knew that I was married, for goodness sake. He'd hardly be likely to ask me for a date if he thought that Rory and I were still living together. I glanced down at my hand. I didn't wear my wedding ring any more. When I'd taken it off first, there was a faint pale line around my finger and I'd felt naked without it. But I couldn't still wear it when it didn't mean anything. Hugh wouldn't know that. So why did he want to meet me for lunch? Anyway, if he had wanted to ask me out (ask me out, what a juvenile expression!), he could have done so any time over the past seven years.

Come on, Jane, I said to myself. Get a grip. But all through the afternoon, as I wrestled with Claire's presentation document, his face swam before me, ruffling me, unsettling me.

I worked until seven o'clock. I phoned Mam to say I'd be late and Clodagh answered the phone. She told me that she was the best in her class at spelling and proceeded to go through her list of words beginning with W.

"You're very clever," I told her proudly.

We bought takeaway pizza on the way home, hot and dripping with melted mozzarella cheese. Clodagh adored pizza although Mam always gave out to me when I bought it. She didn't believe that anything other than chops and vegetables was the right food for a growing girl. I reminded her frequently of the experiments she had done on me, bringing home trial runs of some very dubious fast food from the supermarket when she'd worked there. She dismissed this as irrelevant and reminded me that there was always meat in whatever she had brought home. I remembered some of the stuff that I'd eaten and doubted very much if the meat it claimed to contain had ever actually been part of a living animal, but it was no use, Mam was adamant. She'd always fed me properly. She'd never have made it as a vegetarian.

Clodagh, on the other hand, loved vegetables. Not green ones, but mushrooms and tomatoes and peppers and sweetcorn – all of which were on the giant-sized pizza we took home.

We ate it in front of the fire watching TV, getting topping all over our fingers and our faces and we giggled as we fought over the last piece. Like two children.

I checked her homework for her while she played *Sensible Soccer* on her Nintendo. She still loved soccer and watched it avidly on TV. I thought it might be a link with Rory that she wanted to keep. She supported Liverpool, although, she told me, she fancied Ryan Giggs.

She never played with dolls. She liked toy cars, football and computer games. She loved dressing up, but preferred wearing jeans and trainers. She played quite happily with both the boys and the girls on the road and was much more self-confident than I'd been as a child. She didn't let anyone mess her around. But when she went to bed, it was with her blue teddy bear tucked into the quilt beside her.

I hoped that I'd made the right decision about the holiday. I knew that I'd never forgive myself if she found out that she'd had the opportunity to go and I hadn't let her. But I was terrified that she'd prefer Rory and Amanda's company to my own, and that when she came back she'd ask me if she could stay with them more and more and then one day would move in with them altogether.

It was an unlikely scenario, I knew that. All the same, Amanda and Rory earned more than £100,000 a year between them, lived in a beautiful duplex apartment near Blackrock and would be able to give Clodagh everything she needed without even thinking about it. That's what scared me. If Rory ever decided that he wanted to have custody of Clodagh, I wondered whether any judge would really think me a more suitable parent. Sometimes I'd worry about it as I lay in bed at night, listening to the sounds of the house settling, creaking floorboards and strange gurgles from the cistern. It was never so bad in the daytime, when Clodagh and I were a kind of partnership, but I hated the nights. I'd always been a bit afraid of the dark and all my worst imaginings came to me then. I never dreamed good things at night any more.

31

March 1994

(UK No. 2 – The Sign – *Ace Of Base)*

I met him in the National Gallery again, by accident not design. It was one of those typically March days, one minute a blue sky and blazing sunshine and the next grey clouds and hailstones. I was walking back to work, past the gallery when the hailstorm began. I hurried inside to shelter. Lots of other people had the same idea and the rooms were full of people who probably otherwise wouldn't be there, so that there were groups in front of the paintings. I went to mine.

The nun was still there, still looking serenely out from her field of flowers. I thought of Leech painting his wife as a nun and wondered why their marriage had broken up. I sat on one of the seats and looked around me, still shivering a little from the sudden blast of cold. Then he walked past me, from the restaurant towards the door.

I thought he hadn't seen me at first because he

strode by, hands deep in his pockets, staring at the floor. He stopped suddenly, spun around on his heels and looked back towards me.

His eyes lit up in recognition and he walked back to me, smiling. "Hello again," he said as he squashed himself between me and an elderly gentleman in a waxed coat. "How are you?"

"I'm OK," I said. "And you?"

"Great." He smiled.

We looked at each other for a while. I felt that I should say something to him but I didn't know what. He just looked at me.

We both started to speak at the same time and broke off.

"You first," he said. I shook my head. "No, you."

"I was going to ask you if you'd like to lunch with me sometime," he said. "Since you gave me the bum's rush the last time."

"I was surprised you phoned," I said. "That you even knew where to phone."

He looked surprised himself. "That was easy," he said. "The name-plate was on the railings."

"Oh, I see." I couldn't believe he'd noticed the name-plate, or remembered it.

"So?"

"Why did you ask me?" I turned to him. "Why do you want to lunch with me at all."

"I like you," he said simply. "I always have."

"But I'm married," I told him. "You know that." I didn't want to tell him about Rory and me. I wasn't able to. I was afraid that he'd think that I was looking for someone if I told him about Rory. I didn't want him to think that. I wasn't looking for someone. Not like that.

He looked resigned. "I know you're married, Jane, that's not the issue. I'm not trying to have an affair with you or anything. For God's sake, I saw you in bed and didn't try to have an affair with you."

I laughed. "I don't think anybody could have, just then." I looked at him seriously. "But there's no point in us having lunch, Hugh." It was the first time I'd ever said his name to his face. It felt strange. "What good would having lunch with me do?"

"I'd enjoy it," he said, simply. "You make me smile."

I looked at him in astonishment. "Me? Don't be daft."

I didn't think I made him smile. Any time I ever met him, I seemed to be in floods of tears. Around us, people walked up and down the gallery's polished floor. People sat down or got up from the seat beside us and yet they only registered in the outer reaches of my mind. I liked Hugh. But what was the point in getting to know him? And if, by the remotest chance we started to have a relationship (I hated that word), where could it possibly go? I had a seven-year-old child, I had to be realistic about things.

"Why are you so afraid of a simple lunch?" asked Hugh.

I stared at my shoes. There was a ladder beginning in my tights. I twisted that leg behind my other leg to hide it.

"I don't think it would be a good idea." I stood up. "I'm sorry."

He stood up too and walked towards the door with me. We walked side by side out of the gallery and on to the street.

"Are you happy?" he asked suddenly.

I was horrified to find tears in my eyes. "Of course I'm happy," I said, as a huge tear slid down my cheek. I turned away from him to hide it and hurried up the street. I felt him standing there, watching me. Please don't follow me, I prayed. Please don't.

For once, my prayers were answered. He allowed me to walk away from him without doing anything about it. Part of me wondered whether he would ring again, to apologise perhaps, or even to ask to see me. But he didn't. I didn't hear from him at all, and I told myself that it was just as well.

Clodagh and I went to the supermarket to get her photograph taken for her passport. She twirled around on the seat with excitement and stuck her tongue out in the last photo.

"What's this meant to be?" I asked in mock severity.

"A present for you," she told me.

"Some present," I said.

She still crossed off every day on the calendar. She smiled in satisfaction and said "only ten more days, only nine more days," while I tried not to let her see that it bothered me.

David Norris rang towards the end of the month to tell me that Lucy had given birth to a baby boy. Mother and child doing well, he told me.

She was in Holles Street, so I walked down the next day to see her. She sat propped up in the bed, reading *Hello!* magazine and looking fantastic. I hugged her and peeped into the little crib where the baby lay sleeping.

He was lovely, still wrinkled, not yet grown into his skin. He opened his eyes as I looked down at him, navy blue staring up at me. I touched his cheek. The skin was soft as a peach, the sort of skin I'd die for now.

"He's gorgeous," I whispered to her. "And you, you bitch, you look brilliant."

"I'm actually knackered," said Lucy. "I've muscles where I never knew muscles existed before. I feel like every organ in my body has been taken out and put back in the wrong place."

I laughed at her.

"It's no laughing matter," she said. "I'll never be able to walk properly again. And," she hissed, "I've got stitches."

I shuddered. "I don't want to know, Lucy," I said. "I've been though this already."

"Yes, but you at least did it in style," objected Lucy. "You were carted away in an ambulance and knocked out for the entire episode. None of this pushing and shoving business for you."

I grinned at her. "Was it absolutely awful?"

"They say you forget," she told me darkly. "But I'll never forget."

"Never mind," I grinned. "Have you thought of a name for him yet?"

"We keep tossing names around," said Lucy. "But

we can't agree on one yet. The poor child will be known as X for the rest of his life, as far as I can see."

"Loads of names will go with Norris," I told her as I sat on the edge of her bed and idly flicked through her magazine. "God, doesn't Cindy Crawford look fantastic?"

"Jane, please don't show me pictures of supermodels," complained Lucy. "I know I never looked like them but now I know I never will. It's a very depressing thought."

"Sorry." I put the magazine on a shelf. "So what names have you come up with?"

She sighed. "David wanted to call him Nicholas!"

Lucy's married man. I laughed. "So what did you say?"

"I told him that he could call him after the bloke that first groped me in the back seat of a car if he wanted to, but that it wasn't my favourite name."

"So what others?" I asked.

"I'm not sure yet; we're going to make up our minds soon, though. We'll have to."

I stood up. "Whatever you call him, he's a darling," I said as I peeked in at him again. "And he doesn't look a bit like either of you."

"I know," she said, "although I tell David that he looks like him after a few pints."

"I'd better get back to work," I said regretfully. "But I'll call in and see you again."

I hurried back up the square to the office, thinking about Lucy and David and how happy they were, truly delighted that she had such a lovely baby. It made me think of Clodagh, and how she'd been as a tiny scrap. And of Hugh McLean, who had visited us. I couldn't get Hugh McLean out of my head, although I tried to blank out thoughts of him every time they appeared. But I'd be in the middle of typing something, or answering the phone, and then suddenly I'd hear his voice in my head, or see his face in front of me as clearly as if he were really there. And I'd stumble over whatever I was doing and make a mess of it.

It was like being a teenager again, although if I were a teenager I could say that I had a crush on him or something. But I was too old for crushes! Too mature to act like a schoolgirl! Anyway, I didn't fancy him and I wasn't attracted to him. Not in that sort of way. I told myself this over and over again. There was no room in my life for men any more. They brought nothing but grief.

I thought about them all. Every man I'd ever known had made me cry. Jesse, Dermot, Richard – even Frank, Mr Nice Guy, had left me to pursue his career. And Rory had never stopped making me cry. Even now, when I didn't love him any more, a film or a song might remind me of a time when we *did* love each other, when everything was all right. I'd suddenly ache for something that I knew now I could never have.

They went on holidays the Thursday before Easter. The flight was in the morning so I took time off work and drove Clodagh to the airport to meet Rory and Amanda there. I could have brought her to their apartment the night before, but I didn't want to do that. I was shaking as I put her case into the boot of the car. She looked confident and self-assured as she clambered into the back seat, neatly dressed in her best jeans, jumper and jacket and wearing her Nike trainers. She had her own bag with her spending money in it and her passport.

It took no time to reach the airport. I parked in the short-term car park and walked with her to the departures area. She held my hand and I was comforted by the warmth of it in mine.

"I'll bring you back a present," she promised as we walked through the sliding doors. "I'll get you something really nice."

"Thank you." I scanned the crowds for Rory.

He was near the escalators and he was on his own. For a brief moment I thought that maybe Amanda had decided not to go, but that was ridiculous.

"Hello, there," he called and Clodagh waved at him. I looked around for Amanda.

"She's in the café upstairs," said Rory. "She thought you'd prefer it if she was upstairs."

"I don't mind," I said, nonchalantly, although my heart thumped and I was still shaking. I looked at Clodagh. "You be a good girl," I told her.

"I will." She stared at me solemnly.

"And do whatever your Daddy tells you."

"I will."

"And don't be any trouble."

"I won't."

"And have a good time."

She beamed. "Of course I'll have a good time."

"OK, then." I dropped down to her level. "Give me a kiss."

She flung her arms around me and kissed me, wetly, on the cheek. "Why don't you come too?" she whispered. "They'd let you come."

"I'd love to," I said, "but I have to go to work."

"Please come."

"I can't. You won't miss me, Clodagh, you'll be too busy having fun."

"I s'pose so," she said, as she unwrapped her arms from around my neck. "But I'll remember you all the time."

"Good." I planted a kiss on top of her head. "So I'll leave you with Daddy." I stood up. "Look after her," I said to Rory.

"Of course I will," he said. "She's my own daughter. I'm not going to let anything happen to her."

I knew that he meant it and I knew that he would take care of her. But it was still hard to turn away from them and walk out of the building back to the car. I kept wanting to run back, especially to see Amanda. I didn't want her to touch Clodagh but I knew that I was being silly. I was proud of the fact that I'd let Clodagh go with them. But I still felt sick inside.

I dropped around to Lucy that evening, unwilling to sit at home on my own yet. She was feeding baby Andrew, patiently holding him against her, watching him carefully.

She smiled as I came into the room. "I'm not very good at this yet," she said, "but I'm going to persevere for a while."

"How are you feeling?" I asked as I sank into the armchair opposite her.

"Great," she said, and she did look wonderful. Her golden hair shone in the warm light of the lamp beside her, and her skin was clear and flawless. She looked about twenty.

"You look fantastic," I said enviously. "How do you do it?"

"Make-up," she laughed. She looked at me intently. "How did it go this morning?" She knew how I felt about it, she'd been very sympathetic but had agreed with my decision to let Clodagh go.

"I was sick leaving her at the airport," I said. "I wanted to stop her and say I'd changed my mind, but I couldn't do that. She was looking forward to it so much. And Rory will be good to her."

"But the idea of another woman with your child . . . " Lucy lifted Andrew gently on to her shoulder and rubbed his back.

"I know." I bit my lip. "But she's seven years old, Lucy, and she's a person herself. I can't try to stop her from seeing Amanda. If we lived in England, Rory and I would probably be divorced by now and he'd have married Amanda, and there'd be nothing I could do about it."

"Will he stay with her, d'you think?" asked Lucy.

"I don't know." I stood up and paced across the room. "I think he loves her but who knows, really. I thought he loved me."

We were silent for a moment. The clock on the mantelpiece ticked rhythmically. I pulled at my fingernails.

"Why do you think he got off with her in the first place?" asked Lucy.

"Why did Rory ever do anything?" I asked. "He loves new things all the time, Lucy. That's why I can't be sure whether or not he'll even stick with Amanda. He used to change the car nearly every year. He was the one who wanted to move house. He was always looking for new things to buy. He changed his friends a lot. Except for the management at the bank, he went through phases of blokes being his best mate. He's not a very constant sort of person."

"But you are," said Lucy. "So you'd think it'd work out, really."

"You are the most constant thing in my life." I sat down again. "You're the only person I know that I still feel comfortable with. You never criticise or accuse me or try to change me."

She laughed. "That's because I know you. Anyway, you don't do any of those things to me either. That's why we're friends, stupid."

I smiled. "Suppose so."

She handed the baby to me while she went upstairs. I cradled him in the crook of my arm. He was lovely, so small and so innocent. It was such a shame that he had to grow up, I thought. Into a person. Being a boy, he'd probably break some poor girl's heart. Why couldn't life be easier?

"You look very natural," said Lucy as she came back into the room, a book in her hand. "Sure you wouldn't like another one?"

I shook my head. "Out of the question," I said.

"But if it wasn't out of the question?"

"It is," I told her. "There's no point in thinking about it."

She handed me the book. It was a photograph album.

"Our Debs' Ball," she said, "and our first holiday together. Remember?"

I looked at the pictures of us all. Lucy, the Quinlans, Stephanie McMenamin, Jenny Gibson, Louise Killane, Anne Sutherland, Camilla McKenzie, Martha Sheridan. We were all smiling, delighted with ourselves. And the holiday snaps. Lucy and Wim, Jaime and me. I closed my eyes as I remembered losing my virginity to Jaime.

"Great holiday," I said, reliving the moment.

"Jane O'Sullivan, you're practically there again!" Lucy prodded me in the ribs.

"I remember it all so clearly," I said. "We were on the beach. I got sand in my hair."

"And you came back with a smile like a Cheshire cat," she told me. "I knew that you'd done it."

"Lucy!"

"Well, you had the glow," she said.

I leafed through the photograph album, smiling at its memories.

"Don't you miss the sex?" asked Lucy suddenly.

I blushed furiously. "What a question," I mumbled.

"Well, don't you?"

Lucy had always loved it. More than me, I thought.

I made a face at her. "Sometimes."

"Have you gone out with anyone in the last four years?" she demanded.

"Don't be ridiculous," I said. "How could I?"

"Easily," she told me.

"Lucy, you'll find out for yourself when Andrew is a bit older. You don't have a life of your own when you've got a kid. And I'm all that Clodagh has. I don't have time to go around meeting men."

"You should make time," said Lucy. "It's not good to be alone."

"That's rubbish," I said. "There's nothing wrong with being alone. I'm quite happy."

"You think you are," she said. "But you're only coping, Jane. There's a difference."

"Lucy, I'm perfectly happy. I enjoy my work, I get on well with my colleagues, I have a good relationship with my daughter. I have a nice house, a car that goes and a cat that curls up on my lap at night. What more could a girl ask for?"

She was silent for a moment. I'd stumped her now, I thought. Because if you were happy, then there wasn't any more that you needed. And I was happy.

"When we were younger, you always wanted boyfriends," she said.

"That was different," I objected. "That was to prove something."

"But don't you miss the companionship?"

I leaned back in the chair. "That is where your entire argument falls down," I told her. "Rory gave me bugger-all companionship in the last couple of years of our marriage. Obviously because he was giving it all to Amanda Ferry. Golf trips that were supposed to be with the lads – he was taking her away. And I never even guessed, Lucy. Not once. Christ, I was stupid." I shook my head at my own naiveté. "And when he wasn't with her, he was with people from the bank. So when he came home, all he did was flop down on the sofa and fall asleep. Call that companionship! All he did was get in the way, really."

"So why didn't you get out sooner?"

"Because I thought marriage was like that," I said. "Anyway, who cares now? I don't."

She gazed at me sympathetically but I was immune to her sympathy. I was perfectly happy as I was, and I wasn't going to let her make me feel in some way inadequate because there wasn't a man in my life.

"We should go to the fortune-teller again," she said suddenly.

"Oh, come on, Lucy!" I cried. "That's a load of crap and you know it."

"She told me about Andrew," said Lucy, obstinately. "She's been right about everything."

I'd never been back to Mrs. Vermuelen after my first visit, I was too scared. She'd been right about some things and I didn't want to know about my future from her. Anyway, I still didn't believe in fortune-tellers. But Lucy went regularly and said that the woman was always right.

"Maybe," I said finally. Lucy's silences were more persuasive than her words.

David came back just as I was leaving. He kissed Lucy, picked up his son and held him close. David was still one of life's sensitive souls. I envied Lucy, but there weren't many Davids around.

It was raining as I drove home. The windscreen

wipers scraped back and forwards, pushing the water away. I hated this sort of weather and I detested driving in it. Car headlights dazzled me as I drove along the coast back towards the toll bridge. I could feel the wind whipping down the river as I drove across the bridge and a blast of icy air hit me as I rolled down the window to toss the change into the basket.

The house was cold and dark. It felt completely different without Clodagh, as though a whole chunk of it was missing. I wondered if my mother had felt like that when I left home. I pressed the button and the central heating sprang into life. The water whooshed through the pipes and immediately made me feel less alone.

Junkie was sheltering under the windowsill. I opened the kitchen door and he shot into the kitchen, an angry ball of wet fur. He slid across the tiled floor and crashed into his food bowl. He sat down and licked his fur, trying to rearrange it. I put some more food into the bowl and he fell on it ravenously.

I made myself a cup of coffee and brought it into the living-room. I switched on TV and gazed unseeingly at the screen. Junkie followed me in and climbed on to my lap. I sat there like a grandmother, sipping coffee and rubbing the cat's fur. It was soporific.

Did I need a man in my life? Was there room for one? Was there a part of me that needed one? What were they worth after all? None of them had ever done me any good.

I thought of Hugh McLean again, as I knew I

would. He wanted to know me, but why? It was stupid of him to say that it was because I made him smile or because I interested him. Men didn't want to meet women for lunch because they interested them. They only wanted to meet women because they fancied them. Because they wanted to go to bed with them.

The idea that Hugh might want to go to bed with me gave me a sudden glow. Had I been missing out for the last few years? No, I decided suddenly. I hadn't. It would be all moonshine and gossamer for a while and then suddenly it would all go horribly wrong, and I just wasn't going to let that happen to me again. It didn't matter who it was. Whether they seemed nice or not. Men hurt you, that was all they knew what to do. They wined you, dined you, took you to bed and left you. And it would never be any different.

The sun slanted through the chink in the bedroom curtains. I could see the fragments of dust float in the air. I yawned suddenly and stretched out in the bed. The stretch went from my fingertips to my toes.

The bedroom door opened and he stood naked before me. Each muscle on his body was clearly defined. I gazed at him, enjoyed looking at him.

"Do I meet with your approval?" he asked.

He opened the curtains. The Mediterranean sun spilled into the room. I blinked at its brightness. He opened the windows and the scent of bougainvillaea filled the air.

He sat on the bed beside me. He touched my forehead and traced a line slowly down my face, my neck, between my breasts where he paused for a moment, looking at me. Then his finger moved lower, slower. I flinched involuntarily as it reached the base of my stomach. He smiled.

I reached for him and pulled him closer to me. He smelled of shower gel and Paco Rabanne. His face was smooth, clean-shaven. I touched his arms, the muscles were strong and hard.

He made love to me and I cried out with the joy of it and the passion. We lay together when it was over and he lit a continental cigarette. The smoke spiralled above me, blue and pungent.

"I have to go," he said, and I nodded. I didn't know who he was. I'd never seen him before. I didn't want to see him again.

When I woke the next morning the rain was still beating on the window, drumming heavily against the glass. Junkie was curled into a little ball at my feet, purring with pleasure. I blushed as I remembered the dream. I'd blame Lucy for it, I thought, for reminding me of desires that I didn't need to have any more. I pulled the duvet around me and stayed in bed until the afternoon.

32

April 1994

(UK No. 1 – The Real Thing – *Tony Di Bart)*

I wanted to collect Clodagh from the airport, but Rory said that he'd drop her back to the house. He'd leave Amanda home first, he told me, and then call in with Clodagh. I spent all day waiting for her return. The flight was delayed by almost two hours – I rang the airport a few times to check on its progress.

I made shepherd's pie for her dinner because it was her favourite meal. I kept reminding myself that she would probably be tired and cranky and would want to go to bed straight away.

They arrived home about nine o'clock. I had the central heating on all day so that the house would be warm enough for her. Rory held her in his arms. For a horrible moment I thought that something was wrong, but I could see that she was only sleeping.

"She's exhausted," he told me. "She didn't sleep on the plane, she insisted on watching the movies, but with the delays and everything she hasn't slept since yesterday. She fell asleep in the car."

He carried her upstairs. I eased her out of her clothes. She didn't wake up, even when I slipped her pyjamas on to her.

"Did she have a good time?" I asked.

Rory nodded. "A ball," he told me. "She enjoyed everything. Went on as much as she possibly could in Disneyworld. Wanted to go jet-skiing in the Bahamas – we didn't let her, of course, although she had great fun on the banana boat."

"Banana boat?" I asked.

"Oh, a floating thing shaped like a banana," he explained. "You sit on it and it's pulled along by another boat. Goes quite fast. She had a great time on that. Met a few American kids on the beach, so she can speak a bit of Spanish, now!"

"Did you enjoy it yourself?"

We were like strangers, really. Such courtesy, I thought. Never there when we lived together.

"I'm knackered," he admitted. "Looking after her is a full-time job."

"I'm glad you think so," I said. "And how is Amanda?"

"Fine," said Rory. "She had a good time. She was very good to Clodagh."

I looked around uncomfortably. "Good."

"They got on very well."

"You and Amanda can have one of your own," I said tartly.

"We might," said Rory. "Clodagh has made us think that we might."

His words made me feel sick. I could cope with the idea of them living together, but the idea of them being a family was completely different. Then Clodagh would have a half-brother or sister. I supposed they'd want me to let her stay over, then. Well, I wouldn't. She was mine.

"Amanda'll be wondering where you are," I said. "And you're probably tired yourself. Maybe you'd better be going."

He did look tired. He stood up. "Thanks for being good about it all," he said suddenly.

I stood up, too. "It's OK."

We were face to face. His eyes were still the same colour blue, still attracted me. Don't, I whispered to myself, fighting the urge to touch him. You don't love him any more.

He leaned towards me and kissed me on the mouth. I was shocked that he would think the same as me. I returned his kiss, remembering the familiarity of him, the taste of him. It would be easy, I thought wildly, to get him back. I could make love to him now, and then he would come back to me and it could be as it was before.

He held me closer to him and I could feel myself hungry with desire. We could be together again. I would forget everything that had happened. We were husband and wife still. He could move in tomorrow, and it wouldn't matter because we were still Rory and Jane McLoughlin. We'd a perfect right to be together. Clodagh could have her parents back, her family back. She would love that.

He began to unbutton my blouse. His hand

slipped beneath the cotton of my bra, touching my breast. I trembled. He groaned softly. I pressed against him and he slid the blouse from my shoulders.

"Oh, Jane," he said.

If he hadn't spoken maybe it all would have been different. If he'd said nothing, perhaps we would have made love there and then on the rug of the living-room floor, naked in front of the flickering gas fire. And then my life would have fitted back into the groove from which it had been so unfairly shaken. I could have become Jane McLoughlin again.

But he said "Oh, Jane" and his words pierced through my desire and into the part of my brain that was practical and intelligent. I pulled away from him and started to rebutton my blouse.

"What's the matter?" he asked.

I stared at him. "What's the matter!"

"You wanted to, I wanted to. Where's the harm?"

I stepped back away from him, folding my arms in front of me.

"You left me for another woman," I said. "You changed everything."

"You're still my wife," he said.

"Don't be stupid," I said.

"You still want me."

I clenched my fists until my nails dug into my palms. "No."

"Oh, come on, Jane. You were shaking with want for me."

I was shaking still. "No," I repeated.

He stepped towards me. "Why not?"

"Because you're living with Amanda," I said. "You

know that. You've been living with her for years. You've been on holiday with her. You can't surely expect me to – " I broke off. "Don't you love Amanda any more?" I asked.

He shrugged. "Oh, I love her," he said, offhandedly.

"Then why?"

"Because I still love you too, Jane."

"Don't be ridiculous."

"You're so desirable," he said. "You were always so desirable. From the first moment I saw you, I wanted you. That first night I wanted to fuck your brains out."

"Rory!"

"Sorry," he said. "But it's true. You had a great body and you used it, Janey. Then you went all uninterested."

"I was uninterested because you were," I said. "You were never around. How could I stay interested in someone who was never there?"

"I'm sorry about that," he said. "I was wrong."

"And you're wrong now," I said. "It's over between us, Rory."

"Is there someone else now?" he asked.

"No," I said.

"Stands to reason," said Rory.

"Why?"

"You practically fell on me," he said. "You wouldn't have done that if you were getting it regularly."

"I think you'd better go." I thought I was going to faint.

"You think you're in the movies," he said. "People don't go just because you ask them to."

I swallowed. "Do you want to stay?"

"I want to make love to you," he said. "You want to make love to me."

"No, Rory, I don't."

He looked at me quizzically. "You'll turn into a dried-up old maid," he said, "and nobody'll want you."

"Rory, will you please leave."

"Poor old Jane, they'll say. Frigid."

"I'm not frigid," I said.

"Not yet. You're still hot stuff now, Jane. But give it another few years. Then you'll be forty and you'll have no chance."

"Why do you bring everything down to your level?" I asked. "I think you should go, Rory. I'm sure Amanda is anxiously waiting for you."

He laughed suddenly. "It was a good try, though, wasn't it?"

"Brilliant," I said, trying to keep my voice under control. "Thanks for giving Clodagh a great holiday. Now will you go?"

"Suit yourself." He tucked his shirt back inside his jeans. "See you, Jane."

I stayed where I was. I heard the front door close and his car roar down the road. Then I poured myself a brandy and port and knocked it back in one go. My legs buckled beneath me and I collapsed on to the sofa.

Clodagh woke up at midday on Sunday. She insisted

on wearing her American leggings and her Miami Dolphins sweatshirt and put her baseball cap on her head backwards. She told me her stories about the States, about the fun she'd had and the places she'd seen. But most especially about Disneyworld, and the great time she'd had there. Rory and Amanda had indulged her completely. They'd gone to Paradise Island in the Bahamas where she'd spent every day on the beach. She looked tanned and healthy and she hadn't burned. Amanda had made her wear suntan cream, she told me. And a hat. She was a real nag. I laughed at that, although with some reservations, because it seemed to me that Amanda really had taken good care of her and I suppose that I'd half hoped that Amanda wouldn't have given a curse what Clodagh did.

"Did you like her?" I asked curiously.

"She was OK," said Clodagh laconically. "She played loads of games with me and she let me buy loads of clothes. But it wasn't the same as being with you," she added.

"I'm glad to hear it," I said. "Now, come on, we're going over to Granny's for our lunch."

Clodagh complained about the cold although the weather was improving and the evenings were getting brighter. The cherry blossom tree in the front garden was laden with pink flowers which spilled down on to the grass and swirled on the driveway whenever the breeze picked up. I liked the way the evenings were getting longer, it made me feel as if I was emerging from a long tunnel. I always felt like this when winter finally began to give way to spring and the leaves reappeared on the trees. I loved waking up to a sunlit bedroom instead of the inky blackness of a December morning. I'd more energy in the springtime too, I became more optimistic.

I tried to forget about Rory's advances. It wasn't something I wanted to think about, or talk about, even with Lucy. I'd been afraid that I might give in to him, and that would have been a terrible mistake. But he'd said things that could be true and they niggled at me.

Was I becoming a dry old maid? Surely that was an outdated idea? I had a full and active life and I didn't need Rory to lecture me about it. Of course I didn't get out much after work, and maybe that was a problem. When I thought about it, I realised that it was ages since I'd been to the pub (except for a sandwich at lunchtime), or to the cinema or to a play. Maybe it was time to get out and about a bit more. But I couldn't abandon Clodagh, that wouldn't be fair.

I looked at the calendar. Lucy, myself and the twins hadn't got together since New Year. I'd been in Les Jumelles a couple of times since then, but the shop had been incredibly busy and the twins hadn't any time for idle gossip. The thing to do was to get them over to the house for a dinner party. Or better still, go out to dinner some evening. That was my problem; all my entertaining, such as it was, was conducted from home. I needed to be outside these four walls. I rang Lucy and asked her what she thought.

"Great idea," she said. "Leave it until the end of

the month, because Andrew will be on bottles by then and I'll be able to dump him on David for the night."

"Lucy, you don't dump your child," I told her. "I'm sure that's not a politically correct way of putting it."

"I shall leave my husband to do his share of the joint parenting of our child," she amended.

I rang Brenda at home. "Love to," she said.

We arranged the party for a Saturday night so that the twins could come and sleep late on Sunday. I was surprised at how much I was looking forward to it.

"Pick somewhere around the canal," said Lucy. "Then I can come across the tollbridge and we won't have to struggle with parking in town."

"We should have it in Temple Bar," I said. "That's the in place to be."

"Yeah, and they'll ask us for our bus passes or something," said Lucy.

So we met in Searson's, which we'd done so often before. It seemed like a different pub altogether.

"Isn't this like old times?" grinned Brenda, as she came back to the table carrying glasses and mixers. "How's the baby, Lucy?"

"He's great," she said proudly. "Although I don't know where the phrase 'sleeping like a baby' comes from. My baby doesn't sleep."

We laughed. It was good to be together again.

The pub filled up fairly quickly and a blue smoke haze drifted through the lounge. We'd booked a table in the Malaysian restaurant next door for nine o'clock.

"Time to get a few drinkies in first," Grace said. "A very important element of a girls' night out."

"Does anyone have any news?" I tipped my Coke into the glass of Bacardi in front of me.

"Don't look at me," said Lucy. "I've done my bit. It's time for the twins to do something. Like open a chain of shops, maybe. Buy out Brown Thomas, for instance."

Grace Quinlan blushed furiously and Brenda looked down into her glass of vodka. Both girls looked so embarrassed and guilty that we knew there was something they had to tell us.

"What?" asked Lucy, staring at them. "You've done something, haven't you?"

They looked at each other and giggled. When they did that it was hard to imagine that they ran a very successful shop and made expensive clothes to order for influential people. They looked exactly as they'd done the day they got into trouble at school for pretending to be the opposite twin. It caused great consternation at the time, because the one difference between them was that Grace could sing while Brenda could not. We'd had a practise for the school musical that day, some operetta which I couldn't remember now, but Grace had to sing a solo and when Brenda stood out front and belted out the number in one note, the music teacher had thrown a fit.

"So?" I asked, looking at them. "What have you done now?"

"We're getting married," said Grace, and burst into a fit of giggles again.

Lucy and I exchanged looks. It was hard to take them seriously.

"To whom?" I asked, "each other?"

Brenda looked at me. "Don't be stupid," she said.

"Well, Brenda, I just find it hard to believe," I said. "I didn't know you were going out with anyone. So are both of you getting married? Or just one of you?"

Lucy stared at them with her mouth open.

Brenda looked offended. "If we'd realised that you'd be so surprised – " she said.

"Not surprised, shocked," I amended. "Come on Brenda, tell all."

It was almost too good to be true. They'd gone to an Irish fashion presentation in London earlier in the year. There'd been a reception afterwards, lots of Irish people milling around. Brenda had met a man from the promotions board. Nice guy, she said, his name was Robert Driscoll. He said he'd look her up when he was back in Dublin. He was back two weeks later, his younger brother in tow because he knew Brenda had a twin sister and he thought that a double date might be better fun. Grace and Damien got on like a house on fire.

"Love at first sight," said Brenda.

"Are you sure?" I asked, in disbelief.

"Why shouldn't I be?" she said.

Lucy and I were flabbergasted. All their lives, the twins had been a unit on their own. Now, finally, they were getting married. It was almost impossible to believe.

"Are you sure one isn't doing it because the other is?" asked Lucy.

Brenda smiled. "Absolutely not," she said. "Really, Lucy, it's true."

"Where are your engagement rings?" asked Lucy. Like doubting Thomas, she wanted proof.

The twins opened their bags and took out jewellery boxes. Identical solitaire diamonds, glittering in the light, nestled in red velour.

"Why aren't you wearing them?" I asked.

The twins slipped them on. "We wanted to tell you before you saw them," said Grace. "We couldn't just walk in and flash them at you!"

"It's fantastic news," I said. "I'm thrilled for you both."

"Thanks, Jane," said Brenda. "And believe me. We're both madly in love."

They looked it. There was a sparkle about them that made them radiate happiness. I'd seen the sparkle earlier but I'd thought, enviously, that it was because they were busy at work and having a good time being free and single.

"I'm stunned," I said. "So tell us all about your fiancés!"

Robert, the older brother, was a promoter of Irish goods abroad. They'd heard of him before, but never met him. Damien, the younger by two years, was a photographer. They'd seen his credits on pictures. So, Grace said, they weren't completely unknown to them. The twins spoke with all the excitement of first love. They fell over themselves to tell us about them.

"So are you going to have a double wedding?" I asked.

"Absolutely," said Brenda. "At the end of the summer. We haven't set an exact date yet. We haven't decided what sort of do we'll have."

"I can't believe it," I said, "it's incredible."

"I wish you'd stop saying that you can't believe it." Grace looked amused. "Why shouldn't two men find us completely and utterly desirable?"

"No reason at all," said Lucy. "What astounds us is that you found two eligible men out there. You know how it is when you hit thirty. They're all either married or gay."

We ordered another round of drinks and then went into the restaurant for our food. There was no other topic of conversation besides the twins' news. Lucy and I tried on their engagement rings. I liked the look of the diamond on my engagement finger again.

The waiter brought us menus. We'd chosen Malaysian because none of us had ever eaten Malaysian food before. We hadn't a clue what anything was so we told the waiter to bring a bit of everything, as long as it wasn't too hot.

"And a bottle of Chablis," I added. I still ordered it automatically. It had been Rory's favourite wine and I'd grown to like it.

"Where are you going on your honeymoons?" I asked, as we sat back in our seats.

"I'm not sure," said Grace.

"Are you going to different places?" Lucy asked.

"We haven't really thought about it properly yet," said Brenda.

"And have you bought different houses?" I asked.

"Give us a break!" laughed Grace. "We will, but not yet!"

"My God," said Lucy. "That'll be the first time ever."

"Will you be able to cope apart?" asked Lucy.

"Definitely," they replied in unison.

The meal was great. Satay chicken on wooden skewers and neat little spring rolls with an individual bowl of sweet and sour sauce for starters; then beef in a coconut sauce which sounded awful but tasted gorgeous, and prawns and chicken. We asked for bowls and chopsticks for the authentic look.

"Means I'll hardly get any food," complained Lucy, who wasn't great on coordination.

The restaurant was busy. There was a steady hum of conversation and the waiters and waitresses scurried around serving customers. I'd driven past the Copper Beech on the way to meet the girls, detoured especially to briefly stop in front of it. It was unchanged, the iron sign still swung over the door. I'd grown hot with remembered rage as I paused before driving on.

I wondered if they'd remember me if I went in. If the woman at the desk was still the same, and whether she'd shudder at the sight of me. I'd never found out what had happened afterwards. Rory would never speak about it and I couldn't blame him.

When Rory and Amanda moved in together, Amanda changed jobs. She went to work for another, smaller, bank. Still as a dealer, still earning good money. Was she really thinking about having a baby with Rory? The thought made me go hot and cold.

"Wake up, Jane," said Grace. "We're talking to you."

"Still dreamy old Jane," laughed Lucy. "What were you thinking about?"

"Oh, nothing," I said lamely. "What are you talking about?"

"You see," said Lucy, "you go off into a little world of your own. We're discussing whether or not to go to a night club."

"A night club!" I looked at them in horror. "You must be joking!"

"There speaks the sensible one," laughed Brenda. "The mother of the seven-year-old."

"Do you want to go to one?" I asked Lucy. "I haven't a clue where we should go."

"It was a joke, Jane." Lucy grinned. "You really are hopeless."

But they were laughing with me, not at me, and I didn't mind.

It was past one when I got home. Clodagh was spending the night at my parents' house, which was what she always did on the rare occasions I was out late. The last time had been New Year's Eve.

Although the house was empty now, the feeling was different than when Clodagh had been on holiday with Rory and Amanda. I knew where she was now, that she would be asleep. While she'd been away, I lay in my bed and kept working out what time it was in the States so that I could imagine what she might be doing.

Junkie sidled up to me and rubbed against my legs. I bent down and scratched him under the chin and he stretched his neck, purring with pleasure. He sat down in front of his food bowl and looked expectantly at me.

"You can't possibly want food," I said. "I fed you

before I went out." But I put some food into the bowl and he ate it, gulping it down as though I might take it away before he finished.

I leant against the worktop and waited for him to finish. He would go out for the night tonight, he'd been in all evening, sleeping as he usually did, curled up in the turn of the stairs.

I was still amazed by the twins' news. I couldn't believe that they'd actually got themselves engaged. It was incredible. I'd always believed them to be completely uninterested in men. The occasional date for one or the other, sure, but never anything more serious than that. Sometimes Lucy and I had discussed what it would be like for one twin if the other married. She would be bereft, I said, dysfunctional. They would have to marry other twins, we'd decided, and it was hard enough to find one eligible man.

But they'd managed it. It just went to show that if you waited long enough the right man – or men – would come along.

And what sort of man are you waiting for, I asked myself, as I sat in front of the mirror wiping away my make-up. What sort of man could fit into my carefully constructed new life?

Nobody. I didn't care what the others were going to do. I didn't care how many daydreams or even ordinary dreams I had about men. I didn't care if Rory called me a dried-up prune. I didn't care that sometimes I sat at home and felt my aloneness cling to me. I didn't care that I was a single parent. I didn't care about any of that.

It would be so nice, though, to have someone in

the bed beside me. That was the time I felt it. When I lay in the double bed, using only a sliver of its actual size. I didn't curl up. I slept in a straight line either on my stomach or on my side. It would be wonderful to have somebody to hold me, then, and to protect me from the things that kept me awake.

I kept on having the dream again. Of the man I didn't know, making love to me. It frightened me. That I didn't know who he was. That I enjoyed the lovemaking so much. That I needed to dream the dream in the first place.

I don't want to need someone, I said to myself, holding on to the corner of the pillow as I'd done when I was very small. I can do it all by myself. Other people only let you down. I can depend on me, only on me. And Clodagh depends on me too. I don't have time for weakness or for wanting things I can't have.

Stop dreaming, Jane, I told myself firmly. Dreams don't come true.

33

May 1994

(UK No. 15 – Inside – *Stiltskin)*

It was my favourite month. The air was warm again, the trees were dressed in shining green leaves and the flowers had come into bloom in the garden. My Californian lilac bush, something I'd grown in every place I lived, was covered in bright blue flowers with little yellow pinpricks of pollen. Junkie lay in its shade and ignored the occasional early bee which hovered in front of it, his head casually across his front paws.

The sun streamed through the bedroom window, making it easier to get up. Clodagh talked about school holidays and I wondered where I should bring her this summer. I wanted to take her somewhere myself. I wasn't trying to compete with Rory and Amanda, I said to my reflection in the bathroom mirror, I was doing my own thing as a mother.

I always got up earlier in the summer and I made an extra bit of effort to look good. God only knew why, there wasn't anybody in the office to look good for. But I liked looking well for me. I wore brighter clothes and coloured shoes. My winter wardrobe was greys and black. My summer wardrobe was a rainbow of colours, and I didn't care if they clashed with my hair. Today I wore a red and cream check suit and a cream hair-band in my hair to keep it out of my eyes, to let the sun get at my wintry pale forehead.

"You look pretty." Clodagh came into the bedroom. Sometimes I could see myself in her now, especially when she was dressed in the St Attracta's uniform.

"Pull your socks up," I said, "don't leave them hanging around your ankles like that."

She sighed deeply and pulled up the socks. I stifled a grin. I was sure that I was echoing my own mother, I'd caught myself doing it so many times that it was scary.

"Come on," I said, "let's go."

I dropped her to school and drove on to the office, playing my kd lang tape at full volume. I didn't expect to be busy today and I planned to go down town at lunch-time and do a bit of shopping. I hadn't been in town in ages because the weather hadn't been good enough, but I was looking forward to a stroll down Grafton Street and some window-shopping. I never came into town on Saturdays any more, it was too crowded and Clodagh hated it. Even though she liked clothes, she wasn't like some other children I knew who positively enjoyed trying things on. Whenever we went to town, she dragged out of my arm and wanted to go into Virgin Megastore or

HMV to look at the computer games. When it came to clothes she usually came home and told me what she wanted and I tried, when possible, to get it for her.

But today would be shopping for me and for me only. I needed some new blouses, a lightweight skirt and maybe a jacket. Nothing designer, just something practical and smart for the office.

I left the office at half twelve and strolled to the Stephen's Green Centre.

It was bright and crowded. Although I didn't like huge crowds, I enjoyed the bustling of the centre, of people in good mood with things to do and places to go. I wandered through the shops humming to the music. Funny how they were always playing seventies music these days; it was amusing to know all the words from the first time around.

"Money, money, money,
Must be funny
In a rich man's world."

I took the escalator to the first floor and leaned over the railings to look at the crowds below. I loved doing that, watching people when they didn't know that you could see them. Often you saw somebody you knew, like the dark-haired girl sitting at a coffee shop who used to work in the bank. I couldn't remember her name but she'd been in the Settlements Department when I was there. She'd joined when I was on maternity leave.

Then I saw Hugh McLean. He was leaning against a shop window reading *The Irish Times*. I recognised him straight away, although he looked unusually smart. He was wearing a suit and tie. It was a good suit, the jacket was a neat fit and the trousers had a knife-edge crease down the middle. His tie was a splash of colour. As I watched him, he folded the newspaper and glanced at his watch.

It was one-fifteen. I left the balcony and walked down the stairs. If he was still there when I got to the bottom, I'd talk to him. That was the sort of mood I was in. The stairs were crowded with people, all of whom seemed to be going in the opposite direction to me.

He was still there. I thought about walking by, but that would be silly. I knew this man and I could say hello to him, there was nothing strange in that. I'd been stupid up until now. There was nothing wrong with knowing men, and he had said that men and women could be friends without it meaning anything. So I'd say hello to him, and we would chat casually and that would be that.

"Hi," I said. My voice broke as I spoke and I cleared my throat and started again. "Hi."

He looked up, surprised. "Jane. How are you?"

"I'm fine," I said. "And you?"

"I'm equally fine. What are you doing here?"

"Shopping," I said. "Browsing, really. And you?"

"Nothing much," he replied.

We stood there awkwardly, neither of us sure what we were going to say next. The last time I'd seen him, I'd been crying. He was used to seeing me crying, not like this, not cheerful and relaxed. I realised that he had never seen me cheerful and relaxed before.

I smiled at him. "Nice seeing you. I'd better get on and do my shopping."

I turned away from him as the girl approached. She was drop-dead beautiful. Her hair flowed around her shoulders in a riot of chestnut curls and she wore an elegant terracotta-coloured suit. She was taller than me, even in her flat Italian shoes.

You cannot possibly be jealous, I told myself, as she kissed him full on the lips.

"Jane!"

I turned back to him. The girl was holding his arm. "I'll see you again, Jane," he said.

I nodded but I didn't think so. Not with that girl on his arm.

I spent more than I meant to. I bought a suit, like the one Hugh's girlfriend was wearing and a pair of jeans that hugged tight, but not too tight. I was probably being a bit optimistic about the jeans, but what the hell. At the last minute, I saw a floral body in Knickerbox which I thought would look great with the jeans and I bought it. I walked back up to Merrion Square, swinging the plastic bags as I went.

So he had a girlfriend now, I thought. He'd probably had a girlfriend for ages. Maybe even when I'd last met him. So if he had a girlfriend, and if she was as beautiful as the girl in the shopping centre, then there was no real reason for him to ask me out. Not for the sort of reasons I'd imagined. He really did only want to get to know me because – why? My mind, perhaps. Seeing the girl had helped me put everything in perspective. Up until now, I'd been looking at things purely from my own point of view. Strangely, today I could see things clearly for the first time in ages. It was though a cloud had lifted from me.

I half thought he might phone that afternoon, although there was no reason why he should. All the same, I kept anticipating the ring of the switchboard and I answered every call with such efficiency that the light had hardly flashed before I was talking. But he didn't call and it didn't matter.

There was an exhibition of our art class's paintings that evening in the community hall. I told Brenda and Grace that they would have to show up to give a bit of moral support and pretend at least to want to buy one of mine. I'd three in the exhibition. They were all of Junkie. One of him stretched on the windowsill in the evening sun, eyes tightly closed. One of him curled up under the cherry blossom tree, paws covering his head. And one of him on his hind legs as he tried, unsuccessfully, to catch a butterfly. They were watercolours, nothing special, but pretty. I'd never bought a painting myself but I hoped against hope that someone would buy mine.

The twins showed up around eight. They were meeting the Driscoll brothers a little later. They hung around my paintings impressively until an elderly lady who had been dithering beside the one of Junkie on the windowsill finally took it up and bought it.

In the end I sold them all, which was thrilling. Clodagh and I went for a pizza on the strength of my earnings.

"Are you famous?" she asked, as mozzarella dripped down her chin.

"Practically." I grinned. "You can call me Picasso from now on."

"Who's Picasso?" she asked.

I told her.

"Did he paint cats?"

"Possibly," I said. "Although you mightn't recognise them."

He phoned the following week. I was busy at the time, but not so busy that I couldn't talk to him.

"Want to meet for lunch?" he asked.

"OK," I said.

"Today?"

"I can't today," I told him. "But tomorrow, maybe?"

"OK," said Hugh. "The Gallery?"

"What time?"

"Better be there early if we want a table. Half twelve?'

"Sounds great. I'll see you there."

"OK."

I exhaled slowly. I still wasn't sure what I was doing or why. Maybe it was the twins. Maybe hearing about their engagements had made me feel that I should try again. But try what, exactly? And what did he want me to try? Oh Jane, I told myself, you're an awful idiot.

I spent ages trying to decide what to wear. First I put on my new suit but decided that it looked far too new and too much as if I was making an effort for him. Besides, it was the same make as his girlfriend's. This was a friendly lunch. Nothing else. I wore my safe, green linen suit and a plain cream blouse. But I was nearly late for work because I spent so much time styling my hair, and I wore my favourite drop pearl earrings, the ones Rory had given me for our fifth wedding anniversary. I didn't wear my rings.

It was colder today, a sudden return to wintry weather. I wore my leather jacket over my suit and pulled it around me as I hurried down the street to the Gallery. I looked around for Hugh but I didn't see him at first. I walked through the rooms.

He was standing in front of the convent garden painting. He was smiling as he looked at it.

"Hello, Hugh," I said. The second time I'd used his name.

"Hello, Jane." He smiled at me.

I liked his face. It was a better face now that it was older, it suited him more. It was long, and still lean, lightly tanned. His eyes were brown pools, set deep. He wasn't wearing glasses today.

"Let's go, shall we?"

We walked in silence to the restaurant. We were early and it was still quiet.

"What would you like?"

"Lasagne and salad," I said.

"Same for me," ordered Hugh. We pushed our trays along the chrome counter.

"Would you like some wine?" he asked.

"Are you having some?"

"Yes," he said.

I took a small bottle of Chianti.

Hugh paid for lunch. I wanted to split the bill.

"No," he said. "I've asked you loads of times. It has to be my treat."

"I'd prefer if we split it," I said. "Really, Hugh." The third time. It was getting easier to say his name.

"Really, Jane," he said. "It's not as though I'm exactly pushing the boat out here."

I looked doubtfully at him. "But I'd feel better about it."

"Why?"

"I don't know, I just would."

He carried his tray to a table and sat down. I followed him, clutching my money in my hand.

"Put it away, Jane," he said. "It's my treat."

I sighed. "OK."

Now that we were face to face, I couldn't think of anything to say. It was exactly as it had been when I was younger, I was completely tongue-tied. How crazy, I thought. I'm a mature adult. He's a mature adult. There must be something we can talk about. I busied myself with my food, although I kept looking at him furtively. He was relaxed as he cut his lasagne with a fork, oblivious to me.

The restaurant was already filling up. The hum of conversation was getting louder all the time. If it got too busy, they would put other people at our table. We wouldn't have a chance to talk but it didn't seem to bother him.

"How are the bookshops?" I asked, after what seemed like an age of silence.

He looked up at me. "Great," he replied enthusiastically. "We're half thinking of opening one in the city centre, but rents are astronomical and I'm not sure about the demand. It's cut-throat in town at the moment."

"Does your sister still work with you?"

"Denise?" he asked. "Yes, she manages the Sutton

shop. Janet does the Dún Laoghaire one and I do the one in Rathmines."

"Janet is the sister with the baby, isn't she?"

He grinned. "She's had another one since you were in hospital," said Hugh casually, "a boy. They named him after me, which I think is incredibly silly. I don't believe in calling children after anyone else. He's four."

"I don't have any other children," I said as I took a mouthful of wine.

It was months since I'd had wine at lunch-time. It was going straight to my head; I was seeing things at a distance, hearing things through cotton wool.

"Is Denise married?" My voice seemed to belong to somebody else.

"Oh, yes," said Hugh. "She was married a couple of years ago. No children yet, although she probably will have them one day."

"Is there anyone else in your family?"

He smiled at me. "No."

"You're not married, then?"

"No."

"Not engaged?"

"No."

"Going out with someone?" I could see her clearly, the chestnut hair, the perfect body, holding his arm in a possessive grip.

"On and off."

"On or off at the moment?"

"Midway," he said. His eyes crinkled with amusement . . . I felt like a child caught with a hand in a jar of sweets.

"The food is nice here, isn't it?" I said.

"Yes." He still sounded amused.

I took a slug of wine and almost drained the glass.

"Do you mind if I sit here?" The elderly man had already placed his tray on the table beside us. Hugh looked up at him. "Not at all," he said.

"I don't want to interrupt," said the man.

"It's no problem," I said hastily.

He took his plate of fish and potatoes and put it carefully on the table. He sliced the potatoes into even pieces and popped a piece into his mouth, chewing carefully. I couldn't help watching him and I knew that Hugh was watching me. I smothered the desire to laugh.

"Are you finished?" asked Hugh, seeing that I'd put down my knife and fork.

I nodded.

"So am I." He pushed back his chair.

"Oh, please don't leave because of me." The elderly man looked perturbed.

"Not at all," said Hugh. "We were leaving anyway. We're quite finished."

We went back into the gallery and strolled towards the exit, saying nothing. I stopped in front of another painting I liked.

"The Ladies Catherine and Charlotte Talbot," read Hugh. "Why do you like it?"

"Because they're only children," I said. "Can you imagine what it was like to be a child back in 1700? Dressed up like that?"

They wore miniature adult dresses. The older child's dress was a blue and gold outer skirt over pink and gold beneath. A gold-coloured shoe peeped from under the dress, a gold buckle and a red heel. The younger girl's dress was a lighter material in green and cream. She had flowers in the apron of the dress and her sister was taking one. I could just see Clodagh in those circumstances, jeans, T-shirt and trainers. She wouldn't have bothered gathering flowers, either.

I looked at my watch. "I'd better get back," I said.

"Sure," said Hugh.

We walked in silence back to the office. The lunch hadn't been as I'd expected. I thought he'd try and get me to go to bed with him. I was so stupid, I told myself as he said good-bye. Really bloody stupid.

I messed up my work that afternoon because of the wine. It made me incredibly sleepy. I couldn't believe that a glass and a bit could do so much damage. I drank loads of water from the dispenser and made myself half a dozen cups of coffee.

"Who was the guy I saw you with coming back from lunch?" asked Claire. She sat on the corner of my desk with a red file in her hand, swinging one of her shapely legs backwards and forwards.

"Nobody in particular," I muttered as I slapped away at the keyboard.

"Very good-looking, from what I saw of him." said Claire. "Is he married?"

"Why on earth do you want to know that?" I asked, startled into looking up at her.

"Just wondered," she said. "All the good-looking ones usually are."

"And so are you," I said. "And me."

She stared at me. "You don't seriously consider yourself still married to that bastard, do you?' she asked.

"You mean Rory?"

"Of course I mean Rory!" She actually looked quite angry.

"I am married to him," I said. "I might not want to be and he might not want to be either, but we are."

"You're quite mad," said Claire.

I tapped furiously at the keys on my keyboard.

"He tried to make love to me again," I said quietly. She stopped swinging her leg and looked at me.

"Rory did?"

I nodded.

"And what did you say?"

"No."

She breathed a sigh of relief. "Thank God for that."

"Maybe I should have let him."

"Jane, are you in your right mind? He left you with a three-year-old kid, for God's sake! He's been living with some other woman for the past four years. Why would you want him back?"

"I don't know," I said. "I don't know."

"Take a week off," she advised. "And see a shrink."

She walked back to her office and slammed the door shut behind her. She had always cared about me. She had been very good to me. I leaned my head against the VDU. I should never have gone to lunch with Hugh McLean.

Clodagh and I went to a christening on Sunday. It was my cousin Laura's child, her third. Laura was the only girl in the family that had her first baby before she'd married. She'd only been twenty at the time. She didn't marry the father of baby Ben, but another guy, Séan Riordan, someone she'd only known for a couple of months. They seemed happy and this was their second child together. The first had been a boy, now aged three, whose name was Joe. This christening was for their daughter, Alexandra.

Declan and his wife, Anna, were the godparents. He hadn't married his crazy girlfriend, Ruth, but had chosen instead the sensible, pragmatic Anna. I hadn't seen them in ages. The last time I'd seen her Anna had looked middle-aged, but today she looked great. She'd coloured her hair, was wearing a fabulous new suit and had lost weight. Declan was extremely attractive with his silver-grey hair and light grey suit. They sat either side of Laura and Séan and smiled down at baby Alexandra.

There were four other babies being christened that day. I listened to the drone of the priest as the sun shone through the stained glass windows and fell in dappled drops on to the altar. Alexandra roared as the water was poured over her.

Ben shuffled in his seat. He was very uncomfortable in his suit and tie and he pulled at the tie every so often. Each time he did his grandmother, Aunt Kathleen, shoved him in the back. Joe played with a Transformer toy. Declan and Anna's two children sat in solemn silence as they watched the ceremony. Richard was ten years old, a tall gangly child, usually awkward and ill at ease. Rebecca was a pretty little thing, a year older than Clodagh, with the McDermott gold hair and tumbling curls. Clodagh sat beside me, yawning.

"Is it over yet?" she asked, as Alexandra's yells tore through the church.

"Soon," I whispered.

"Did I cry?"

I looked down at her. "No," I said.

She'd been the best behaved baby at her christening. When the water hit her head, she'd opened her eyes in shock and her face had puckered up into an parody of a cry, but she'd been quiet.

"That's my girl," Rory had murmured proudly.

We went back to Laura and Séan's house. It was in the Riverview estate, a few doors down from the house that Stephanie McMenamin had bought when she married Kurt Kennedy, straight after school.

The younger members of the family, freed from the need to be quiet, raced into the garden and started chasing each other around the lawn.

The aunts sat together, chattering away and, as always, argued about some event in their past.

"You're wrong, you know, Liz, it was after John's wedding."

"No, absolutely not, it was before. Because they went to Blackpool for their honeymoon."

"I like your dress, Jane," said Laura as she sat down beside me. "It's really pretty."

"I got it in town last month," I said. It was taupe linen, buttoned up the front and reached almost to my ankles.

"It makes you look incredibly thin." Laura stubbed her cigarette in the ashtray beside her.

"I'm not thin," I said, "I wish I was."

"You look fabulous," said Laura.

"You're not bad yourself," I told her, although I was sort of lying because Laura looked washed-out. Her hair had lost some of its shine and her skin was dull.

"I'm so tired," she said. "For some reason, the baby keeps waking up at three in the morning and won't go back to sleep."

I nodded sympathetically.

"It's funny, isn't it," mused Laura. "After all the things we said we'd do as kids, we've ended up like our parents."

I looked at her.

"Me, for instance," she said. "Three kids, just like my own mother. And you, like yours, with one."

I laughed. "Never thought about that," I said. "But the difference with me is that I don't have a bloody husband any more."

"And the difference with me is that my oldest kid has a different father."

Aunt Elizabeth came over to us, camera in hand. "I want to get a photo of my favourite nieces," she said.

"I'm not your favourite niece," I objected.

"All my nieces are," she said.

I sighed but moved closer to Laura. The flash lit up the room. Alexandra wailed for a moment but then stopped. The sounds of the children playing wafted through the open window.

"Get away from my swing!"

"No!"

"Give me that ball!"

"It's mine!"

"Mine!"

"It's not yours, go away, I'm telling my Mam."

Laura walked over to the window.

"Keep it down out there," she called. "Ben, let Joe have the ball."

"It's my ball," objected Ben.

Joe started to cry.

"He's a cry-baby," said Rebecca calmly. "He's always crying."

While they were arguing, Clodagh took the ball and ran to the end of the garden. "It's mine now," she said.

"Clodagh," I called warningly.

"Anybody want some tea?" Mam came into the room carrying a tray laden with cups and saucers and a huge teapot. The women fell on it gratefully, the men ignored it.

I sipped a glass of wine. I was trying to get back on to wine, I'd had a revolting headache after my lunch with Hugh and I knew that it was because of the Chianti. I'd once drunk bottles of the stuff, with no ill-effects whatsoever. I was losing my touch with drink. And if, on the remotest off-chance, I went out to lunch with Hugh again, I didn't want to be made emotional and soppy by a single glass of wine. I wanted to have my wits about me. If I had any left.

34

June 1994

(UK No. 15 – Love Is All Around – *Wet Wet Wet)*

I flicked through the travel brochure and looked at the pictures of apartments in the sun. Impossibly blue skies were mirrored in impossibly blue pools while scantily-clad people sunbathed. I was trying to find a picture of the San Carlos apartments in Cala d'Or, Majorca. I hoped they actually existed. I was a bit worried that they didn't appear in any of the brochures I'd picked up at the travel agent's. The San Carlos apartments were where Clodagh, Mam and I were going for a two-week holiday, and they weren't in the regular brochure because the tour operator had only recently obtained a number of them. It was a spur-of-the-moment holiday, at Mam's suggestion. Dad, Mr. McAllister and a couple more of their friends were going to the States for the World Cup, and Mam felt that she should have a holiday too. So she asked me what I thought. I was more than happy to go on holiday and started to scout around for something. I'd seen the ad on the back of *The Irish Times* the previous week – a special offer – and I'd decided to go for it. What a turn-up, I'd thought, as I booked the tickets. Going on a sun holiday with my mother!

Claire walked into the office and I hastily thrust the brochure into my desk drawer. She'd been in a foul humour all week with an abscess on her gum which wasn't getting any better. She'd already been to the dentist during the morning and now she looked pale and ill.

"How are you feeling?" I asked solicitously.

She grunted. "Not great. Don't ask me what he did to it." She took her diary from her office and brought it out to me. "Can you cancel the rest of my appointments, Jane? Or try to, anyhow?"

I took the diary. "I'll do my best." Claire's schedule was always full. She was the hardest-working person I'd ever met.

"Claire?" I called to her. "Is this for real?" I pointed to Hugh McLean's name, an appointment for four o'clock.

She looked puzzled. "Of course it is," she said. "He's a new client."

"When did he phone you?"

"Early last week," she said. "Actually, he called quite early in the morning. Before you were in. Why?"

"No reason," I said. "I know him, that's all."

"Do you?" Claire's face lit up. "Well, if you know him, Jane, maybe you can meet him."

"What!"

"I don't see why not," she said. "He only wants to talk about some of his personal investments. He's looking for a valuation on some shares and a comparison of some products. You can find out exactly what his portfolio is and I'll do the work. I'd prefer not to cancel a new client."

I looked uncomfortably at her. "I'm not sure he'll want to talk about his personal finances to me," I told her. "I don't know him that well."

"See how you get on." She massaged the side of her cheek. She hadn't read any of the signs, totally unlike her.

I rang the list of clients and rescheduled her appointments. I didn't know what to do about Hugh. He hadn't called me since our lunch. I'd been mistaken about him, he obviously wasn't interested in me. Like all men, I thought bitterly, meet you and discard you. I knew I was being irrational about him, but I couldn't help it. Perhaps it would be easier to ring him and put him off. He wouldn't want to talk to the office manager about anything as important as his shares, anyway.

I phoned the number in Claire's diary.

"CityBooks." The girl's voice at the other end was bright and cheerful. "How can I help you?"

"I'd like to speak to Mr McLean," I said. "I'm calling from Renham Financial."

"I'm sorry, but Mr McLean isn't in the store today," she told me. "If you'd like to leave a name and number, I can get him to call you on his return."

"Is he due back today?" I asked.

"I'm afraid not," she said. "He's at meetings all day."

"No problem," I said. "I can get him again." I

replaced the receiver and rubbed my nose. Well, he'd have to meet me and talk about the sordid details of his financial life. Tough.

At three o'clock, I went into our small bathroom and did my face. Liquid powder make-up, hazel eyeshadow, scarlet lipstick. And lash-lengthening mascara. I wasn't going to let him see me looking anything other than my best.

Claire had gone home at lunch-time but I bumped into Stephen as I came back into the main office. He stared at me. "What have you done to your face?" he asked.

"I'm meeting one of Claire's clients," I told him. "I thought I'd better put on a bit of make-up."

"Very nice," he said, vaguely. "You look different."

"Thanks." I decided to take it as a compliment.

"I'm leaving the office now," said Stephen. "I've got a meeting at the Westbury in fifteen minutes and I don't think I'll be back here this evening. So I'll leave you to lock up if that's OK, Jane."

"Sure," I said. "Have a good weekend."

"You too." Stephen hurried out of the building.

Hugh McLean arrived on the dot of four. I buzzed the intercom to let him in to the building. He was carrying a bunch of flowers. "For you." He handed them to me.

"What for?"

"Does there have to be a reason?"

I buried my head in the bouquet. The scent was wonderful.

"I was trying to contact you earlier," I said in my

best office manner. "Claire has gone home sick. Toothache. She can't meet you and I was going to cancel. She suggested that I talk to you instead, but obviously that's ridiculous."

"Why?"

"Because I'm not an expert on financial matters," I said. "I can't tell you what you should buy and sell. I can tell you the value of what you currently own, but that's not necessarily a great deal of use to you."

"That's partly what I need to know," said Hugh. "Why don't you do that, anyway?"

I got up from the desk and switched the telephone to Claire's office. Her room was small but neatly decorated in pale blue and cream. Her desk was white ash, empty of paper because she was so tidy. I switched on her computer terminal.

"Do you want to tell me what you have?" I asked.

He handed over a sheet of paper. I looked through his investments and then up at him again. His holdings were much greater than I'd imagined. If he wasn't exactly rich, he was very well-off.

"Some of them were left to me," he said, seeing my expression.

I nodded wordlessly. When I'd finished his valuation, I pressed "print" and handed him the results. He smiled when he saw them.

"Good," he said. He sat back in the chair and looked around the room.

"How long have you worked here?" he asked.

"Four years," I replied.

"Like it?"

I nodded. "It's a good company and they're good

employers. I've got a decent job here, I'm a shareholder now."

"Never think of changing?" asked Hugh.

I shook my head. "I'm good at this," I said. "Most of the time."

Hugh glanced at his watch. "What will you be doing for the rest of the afternoon?" he asked.

"Nothing much," I said and pressed a few keys on the computer simply for something to do.

"Would you like to come for a drink with me?" asked Hugh.

"I can't I'm afraid," I said, keeping my voice businesslike. "I have to pick up my daughter from my mother's house after work. They're expecting me by five-thirty."

"It's only four-thirty now," he said. "A quick drink and you can still be on time."

"I have to lock up the office at five," I told him. "Everybody else has gone for the weekend."

"So we're alone together?" he said.

I stared at him. "In this office, yes," I said.

He grinned at me. "What fun."

"I don't see anything funny in it," I said nervously. "What did you have in mind for fun?"

"You, me, a little hanky-panky on the boardroom table?"

"Really," I said. "I think – "

"Jane, Jane!" He held up his hand. "I'm only joking."

His eyes were twinkling but I was annoyed with him.

"Well, it's not something to joke about," I said

coolly. "You really shouldn't make those sort of jokes."

"Then you really shouldn't wear those sort of clothes," said Hugh.

I smoothed down my light woollen skirt with my hands. It was short but not too short. It fitted me perfectly, though, and I knew that it looked good on me. I wore it with a short-sleeved angora jumper in pale lilac which plunged rather more than I liked at the neckline but which had never given rise to any comment in the office before.

"Those sort of remarks aren't very businesslike." I tried to keep my voice steady.

"Who cares?" asked Hugh.

I wondered whether he had been drinking. There was a devil-may-care attitude about him that I'd never seen before. "I do," I said. "I'm a married woman, you know."

Hugh came and sat on the edge of the desk, closer to me. I pushed Claire's swivel chair back from it and away from him.

"I find your marital state very interesting," said Hugh lazily. "It doesn't stop you from lunching with me, from flirting with me, but you use it like a shield against me."

"I've never flirted with you," I said, as I got up from the chair and walked across the room. "And you were the one who asked me to lunch, even though you knew I was married. So don't give me that crap. You're the one who keeps coming on to me."

"Do I?" he asked. "I thought I was being nice to you."

"You're all the same," I cried. "Bastards, all of you!"

He looked at me, astonishment in his eyes, as I ran out of the office and down the corridor to the bathroom, slammed the door behind me and pulled the lock firmly across. I'd never meant to flirt with him, I'd thought he'd fancied me and that had given me a bit of a boost, but I didn't want him to think that I wanted anything more. I was hopelessly confused about what I did want. Tears of embarrassment coursed down my face, leaving black track marks of mascara on my cheeks.

"Jane!" He knocked on the bathroom door. "Are you in there, Jane?"

"Go away," I said. "You can leave the office, just close the door behind you."

"Jane, don't be silly. Come on out."

"No," I said.

"Jane, this is ridiculous."

"I know," I said. "You've made it ridiculous."

"Jane I'm sorry if I teased you. I didn't mean to, you know."

"Oh really?"

"Really. Jane. Come out."

But I wasn't going to come out. Even if I wanted to, I was too self-conscious. And my face was a blotchy mess. God, I thought, you'd think by now I'd be able to function as a human being. Would I ever grow up? Frank had done this to me once when we'd had a row. I'd locked myself into the kitchen at home then, as far as I could remember. The whole situation was farcical and I began to giggle helplessly. So much for my sophisticated office manager function!

It was quiet outside. I hadn't heard the office door close but I presumed he must have gone. I looked at my watch. I'd give him another five minutes and then I'd have to leave anyway. I splashed some water on to my face and scrubbed away the mascara with toilet roll. I still looked as though someone had given me a couple of black eyes.

I slid back the bolt on the door and walked outside, feeling like someone in a spy movie. He was sitting at my desk.

"Hi," he said.

I bit my lip. I'd rubbed off the lipstick.

"I thought you'd be gone."

"I couldn't go, not after making you cry yet again!"

I rubbed the side of my face. "I'm sorry about that," I said. "I've been really stupid."

"I suppose I should be apologising – yet again!" He smiled at me and his brown eyes glinted. "I really don't mean to upset you, Jane and I was only joking. But it was in bad taste and that's what I'm sorry about."

My heart was doing somersaults. This is crazy, I thought. He thinks I'm trying to have some sort of affair with him and he's trying to let me down nicely. And I think that he's trying to have some sort of affair with me. But I don't want to know someone who'd try and have an affair with a married woman. And I'm probably all wrong about him, anyway. I was always useless with men, absolutely hopeless. "It's OK," I said. "Really."

"Well, look," said Hugh. "I'll leave you alone and

never bother you again if you'll just do one thing for me." He stood up. "Only one thing."

"Sure," I said, and smiled at him. "I'll be pleased to."

His kiss took me by surprise. His head bent towards me and suddenly his lips were on mine, soft and gentle, exploring mine. I gasped as his arm encircled my waist, drawing me closer to him. I breathed his aroma, tasted him, wanted him.

He held me even more tightly and I held him too. It was so long, so bloody long since I'd held anyone like this, been held like this. But he broke away from me first, still holding me, as he looked down at me breathlessly. He let me go so abruptly that I almost fell.

"I just wanted to see what it would be like," he said.

I steadied myself by clutching at my desk. His eyes were almost black now and the hint of amusement was gone. I couldn't speak. I opened and closed my mouth but no words came out.

"But I shouldn't have done it." He turned on his heel and walked out of the office.

The flight to Palma was delayed. We'd been sitting at Gate B27 for the past half-hour, and now it looked like we'd be there for at least another hour. People grumbled, muttered under their breaths and talked about the small print in the insurance policy.

"Hopefully we will be boarding the flight in about an hour," said the slightly distracted air hostess.

"Why aren't we going?" asked Clodagh. "I want to go now."

"Because the plane isn't here yet," I said. "You can't go until the plane arrives."

Mam had never been on a sun holiday before. She hadn't been out of the country in over five years and her last flight had only been as far as Manchester. We'd gone to the Isle of Man when I was small, but by boat, not by plane. She fussed around with her bags and took out her magazine. "This was for the plane," she said. "I'll have nothing to read on the journey."

"It's not a very long flight." I slipped my Walkman earpieces from my ears. "They'll be interrupting you, serving you drinks and duty-free and food."

"And the movies." Clodagh looked up from her Gameboy for a second.

"There won't be any movies on this plane," I told her.

"There was with Daddy," she said petulantly. "I'm not going if there isn't a movie."

"Then you can just stay here," I said, my patience close to snapping. "In the airport, for two weeks."

Her lower lip trembled and she looked to Mam for support. "You'd better be good." Mam used her peacemaking voice.

I put the headphones back on again. I was trying to learn some Spanish.

"Donde esta la Oficina de Turismo, por favor," I repeated to the tape. *"Donde estan los servicios?"*

"You've asked where the toilets are." Clodagh pulled me by the sleeve. "*Los servicios* are the toilets."

I sighed and switched off the tape.

The plane arrived eventually and we filed on.

Unfortunately, I didn't qualify for preferential treatment under the "women and young children" rule any more, but Clodagh hopped around begging me to get up from my seat and join the queue.

"We have to wait until it's our seat number," I explained, giving her a boarding pass. "When they call these numbers, then we can board."

Finally we were on the plane, seat belts fastened and ready to go. Clodagh peered out of the window. She wasn't impressed by the 737, she wanted a Jumbo. They'd flown to Florida in a Jumbo. But she liked the roar of the engines and the thunder of speed as we accelerated down the runway and cleaved our way through the clouds and up to the blue sky above.

"Of course, I've done all this before," she said as she undid her tray and pulled it down from the seat in front.

"I'm sure you have, lovey." Mam was indulgent.

I didn't enjoy the flight. There were too many children, all over-excited, all trying to run up and down the aircraft. I wouldn't let Clodagh out of her seat and she cried with frustration. We spent the entire journey quarrelling and, when we finally landed in Palma airport she refused to get out of the seat.

"Stay here then," I said, as I lifted our hand luggage out of the compartment. "I don't care."

"Oh, Jane, you're not being very nice to her," said Mam. "Come on, Clodagh, you don't want to miss the beach, do you?'

My daughter obeyed my mother and got out of the seat.

"Have a nice holiday," smiled the hostess as we stepped out of the plane.

A blanket of heat engulfed us. I felt beads of sweat beginning to prickle the top of my forehead and I inhaled warm air and jet fumes.

"It's hot," said Clodagh in surprise.

"Of course it's hot," I said in delight. "You're in the sun."

"It's very humid." Mam looked around and fanned herself with her magazine.

There was a baggage handlers' strike at the airport, and the arrivals hall was chaotic with people and luggage all over the place. I held on grimly to Clodagh. If she disappeared into the maelstrom, I would never find her.

The dispute was resolved while we waited but it was still an hour before our luggage appeared. We struggled outside to where the coach was waiting. The tour rep looked harassed.

The coach started up and chugged out on to the motorway. The rep blew into the mike a couple of times and then welcomed us to Majorca.

"I'm sorry about the hassle at the airport," she said. "There wasn't anything we could do about it. I hope it won't spoil your holiday."

"What's left of it," muttered a man behind me. "We're already over three hours late."

A muted rumble of agreement came from the back of the coach. People talked about suing the company and the airline and just about everyone. I leaned my head against the coach window and gazed outside as we sped along the motorway.

We were the second stop, which was a great relief because Clodagh wanted to go to the loo. It was a lovely block of apartments, only three storeys high, purple and pink flowers tumbling over the balconies.

Mam was exhausted and flopped on to the bed. Clodagh, after her emergency trip to the bathroom, rushed out on to the balcony. We overlooked the pool and she squealed in delight when she saw it. It was kidney-shaped, with a small wooden bridge across the narrowest point and a tiny bar nearby.

"Look!" she cried. "Can I go swimming?"

"I have to find your things first," I said.

"Oh, please now. Please."

I grinned at her. "All right." I slapped some sun cream on her before she ran out. "Be careful."

She gave my words the weight they deserved. Clodagh was a superb swimmer, much better than I'd been at her age. As I looked out of the window, she ran to the pool and dived in, cleaving the water cleanly. I sighed with relief. She was happy, anyway.

"Are you OK?" I asked Mam, who lay on the bed, eyes closed.

"Just hot," she said.

"Well, change into something lighter," I told her. Mam had insisted on wearing Irish clothes, although I'd told her she'd melt in Majorca. "Why don't you have a shower?" I suggested. "That'll cool you down."

She went into the shower while I unpacked the cases and put away the clothes. So organised, I smiled to myself. When I'd gone on holidays first, I'd always lived out of the case. Now everything was neatly hanging in its place. I left out a light blouse and skirt for Mam and changed into shorts and a T-shirt. I looked out of the window again. Clodagh was deep in discussion with a couple of children, so I didn't have to worry about her.

"I think I'll go downstairs for a while," I called in to the bathroom.

"Don't forget to put on some sun protection," shouted Mam over the hiss of the shower.

What did she think I was? I'd been to the sun so many times and she'd never been at all, yet she was the one telling me what to do. I shook my head.

There were some sun loungers in the shade and I sat down, allowing the heat to warm me through to my bones. It was blissful. I smoothed Protection 8 on to my face, arms and legs and stretched out on the lounger.

"Jane."

I looked up, my sunbathing disturbed. Hugh was standing over me, casting a shadow across my body.

"Hello," I said, not at all surprised that he was there. I'd always expected him to be there. He sat down on the edge of the lounger and ran his finger gently across my forehead.

"Hot?" he asked.

I nodded, lazily.

"Want to get into the pool?"

"Maybe."

"I want you in the pool, Jane. And out here on the grass. And upstairs in the apartment. Everywhere."

He bent towards me, his mouth met mine again and I recognised the familiarity of his lips.

I woke with a start, flustered by the intensity of the dream. The sun had dipped behind the apartment building and caused a shadow to fall over the lounger. It wasn't any colder, just shady, but I pulled myself upright and looked around me.

"Hello," said Clodagh, seeing me move and running towards me. "I thought you were going to stay asleep forever. Like the sleeping princess."

"I thought I was, too," I said. "Are you having a good time?"

She nodded vigorously. "They're my friends over there," she said. "Natasha and Sonia and Martin. They're from Croydon. That's in England."

"Good," I said. "Do you need any more sun cream?"

"On my nose." She rubbed some on. "They can't swim as good as me."

"You're the best," I kissed her and hugged her wet body against me. She squirmed away from me and ran, yelling, to the pool again.

Mam joined me from her seat under a nearby palm tree.

"Have you got used to the heat yet?" I asked.

"No," she said, "but I'm working on it."

The San Carlos complex was fantastic. The three apartment buildings formed a circle around the pool and garden area. There were two restaurants in the complex itself and a small supermarket. Games were organised for the children, so I hardly saw Clodagh during the day and she was enjoying herself far too much to want to hang around me. Mam went to afternoon dances in the ballroom of the San Carlos hotel next door. Every day the sun blazed down on top of us, and every day we went a little browner. Mam was worried about tanning. It wasn't safe, she warned, we were doing irreparable damage to our skin. But she still sat in the evening sun because there was nothing more soothing or relaxing than the warmth of its rays caressing your shoulders as you sipped a cooling drink.

Some days we went to the beach. Cala d'Or was a series of little coves, with sand running back deeply from the sea. We went to them all, Serena, Esmeralda, Es Forti and Cala d'Or itself.

The Spaniards themselves holidayed in Cala d'Or, the rep told us, and I believed it because there were far more Spanish people there than at any of the other resorts I'd ever gone to. They ran around the beaches chattering to each other, the words unintelligible. I was still trying to learn Spanish but, every time I switched on the tapes, I would be lulled to sleep by the voices repeating the phrases. I still hadn't got much further than asking where the toilets were.

Each night, we ate in a different restaurant. Clodagh loved eating in restaurants, she enjoyed sitting on the terrace with a menu in her hand, having the power to decide exactly what she wanted to eat. Mam kept wanting to eat paella, which I didn't like but which they'd only do for two people. "You have to, Jane," she said, "it's what the people themselves eat."

She'd become immersed in Spanish culture and

robbed my Spanish tapes whenever I wasn't using them. She did all the ordering of the meals, assisted by Clodagh. The waiters humoured them and I shook my head and stared into the distance when I ended up with squid instead of pork chops and octopus instead of chicken.

"It's all part of the experience," said Mam, as she broke a prawn in half.

We stopped at the bar beside the crazy golf every evening so that Clodagh could play while we chatted. The barman got to know us and had our drinks sent over to us straight away. Bacardi for me, Tia Maria for Mam and Fanta lemon for Clodagh. I liked talking to Mam in the evenings, although I hated it when she talked about Rory.

"He ruined your life," she said, after too many Tia Marias one night.

"No, he didn't."

"Of course he did," she told me. "If it wasn't for him, you'd be happily married now."

"How do you know?" I asked. "I could have married somebody much worse and been even more miserable."

"Do you mean you're miserable now?"

"Don't be silly," I told her. "Of course I'm not miserable. I was more miserable when I was married to Rory, only I didn't realise it at the time. But now, I'm happy. I've got a wonderful daughter." I looked across at Clodagh who had nearly brained a German girl with her golf club.

"But he abandoned you," said Mam. "That was a terrible thing to do."

"Mam," I said, "our marriage was falling apart long before Amanda Ferry."

"You could have saved it," she said, "if it wasn't for her."

"Maybe. Maybe not. How does anyone know?"

"I don't like to see you on your own, Jane. It's not right."

"And why not?"

"Because every woman needs a man."

"Oh, spare me that rubbish!" I exclaimed. "It was that sort of thinking that made me marry Rory in the first place. Surely you don't believe that? Not in this day and age."

"You'd be happier with a husband," she said decisively.

"I wouldn't. Anyway, I can't marry again."

"You could always live with someone."

"Maureen O'Sullivan!" I cried. "You can't possibly mean that. I thought you'd die rather than see me shacked up with someone."

"I didn't mean it like that," she objected. "You know what I mean. In a proper relationship."

"You sound like Oprah Winfrey," I teased.

"I only want what's best for you, Jane," she said. "I've always only wanted that."

"I know," I said and squeezed her arm.

The barman came and sat down with us. It was a smallish bar, never very crowded. He preferred it that way, he told us in excellent English. He didn't want to be overrun with tourists.

"Are you from Cala d'Or?" I asked.

He laughed. "No, from the mainland. Barcelona."

"Really?" I asked. "I've been to Barcelona."

So we exchanged conversation about the sights of Barcelona and the people and the buildings, and we had a thoroughly enjoyable time while my mother went behind the bar and served the tourists.

He asked me to dinner a few nights before we went home. I told him that I couldn't possibly, but Mam pushed me into saying yes. "You've only got one life," she said. "Have a bit of fun."

I couldn't believe my mother. She'd never talked to me about having fun, before. Her life had always seemed to be about responsibilities, this was a completely new side to her. So Mam and Clodagh went into the town to eat while Javier brought me in his Renault Clio into the mountains and to a Spanish restaurant where there were no tourists.

It was a small restaurant with ceramic tiled walls and quarry-tiled floor. The meat was on display in a refrigerated unit and you walked up to pick the piece you wanted. Then the chef took it away and cooked it. I had steak, very unSpanish, but so beautifully cooked that it fell apart when I cut it.

"So why are you here alone?" asked Javier.

I sipped the Viña Sol. "Hardly alone," I smiled. "Three generations of women in my family together."

"But you have no husband?"

"We don't live together any more."

"I am sorry to hear that," he said. "It is a sad thing."

It was wonderful to have dinner with a man again. The independent woman idea was great, but I enjoyed being part of a couple. Javier was completely charming and utterly disarming. He complimented me on my dress, my hair, my suntan. He agreed with me on music and on films. He made me feel like the most important person in the world. And the best part was that I knew that I would never see him again, that this was one night that I could have all to myself.

We sat on the verandah outside the restaurant.

"Where do you live?" I asked, idly, looking down at the white lights of the resort below us while the cicadas chirped in the background.

"An apartment," he said. "It's not a very nice apartment. But it is functional."

He draped his arm over the back of my chair. I'd expected it and so I didn't react. Then he leaned towards me and kissed me on the cheek.

The cards were on the table, I thought. It was my decision and mine alone. I could go to bed with him. Dangerous, perhaps. No contraception, what about AIDS? I could thank him for a nice evening and go home. I didn't know what I wanted to do.

"I would not want to bring you to my apartment," he said, as we got into the car. "It is too small. Not right for you."

"Where do you want to bring me?" I asked.

"To my boat," he said.

"Your what?"

"My boat, it is tied up at the Marina."

We drove to the Marina and to his boat. It was a small speedboat, black and sleek. I raised an eyebrow at it.

"Expensive?" I asked.

"My hobby," he answered.

I stepped into the boat, shaky from its movement and from the Viña Sol. Was I a total slut? I wondered. Would I burn in hell for ever?

He was a considerate lover. He brought me places I hadn't been in years, filling a need that had been dormant within me. We moved in rhythm with each other and in rhythm with the rocking of the boat on the water. When I cried out, my cries were echoed by the seagulls overhead.

It was dawn by the time I crept back in to the apartment. I closed the door quietly behind me, wincing as it clicked. I tiptoed to the balcony and gazed out at the lightening sky tinged with orange. The waves broke gently against the sand in the distance. I smiled with pleasure.

"Did you have a good time?" I jumped guiltily as Mam's voice reached me. I peered back into the apartment. She was standing in the living-room, looking out at me.

"Yes," I said, conscious of my rumpled dress and tangled hair.

"Good," said my mother calmly, and went back to bed.

35

July/August 1994

(UK No. 3 – Love Ain't Here Anymore – *Take That)*

I returned home from holidays tanned, happy and full of energy. I busied myself around the office driving Claire and Stephen nuts with my enthusiasm. Files that hadn't been checked in an age suddenly received my full attention, I made back-ups of the hard disk in the computer and I updated everyone's diaries so that no important meetings could be overlooked.

Every day that the weather was fine, I ate my lunch in the park in Merrion Square. I sat under a tree with my sandwiches and tin of Coke, read *Cosmopolitan* and *Marie Claire* and stretched my dusty brown legs to the faint Irish sun.

I hadn't felt so good in ages. I couldn't believe it was because of three nights of passion with Javier, but that had to have had some effect. I suppose it was the excitement of finding myself desirable in a purely physical way that I'd enjoyed so much. Nor did I care that, on the two occasions I'd gone to the sun without a husband, I'd had a holiday romance. Lifelong commitment was all very well, but a brief flirtation with passion was fun. It was great to have fun again.

Even Clodagh noticed the difference in me. She told me that I looked more sparkly and that I was laughing more. Mam hadn't said a word to me. The second night I'd met Javier – not until eleven o'clock – she'd told me simply to be careful and have a good time. She was a revelation to me. Instead of acting as my mother, she was my accomplice. I'd thought that she would lecture me, tell me that I was (at the very least) committing some sort of sin, that I could end up in all sorts of trouble, but she didn't. I was grateful to her, and for the first time in my life I appreciated her.

So when I got the phone call from Amanda Ferry one afternoon two weeks after our return, I didn't start shaking and quaking as I think I would have done earlier, but was able to talk to her in quite a sensible way. She was the one who sounded nervous, unsure of her ground.

"I wondered if we could meet for a chat," she said. "It's nothing exactly important, Jane, but I'd appreciate it very much."

A year ago – six months ago – I would have dropped the phone and fled sobbing to the toilet. Now I listened to her calmly and said "Sure, where and when?"

She didn't want to meet in town, she said. Or in Blackrock or Dún Laoghaire. Perhaps somewhere closer to me? Somewhere we could have a private conversation? I was intrigued. I wondered if she wanted to tell me that she was pregnant, carrying

Rory's child. I didn't know how I'd feel if that were the case.

We decided on Johnny Fox's because the evening was bright and clear even if the air was cool. I drove up the mountains and parked opposite the pub. There was a wooden table outside and I sat there and waited for my husband's lover.

She was ten minutes late. Her bright red Alfa hurtled into the carpark, sending up chips of gravel and sliding to a halt near the wall.

She was still very attractive, I thought enviously. Her dark curtain of hair was natural, no need to hide any grey there, and she wore a pair of pink cotton leggings and a long, white baggy jumper which emphasised the trimness of her figure.

"Bitch," I thought, sipping my Budweiser.

"Hello, Jane," she said as she sat down beside me. "I'm sorry I'm late, I took the wrong turning."

"No problem," I said. "Would you like a drink?"

"I'll get you one. What'll you have?"

"I'm OK for the moment." I indicated my glass. "But let me buy you one."

She shrugged slightly, said she'd have a vodka and white, and I went into the bar to get the drink. When I came back, she was gazing out over the city while she puffed at a cigarette with short, jerky breaths.

Closer to, she was still attractive, but her face owed as much to art as to nature. The smooth skin was helped by her make-up, the colour of her eyes accentuated by kohl. She pushed her hair behind her ears in a jangling of silver bracelets and earrings and took a deep drag of the cigarette.

"Thanks," she said, as I put the drink down in front of her.

We sat looking at the view together. I wasn't going to make whatever it was easier for her, although I was consumed with curiosity. I didn't think she could possibly be pregnant. For one thing she was far too thin, and nowadays it was practically a crime to be pregnant and either drink or smoke, let alone do both.

"I suppose you're wondering why I wanted to see you." She sipped the vodka, leaving the mark from her glossy lips on the edge of the glass.

"I am interested," I admitted.

"It's not awfully easy for me to talk about," she said. She tapped ash into the ashtray and looked around us as though checking that we were alone.

"Why don't you just spit it out?" I suggested. "It's easiest that way."

So she told me, amid much puffing of her cigarette and drinking of her vodka and shredding of the beermat in front of us, that she thought Rory was having an affair.

"He's never in." Her voice quavered. "And he's spent half the summer in the States at that fucking World Cup."

I hid a grin. It didn't seem that long since I'd complained about the very same thing. God, I was glad that I wasn't living with Rory any more. I wished that I could divorce him, not to get married again, but to know that he was finally, irrevocably, out of my life.

"Has he been making any surreptitious phone calls?" I asked. "You know the sort, where he puts the phone down as you walk into the room?"

She shook her head. "Not that I know of. Oh, Jane, I'm sorry to have dragged you up to talk about this, but you've always been so good about it and I really don't have anyone else I could possibly turn to." A tear slid down her face, along her chin and plopped into her empty vodka glass.

I found it hard to believe that I was sitting here listening to the woman who had stolen my husband crying because he might be having an affair with somebody else. It had the hallmarks of a comedy, but there was nothing comical about the way Amanda sobbed quietly beside me.

"Even if he is having an affair, there's nothing much I can do about it," I said. "If I wanted to."

She looked at me, her eyes red. "I thought he might be having it with you," she said starkly.

"With me!" I looked at her in amazement. "Amanda, the bastard left me!"

"But he talks about you," said Amanda bitterly. "All the fucking time. Jane this and Jane that, and Clodagh this and Clodagh that, until I want to throw something at him."

"Rory does?"

"All the time," she said again. "So I thought maybe he wanted to get back with you and maybe you were encouraging him. I had to find out, Jane, to see where I stood."

I shredded a beer mat myself. The scene in my living-room, when he'd tried to make love to me the night they'd come home from the States, was clear and fresh in my mind. I could see him now as he stood in front of me, mocking me.

"I'm not having an affair with him," I said. "If you can have an affair with your own husband. Maybe I would have tried to get him back once, but not now. I don't love him any more."

And this time, maybe for the very first time, my words were true. Other times, I'd told myself I didn't love him. Other times I'd been afraid that I might still love him. Still more times, I'd ached with a need for him that might have been love. But today I knew that I didn't love him any more, would never love him again. Even if he knocked on my front door tonight, carrying flowers and chocolates and airline tickets to somewhere wonderful, I would simply be bored by him. I'd moved on from Rory and I felt that a weight had been lifted from my heart.

The smoke from Amanda's cigarette spiralled in front of me. Poor Amanda, I thought.

"Surely you're out and about a lot," I said brightly. "Maybe it's just that your lives aren't coinciding very much at the moment. And I bet half your dealing room has gone to the World Cup."

Nearly all of Dublin's financial powerhouses had been practically closed during the Italian adventure, and I expected that it was the same this time around.

"Oh, yes," she said. "The lads are jetting back and forward like nobody's business. But Rory has stayed over there. He's been there for almost a month! He says he's meeting clients and I suppose he is, but it's not fair." She looked guilty for a moment. "I rang your office earlier and they said you'd been on holidays. So I thought that maybe you'd gone to the States with him."

"Good God," I said in amazement. "I was in Majorca with my mother and my daughter."

She started to giggle suddenly, slightly hysterically, and I laughed too.

"I really don't think he's having an affair, Amanda," I said, hoping to God I was right. "The last time I talked to him, he said that you and he were thinking of having a baby."

She lit another cigarette from the butt of the first. "Really?"

"He said that you'd thought about it when you brought Clodagh on holiday."

"I do want a child," she admitted. "But he won't talk about it to me. When I mentioned it to him, he said that he already had a perfect child and he didn't need another one."

I was furious at Rory's cruelty. I signalled a barman to get us another drink.

"How badly do you want a baby?" I asked. "I always thought you dealers wouldn't have time for all that."

"Oh, I wouldn't go on dealing if I had a baby!" Amanda looked shocked. "I couldn't, I'd be too tired. God, it's tiring enough half the time. I'm twenty-nine Jane, and I want to have one now."

"And give up work?" I said.

"For a while."

"I can't believe that Rory isn't interested," I said. "I'd a massive row with him because I wanted to go back to work after Clodagh. The only reason I didn't was because I went back in to hospital to have my appendix out and I was too knackered to go back.

Then, when I did eventually decide to return, he was dead set against it. I'd have thought he'd be thrilled to have you at home with your baby."

"Apparently not," she said.

"What about his mother?" I asked. "The wonderful Eleanor?"

She made a face. "Eleanor doesn't like me very much."

"Good," I said. "The old cow never liked me very much either."

We had another drink as dusk fell and the lights of the city came on below us. There was no real comfort I could offer Amanda, because I didn't honestly know whether Rory was seeing someone else or not. I was a bit surprised, because in one of our bitter recriminatory conversations he'd told me that Amanda was everything he had always wanted in a woman. I couldn't believe that it had all changed for them so soon.

I waited until she had driven away before I started my own car, afraid that maybe she was so upset that she would stay and drink some more and have an accident on her way home. I laughed at myself for my concern. But I was concerned about her. Regretfully, I rather liked her.

Lucy was stunned when I phoned her the following evening.

"Didn't you want to scratch her eyes out?" she asked.

"Not really," I said. "To be honest, I felt sorry for her."

"Jesus, Jane," said Lucy. "That's above and beyond the call of duty."

"Well, I did," I told her. "The poor girl is going through exactly what I went through, and even if she was once my worst enemy, I wouldn't wish it on her now. Rory can be such a bastard when he wants to be."

"So you don't care that she wants to have a kid?"

"No," I said. "She can have a dozen of them and I still wouldn't care."

"Jane," said Lucy. "I think you're over him."

"Lucy," I said. "I know I am."

So there I was, thirty-four, and out of love with my husband at last. I could even play the songs that we had danced to without wanting to cry, to hold my head in my hands and wonder what had all gone wrong and why.

I sold another painting. I'd been commissioned to do it by a woman who'd seen one of the ones I'd done of Junkie and wanted me to do one of her own cat. So I did and she paid me for it, and I went to Les Jumelles to spend the proceeds on an outfit for Brenda and Grace's weddings.

The shop was crowded when I called in on Saturday afternoon with Clodagh, who wanted to be somewhere else.

I looked through the racks of clothes for something simple but elegant. I still found it hard to believe that the twins were actually getting married.

I found the outfit I wanted, a floaty chiffon dress with faint cream and pink flowers and a pale green jacket to go over it. It conjured up pictures of English country lawns and afternoon tea and it made me look serene. It took more than my pay cheque for the painting to pay for it, but it was worth it. I bought a hat too, a kind of cloche in the same green as the jacket, and I thought that it finished my outfit perfectly.

"You look like Mia Farrow in *The Great Gatsby*," said Brenda. "It suits you."

"I hope I'm a bit more robust than Mia Farrow," I said. "And I always thought Daisy was a dopey character."

"Jane, girls who are dressed like nineteen-twenties rich young ladies don't go around using words like dopey," complained Brenda. "You don't live the part."

"It doesn't matter about me, once you do," I returned. "How are the preparations going?"

Brenda groaned. "Next month," she said, "and we're up to our eyes. I don't know how we'll get through it at all."

"What about your own dresses?"

"Oh, we've got them," she said. "We didn't even attempt to make them, wedding dresses are so much fuss and I know it's silly, but we don't want the bother. Besides which – " she broke off.

"What?" I asked.

"Nothing," she said. I looked at her. The twins were up to something, I knew it by the expression on her face, but she suddenly distracted me.

"Guess who was in here the other day?" she said. "Stephanie McMenamin. Stephanie Kennedy, I mean. She's improved again, she looked absolutely wretched for a while, but she'd had her hair done and she'd dumped her kids with someone, so she had a bit more of a spring in her step."

"Good," I said.

"You look great too," observed Brenda, "colour in your cheeks and a bit of a spring in your step, too. Have you been getting up to anything?"

I blushed wildly and looked at her in confusion. She stared at me with delight. "You *have* been getting up to something!"

"Not at all," I said, composing myself, "it's just the tan from my holiday."

But Brenda continued to grin as she wrapped my jacket and dress in soft white tissue paper and slid it carefully into the bag.

I felt as though I were tying up all the pieces of my life. As though, quite suddenly, they were all falling into place and all finally making sense. Good things had happened to me and horrible things had happened and – not that I believed in a great plan or anything, any more – they were all part of what made me be the person I was. And I was an OK person. Not the loveliest in the world, or the most intelligent, or the luckiest or the most miserable. Still pretty average, really, but content with that.

The only part of my life that I hadn't tidied up was the part of it where Hugh McLean lurked. I didn't know what to do about him. I'd misread his signals time and time again. I still didn't know exactly what he'd wanted from me – a quick fling seemed the most likely thing, and yet he wasn't the type of person who'd want, quick fling. And he wasn't the kind of person who would deliberately try to break up someone's marriage. I wished I could figure him out and then forget him, but I couldn't quite do that. I hadn't dreamed about him for quite a while, though, which was a relief.

I'd put him to the back of my mind when Claire came out of her office, holding his file.

"Did you send off the analysis of this client's portfolio I did for him?" she asked me.

My heart missed a beat when I saw his name. "Of course," I said. "I sent it the following Monday."

"I think I should give him a call," she said. "I forgot about him a bit, the file had somehow gone to the bottom of my pile. Can you get him for me, Jane?"

"Wouldn't you like to call him yourself?" I asked.

"But you spoke to him for me, didn't you?" said Claire. "So you should call him and then put him through to me. OK?"

"OK," I said, with leaden heart.

I didn't want to do this. I didn't want to ring his number and ask for him. I hoped against hope that he would be out of the shop and that the girl would take a message because then I could leave the number of Claire's direct line with him to phone. An absolutely taboo thing to do, to give either Claire or Stephen's direct line to anybody, but I'd do it and hang the consequences.

I punched the numbers on the phone and listened to the dialling tone.

"CityBooks."

"Shit," I thought as I heard his voice.

"Is that Hugh McLean?" I asked. What a way to talk

to someone who has kissed you the way Hugh had kissed me.

"Yes," he said. "What do you want, Jane?" His voice was cool, impersonal.

"I've a call for you from Claire Haughton, one of our partners," I said. "You were due to meet Mrs Haughton the day you called in to our office. She asked me to get you on the line."

"Does Mrs Haughton know about us?" he asked, calmly.

"Us?" I squeaked.

"You know, about me chasing you around the office and you locking yourself in the Ladies. That little incident," he said.

"No. Absolutely not. Nothing," I assured him.

"Can you ask Mrs Haughton to call me back tomorrow?" asked Hugh politely. "I'm quite busy right now and I don't really have the time to talk to her."

"Certainly," I said. "Is any particular time convenient?"

He considered for a moment.

"Perhaps it would be better if you arranged an appointment for me with her," he said. "I'd prefer to meet her face to face, especially as there are a couple of things I need to chat to her about. Tomorrow afternoon would suit if she has a free moment. Otherwise, Friday?"

I called up Claire's appointments on the VDU. Her diary was full for the next day, but she could see him directly after lunch on Friday.

"Sounds fine," he said. "Thank you for calling, Mrs McLoughlin."

It sounded strange being called Mrs McLoughlin. Most people who knew me called me Jane. When I left a name with anyone, any more I reverted to Jane O'Sullivan.

I told Claire that Hugh McLean had made an appointment to see her and she was delighted.

"Means we've probably nailed him as a client," she said. "Well done, Jane."

I wasn't sure she'd say well done if she knew exactly how Hugh and I had parted. It was not what she'd call professional. And Claire was very professional.

I was in a complete flap all day Friday. My new, composed, self had disappeared under the stress of knowing that Hugh would be in the office. It wasn't, of course, that there was anything between Hugh and me; it was embarrassment at meeting him again, at having to be polite to him. I dressed down deliberately. I wore an old, very plain, white blouse and an ankle-length pleated skirt. I didn't wear any make-up and only a little *L'Air du Temps* behind my ears. I looked demure.

I walked around the square at lunch-time, although the sky was grey and my light cashmere cardigan wasn't really warm enough in the easterly breeze. I rehearsed how I would greet him, how I would keep my composure, how I would be totally unfazed by him. It was an embarrassing situation, I told myself, but I could handle it with dignity and with self-respect. I would be totally in command.

It was exactly a quarter to two when I arrived back at the office. Hugh was due at two. Claire was already in her office making notes. I typed up some reports for Stephen, keeping one eye on the clock, and the other on the door. Stephen's writing was big and florid and much easier to decipher than Claire's, which was small and neat.

I was under the desk retrieving a page which had floated to the floor when Hugh came into the office. I heard the door open and I straightened up and whacked my head off the corner of the desk. For a moment I knew what they meant by seeing stars. The room spun around and my eyes filled with tears of pain.

"Are you all right?" he asked, concern in his voice.

"Yes," I gasped. "Just got a shock, that's all." I took out a tissue and wiped my eyes. Brainy idea not wearing make-up, I thought, if I had done, I'd have mascara running down my face again!

"I've an appointment to see Claire Haughton," said Hugh.

"I know you have," I said, "I made it."

His mouth twitched. I couldn't believe that he was laughing at me. I buzzed the intercom and told Claire that Hugh McLean was here to see her. "Send him in," crackled her voice.

"Do you want to go in?" I asked. "The second door – "

"I know which office," he said. "Thank you."

I was furious with him and with me. Why had he chosen that moment to come in to the office? Why was it that whenever I planned anything, tried to have everything just so, it never worked out like I'd expected. I sat in front of my screen, bleary-eyed from the knock on the head. I rubbed it gently, there was a bump at the back like a golf-ball. I'm probably concussed, I thought gloomily.

"Jane, can you bring in some coffee?" said Claire's voice over the intercom. I made a face but brought in coffee and biscuits. Hugh was sitting opposite her, looking relaxed. He was wearing the same suit as he'd done the last time, I noticed. Probably his only suit. It was the one as I'd seen him wear in the Stephen's Green Centre, too. I felt better when I noticed that. He wasn't one of the sharp businessmen who wandered around the bank, the kind Rory associated with. Usually Hugh looked unkempt and uninterested in suits. He was a jeans and sweatshirt sort of person. I wasn't going to let him intimidate me.

I put the tray with the coffee and the cups and the Afternoon Tea biscuits on Claire's desk. Hugh was wearing his tortoiseshell glasses today. There was a fingerprint in the middle of one of the lenses.

He was with Claire for about half an hour. I sat at my desk and did my work but with only half my brain on it. I could hear the gentle hum of conversation coming from Claire's office, and the occasional laugh.

She escorted him to the outer office and shook his hand. "I'm pleased to have met you," she said. "I look forward to doing business with you."

"Thanks," he said. He looked at me for a moment. "Do you mind if I make a call?"

"You can use my office if you want some privacy," said Claire, waving at her open door.

"Not at all," said Hugh, "I simply want to call my office. This phone will do fine."

Claire smiled at him, a wide beaming smile that I'd never seen before. I wondered if he had that effect on everybody, made them feel good? Hold on a minute, I told myself, he doesn't make you feel good, does he?

He phoned the bookshop and spoke to somebody there. I didn't listen to the conversation, I kept my head buried in a file, reading it carefully, totting up columns of figures.

I heard him replace the receiver. "Thank you, Mrs McLoughlin," he said.

I looked up at him, green eyes meeting brown. "O'Sullivan," I told him. "My name is Jane O'Sullivan."

The switchboard blinked at me and I answered it. I could see him still standing in front of my desk. I put the call through to Claire.

"Why have you changed your name?" he asked.

"Oh, I've just reverted to what it was before," I said casually. "That's all."

"Why?"

"You remind me of my daughter," I said. "Always asking questions."

"I think we should talk," said Hugh.

I was sort of in control. Not completely, because my hands were shaking just a little and I could feel the beat of my heart, but he wouldn't have seen any of this.

"Talk about what?" I asked.

"Us," said Hugh.

I stared at him. "There is no us," I said, as I hit the wrong key on the keyboard and obliterated half my work.

"Why not?" asked Hugh

I shrugged.

"Meet me." He looked carefully at me.

"Is there any point?"

"Meet me."

"When?"

"Tonight."

"You seem to think that I can take off whenever I like," I said. "I'm taking my daughter to her ballet class tonight."

"While she's at ballet. You could meet me then. I do want to talk to you, Jane."

"All right." I was still in control. "If you like. I'll meet you in the Rathfarnham Orchard at seven. Sharp."

"OK," said Hugh. "See you then."

He left the office and I released the breath that I seemed to have been holding ever since he had first entered. What had I done? I asked myself. And more to the point – why had I done it? It wasn't as though I was in Spain any more. I couldn't blame the sun or the sangria for being silly. But I wanted to go out with him. To see what it would be like. To get him out of my system. I couldn't count the lunch at the National Gallery, that was completely different.

It was a rush to get home, get Clodagh's things together and get out again that evening. She lost her shoes and her leotard and her bag. I ran around looking for them while trying to smudge a bit of lipstick on my lips and rummage for my thin gold chain and tiny pinhead stud earrings. I was still going for the demure look. I kept the skirt long – my ecru linen, and the top chaste – an oatmeal knit. I thought

I looked particularly sensible in that outfit. I chivvied Clodagh until she yelled at me and finally bundled her into the car and drove down the road to her ballet class. I wouldn't have very much time with Hugh McLean. Her class was over at eight.

The sun shone on the white walls of the pub. I should have said that I'd meet him outside. It seemed a pity to go in out of the light. But it was still cool and I probably would have shivered my way through our conversation.

I pushed open the doors and peered into the interior of the lounge. He was sitting on a stool at the bar and I caught my breath. I'd tried to pretend that he wasn't that attractive, but he was. I wished that he didn't look so desirable, my knees had turned to jelly.

I walked over to him and sat on the bar stool beside him.

"Glass of Bud," I said to the barman. Hugh closed his book and looked at me. He was reading *War and Peace*.

"Hello, Jane O'Sullivan," he said. "Glad you could make it."

"I can't make it for long," I said. "I've to pick up Clodagh at eight."

He glanced at his watch. "So what are you doing – giving me an hour to make my pitch?"

I shook my head. "I don't know what you mean," I said. "I don't really know why I'm here at all."

He ran his finger around the rim of his beer glass. "I have to confess I'm not too sure about it myself," he said.

"You asked to meet," I told him. "What do you

want?" I knew that I was being very rude but I couldn't help myself. I thought that if I was rude, then he wouldn't realise how nervous I was.

"The last time I saw you, you were Jane McLoughlin," he said. "Now you're Jane O'Sullivan. O'Sullivan is your maiden name, I suppose?"

"Maiden name," I echoed. "Sounds sort of spinsterish, doesn't it. My friends are always telling me that I'll end up a dry old spinster."

"Why should you do that?" he asked.

"Because." I sighed deeply. I wanted to tell him and I didn't want to tell him. I was afraid of breaking the shell I had built around myself. But Javier had already cracked the shell. I pulled at a fingernail.

"Don't." He caught my hand in his. "You'll be sorry afterwards. I always am."

His hand was warm and dry. I resisted the urge to pick it up and kiss it.

"I left my husband," I said, and then corrected myself. "No. My husband left me. Another woman." I thought about Amanda and smiled to myself. Not a victorious smile, just a knowing smile.

"Quite some time ago," said Hugh.

I flashed him a glance. "How would you know how long ago?" I asked.

"I heard," he said.

I took my hand from his. "How did you hear?"

"Dublin is a small city," he said.

"But not that small," I replied. "So how?"

"My company is a client of your – ex-husband's bank. I discovered it in discussions with somebody there. Purely by chance, Jane."

I was furious. How dared people talk about me. "How by chance?"

"It was my fault," he admitted. "I said I'd met you at the Christmas party. The person concerned said it was your last, that you and Rory had split up."

"I see. And did they tell you why?"

He shook his head. "I didn't ask. I don't care why."

"So you knew, when you met me, when you phoned me?"

"What do you take me for, Jane? Do you really think I'd try and pinch another man's wife?"

I didn't know quite what I felt. Relief, perhaps, because that was the one thing that had truly bothered me about Hugh. He knew that I was married but he'd still kind of chased me. And I wasn't happy about him being that sort of person. But he hadn't chased me as a married woman, he'd known that I wasn't living with Rory any more.

He was watching me carefully.

"But why do you want to – " I broke off, unsure.

"See you?" he supplied.

I shrugged. "Whatever."

"Jane, I told you before. I like you. I liked you when I thought you were married, but I like you better now you're not. I kissed you once because I wanted to, but it was the wrong time and the wrong place. I know that I keep making you cry – for which I'm eternally sorry – but I promise that I won't always make you cry. And I like the way you fight me all the time."

I laughed. "You'd get bored with that soon enough."

"I only want to get to know you better," he said. "Nothing more."

"Nothing?" I said.

"Not yet, anyway," said Hugh.

"So what are you suggesting?" I asked.

"A couple of dates," said Hugh. "You know what dates are? Dinner, theatre, movie, drink – that sort of thing."

"And nothing else?"

"Not unless you want to, of course."

I might want to, I reflected, but that wasn't the point. Hugh was a nice man but did I want somebody in my life? It wasn't like Javier, I couldn't just dump him after a few days. And I was trying so hard, so very hard to get it all together all by myself. I could hear them say: "Don't end up a dry old maid, Jane," but I still wasn't sure. I couldn't be convinced. I didn't want this possibility,. this dream to be as uncertain as all the rest.

"A date, then," I said cautiously. "Nothing extravagant."

"Nothing extravagant." He drained his glass. "I'll phone you, shall I?"

I'd thought he would fix up something there and then. I was a bit surprised. "OK," I said.

"Fine." Hugh got down from the bar stool. "Well, I'll leave you in peace and I'll be in touch." He glanced at his watch. "You've plenty of time to pick up Clodagh." He smiled at me and walked out of the pub.

36

September 1994

(UK No. 2 – Always – *Bon Jovi)*

The blue and white KLM DC-11 banked slowly, tilting so that we could see the silvery sheen of the water beneath us and the tiny sail of a boat below. Our side of the plane was in shadow while the evening sun poured through the opposite side in great golden shafts. We were suspended for a moment between the sea and the sky and then the aircraft steadied itself, straightened up and began to drop slowly and gracefully towards the island.

We seemed to skim over the water only a few feet below us. I wondered, briefly and agonisingly, if the pilot had made a mistake but then quite suddenly the runway was beneath us and the plane bumped on to the tarmac, screaming as reverse thrust was applied to the engines and the aircraft jolted down to a slow roll.

The terminal building of Flamingo Airport was to our left, a bright pink building which was no bigger than a supermarket. Palm trees waved gently in the sea breeze and already I could sense that the air outside was warm.

The flight attendants opened the doors and the passengers scrambled to take down their luggage from the bins above. I stood up and stretched. Although this was by far the biggest plane I'd ever flown on, it was nearly twelve hours since we'd left Schipol Airport in Amsterdam. The delay in Caracas had been the worst. We wandered around the Venezuelan airport for almost an hour, looking at touristy dolls and T-shirts without wanting to buy anything. All the same, I could say I'd been to Venezuela now, and nobody need ever know that I hadn't been outside the rather grim terminal building.

But we were here, in Bonaire, the tiny Dutch Antilles island where Brenda and Grace were going to marry Robert and Damien and where Lucy and I were to be their witnesses.

We'd been shocked when the twins told us of their plans, although we understood why they wanted a Caribbean wedding. They didn't want hordes of relatives and they didn't feel that it was appropriate to have a wedding at home without inviting them. So they'd thought of the Caribbean idea – a holiday and a wedding all in one, as Brenda had put it.

None of us had heard of Bonaire before but Robert and Damien, both keen scuba divers, decided that this was the island for them. It was a scuba diver's paradise, with thousands of exotic fish and coral formations that could only be matched by the Great Barrier Reef. The twins agreed, they didn't much care where they went as long as the sun shone and the wedding was legal.

Then they'd sprung their bombshell. They wanted some friends to join them. They didn't want to get married completely on their own and they thought that Lucy and I would like the holiday.

"We can't come on your honeymoon!" Lucy objected, even as I watched her mentally calculate the cost of a transatlantic flight.

"We're not asking you to come on our honeymoon," said Grace. "We'll be spending a few days on Bonaire – to fulfil the residency requirements, and so that the lads can dive, but then we're going on to Aruba and Curacao. We'll be in the Dutch Antilles for two weeks. We're suggesting that you spend a week in Bonaire. At a different hotel."

"A week!" I did some mental calculations myself. "I can't really – "

"Our treat," explained Brenda.

We stared at her speechlessly. Lucy was the first to find her voice. "You mean – you want to pay?"

"We're getting a good deal," grinned Grace. "Damien is going to take hundreds of photographs, and one of the hotels has offered us very inexpensive accommodation, by way of encouraging him to do a bit of Bonaire promotion. We've got another good deal on flights, so don't think that it's costing us the earth. Besides," she put her arms around our shoulders, "we want you to be there. You've always been our friends, through everything. We were at both your weddings, we want you to be at ours."

I felt tears of affection prick the back of my eyes.

"I don't know what to say." I was absolutely stunned.

"Say you'll come," said Brenda.

"There's one other thing," added Grace. "We don't expect you to come on your own, Lucy; after all, David would probably love the holiday too. So he's included in the package." She looked at me and her eyes twinkled. "As is anyone you might want to bring, Jane."

I blushed to the roots of my hair and the others giggled. I'd told them about Hugh. My friend. Who was a man. Just a friend, though.

I still wasn't sure about Hugh and me. I didn't know whether we had a relationship or, if we had, where it might lead. I'd been out with him three times. To the cinema once, *Sleepless in Seattle,* at which I sniffed covertly – Hugh proffered a slightly crumpled tissue beneath the cover of the giant-sized popcorn; to a classical recital which was moving (but not, thank goodness, tear-jerking) and to dinner in Dobbins, which was the nearest we'd got to a romantic evening. And in those three nights, he'd never once tried to do anything more than kiss me lightly on the cheek when I got out of his car. He always refused the offer of a cup of coffee, or a night-cap, and he left me wondering. I couldn't believe that he'd once kissed me, passionately, on the lips. I could only assume that he had done it for a reason of his own which I couldn't yet fathom. If he'd wanted me physically then, it didn't seem as though he wanted me physically now.

Yet it was good to go out with him. Javier had

reminded me of how much I enjoyed turning up at a restaurant on the arm of a man, even one who had a paperback in his suit pocket, pulling the jacket out of shape. It was nice to be part of a couple.

He met Clodagh the night we went to the recital. I felt strange about him coming to our house, but he said that he'd collect me and I thought that Clodagh should meet him. Just in case.

She gazed at him with undisguised interest and he told her that he was pleased to meet her. She asked him questions, silly inconsequential questions, but he answered them seriously, making no concession to her age.

"Where are you going?" she asked us.

"To a concert," I said as I slipped my jacket around my shoulders. "You're to be good while we're out, no giving any trouble. Do what Anne tells you." Anne was her current baby-sitter, the girl next door.

Clodagh yawned, bored with my orders. "I always do what I'm told," she said.

When we returned, at midnight, she was awake. I peeped around her bedroom door as I always did and she stirred slightly in the bed. I walked over to look at her. Her eyes were open, focussed.

"Is he your boyfriend?" she asked.

"I don't know," I answered.

"Amanda is Daddy's girlfriend," she told me. "So I suppose you should have a boyfriend."

"Do you like Amanda?" I asked.

"You're always asking me that." Clodagh snuggled down under the covers. "She's OK. I like your boyfriend."

"Do you?"

"He's nice," she said, as she closed her eyes. "Not as nice as Daddy," she added, opening them again. "But he'll do."

Despite Clodagh's approval, I didn't feel as though I could ask Hugh to come to Bonaire with me. Brenda and Grace urged me to do it. I knew that they thought it would be the ultimate in romance if I went to a wedding with Hugh McLean. Especially a wedding in such wonderful surroundings.

So I mentioned it to him, very casually, over the phone one evening.

"They suggested what!!" he exclaimed.

I repeated it for him. "Of course you probably wouldn't be able to go anyway," I added. "Even if you did want to."

"Do you want me to?" he asked. "Would you like me to be there?"

I'd thought all afternoon about it, picturing myself on the Caribbean island with him and without him, watching the girls get married with him and without him, sitting in a restaurant sipping Piña Coladas with him and without him. If I wanted him to come, I wanted it to be for the right reason. Because I wanted him, Hugh, not just anyone. Although I couldn't trust myself to think it through properly, I wanted him to be with me. I didn't want to allow myself to think that I might be falling for him, because that would be crazy. I would be falling into the same old trap again, trying to live a dream that couldn't possibly come true. It was different for other people. Lucy was lucky. Maybe Brenda and Grace would be lucky. But my men had always been disastrous. Maybe that was my fault, but I wouldn't let myself be hurt again. That was why I was happy with Hugh, because he didn't try anything.

"I'd like you to come," I said hesitantly. "But, you know, as my friend." I put a wealth of meaning in the word "friend".

"I see," said Hugh. "I'm not sure if I can make it, Jane."

"Please," I said, surprised at how much I actually did want to come. "I'd like it if you did, Hugh."

He thought for a moment. "OK," he said. "But I'm paying my own fare."

Brenda was delighted he was coming and told me that they wanted to pay for him, they were paying for David, they had the money for God's sake. But Hugh was adamant, he would pay for himself and the twins had to allow him.

He stood beside me on the tarmac as we looked up at the huge plane that had carried us halfway around the world. The warm air touched my neck and I shivered with the pleasure of it.

Brenda and Grace had arranged to meet us and bring us to our hotel. "You lot are in 'The Golden Necklace'." she told us. "We're in the one a little further away."

"I don't care if we're on a shack on the beach," declared Lucy, as she hugged me with excitement. "This is absolutely fantastic. Aren't the girls the best in the world!"

It took a while to get through immigration. Lucy had lost the form they had given her to fill in on the plane. She finally found it, stuck in her wallet with the pictures of Andrew, and she pulled it out, scattering photographs over the immigration desk. The coloured lady behind the desk picked up the photos and smiled.

"Your baby?" she asked.

Lucy nodded.

"Lovely, lovely," she said as she stamped the form and waved us through.

We collected our luggage and walked outside. The twins and the Driscolls were waiting for us. Robert Driscoll allocated the taxis, and we were driven to the hotels; Lucy, David, Hugh and I to The Golden Necklace which was only a few minutes drive from the airport, and the twins and their fiancés to the larger, more modern Turtle Bay, a little further along the coast. The island was only twenty-seven miles long and, we discovered, almost a third of that was given over to a nature reserve.

Bonaire was a Dutch Antilles island. Apartments and houses built in the tall and narrow Dutch style jostled against the low, whitewashed, more usual Caribbean houses. The signs were a mixture of Dutch and the local dialect, Papiamento. It gave me the strangest feeling to find continental Europe in the middle of the soft, blue sea.

We checked in to the hotel, already warm, definitely tired but happy to have arrived. Lucy wanted to phone home to check on Andrew. Her only worry about the holiday was leaving Andrew with her mother. There were half a dozen phones at reception. I'd phone Clodagh in the morning, I said, before the wedding, when I knew that she would be in. Hopefully, she would be in bed by now.

The bellboy, tall and gangly and wearing the hotel uniform of brightly coloured floral shorts and shirt, showed us to our rooms. They were simply furnished, tiled floors and stone walls but when I opened the balcony and stepped outside, I caught my breath at the beauty in front of me.

A coconut tree swayed outside the window, the nuts clustered in the heart of the tree almost close enough to touch. Through the waving fronds, I could see the expanse of pure white sand which led into the azure blue sea. It was unspoiled and exquisite. It made the brochures look tacky.

Hugh stepped on to the balcony behind me and rested his hands on my shoulders. "Perfect, isn't it," he whispered in my ear. I nodded, watching as a heron suddenly swooped from the sky and, pulling its body into a long white spear, entered the water, then emerged with a fish between its beak.

"Did you see that!" I exclaimed. "Did you?"

"Yes," he said. "Fantastic." He let go of my shoulders and leaned over the edge of the balcony. "There's a swimming pool over there." He waved to the left. "If you want to go swimming."

"In a pool," I said scornfully. "When that sea is there. You must be joking."

"Do you want to go for a swim?" he asked.

"Absolutely."

"Come on, then."

"Before unpacking?" I asked doubtfully.

"The cases will still be here when we get back," he laughed. "Come on, Jane."

I opened my case and found my swimsuit. I held it in my hands, undecided. I was undecided about a few things, now that we were actually here.

The room had two huge double beds. I didn't know what sleeping arrangements Hugh intended. If he behaved the way he usually did, it would be separate beds and a goodnight peck on the top of my head, but I couldn't be certain about that. And I wasn't sure about changing into my swimsuit in front of him either. He'd see my scars, for one thing and my flabby stomach which all the work in the gym couldn't get rid of, for another.

Hugh disappeared into the bathroom and emerged wearing a pair of fluorescent pink shorts and a lime green T-shirt. "What do you think?" he asked. "Suitable attire?"

"Fantastic." I dived into the bathroom myself. My swimsuit was black with tiny white dots. It hid a multitude, although it did plunge daringly between my breasts. I pulled a multicoloured sarong over it and slid into a pair of sandals.

"Nice," said Hugh appreciatively, as I pushed open the bathroom door.

We walked through the hotel and out to the beach, which was hotel property. There were a few deserted sun loungers and half a dozen people sat in the now-fading sun at the end of the pier.

"Do you think it'll be warm enough?" I asked as I looked longingly at the silky blue water.

"Don't be ridiculous," said Hugh and strode in. He

dipped down beneath the surface and bobbed up again. "It's wonderful!"

I undid my sarong and draped it on one of the sun loungers. Then I ran into the water, sending up a shower of silver spray. I dived beneath it myself and struck out strongly. It was beautiful, warm and enticing.

Hugh swam out to me and I turned as he caught up with me. "You're a good swimmer," he said, in surprise, treading water.

"I love swimming," I told him. "I used to do a lot of it when I was younger, then I got out of practise. But Clodagh and I go every Saturday now. It's not the same though, is it, swimming in a pool full of chlorine as swimming in the Caribbean sea?"

I loved saying Caribbean. It sounded so exotic, so romantic.

Even more romantic than The Med, I thought, deliriously.

"I'll race you to that buoy over there," said Hugh, and I nodded.

He was a strong swimmer too, but he only beat me by the length of his body. I caught up with him and grinned. "By the end of the week, I'll be beating you."

"Want to bet?" he asked as he made for the shore.

He floated lazily and I swam over to him.

"Enjoying yourself?" I asked.

"Wonderful," said Hugh. "Thanks for asking me to come."

"Thanks for coming," I said.

I kissed him. I couldn't help it. He righted himself

in the water and looked at me, his eyes dark, unfathomable. Then he smiled suddenly and they were lighter, carefree.

"Come on," he said, "we'd better go back."

I followed him out of the water and we sat for a while on the sand as the sun sank below the horizon in a flaming ball of orange and red, which spilled across the sea in an ever-increasing pool of colour. When it disappeared, quite quickly because the sun sets quickly in the Caribbean, we went back to the room and I showered and changed for dinner.

We were to meet Lucy and David for dinner. It would be the first time that we'd got together properly as couples, although Hugh and David had engaged in long and deep conversations at the airport and during the flight while Lucy and I watched the movie. I'd wondered, uneasily, what they were talking about.

The hotel restaurant was built jutting out over the sea. The water lapped beneath us and boiled with the fighting of the fish for the scraps that the diners threw from their tables. Lucy threw a bread roll into the water and watched as a cauldron of fish demolished it.

"Unreal," she said in wonderment.

We had the obligatory conch chowder for starters, although I wasn't sure that either Hugh or I should have it, its aphrodisiacal properties were probably wasted on us. Then we had a local chicken dish, washed down with Californian chardonnay, followed by some fresh fruit.

"Superb," said David as he spooned the last piece of mango from the plate.

"Magnificent." Lucy dabbed her lips with her linen napkin. "I could grow to like this."

"Me too," I said as I yawned widely and covered my mouth in dismay. "Sorry." I looked around at them. "I suddenly feel exhausted."

David looked at his watch. "Not surprising," he said, "it's three in the morning at home."

"Is it really?" asked Lucy. "No wonder I feel tired! I know I slept on the plane and so I thought I should be OK, but I'm terribly sleepy."

My yawn had set up a chain reaction.

"Stop it," ordered Hugh. "I'm having a wonderful time and I don't want to go to bed yet."

"Could be more wonderful there," muttered Lucy and I kicked her, hard, under the table. Her muffled "ouch" didn't go unnoticed but Hugh pretended to ignore it and took a cigar from his shirt pocket. He offered one to David and they both lit up and smoked while Lucy and I gazed into the sea and looked at the fish.

"Will we have a nightcap and then go to bed?" she asked eventually.

We got up from the table and walked down to the bar, which was practically on the beach. The barman was making cocktails, like Tom Cruise in the movie, shaking and jiving to the music from his ghetto blaster. The music wasn't terribly loud. I guessed the residents wouldn't want their peaceful idyll shattered by Salt-n-Pepa.

The men talked together while Lucy and I took our drinks down to the beach.

"Aren't the twins just great?" Lucy sipped her

Margarita. "Who else would have arranged something like this?"

I shook my head. "I'm so happy for them. They're such wonderful girls and I never, ever would have believed that they'd get married."

"Just goes to prove," said Lucy, "there's somebody out there for everyone."

I stirred my Long Island Iced Tea with a straw. "Maybe."

"Oh, Jane." Lucy kicked off her shoes and buried her feet in the sand. "You know I'm right. What about you and Hugh?"

"What about us?"

"Isn't he right for you?" she asked. "He's come on this holiday, you asked him to come. Surely that means – "

"I don't know," I interrupted her. "I don't know, Lucy."

"But Jane – "

"It's not that sort of relationship," I said.

"What!!"

"We're friends, that's all."

"Don't give me that, Jane. How could you be 'friends' with someone who looks like that? Besides, he's a nice bloke. He's kind and considerate and he treats you well."

"You found out all that on the flight over?" I asked amused.

"I can see it, Jane," she said. "Same as I could see that Rory McLoughlin was a shit and always would be. But Hugh is different. Believe me."

"Why didn't you ever like Rory?" I popped a maraschino cherry into my mouth.

"Because he stood you up," she said. "Remember, the night you were meant to meet him in Searson's? And you came home and found me in bed with Nick?"

I shuddered at the memory.

"That bastard could have contacted you somehow," she told me. "But he didn't. He knew you'd be in Searson's waiting for him, but he didn't even bother to call. I know it all sort of went out of your head because of me, but I never forgot. And even though I couldn't say anything then, it bothered me. If he could stand you up when you were still mad about each other, what could he do later? That was the way I saw it."

"I see," I said.

"And he was such a pompous prick," she said, using language that I rarely heard her use. "Every time we met, he was always trying to prove that he was more intelligent, richer, knew more than anyone else in the company. And whenever you'd say anything, he'd sort of put you down."

The tirade stopped. I looked at her thoughtfully. "Did you always think that?" I asked.

She nodded.

"And you never said anything?"

"He was your husband, Jane."

"Oh, Lucy," I said, and put my arm around her. "I'm glad I know you."

"Don't get soppy," she said. "Look, do you want another drink?"

I surveyed my glass. "I'd better not," I said, "I'm falling asleep as it is."

"Don't fall asleep before you have brilliant sex with Hugh," she told me. "It'd be such a waste."

Just then, David and Hugh arrived down on the beach with another drink. I groaned but drank it anyway. I felt my eyes close and I leaned against Hugh for support.

"Jane, what have you done with my shirts?"

"Ironed them, of course."

"My white ones?"

"Yes."

"Where's my green one?"

"The one you put in the basket on Monday?"

"I only have one green shirt."

"It's not washed yet."

"For Chrissake, Jane, it's not as if I ask that much of you. A meal on the table in the evening and a clean shirt every morning. My God, what else are you doing all day?"

"It's only Wednesday. Why would I have washed your Monday shirt already?"

"Because that's what you should be doing. Look, I'll be late home this evening, I'm meeting a client."

And Rory slammed the front door, the car door and gunned down the road.

I felt myself being lifted from the sand and carried to the hotel room. I knew that somebody, no – I knew it was Hugh – had placed me gently on the bed. I opened my eyes and saw him there, looking at me. I reached up and tried to touch his face but I couldn't quite reach and I couldn't speak either.

He slid my cotton blouse over my head and eased my skirt down my legs. So, I thought, he'll take advantage of me in my exhausted state. He pulled the sheet from the bed and rolled me underneath.

"Sleep well," he said and kissed me on the forehead.

"Shit," I thought, before drifting into deep, dreamless sleep.

Brenda and Grace married Robert and Damien at four o'clock the following afternoon. We arrived at the Turtle Bay at half past three to find them sitting at the beach bar sipping long, interesting-looking cocktails.

"It's for the pre-wedding nerves," Damien explained, his boyish grin wide and cheerful.

"Come on," said Robert, "have one."

So we sat down and drank a cocktail each until it was time for the wedding.

The ceremony was conducted in the gardens of the hotel, a lush oasis of verdant lawns and tropical flowers. The officiating magistrate was a local woman, about fifty, her frizzy hair like a grey Brillo pad on top of her dark skin. She smiled broadly at us as she stood beneath the bower of pink, purple and yellow flowers. Behind her, a tiny fountain sent jets of sparkling water shooting to the sky so that they fell back to earth in diamond droplets, catching the sun and exploding into a rainbow of colours.

The twins were beautiful. Dressed exactly alike in white linen, with tiny red rosebuds twisted into their hair, they looked cool and virginal. The Driscoll brothers wore white suits, with black bow ties, which reminded me a little of characters in a James Bond film I'd once seen. Birdsong echoed around the garden, the ghetto blaster was quietly playing The Four Seasons.

When the magistrate asked, "Do you, Brenda, take Robert" and she replied "I do", I felt my eyes water and a tear slid gently down my cheek.

"Goose," murmured Hugh and slipped me another crumpled tissue. I sniffed and wiped my eyes, then cried again when Grace and Damien were pronounced husband and wife.

"You may kiss the brides!" The magistrate beamed at them and the Driscolls caught the twins and kissed them long and hard, to applause from the four of us and the small crowd which had gathered to watch the ceremony.

We signed the register, Lucy and I, and hugged the twins and their husbands. It was one of the most joyous occasions of my life.

We went for a celebratory drink in the Turtle Bay's terraced restaurant. A table was set out for us, decked in a bright pink tablecloth and laden with an arrangement of tropical fruit in a huge ice bowl which glistened wetly in the afternoon sun.

We didn't think we were very hungry, but we fell on the seafood starters and the tropical kebabs as though we hadn't eaten in days. Robert opened bottles of champagne and we toasted each other in a silly, happy banquet that lasted until dusk fell around us and the sun slid again into the sea.

Later we went down to the beach again, carrying bottles of champagne and ice buckets, and sat at the edge of the water, letting it run between our toes and wash over our feet.

"This has been a marvellous day." Grace lay back and got sand all over her beautiful dress.

"It's definitely the way to get married," agreed Lucy. She turned to David. "If I ever divorce you, you'll find me here marrying one of the divers."

We laughed. We'd seen lots of divers today, strong and muscular men carrying full aqualung equipment as though it weighed nothing.

"It would have been the thing to do, ourselves," commented David.

"Your wedding was good fun, though," said Grace.

"Sure it was." I nodded in agreement.

"God, Jane," said Lucy, "I bet you can never think of my wedding with anything other than horror!"

"Why?" asked Hugh. He'd been quiet all day, keeping just a little bit distant from the revelry, and I jumped now as he spoke.

"Because Jane practically had her baby at my wedding," said Lucy.

"Did you?" Hugh looked at me.

I nodded. "I almost gave birth to Clodagh in a marquee in Stillorgan," I told him. "It was not the best experience of my life."

"You didn't look too bad on it," he said.

There was silence in the group as the twins and Lucy looked at me in astonishment.

"How d'you know what Jane looked like?" asked Lucy. "You wouldn't have known her then."

Hugh and I exchanged glances and I answered. "Hugh actually called into my room in the hospital by mistake," I said. "He was visiting his sister, who'd had a baby too. That's when I first met him."

"Eight years ago?" said Grace.

Hugh cleared his throat. "We didn't exactly know each other," he said. "It wasn't as though we were friends then, or anything."

"All the same, isn't it a small world." Brenda looked at me strangely. "That eight years on you're sitting here beside Jane, at our wedding."

"Isn't it?" said Hugh equably.

"Anybody want a top up?" Damien brandished the bottle of champagne.

We held out our glasses to him, although I didn't really think that I could drink another drop.

"What are your plans for tomorrow?" Lucy asked Brenda.

"Nothing," she said. "We're going to lie here and bask in the sun, then we go to Aruba the day after."

"David and I have joined up for a diving class," said Lucy. "I'm terrified, but it sounds like such fun, and they were showing a video of the marine life in that diving shop we were in this morning. I have to have a go. Are you going to give it a try, Jane?"

"Probably," I answered, "but I didn't put my name down yet." I looked at Hugh. "Do you want to try?"

"Sure," he said. "We'll sign up for tomorrow afternoon."

The moon appeared on the horizon and cast its white light on to the water in front of us.

"Don't want to be party-poopers or anything," said

Lucy, "but David and I are going back to our hotel. Maybe have a drink there, have an early night."

Guffaws greeted this statement and Lucy blushed furiously. David grinned at her. "It's all this romance," she said. "It's getting to me."

"OK, then," said Brenda, "We'd better throw our bouquets."

"Don't be daft," I said. "There's only Lucy and me here."

"Come back up to the bar," said Grace. "We can do it properly there."

We stood up and brushed the fine, white sand from our clothes. A great cheer greeted the twins as they walked into the bar. Brenda spoke to the barman and he shouted out to the crowd that the brides were going to throw their bouquets and all the ladies should gather around.

"You too," hissed Lucy as she pulled me into the group.

"There's no point in me being here," I objected. "It's not relevant to me."

But I stood beside her as Brenda and Grace stood up on the narrow bar, balancing carefully in their high-heeled shoes, and casually threw their bouquets into the crowd.

It was inevitable, I suppose, that I'd catch Brenda's because she had thrown it directly at me. I grinned at her and waved.

"Free drink for the lucky ladies," ordered the barman and presented me and the girl who had caught Grace's flowers with Piña Coladas.

Lucy and David disappeared.

"Come on," whispered Hugh, "we should go, too."

We hugged the twins, told them to have a great time in Aruba and promised to meet them at the airport when they got home.

"We're delighted you came," said Brenda, "and it was lovely to meet you, Hugh."

"Thanks for asking me." He kissed the twins on the cheeks and shook hands with the Driscoll brothers.

Hugh and I walked in silence along the beach towards The Golden Necklace. I was light-headed from the sun and the champagne and still tired from the flight the day before. It had been a wonderful day.

I stumbled in the soft sand and Hugh caught me by the arm to steady me.

"You OK?" he asked, and I nodded but I held on to his arm, enjoying the warmth.

A diving jetty separated our hotel from the Turtle Bay. Coloured lights along the jetty danced in the night-time breeze. The diving boats bobbed in the water, waiting for the morning. Suddenly, I didn't want to go back to the hotel yet.

"Can we sit on the edge of the jetty for a while?" I asked.

"Sure," said Hugh.

We strolled along the wooden planks to the end of the jetty and sat there with our legs dangling over the water. In the distance I could see a fluorescent purple light under the sea. "It's a night diver," explained Hugh. "Some types of fish only come out at night."

"I'd be scared to dive in the dark." I shivered at the thought.

"Cold?" asked Hugh and put his arm around me.

I sat, immobile, in the circle of his arm. I could feel the rise and fall of his body beside me. Thousands of sensations surged through me. I moved towards him, very slightly, unsure of myself and of him.

"Cold?" he asked again. I looked up at him, into his brown eyes, half hidden by the shadows of the night.

"A bit."

He held me tighter. "Still?"

"A bit," I said, again.

He face was close to mine and I could hear his breathing now and smell his aftershave. I leaned my head towards him and I saw a flicker in his eyes before we kissed.

I'd been kissed more passionately before, more intensely before but never more urgently. Never with more unspoken promise, unspoken desire. And as we kissed, the ice that I'd tried to keep around me since Rory suddenly melted and coursed through me in a torrent of hunger and longing.

"My God," said Hugh, as we parted. He held my shoulders, looking at me fiercely. "Do you kiss like that all the time?"

"No," I said. "Only when I want to." And I kissed him again.

"I love you," he said, when we parted again.

I disentangled myself from his embrace and stood up. Hugh stood beside me. I gazed into the darkness of the sea and watched the reflection of the jetty's lights on the water. Hugh was close to me, but not touching me.

"Did you mean that?" I whispered, afraid of his answer.

He stood behind me, and wrapped his arms around me. "I never say anything I don't mean."

"But love?" I murmured.

"I loved you from the first moment I set eyes on you," said Hugh. "Crazy though that may seem to you, Jane. With your eyes all red and puffy in your hospital bed. You'd just had another man's baby and I wanted to kill him for leaving you on your own."

"Don't be daft."

"And I loved you when I saw you at the Park Hotel, and again at your Christmas party, and I've wanted you every day in between."

I turned, still held by him. "But you can't have loved me."

"I loved you," he said. "Don't ask me why, Jane, because I don't know. What makes people fall for each other? When I talked to you, I knew. And I couldn't do a damn thing about it."

"Really?"

"Really, Jane. And it's not just because you interest me or intrigue me or anything, it's just that I think we fit together. I know that might not sound the most romantic thing in the world, but it's true. And maybe you're still not ready to love someone." He held me closer. "I'll wait."

But he didn't need to wait, because I knew that I

loved him too. He was the right person for me. It was though I'd found another part of me.

"I love you." I said. The words sounded strange but right.

The mauve light of the night diver moved out towards the sea. The reflection of the jetty's lights rippled on the surface of the water. The air was still.

Then Hugh led me away from the pier, out of the night and into his life.

My lover and I sat side by side on the white Caribbean sand. The setting sun shattered into a thousand glittering diamonds as it hit the turquoise blue of the sea, and the only sound was the rhythmic thud of the waves as they broke upon the shore.

My lover and I sat in silence. There was no need for words between us. The only ones that mattered had already been said.

The End